NIrV

THE LITTLE KIDS'
Adventure
BIBLE

Features written by:

Lawrence O. Richards

zonderkidz

NIrV **THE LITTLE KIDS'**

Adventure

BIBLE

This NIrV Bible was given to

Name:

_____

_____

On:

_____

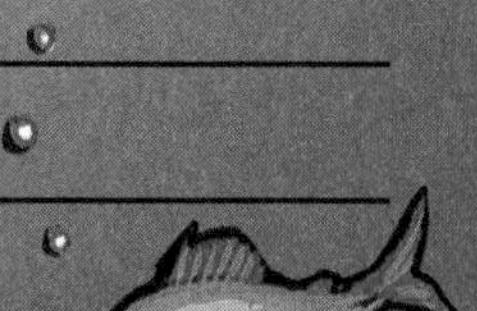

_____

By:

_____

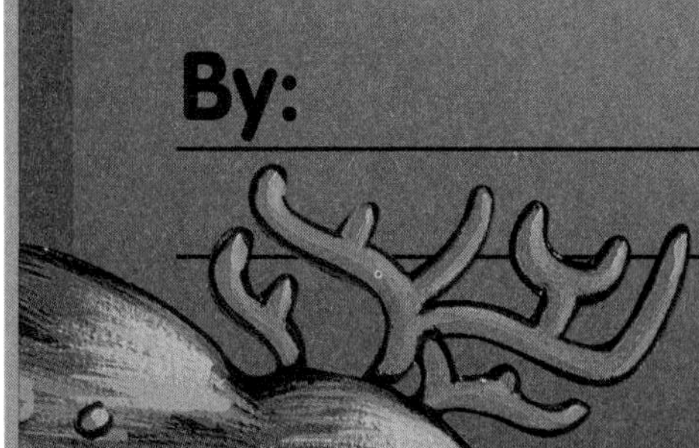

_____

About the BIBLE

QUESTION: What is the Bible?

ANSWER: The Bible is a book that tells us about God.

It shows us what he is like, what he has done and what he wants us to do. It tells us about ourselves—about how God made us and about how sin came into the world. It tells us about Jesus, who came to show us how much God loves us and wants to forgive our sins.

QUESTION: How was the Bible written?

ANSWER: The simplest answer is: God wrote the Bible.

But he used humans to write down what he wanted us to know. We can trust God that he worked in the writers so that they wrote down what is really God's Word, even though God let each writer use his own personality and style.

QUESTION: Who are these people and who wrote the Bible?

ANSWER: The people who wrote the Bible lived a long time ago.

Some, like Moses, lived as long ago as 3,500 years. Others, like John, lived about 1,900 years ago. In lots of ways they were people just like we are... people who had doubts, people who did some bad things and some good things. God used them to write down words that tell us about him and his love for us.

QUESTION: Why is the Bible important to me?

ANSWER: The Bible is one of the most important ways that God uses to talk to you and let you know that he is real.

The Bible is more than just a bunch of old stories about some people who lived a long time ago. It is God's love letter to you, assuring you that he is interested in you and will take care of you every day.

You will be pleased to know that a portion of the purchase price of your
new NIrV Bible has been provided to International Bible Society to help
spread the gospel of Jesus Christ around the world!

Contents

New Testament

WELCOME!

to the
Little Kids'
Adventure
Bible

Welcome to the great adventure of reading, exploring and discovering the Bible.

Are you looking for adventure? Do you want to discover God's Word and apply it to your life? Then the *Little Kids' Adventure Bible* is especially for you.

Each feature of the *Little Kids' Adventure Bible* is made to show you the wonderful messages and promises in God's Word. Take a few minutes to read about these features. Then you will know the best way to use your Bible.

Features You Should Know About

Words to Treasure

The best way to live for Jesus is to know what the Bible says. Memorize these verses from "Words to Treasure."

In the beginning, God created the heavens and the earth.
Genesis 1:1

DID YOU KNOW?

What does create mean?

The word *create* means to "make something new." Genesis tells us that God is the creator of all things. You can find many things that God created in the book of Genesis.

Did You Know?

This feature points out many interesting facts that are found in the Bible. Learn them all and tell your parents, teachers and friends what you learn!

Life in Bible Times

Do you ever wonder what it was like to live in the times of Noah or Samson or Jesus? What kind of food did they eat? Where did they sleep? What kind of work did they do? "Life in Bible Times" will tell you—and show you! Each of these exciting features includes a picture.

Let's Live It!

It is important to read and memorize God's Word. But what really counts is *living* it, letting the Bible affect how you work, play and live. "Let's Live It!" tells you what the Bible has to say about your life RIGHT NOW!

People in Bible Times

The Bible is full of wonderful people. "People in Bible Times" helps you learn about these real-life characters and their true stories. It might be fun to try to imagine yourself in their situations. What would you do?

PEOPLE IN BIBLE TIMES

Adam

Adam was the first human being. God created Adam in his own image. That means that in many ways Adam was like God. God made Adam from the dust of the earth. God placed Adam in the Garden of Eden to take care of it.

viii

Section Introductions

If you need the basic facts about a section of the Bible (who wrote it, where it took place, why it was written), you'll find that information there. You'll find ten section introductions throughout this Bible.

The Books of the Law

Genesis Exodus Leviticus Numbers Deuteronomy

The first five books of the Bible are the books of the Law. In these books are many stories. There are stories about how God created the world. There are stories of how the nation of Israel began. And there are stories about the people that God chose to lead Israel: Abraham, Isaac, Jacob, Joseph and Moses.

One very important story is about how God gave his people the law. His laws are rules to help people live the way that he wants them to live. The laws help people love God. They help people love each other. You can read about God's laws in these books. Moses wrote these books almost 1500 years before Jesus lived.

Activities

If you want to not only read the *Little Kids' Adventure Bible* but also do something with what you've learned, turn to the list of activities at the back of the Bible (page 424). You'll find many ideas for things to discuss, to do, and to make.

Dictionary

When you're reading the *Little Kids' Adventure Bible*, you may come to a word that you don't understand. Be sure to take a minute to look it up in the dictionary at the back of your Bible (page 426). Read the meaning of the word so you can better understand God's message.

Where To Start

Don't worry about where to start. Start anywhere. Go through the Bible and see what features interest you. Then begin exploring and reading both the features and the Bible text. Use the *Little Kids' Adventure Bible* every day to begin the great adventure of living for Jesus!

If you have any questions or comments about this Bible, please write and tell us.

The Editors
ZonderKidz Bible Publishers
5300 Patterson Ave., SE
Grand Rapids, MI 49530

Note to parents and teachers:
The special features of the *Little Kids' Adventure Bible* can be used as a teaching or devotional tool by parents and teachers but also may be used to encourage children to explore the Bible on their own and to have their own quiet times with God.

A Word About the New International Reader's Version

Have You Ever Heard of the New International Version?

We call it the NIV. A lot of people read the NIV. In fact, more people read the NIV than any other English Bible. They like it because it's easy to read.

And now we are happy to give you another Bible that's easy to read and understand. It's the New International Reader's Version. We call it the NIrV.

Who Will Enjoy Reading the New International Reader's Version?

We made sure that people who are just starting to read could understand and enjoy the NIrV. Children will be able to read it and understand it. So will older people who are learning how to read or those who are reading the Bible for the first time. So will people who have a hard time understanding what they read. And so will people who use English as their second language. We hope this Bible will be just right for you.

How Is the NIrV Different From the NIV?

The NIrV is based on the NIV. The NIV Committee on Bible Translation (CBT) didn't produce the NIrV. But several members of CBT worked hard to make the NIrV possible. We used the words of the NIV when we could. When the NIV words were long, we used words that were shorter. We wanted to use words that are easy to understand. We explained words that might be hard to understand in a dictionary at the back of the Bible. We also made the NIV sentences much shorter.

Why did we do all of those things? Because we wanted to make the NIrV really easy to read and understand.

What Other Helps Does the NIrV Have?

We decided to give you a lot of other help too. For example, sometimes a verse is quoted from another place in the Bible. When it is, we put the Bible book's name, chapter and verse right after the verse that quotes another place.

We separated each chapter into shorter sections. We gave a title to almost every chapter. Sometimes we even gave a title to a section. We did it to help you understand what the chapter or section is all about.

Sometimes the writers of the Bible used more than one name for the same person or place. For example, in the New Testament the Sea of Galilee is also called the Sea of Gennesaret and the Sea of Tiberias. But in the NIrV we decided to call it the Sea of Galilee everywhere it appears in the New Testament. We did it because that is its most familiar name.

We also wanted to help our readers learn the names of people and places even in verses where those names don't actually appear. For example, when we knew that "the River" meant "the Euphrates River," we used those words even in verses where only the words "the River" are found. When we knew that the name of "Pharaoh" in a certain verse was "Hophra," we wrote his name in that verse. We did all of those things because we wanted to make the NIrV as clear as possible.

Does the NIrV Say What the First Writers of the Bible Said?

We wanted the NIrV to say just what the first writers of the Bible said. So we kept checking the Greek New Testament as we did our work. That's because the New Testament's first writers used Greek.

We used the best and oldest copies of the Greek New Testament. Earlier English Bibles couldn't use those copies because they had not yet been found. The oldest Greek New Testaments are best because they are closer in time to the ones the first Bible writers wrote. That's why we kept checking the older copies instead of newer ones.

Later copies of the Greek New Testament added several verses that the earlier ones don't have. Sometimes it's several verses in a row. When that's the case, we included them in the NIrV. But we set those verses off with a long line. That tells you that the first writers didn't write them. The verses were added later on. You will find the long lines at Mark 16: 9–20 and John 7:53—8:11. Sometimes it's a single verse. An example is Mark 9:44. That verse is not in the oldest Greek New Testaments. So we put the number 43/44 right before Mark 9:43. Then you can look on the list below for Mark 9:44 and locate the verse that was added.

Verses That Were Not Found in Earliest Greek New Testaments

Matthew 17:21	But that kind does not go out except by prayer and fasting.
Matthew 18:11	The Son of Man came to save what was lost.
Matthew 23:14	How terrible for you, teachers of the law and Pharisees! You pretenders! You take over the houses of widows. You say long prayers to show off. So God will punish you much more.
Mark 7:16	Everyone who has ears to hear should listen.
Mark 9:44	In hell,/ "the worms don't die,/ and the fire doesn't go out."

Mark 9:46	In hell,/ "the worms don't die,/ and the fire doesn't go out."
Mark 11:26	But if you do not forgive, your Father who is in heaven will not forgive your sins either.
Mark 15:28	Scripture came true. It says, "And he was counted among those who disobey the law."
Luke 17:36	Two men will be in the field. One will be taken and the other left.
Luke 23:17	It was Pilate's duty to let one prisoner go free for them at the Feast.
John 5:4	From time to time an angel of the Lord would come down. The angel would stir up the waters. The first disabled person to go into the pool after it was stirred would be healed.
Acts 8:37	Philip said, "If you believe with all your heart, you can." The official answered, "I believe that Jesus Christ is the Son of God."
Acts 15:34	But Silas decided to remain there.
Acts 24:7	But Lysias, the commander, came. By using a lot of force, he took Paul from our hands.
Acts 28:29	After he said that, the Jews left. They were arguing strongly among themselves.
Romans 16:24	May the grace of our Lord Jesus Christ be with all of you. Amen.

What Is Our Prayer for You?

The Lord has blessed the New International Version in a wonderful way. He has used it to help millions of Bible readers. Many people have put their faith in Jesus after reading it. Many others have become stronger believers because they have read it.

We hope and pray that the New International Reader's Version will help you in the same way. If that happens, we will give God all of the glory.

A Word About This Edition

This edition of the New International Reader's Version has been revised so that the gender language more closely matches that of the New International Version. When we prepared this new edition, we had help from people who were not part of the first team. We want to thank them for their help. They are Ben Aker from the Assemblies of God Theological Seminary, Paul House from the Southern Baptist Seminary, and Scott Munger from International Bible Society.

Old Testament

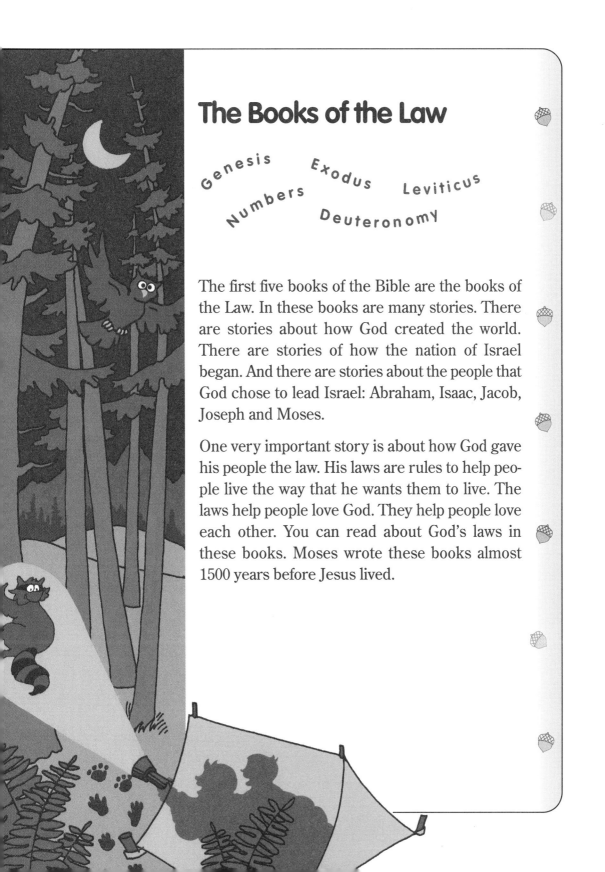

The Books of the Law

Genesis   Exodus   Leviticus
Numbers   Deuteronomy

The first five books of the Bible are the books of the Law. In these books are many stories. There are stories about how God created the world. There are stories of how the nation of Israel began. And there are stories about the people that God chose to lead Israel: Abraham, Isaac, Jacob, Joseph and Moses.

One very important story is about how God gave his people the law. His laws are rules to help people live the way that he wants them to live. The laws help people love God. They help people love each other. You can read about God's laws in these books. Moses wrote these books almost 1500 years before Jesus lived.

The Story of Creation

Genesis 1—2

The Beginning

In the beginning, God created the heavens and the earth. The earth didn't have any shape. And it was empty. Darkness was over the surface of the ocean. At that time, the ocean covered the earth. The Spirit of God was hovering over the waters.

God said, "Let there be light." And there was light. God saw that the light was good. He separated the light from the darkness. God called the light "day." He called the darkness "night." There was evening, and there was morning. It was day one.

God said, "Let there be a huge space between the waters. Let it separate water from water." And that's exactly what happened. God made the huge space between the waters. He separated the water that was under the space from the water that was above it. God called the huge space "sky." There was evening, and there was morning. It was day two.

God said, "Let the water under the sky be gathered into one place. Let dry ground appear." And that's exactly what happened. God called the dry ground "land." He called the waters that were gathered together "oceans." And God saw that it was good.

WORDS TO TREASURE

In the beginning, God created the heavens and the earth.

Genesis 1:1

Then God said, "Let the land produce plants. Let them bear their own seeds. And let there be trees on the land that bear fruit with seeds in it. Let each kind of plant or tree have its own kind of seeds." And that's exactly what happened.

The land produced plants. Each kind of plant had its own kind of seeds. The land produced trees that bore fruit with seeds in it. Each kind of tree had its own kind of seeds.

God saw that it was good. And there was evening, and there was morning. It was day three.

God said, "Let there be lights in the huge space of the sky. Let them separate the day from the night. Let them serve as signs to mark off the seasons and the days and the years. Let them serve as lights in the huge space of the sky to give light on the earth." And that's exactly what happened.

God made two great lights. He made the larger light to rule over the day. He made the smaller light to rule over the night. He also made the stars.

God put the lights in the huge space of the sky to give light on the earth. He put them there to rule over the day and the night. He put them there to separate light from darkness.

God saw that it was good. And there was evening, and there was morning. It was day four.

What does create mean?
The word *create* means to "make something new." Genesis tells us that God is the creator of all things. You can find many things that God created in the book of Genesis.

God said, "Let the waters be filled with living things. Let birds fly above the earth across the huge space of the sky." So God created the great creatures of the ocean. He created every living and moving thing that fills the waters. He created all kinds of them. He created every kind of bird that flies. And God saw that it was good.

God blessed them. He said, "Have little ones and increase your numbers. Fill the water in the oceans. Let there be more and more birds on the earth."

There was evening, and there was morning. It was day five.

God said, "Let the land produce all kinds of living creatures. Let there be livestock, and creatures that move along the ground, and wild animals. Let there be all kinds of them." And that's exactly what happened.

God made all kinds of wild animals. He made all kinds of livestock. He made all kinds of creatures that move along the ground. And God saw that it was good.

Then God said, "Let us make man in our likeness. Let them rule over the fish in the waters and the birds of the air. Let them rule over the livestock and over the whole earth. Let them rule over all of the creatures that move along the ground."

So God created man in his own likeness.
He created him in the likeness of God.
He created them as male and female.

God blessed them. He said to them, "Have children and increase your numbers. Fill the earth and bring it under your control. Rule over the fish in the waters and the birds of the air. Rule over every living creature that moves on the ground."

Then God said, "I am giving you every plant on the face of the whole earth that bears its own seeds. I am giving you every tree that has fruit with seeds in it. All of them will be given to you for food.

"I am giving every green plant to all of the land animals and the birds of the air for food. I am also giving the plants to all of the creatures that move on the ground. I am giving them to every living thing that breathes." And that's exactly what happened.

God saw everything he had made. And it was very good. There was evening, and there was morning. It was day six.

So the heavens and the earth and everything in them were completed.

You're Special

God made us in his own image. We are God's very special creation.

Look at pictures of your mom or dad when they were children. How were they like you? How were they different? Your parents love you very much because you are their child. You are like them in important ways. Ask your mom or dad to tell you why they think you are special.

God made you in his image too. You are special to God. He loves you. Say a prayer to God, thanking him for making you and for loving you very much.

By the seventh day God had finished the work he had been doing. So on the seventh day he rested from all of his work. God blessed the seventh day and made it holy. He rested on it. After he had created everything, he rested from all of the work he had done.

The Very First Man and Woman

Genesis 2—3

Adam and Eve

Here is the story of the heavens and the earth when they were created.

The LORD God made the earth and the heavens. At that time, bushes had not appeared on the earth. Plants had not come up in the fields. The LORD God had not sent rain on the earth. And there wasn't any man to work the ground. But streams came up from the earth. They watered the whole surface of the ground.

Then the LORD God formed a man. He made him out of the dust of the ground. He breathed the breath of life into him. And the man became a living person.

The LORD God had planted a garden in the east. It was in Eden. There he put the man he had formed. The LORD God made all kinds of trees grow out of the ground. Their fruit was pleasing to look at and good to eat.

PEOPLE IN BIBLE TIMES

Adam

Adam was the first human being. God created Adam in his own image. That means that in many ways Adam was like God. God made Adam from the dust of the earth. God placed Adam in the Garden of Eden to take care of it.

The tree that gives life forever was in the middle of the garden. The tree that gives the ability to tell the difference between good and evil was also there.

A river watered the garden. It flowed from Eden. From there it separated into four other rivers.

The LORD God put the man in the Garden of Eden. He put him there to work its ground and to take care of it.

The LORD God gave the man a command. He said, "You can eat the fruit of any tree that is in the garden. But you must not eat the fruit of the tree of the knowledge of good and evil. If you do, you can be sure that you will die."

The LORD God said, "It is not good for the man to be alone. I will make a helper who is just right for him."

The LORD God had formed all of the wild animals. He had also formed all of the birds of the air. He had made all of them out of the ground. He brought them to the man to see what names he would give them. And the name the man gave each living creature became its name.

So the man gave names to all of the livestock. He gave names to all of the birds of the air. And he gave names to all of the wild animals.

But Adam didn't find a helper that was right for him. So the LORD God caused him to fall into a deep sleep. While the man was sleeping, the LORD God took out one of his ribs. He closed up the opening that was in his side.

Then the LORD God made a woman. He made her from the rib he had taken out of the man. And he brought her to him.

The man said,

"Her bones have come from my bones.
　Her body has come from my body.
She will be named 'woman,'
　because she was taken out of a man."

That's why a man will leave his father and mother and be joined to his wife. The two of them will become one.

Adam and Eve Fall Into Sin

The serpent was more clever than any of the wild animals the LORD God had made. The serpent said to the woman, "Did God really say, 'You must not eat the fruit of any tree that is in the garden'?"

The woman said to the serpent, "We can eat the fruit of the trees that are in the garden. But God did say, 'You must not eat the fruit of the tree that is in the middle of the garden. Do not even touch it. If you do, you will die.'"

"You can be sure that you won't die," the serpent said to the woman. "God knows that when you eat the fruit of that tree, you will know things you have never known before. You will be able to tell the difference between good and evil. You will be like God."

What kind of fruit did Adam and Eve eat?

The Bible does not name the fruit. The important point is that Adam and Eve disobeyed God. Genesis 3 tells what happened when they disobeyed.

The woman saw that the fruit of the tree was good to eat. It was also pleasing to look at. And it would make a person wise. So she took some of the fruit and ate it. She also gave some to her husband, who was with her. And he ate it.

Then both of them knew things they had never known before. They realized they were naked. So they sewed fig leaves together and made clothes for themselves.

Then the man and his wife heard the LORD God walking in the garden. It was the coolest time of the day. They hid from the LORD God among the trees of the garden.

But the LORD God called out to the man. "Where are you?" he asked.

"I heard you in the garden," the man answered. "I was afraid. I was naked, so I hid."

The LORD God said, "Who told you that you were naked? Have you eaten the fruit of the tree I commanded you not to eat?"

The man said, "It was the woman you put here with me. She gave me some fruit from the tree. And I ate it."

Then the LORD God said to the woman, "What have you done?"

The woman said, "The serpent tricked me. That's why I ate the fruit."

The LORD God said to Adam, "You listened to your wife. You ate the fruit of the tree that I commanded you about. I said, 'You must not eat its fruit.'

"So I am putting a curse on the ground because of what you did.
  All the days of your life you will have to work hard
    to get food from the ground.
You will eat the plants of the field,
    even though the ground produces thorns and thistles.
You will have to work hard and sweat a lot
    to produce the food you eat.
You were made out of the ground.
    And you will return to it.
You are dust.
    So you will return to it."

Adam named his wife Eve. She would become the mother of every living person.

The LORD God made clothes out of animal skins for Adam and his wife to wear. The LORD God said, "The man has become like one of us. He can now tell the difference between good and evil. He must not be allowed to reach out his hand and pick fruit from the tree of life and eat it. If he does, he will live forever."

So the LORD God drove the man out of the Garden of Eden to work the ground he had been made out of. The LORD God drove him out and

Bad Choices

Adam and Eve made a wrong choice. They disobeyed God. Why did they do it? Adam and Eve made the wrong choice because:

1. Someone said it was all right to do the wrong thing.
2. It looked like a fun thing to do.
3. A close friend did it first.

After Adam and Eve made that wrong choice, they felt guilty and afraid. But it was too late.

Think about what you should say if someone tells you it's all right to do a bad thing. Or if something wrong looks like it would be fun. Or if a friend does a wrong thing first and wants you to do it too. If you can't think of a good answer, ask an older friend or your mom or dad for help.

then placed cherubim on the east side of the Garden of Eden. He also placed a flaming sword there. It flashed back and forth. The cherubim and the sword guarded the way to the tree of life.

The Very First Children

Genesis 4

Cain and Abel

Eve became pregnant and gave birth to Cain. She said, "With the LORD's help I have had a baby boy." Later she gave birth to his brother Abel.

Abel took care of sheep. Cain worked the ground. After some time, Cain gathered some of the things he had grown. He brought them as an offering to the LORD.

But Abel brought the fattest parts of some of the lambs from his flock. They were the male animals that were born first to their mothers.

The LORD was pleased with Abel and his offering. But he wasn't pleased with Cain and his offering. So Cain became very angry. His face was sad.

Then the LORD said to Cain, "Why are you angry? Why are you looking so sad? Do what is right. Then you will be accepted. If you don't do what is right, sin is waiting at your door to grab you. It longs to have you. But you must rule over it."

Cain said to his brother Abel, "Let's go out to the field." So they went out. There Cain attacked his brother Abel and killed him.

Then the LORD said to Cain, "Where is your brother Abel?"

"I don't know," he replied. "Am I supposed to look after my brother?"

The LORD said, "What have you done? Listen! Your brother's blood is crying out to me from the ground."

The LORD put a mark on Cain. Then anyone who found him wouldn't kill him.

So Cain went away from the LORD. He lived in the land of Nod. It was east of Eden.

Noah, the Ark and the Flood

Genesis 6—9

The Flood

Noah was a godly man. He was without blame among the people of his time. He walked with God. Noah had three sons. Their names were Shem, Ham and Japheth.

The earth was very sinful in God's eyes. It was full of mean and harmful acts. God saw how sinful the earth had become. All of the people on earth were leading very sinful lives.

Noah

Noah was a good man who loved and trusted God. He followed God's plans and built an ark. God saved Noah, his family, and all sorts of animals from a flood that destroyed the world.

How long did it take to build the ark?

It took about 120 years. God waited until the ark was ready before he sent the flood. He wanted to save Noah and his family.

So God said to Noah, "I am going to put an end to all people. They have filled the earth with their harmful acts. You can be sure that I am going to destroy both them and the earth.

"So make yourself an ark out of cypress wood. Make rooms in it. Cover it with tar inside and out. Here is how I want you to build it. The ark has to be 450 feet long. It has to be 75 feet wide and 45 feet high. Make a roof for it. Leave the sides of the ark open a foot and a half from the top. Put a door in one side of the ark. Make lower, middle and upper decks.

"I am going to bring a flood on the earth. It will destroy all life under the sky. It will destroy every living creature that breathes. Everything on earth will die.

"But I will make my covenant with you. You will enter the ark. Your sons and your wife and your sons' wives will enter it with you.

"Bring two of every living thing into the ark. Bring male and female of them into it. They will be kept alive with you. Two of every kind of bird will come to you. Two of every kind of animal will come to you. And two of every kind of creature that moves along the ground will come to you. All of them will be kept alive with you.

"Take every kind of food that you will need. Store it away. It will be food for you and for them."

Noah did everything exactly as God commanded him.

Then the LORD said to Noah, "Go into the ark with your whole family. I know that you are a godly man among the people of today.

"Take seven of every kind of 'clean' animal with you. Take male and female of them. Take two of every kind of animal that is not 'clean.' Take male and female of them. Also take seven of every kind of bird. Take male and female of them. That will keep every kind alive. Then they can spread out again over the whole earth.

"Seven days from now I will send rain on the earth. It will rain for 40 days and 40 nights. I will destroy from the face of the earth every living thing I have made."

Noah's Ark

Noah built a wooden ark. It was a kind of boat. When the flood came, Noah and his family were safe. The animals were safe too. The ark was 450 feet long. That is as long as 1½ football fields laid out end to end. The ark was 45 feet high. That's as high as a five-story building. The ark had a long row of windows just under the roof. The door must have been big to allow the large animals to go in.

Noah did everything the LORD commanded him to do.

Noah was 600 years old when the flood came on the earth. He and his sons entered the ark. His wife and his sons' wives went with them. They entered the ark to escape the waters of the flood.

Everything happened exactly as God had commanded Noah. After seven days the flood came on the earth.

For 40 days the flood kept coming on the earth. As the waters rose higher, they lifted the ark high above the earth. The waters rose higher and higher on the earth. And the ark floated on the water.

The waters rose on the earth until all of the high mountains under the entire sky were covered. The waters continued to rise until they covered the mountains by more than 20 feet.

Every living thing that moved on the earth died. The birds, the livestock and the wild animals died. All of the creatures that fill the earth also died. And so did every human being. Everything on dry land that had the breath of life in it died. Every living thing on the earth was wiped out. People and animals were destroyed. The creatures that move along the ground and the birds of the air were wiped out.

Everything was destroyed from the earth. Only Noah and those who were with him in the ark were left.

How long was the world covered with water?

Noah spent about one year in the ark. When Noah came out, he built an altar. He sacrificed animals there to thank God for saving his family.

The waters flooded the earth for 150 days.

But God showed concern for Noah. He also showed concern for all of the wild animals and livestock that were with Noah in the ark.

Noah opened the window he had made in the ark. He sent a raven out. It kept flying back and forth until the water had dried up from the earth.

Then Noah sent a dove out. He wanted to see if the water had gone down from the surface of the ground. But the dove couldn't find any place to put its feet down. There was still water over the whole surface of the earth. So the dove returned to Noah in the ark. Noah reached out his hand and took the dove in. He brought it back to himself in the ark.

He waited seven more days. Then he sent the dove out from the ark again. In the evening the dove returned to him. There in its beak was a freshly picked olive leaf! So Noah knew that the water on the earth had gone down.

He waited seven more days. Then he sent the dove out again. But that time it didn't return to him.

It was the first day of the first month of Noah's 601st year. The water had dried up from the earth. Then Noah removed the covering from the ark. He saw that the surface of the ground was dry. By the 27th day of the second month the earth was completely dry.

Then God said to Noah, "Come out of the ark. Bring your wife and your sons and their wives with you.

"Bring out every kind of living thing that is with you. Bring the birds, the animals, and all of the creatures that move along the ground. Then they can multiply on the earth. They can have little ones and increase their numbers."

So Noah came out of the ark. His sons and his wife and his sons' wives were with him. All of the animals came out of the ark. The creatures that move along the ground also came out. So did all of the birds. Everything that moves on the earth came out of the ark. One kind after another came out.

Then Noah built an altar to honor the LORD. He took some of all of the "clean" animals and birds. He sacrificed burnt offerings to the LORD on the altar.

Their smell was pleasant to the LORD. He said to himself, "I will never put a curse on the ground again because of man. I will not do it even

Thank God

When Noah and his family left the ark, they gave thanks to God. God was pleased. He put a rainbow in the sky. It was his promise that he would never again send a flood over the whole earth. Noah and his family were very thankful. Think of three things you are thankful for.

though his heart is always directed toward what is evil. His thoughts are evil from the time he is young. I will never destroy all living things again, as I have just done.

"As long as the earth lasts,
    there will always be a time to plant
    and a time to gather the crops.
As long as the earth lasts,
    there will always be cold and heat.
There will always be summer and winter,
    day and night."

God Makes a Covenant With Noah

Then God gave his blessing to Noah and his sons. He said to them, "Have children and increase your numbers. Fill the earth."

Then God spoke to Noah and to his sons who were with him. He said, "I am now making my covenant with you and with all of your children who will be born after you. I am making it also with every living thing that was with you in the ark. I am making my covenant with the birds, the livestock and all of the wild animals. I am making it with all of the creatures that came out of the ark with you. I am making it with every living thing on earth.

"Here is my covenant that I am making with you. The waters of a flood will never destroy all life again. A flood will never destroy the earth again."

God continued, "My covenant is between me and you and every living thing with you. It is a covenant for all time to come.

"Here is the sign of the covenant I am making. I have put my rainbow in the clouds. It will be the sign of the covenant between me and the earth. Sometimes when I bring clouds over the earth, a rainbow will appear in them. Then I will remember my covenant between me and you and every kind of living thing. The waters will never become a flood to destroy all life again.

"When the rainbow appears in the clouds, I will see it. I will remember that my covenant will last forever. It is a covenant between me and every kind of living thing on earth."

So God said to Noah, "The rainbow is the sign of my covenant. I have made my covenant between me and all life on earth."

God Confuses the Language of the People

Genesis 11

The Tower of Babel

The whole world had only one language. All people spoke it. They moved to the east and found a broad valley in Babylonia. There they settled down.

They said to each other, "Come. Let's make bricks and bake them well." They used bricks instead of stones. They used tar to hold the bricks together.

Then they said, "Come. Let's build a city for ourselves. Let's build a tower that reaches to the sky. We'll make a name for ourselves. Then we won't be scattered over the face of the whole earth."

But the LORD came down to see the city and the tower the people were building. The LORD said, "They are one people. And all of them speak the same language. That is why they can do this. Now they will be able to do anything they plan to. Come. Let us go down and mix up their language. Then they will not understand each other."

So the LORD scattered them from there over the whole earth. And they stopped building the city. The LORD mixed up the language of the whole world there. That's why the city was named Babel. From there the LORD scattered them over the face of the whole earth.

The Tower of Babel

The tower of Babel was probably a ziggurat (ZIG–ger–at). A ziggurat was a tall building. It was shaped like a pyramid. It had stairs on the outside. These towers often had a temple on top. People went there to try to reach heaven with prayers to false gods. But God wanted the people to love and worship *him*, not false gods.

God Leads Abram

Genesis 12; 15

God Chooses Abram

The LORD had said to Abram, "Leave your country and your people. Leave your father's family. Go to the land I will show you.

"I will make you into a great nation.
　I will bless you.
I will make your name great.
　You will be a blessing to others.
I will bless those who bless you.
　I will put a curse on anyone who calls down a curse on you.
All nations on earth
　will be blessed because of you."

PEOPLE IN BIBLE TIMES

Abraham

Abram, later called Abraham, obeyed God. He left his family and his nation because God told him to go to a new land far away. God promised to give Abraham many children. Abraham believed God's promise. When he was an old man, God gave him a son. This son later had his own children, and in this way Abraham became the "father of many."

So Abram left, just as the LORD had told him. Lot went with him. Abram was 75 years old when he left Haran.

He took his wife Sarai and his nephew Lot. They took all of the things they had gotten in Haran. They also took the workers they had gotten there.

They set out for the land of Canaan. And they arrived there.

Abram traveled through the land. He went as far as the large tree of Moreh at Shechem. At that time the people of Canaan were living in the land.

The LORD appeared to Abram at Shechem. He said, "I will give this land to your children after you." So Abram built an altar there to honor the LORD, who had appeared to him.

From there, Abram went on toward the hills east of Bethel. He set up his tent there. Bethel was to the west, and Ai was to the east.

Abram built an altar there and worshiped the LORD. Then Abram left and continued toward the Negev Desert.

Abram Goes to Egypt

At that time there wasn't enough food in the land. So Abram went down to Egypt to live there for a while.

As he was about to enter Egypt, he spoke to his wife Sarai. He said, "I know what a beautiful woman you are. The people of Egypt will see you. They will say, 'This is his wife.' And they will kill me. But they will let you live. Say you are my sister. Then I'll be treated well because of you. My life will be spared because of you."

Abram arrived in Egypt. The people of Egypt saw that Sarai was a very beautiful woman. When Pharaoh's officials saw her, they bragged to Pharaoh about her. Sarai was taken into his palace.

Pharaoh treated Abram well because of her. So Abram gained more sheep and cattle. He also got more male and female donkeys. And he gained more male and female servants and some camels.

PEOPLE IN BIBLE TIMES

Sarah

Sarah was married to Abraham. She was sad because she did not have any children. God promised Sarah a son. She laughed because she thought she was too old. God kept his promise, and Sarah's son, Isaac, was born (see page 21.)

DID YOU KNOW?

What is a covenant?

A covenant is a promise. It is the strongest possible promise a person can make. God made promises to Abram. God's promises are a covenant.

But the LORD sent terrible sicknesses on Pharaoh and everyone in his palace. He did it because of Abram's wife Sarai.

So Pharaoh sent for Abram. "What have you done to me?" he said. "Why didn't you tell me she was your wife? Why did you say, 'She's my sister'? That's why I took her to be my wife. Now then, here's your wife. Take her and go!"

Then Pharaoh gave orders about Abram to his men. They sent him on his way. He left with his wife and everything he had.

God Makes a Covenant With Abram

Abram had a vision. The LORD said to him,

WORDS TO TREASURE

Abram believed the LORD...
His faith made him
right with the LORD.

Genesis 15:6

"Abram, do not be afraid.
 I am like a shield to you.
 I am your very great reward."

The LORD took Abram outside and said, "Look up at the sky. Count the stars, if you can." Then he said to him, "That is how many children you will have."

Abram believed the LORD. The LORD accepted Abram because he believed. So his faith made him right with the LORD.

God's Promise to Abraham

Genesis 18

Three Men Visit Abraham

The LORD appeared to Abraham near the large trees of Mamre. Abraham was sitting at the entrance to his tent. It was the hottest time of the day.

Abraham looked up and saw three men standing nearby. He quickly left the entrance to his tent to meet them. He bowed low to the ground.

He said, "My lord, if you are pleased with me, don't pass me by. Let a little water be brought. All of you can wash your feet and rest under this tree.

"Let me get you something to eat to give you strength. Then you can go on your way. I want to do this for you now that you have come to me."

"All right," they answered. "Go ahead and do it."

So Abraham hurried into the tent to Sarah. "Quick!" he said. "Get about half a bushel of fine flour. Mix it and bake some bread."

Then he ran to the herd. He picked out a choice, tender calf. He gave it to a servant, who hurried to prepare it. Then he brought some butter and milk and the calf that had been prepared. He served them to the three men.

While they ate, he stood near them under a tree.

"Where is your wife Sarah?" they asked him.

Believe God's Promise

God promised Abram that he would have a son. He would have more children than he could count. Abram was 85 years old and had no children. But Abram believed what God promised. Abram's faith made him right with the Lord.

You can become right with the Lord by believing in God's Son Jesus. If you have never believed that Jesus is your Savior, or if you are not sure, say this prayer. Put a marker in your Bible at this place. Then you will remember what you did.

"Dear God, I believe that Jesus is my Savior. Thank you, God, that I am now right with you, and that you will take me to heaven when I die."

"Over there, in the tent," he said.

Then the LORD said, "You can be sure that I will return to you about this time next year. Your wife Sarah will have a son."

Sarah was listening at the entrance to the tent behind him. Abraham and Sarah were already very old. Sarah was too old to have a baby. So she laughed to herself. She thought, "I'm worn out, and my husband is old. Can I really know the joy of having a baby?"

Then the LORD said to Abraham, "Why did Sarah laugh? Why did she say, 'Will I really have a baby, now that I am old?' Is anything too hard for me? I will return to you at the appointed time next year. Sarah will have a son."

Two Evil Cities

Genesis 19

The LORD Destroys Sodom and Gomorrah

Two angels arrived at Sodom. [They] said to Lot, "Do you have anyone else here? Do you have sons-in-law, sons or daughters? Does anyone else in the city belong to you? Get them out of here. We are going to destroy this place. There has been a great cry to the Lord against the people of this city. So he has sent us to destroy it."

Then Lot went out and spoke to his sons-in-law. They had promised to get married to his daughters. He said, "Hurry up! Get out of this place! The Lord is about to destroy the city!" But his sons-in-law thought he was joking.

The sun was coming up. So the angels tried to get Lot to leave. They said, "Hurry up! Take your wife and your two daughters who are here. Get out! If you don't, you will be swept away when the city is punished."

Where are Sodom and Gomorrah?

The ruins of these cities are probably under shallow water in the Dead Sea. God destroyed the cities because they were so sinful. Today the nation of Israel runs oil wells near where these cities may have stood.

Lot didn't move right away. So the men grabbed him by the hand. They also took hold of the hands of his wife and two daughters. They led all of them safely out of the city. The Lord had mercy on them.

As soon as the angels had brought them out, one of them spoke. He said, "Run for your lives! Don't look back! Don't stop anywhere in the valley! Run to the mountains! If you don't, you will be swept away!"

Then the Lord sent down burning sulfur. It came down like rain on Sodom and Gomorrah. It came from the Lord out of the sky. He destroyed those cities and the whole valley. All of the people who were living in the cities were wiped out. So were the plants in the land.

But Lot's wife looked back. When she did, she became a pillar made out of salt.

Early the next morning [Lot's uncle] Abraham got up. He returned to the place where he had stood in front of the Lord. He looked down toward Sodom and Gomorrah and the whole valley. He saw thick smoke rising from the land. It looked like smoke from a furnace.

So when God destroyed the cities of the valley, he showed concern for Abraham. He brought [Abraham's nephew] Lot out safely when he destroyed the cities where Lot had lived.

Abraham and Isaac

Genesis 21—22

Isaac Is Born

The LORD was gracious to Sarah, just as he had said he would be. He did for Sarah what he had promised to do. Sarah became pregnant. She had a son by Abraham when he was old. He was born at the exact time God had promised him.

Abraham gave the name Isaac to the son Sarah had by him. When his son Isaac was eight days old, Abraham circumcised him. He did it exactly as God had commanded him. Abraham was 100 years old when his son Isaac was born to him.

Sarah said, "God has given laughter to me. Everyone who hears about this will laugh with me."

She continued, "Who would have said to Abraham that Sarah would nurse children? But I've had a son by him when he is old."

God Puts Abraham to the Test

Some time later God put Abraham to the test. He said to him, "Abraham!"

"Here I am," Abraham replied.

Then God said, "Take your son, your only son. He is the one you love. Take Isaac. Go to Moriah. Give him to me there as a burnt offering. Sacrifice him on one of the mountains I will tell you about."

Early the next morning Abraham got up. He put a saddle on his donkey. He took two of his servants and his son Isaac with him. He cut enough wood for the burnt offering. Then he started out for the place God had told him about.

On the third day Abraham looked up. He saw the place a long way off. He said to his servants, "Stay here with the donkey.

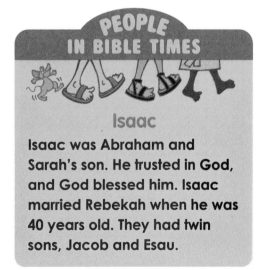

PEOPLE IN BIBLE TIMES

Isaac

Isaac was Abraham and Sarah's son. He trusted in God, and God blessed him. Isaac married Rebekah when he was 40 years old. They had twin sons, Jacob and Esau.

The boy and I will go over there and worship. Then we'll come back to you."

Abraham put the wood for the burnt offering on his son Isaac. He himself carried the fire and the knife. The two of them walked on together.

Then Isaac spoke up. He said to his father Abraham, "Father?"

"Yes, my son?" Abraham replied.

"The fire and wood are here," Isaac said. "But where is the lamb for the burnt offering?"

Abraham answered, "God himself will provide the lamb for the burnt offering, my son." The two of them walked on together.

I will certainly bless you . . . because you have obeyed me.
Genesis 22:17–18

They reached the place God had told Abraham about. There Abraham built an altar. He arranged the wood on it. He tied up his son Isaac. He placed him on the altar, on top of the wood. Then he reached out his hand. He took the knife to kill his son.

But the angel of the LORD called out to him from heaven. He said, "Abraham! Abraham!"

"Here I am," Abraham replied.

"Do not lay a hand on the boy," he said. "Do not do anything to him. Now I know that you have respect for God. You have not held back from me your son, your only son."

Abraham looked up. There in a bush he saw a ram. It was caught by its horns. He went over and took the ram. He sacrificed it as a burnt offering instead of his son.

So Abraham named that place The LORD Will Provide. To this day people say, "It will be provided on the mountain of the LORD."

The angel of the LORD called out to Abraham from heaven a second time. He said, "I am taking an oath in my own name. I will bless you because of what you have done," announces the LORD. "You have not held back your son, your only son.

"So I will certainly bless you. I will make your children after you as many as the stars in the sky. I will make them as many as the grains of sand on the seashore. Your children will take over the cities of their enemies. All nations on earth will be blessed because of your children. All of that will happen because you have obeyed me."

Isaac Marries Rebekah

Genesis 24

Abraham's Servant Finds a Wife for Isaac

By that time Abraham was very old. The LORD had blessed him in every way. The best servant in his house was in charge of everything he had.

Abraham said to him, "Put your hand under my thigh. The LORD is the God of heaven and the God of earth. I want you to make a promise with an oath in his name.

"I'm living among the people of Canaan. But I want you to promise me that you won't get a wife for my son from their daughters. Instead, promise me that you will go to my country and to my own relatives. Get a wife for my son Isaac from there."

The servant took ten of his master's camels and left. He took with him all kinds of good things from his master. He started out for Aram Naharaim. He made his way to the town of Nahor.

He stopped near the well outside the town. There he made the camels get down on their knees. It was almost evening. It was the time when women go out to get water.

Then he prayed, "LORD, you are the God of my master Abraham. Give me success today. Be kind to my master Abraham. I'm standing beside this spring. The daughters of the people who live in the town are coming out here to get water.

"I will speak to a young woman. I'll say, 'Please lower your jar so I can have a drink.' Suppose she says, 'Have a drink of water. And I'll get some for your camels too.' Then let her be the one you have chosen for your servant Isaac. That's how I'll know you have been kind to my master."

Before he had finished praying, Rebekah came out. She had a jar on her shoulder. She was the daughter of Bethuel, the son of Milcah. Milcah was the wife of Abraham's brother Nahor. The young woman was very

PEOPLE IN BIBLE TIMES

Rebekah

Rebekah was a beautiful girl. She was kind too. She agreed to leave her family to marry Isaac. She moved to a country called Canaan. Isaac loved her very much. Rebekah comforted him when his mother died.

beautiful. She was a virgin. No man had made love to her. She went down to the spring. She filled her jar and came up again.

The servant hurried to meet her. He said, "Please give me a little water from your jar."

"Have a drink, sir," she said. She quickly lowered the jar to her hands. And she gave him a drink.

After she had given him a drink, she said, "I'll get water for your camels too. I'll keep doing it until they finish drinking." So she quickly emptied her jar into the stone tub. Then she ran back to the well to get more water. She got enough for all of his camels.

Then Abraham's servant and the men who were with him ate and drank. They spent the night there.

They got up the next morning. Abraham's servant said, "The LORD has given me success on my journey. Send me on my way so I can go to my master.

Then Rebekah and her female servants got ready. They got on their camels to go with the man. So the servant took Rebekah and left.

One evening he went out to the field. He wanted to spend some time thinking. When he looked up, he saw camels approaching.

Praying in Your Heart

Praying in your heart means praying to God without saying anything out loud. Abraham's servant may have prayed in his heart.

Here are some times when you might want to pray in your heart:

1. **When you are afraid of the babysitter.**
2. **When you are about to cross a busy street.**
3. **If your brother or sister is being mean to you.**

Draw pictures of three other times you could pray in your heart.

Rebekah also looked up and saw Isaac. She got down from her camel. She asked the servant, "Who is that man in the field coming to meet us?"

"He's my master," the servant answered. So she took her veil and covered her face.

Then the servant told Isaac everything he had done.

Isaac brought Rebekah into the tent that had belonged to his mother Sarah. And he married Rebekah. She became his wife, and he loved her. So Isaac was comforted after his mother died.

Isaac's Sons

Genesis 25; 27—28

Jacob and Esau

Here is the story of Abraham's son Isaac.

Abraham was the father of Isaac. Isaac was 40 years old when he married Rebekah. She was the daughter of Bethuel the Aramean from Paddan Aram. She was also the sister of Laban the Aramean.

Rebekah couldn't have children. So Isaac prayed to the LORD for her. And the LORD answered his prayer. His wife Rebekah became pregnant.

The babies struggled with each other inside her. She said, "Why is this happening to me?" So she went to ask the LORD what she should do.

The LORD said to her,

"Two nations are in your body.
    Two tribes that are now inside you will be separated.
One nation will be stronger than the other.
    The older son will serve the younger one."

The time came for Rebekah to have her babies. There were twin boys in her body. The first one to come out was red. His whole body was covered with hair. So they named him Esau.

Then his brother came out. His hand was holding onto Esau's heel. So he was named Jacob. Isaac was 60 years old when Rebekah had them.

The boys grew up. Esau became a skillful hunter. He was a man who liked the open country. But Jacob was a quiet man. He stayed at home

among the tents. Isaac liked the meat of wild animals. So Esau was his favorite son. But Rebekah's favorite was Jacob.

One day Jacob was cooking some stew. Esau came in from the open country. He was very hungry. He said to Jacob, "Quick! Let me have some of that red stew! I'm very hungry!" That's why he was also named Edom.

Jacob replied, "First sell me the rights that belong to you as the oldest son in the family."

"Look, I'm dying of hunger," Esau said. "What good are those rights to me?"

But Jacob said, "First promise me with an oath that you are selling me your rights." So Esau promised to do it. He sold Jacob all of the rights that belonged to him as the oldest son.

Jacob gave Esau some bread and some lentil stew. Esau ate and drank. Then he got up and left.

So Esau didn't care anything at all about the rights that belonged to him as the oldest son.

Isaac Gives Jacob His Blessing

Isaac had become old. His eyes were so weak he couldn't see anymore. One day he called for his older son Esau. He said to him, "My son."

"Here I am," he answered.

Isaac said, "I'm an old man now. And I don't know when I'll die. Now then, get your weapons. Get your bow and arrows. Go out to the open country. Hunt some wild animals for me. Prepare for me the kind of tasty food I like. Bring it to me to eat. Then I'll give you my blessing before I die."

Rebekah was listening when Isaac spoke to his son Esau. Esau left for the open country. He went to hunt for a wild animal and bring it back.

Then Rebekah said to her son Jacob, "Look, I heard your father speaking to your brother Esau. He said, 'Bring me a wild animal. Prepare some tasty food for me to eat. Then I'll give you my blessing before I die. The LORD will be my witness.'"

Rebekah continued, "My son, listen carefully. Do what I tell you. Go out to the flock. Bring me two of the finest young goats. I will prepare tasty food for your father. I'll make it just the way he likes it. I want you to take it to your father to eat. Then he'll give you his blessing before he dies."

Jacob said to his mother Rebekah, "My brother Esau's body is covered with hair. But my skin is smooth. What if my father touches me? He would know I was trying to trick him. That would bring a curse down on me instead of a blessing."

His mother said to him, "My son, let the curse fall on me. Just do what I say. Go and get the goats for me."

So he went and got the goats. He brought them to his mother. And she prepared some tasty food. She made it just the way his father liked it.

The clothes of her older son Esau were in her house. She took the best of them and put them on her younger son Jacob. She covered his

God Is Important

Esau had special rights as the oldest son. He could claim promises that God had made to his grandfather Abraham. How did Esau show that God was not important to him?

The way we act shows if God is important to us.

Make up an ending to each of these stories. Be sure your endings show how the person will act if God is important to him or her. Tell your stories to a friend or to one of your parents.

1. Some boys were throwing stones at passing cars. "Come on, Tim," they said. "It's fun. Here, take this stone."

2. "Sarah, I won't come to your birthday party if Cindy is there," Judy said. "Cindy wears old clothes and looks funny."

3. "Hey, Justin," his best friend whispered. "I dare you to take a piece of candy without paying for it."

Think of something you did that shows that God is important to you.

hands with the skins of the goats. She also covered the smooth part of his neck with them.

Then she handed to her son Jacob the tasty food and the bread she had made.

Why was Isaac's blessing so important to Jacob and Esau?

A father's blessing was like a powerful prayer or promise. Whoever had the blessing would be happy and successful. So both Jacob and Esau wanted their father's blessing.

He went to his father and said, "My father."

"Yes, my son," Isaac answered. "Who is it?"

Jacob said to his father, "I'm your oldest son Esau. I've done as you told me. Please sit up. Eat some of my wild meat. Then give me your blessing."

Isaac asked his son, "How did you find it so quickly, my son?"

"The LORD your God gave me success," he replied.

Then Isaac said to Jacob, "Come near so I can touch you, my son. I want to know whether you really are my son Esau."

Jacob went close to his father. Isaac touched him and said, "The voice is the voice of Jacob. But the hands are the hands of Esau."

Isaac didn't recognize him. His hands were covered with hair like those of his brother Esau. So Isaac blessed him. "Are you really my son Esau?" he asked.

"I am," Jacob replied.

Isaac said, "My son, bring me some of your wild meat to eat. Then I'll give you my blessing."

Jacob brought it to him. So Isaac ate. Jacob also brought some wine. And Isaac drank. Then Jacob's father Isaac said to him, "Come here, my son. Kiss me."

So Jacob went to him and kissed him. When Isaac smelled the clothes, he gave Jacob his blessing. He said,

"It really is the smell of my son.
    It's like the smell of a field
    that the LORD has blessed.

May God give you dew from heaven.

May he give you the richness of the earth.

May he give you plenty of grain and fresh wine.

May nations serve you.

May they bow down to you.

Rule over your brothers.

May the sons of your mother bow down to you.

May those who call down curses on you be cursed.

And may those who bless you be blessed."

When Isaac finished blessing him, Jacob left his father. Just then his brother Esau came in from hunting. He too prepared some tasty food. He brought it to his father. Then Esau said to him, "My father, sit up. Eat some of my wild meat. Then give me your blessing."

His father Isaac asked him, "Who are you?"

"I'm your son," he answered. "I'm your oldest son. I'm Esau."

Isaac was shaking all over. He said, "Then who was it that hunted a wild animal and brought it to me? I ate it just before you came. I gave him my blessing. And he will certainly be blessed!"

Esau heard his father's words. Then he began crying loudly and bitterly. He said to his father, "Bless me! Bless me too, my father!"

But Isaac said, "Your brother came and tricked me. He took your blessing."

Esau said, "Isn't Jacob just the right name for him? He has cheated me two times. First, he took my rights as the oldest son. And now he's taken my blessing!"

Jacob Runs Away to Laban

Esau was angry with Jacob. He was angry because of the blessing his father had given to Jacob. He said to himself, "My father will soon die. The days of sorrow over him are near. Then I'll kill my brother Jacob."

Rebekah was told what her older son Esau had said. So she sent for her younger son Jacob. She said to him, "Your brother Esau is comforting himself with the thought of killing you.

"Now then, my son, do what I say. Go at once to my brother Laban in Haran. Stay with him until your brother's anger calms down. Stay until your brother isn't angry with you anymore. When he forgets what you did to him, I'll let you know. Then you can come back from there."

Jacob Has a Dream at Bethel

Jacob left Beersheba and started out for Haran. He reached a certain place and stopped for the night. The sun had already set. He took one of the stones there and placed it under his head. Then he lay down to sleep.

In a dream he saw a stairway standing on the earth. Its top reached to heaven. The angels of God were going up and coming down on it.

The LORD stood above the stairway. He said, "I am the LORD. I am the God of your grandfather Abraham and the God of Isaac. I will give you and your children after you the land on which you are lying. They will be like the dust of the earth that can't be counted. They will spread out to the west and to the east. They will spread out to the north and to the south. All nations on earth will be blessed because of you and your children after you.

I am with you. I will watch over you everywhere you go.
Genesis 28:15

"I am with you. I will watch over you everywhere you go. And I will bring you back to this land. I will not leave you until I have done what I have promised you."

What Is Important?

What are some important things you can ask God for? Jacob wanted three things from God. He wanted God to be with him on his journey. He wanted food to eat and clothes to wear. And he wanted God to return him safely to his father's home.

God gave Jacob the important things he wanted and needed. What area few really important things God has given you? Thank him for these things when you pray.

Jacob Gets Married

Genesis 29

Jacob Gets Married to Leah and Rachel

Jacob stayed with Laban for a whole month. Then Laban said to him, "You are one of my relatives. But is that any reason for you to work for me for nothing? Tell me what your pay should be."

Laban had two daughters. The name of the older one was Leah. And the name of the younger one was Rachel. Leah had weak eyes. But Rachel was beautiful. She had a nice figure.

Jacob was in love with Rachel. He said to Laban, "I'll work for you for seven years to get your younger daughter Rachel."

Laban said, "It's better for me to give her to you than to some other man. Stay here with me."

So Jacob worked for seven years to get Rachel. But they seemed like only a few days to him because he loved her so much.

Laban brought all of the people of the place together and had a big dinner prepared. But when evening came, he gave his daughter Leah to Jacob. And Jacob made love to her. Laban gave his female servant Zilpah to his daughter as her servant.

PEOPLE IN BIBLE TIMES

Rachel

Rachel was a beautiful girl. She was Laban's youngest daughter. Jacob loved her very much. He worked for her father for 14 years so he could marry her.

DID YOU KNOW?

Why did Jacob have to work for Laban?

In Bible times, men gave a gift to the father of the woman they married. Jacob had no money. But he loved Rachel. So he was willing to work 14 years to marry her.

When Jacob woke up the next morning, there was Leah next to him! So he said to Laban, "What have you done to me? I worked for you to get Rachel, didn't I? Why did you trick me?"

Laban replied, "It isn't our practice here to give the younger daughter to be married before the older one. Complete this daughter's wedding week. Then we'll give you the younger one also. But you will have to work for another seven years."

So Jacob did it. He completed the week with Leah. Then Laban gave him his daughter Rachel to be his wife. And he worked for Laban for another seven years.

The Story of Joseph

Genesis 37; 39; 41—43; 45—46

Joseph Has Two Dreams

Jacob [who was also called Israel] lived in the land of Canaan. It's the land where his father had stayed.

Here is the story of Jacob.

Joseph was [Jacob and Rachel's son]. He was 17 years old. He was taking care of the flocks with some of his brothers. They were the sons of Bilhah and the sons of Zilpah, his father's wives. Joseph brought their father a bad report about them.

Israel loved Joseph more than any of his other sons. Joseph had been born to him when he was old. Israel made him a beautiful robe.

Joseph's Robe
People in Bible times liked beautiful clothes. They made their clothes out of black or white cloth. Sometimes they liked to use brighter colors like purple, red, blue and yellow. Joseph's robe was made by sewing colored threads into designs in the cloth. The robe Jacob gave Joseph was more than just a beautiful gift. It probably showed that Joseph had a more important place in the family than his older brothers. This picture shows decorated clothes worn by people in Joseph's time. Joseph's robe probably looked something like this.

Joseph's brothers saw that their father loved him more than any of them. So they hated Joseph. They couldn't even speak one kind word to him.

Joseph had a dream. When he told it to his brothers, they hated him even more. He said to them, "Listen to the dream I had. We were tying up bundles of grain out in the field. Suddenly my bundle rose and stood up straight. Your bundles gathered around my bundle and bowed down to it."

His brothers said to him, "Do you plan to be king over us? Will you really rule over us?" So they hated him even more because of his dream. They didn't like what he had said.

Then Joseph had another dream. He told it to his brothers. "Listen," he said. "I had another dream. This time the sun and moon and 11 stars were bowing down to me."

He told his father as well as his brothers. Then his father objected. He said, "What about this dream you had? Will your mother and I and your brothers really do that? Will we really come and bow down to the ground in front of you?"

His brothers were jealous of him. But his father kept the matter in mind.

Joseph Is Sold by His Brothers

Joseph's brothers had gone to take care of their father's flocks near Shechem. Israel said to Joseph, "As you know, your brothers are taking care of the flocks near Shechem. Come. I'm going to send you to them."

"All right," Joseph replied.

So Israel said to him, "Go to your brothers. See how they are doing. Also see how the flocks are doing. Then come back and tell me." So he sent him away from the Hebron Valley.

Joseph arrived at Shechem. A man found him wandering around in the fields. He asked Joseph, "What are you looking for?"

He replied, "I'm looking for my brothers. Can you tell me where they are taking care of their flocks?"

"They've moved on from here," the man answered. "I heard them say, 'Let's go to Dothan.'"

So Joseph went to look for his brothers. He found them near Dothan. But they saw him a long way off. Before he reached them, they made plans to kill him.

"Here comes that dreamer!" they said to one another. "Come. Let's kill him. Let's throw him into one of these empty wells. Let's say that a wild animal ate him up. Then we'll see whether his dreams will come true."

Reuben heard them. He tried to save Joseph from them. "Let's not take his life," he said. "Let's not spill any blood. Throw him into this empty well here in the desert. But don't harm him yourselves."

Reuben said that to save Joseph from them. He was hoping he could take him back to his father.

When Joseph came to his brothers, he was wearing his beautiful robe. They took it away from him. And they threw him into the well. The well was empty. There wasn't any water in it.

Then they sat down to eat their meal. As they did, they saw some Ishmaelite traders coming from Gilead. Their camels were loaded with spices, lotion and myrrh. They were on their way to take them down to Egypt.

Judah said to his brothers, "What will we gain if we kill our brother and try to cover up what we've done? Come. Let's sell him to these traders. Let's not harm him ourselves. After all, he's our brother. He's our own flesh and blood." Judah's brothers agreed with him.

The traders from Midian came by. Joseph's brothers pulled him up

Family Favorites

Jacob loved his son Joseph the most. He gave him a beautiful coat. The story says that Joseph's brothers hated him. And Joseph only made things worse. He bragged to his brothers about a dream he had.

Do you ever feel like your parents love a brother or sister more than they love you? Ask your parents if they ever felt like that when they were young.

Read this Bible story with your family. Talk about Joseph and his father. How could they have helped their family feel closer and happier?

out of the well. They sold him to the Ishmaelite traders for eight ounces of silver. Then the traders took him to Egypt.

Later, Reuben came back to the empty well. He saw that Joseph wasn't there. He was so upset that he tore his clothes. He went back to his brothers and said, "The boy isn't there! Now what should I do?"

Then they got Joseph's beautiful robe. They killed a goat and dipped the robe in the blood. They took it back to their father. They said, "We found this. Take a look at it. See if it's your son's robe."

Jacob recognized it. He said, "It's my son's robe! A wild animal has eaten him up. Joseph must have been torn to pieces."

Jacob tore his clothes. He put on black clothes. Then he sobbed over his son for many days.

All of Jacob's other sons and daughters came to comfort him. But they weren't able to. He said, "I'll be full of sorrow when I go down into the grave to be with my son." So Joseph's father sobbed over him.

Why is Joseph important?

Joseph saved his family from a famine. He brought them to live in the great country of Egypt. When Joseph was young, his brothers did not treat him fairly. But God helped him become powerful in Egypt.

But the traders from Midian sold Joseph to Potiphar in Egypt. Potiphar was one of Pharaoh's officials. He was the captain of the palace guard.

The LORD was with Joseph. He gave Joseph success in everything he did. So Pharaoh said to Joseph, "I'm putting you in charge of the whole land of Egypt."

Joseph's Brothers Go Down to Egypt

Jacob found out that there was grain in Egypt. So he said to his sons, "Why do you just keep looking at each other?" He continued, "I've heard there's grain in Egypt. Go down there. Buy some for us. Then we'll live and not die."

So ten of Joseph's brothers went down to Egypt to buy grain there. But Jacob didn't send Joseph's brother Benjamin with them. He was afraid Benjamin might be harmed.

Israel's sons were among the people who went to buy grain. There wasn't enough food in the land of Canaan.

Joseph was the governor of the land. He was the one who sold grain to all of its people. When Joseph's brothers arrived, they bowed down to him with their faces to the ground.

As soon as Joseph saw his brothers, he recognized them. But he pretended to be a stranger. He spoke to them in a mean way. "Where do you come from?" he asked.

"From the land of Canaan," they replied. "We've come to buy food. All of us were the sons of one man. He lives in the land of Canaan. Our youngest brother is now with our father. And one brother is gone."

Why did Joseph pretend to be a stranger to his brothers?

Joseph wanted to find out if his brothers had changed. Joseph kept on testing them. At last they showed they really cared for their father and each other too. Then Joseph told them who he was.

Joseph said to them, "I still say you are spies! So I'm going to put you to the test. You must bring your youngest brother to me. That will prove that your words are true. Then you won't die." So they did what he said.

They said to one another, "God is certainly punishing us because of our brother. We saw how troubled he was when he begged us to let him live. But we wouldn't listen. That's why all of this trouble has come to us."

They [travelled back] to their father Jacob in the land of Canaan. They told him everything that had happened to them.

They said, "The man who is the governor of the land spoke to us in a mean way. He treated us as if we were spying on the land. But we said to him, 'All of us were the sons of one father. But now one brother is gone. And our youngest brother is with our father in Canaan.'

"Then the man who is the governor of the land spoke to us. He said, 'Here's how I will know whether you are honest men. Leave one of your brothers here with me. Take food for your hungry families and go.

"'But bring your youngest brother to me. Then I'll know that you are honest men and not spies. I'll give your brother back to you. And you will be free to trade in the land.'"

They began emptying their sacks. There in each man's sack was his bag of money!

Joseph's Brothers Go Down to Egypt Again

There still wasn't enough food anywhere in the land. After a while Jacob's family had eaten all of the grain the brothers had brought from Egypt.

So their father said to them, "Go back. Buy us a little more food."

But Judah said to him, "The man gave us a strong warning. He said, 'You won't see my face again unless your brother comes with you.' So send our brother along with us. Then we'll go down and buy food for you."

Then their father Israel spoke to them. He said, "If that's the way it has to be, then do what I tell you. Put some of the best things from our land in your bags. Take them down to the man as a gift. Take some lotion and a little honey. Take some spices and myrrh. Take some pistachio nuts and almonds. Take twice the amount of money with you. You have to give back the money that was put in your sacks. Maybe it was a mistake.

"Also take your brother. Go back to the man at once. May the Mighty God cause him to show you mercy."

[The brothers] were afraid when they were taken to Joseph's house. They thought, "We were brought here because of the money that was put back in our sacks the first time. He wants to attack us and overpower us. Then he can hold us as slaves and take our donkeys."

The Nile

The Nile is one of the longest rivers in the world. The people of Egypt lived along the northern part of the river at the top of the map. Every year the river flooded over the banks. Its water left rich new soil where crops could grow. When other lands didn't get rain, there were famines. But even with no rain, Egypt still had food because of the Nile River.

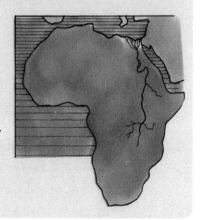

So they went up to Joseph's manager. They spoke to him at the entrance to the house. "Please, sir," they said. "We came down here the first time to buy food. We opened our sacks at the place where we stopped for the night. Each of us found in our sacks the money we had paid. So we've brought it back with us. We've also brought more money with us to buy food. We don't know who put our money in our sacks."

"It's all right," the manager said. "Don't be afraid. Your God, the God of your father, has given you riches in your sacks. I received your money." Then he brought Simeon out to them.

The manager took the men into Joseph's house. He gave them water to wash their feet. He provided feed for their donkeys. They prepared their gifts for Joseph. He was planning to arrive at noon. They had heard that they were going to eat there.

When Joseph came home, they gave him the gifts they had brought into the house. They bowed down to the ground in front of him.

He asked them how they were. Then he said, "How is your old father you told me about? Is he still living?"

They replied, "Your servant our father is still alive and well." And they bowed low to show him honor.

Joseph Tells His Brothers Who He Is

Joseph couldn't control himself anymore in front of all of his attendants. He cried out, "Have everyone leave me!"

So there wasn't anyone with Joseph when he told his brothers who he was. He sobbed so loudly that the Egyptians heard him. Everyone in Pharaoh's house heard about it.

Joseph said to his brothers, "I am Joseph! Is my father still alive?"

But his brothers weren't able to answer him. They were too afraid of him.

Joseph said to his brothers, "Come close to me." So they did.

Then he said, "I am your brother Joseph. I'm the one you sold into Egypt. But don't be upset. And don't be angry with yourselves because you sold me here. God sent me ahead of you to save many lives.

"For two years now, there hasn't been enough food in the land. And for the next five years, people won't be plowing or gathering crops. But God sent me ahead of you to keep some of you alive on earth. He sent me here to save your lives by an act of mighty power.

"So then, it wasn't you who sent me here. It was God. He made me like a father to Pharaoh. He made me master of Pharaoh's whole house. He made me ruler of the whole land of Egypt.

"Now hurry back to my father. Say to him, 'Your son Joseph says, "God has made me master of the whole land of Egypt. Come down to me. Don't waste any time. You will live in the area of Goshen. You, your children and grand-children, your flocks and herds, and everything you have will be near me. There I will provide everything you need.

"'Five years without enough food are still coming. If you don't come down here, you and your family and everyone who belongs to you will lose everything.'"

"Brothers, you can see for yourselves that it's really I, Joseph, speaking to you. My brother Benjamin can see it too.

"Tell my father about all of the honor that has been given to me in Egypt. Tell him about everything you have seen. And bring my father down here quickly."

Then Joseph threw his arms around his brother Benjamin and sobbed. Benjamin also hugged him and sobbed. Joseph kissed all of his brothers and sobbed over them. After that, his brothers talked with him.

Then Joseph sent his brothers away. They came to their father Jacob in the land of Canaan. They told him, "Joseph is still alive! In fact, he is ruler of the whole land of Egypt."

Jacob was shocked. He didn't believe them. So they told him every-thing Joseph had said to them.

Jacob saw the carts Joseph had sent to carry him back. That gave new life to their father Jacob. Israel said, "I believe it now! My son Joseph is still alive. I'll go and see him before I die."

Jacob sent [his son] Judah ahead of him to Joseph. He sent him to get directions to Goshen. And so they arrived in the area of Goshen.

Why did God send Jacob's family to Egypt?

God sent Jacob to Egypt so his family could live in safety. There were many wars and there was nothing to eat in Canaan. But not in Egypt. In Egypt the 70 people in Jacob's family grew and grew. Over the next 400 years, they became a nation of millions.

Then Joseph had his servants get his chariot ready. He went to Goshen to meet his father Israel. As soon as he came to his father, Joseph threw his arms around him. Then Joseph sobbed for a long time.

Slaves in Egypt

Exodus 1

The People of Israel Are Slaves in Egypt

A new king came to power in Egypt. He didn't know anything about Joseph.

"Look," he said to his people. "The Israelites are far too many for us. Come. We must deal with them carefully. If we don't, they will increase their numbers even more. Then if war breaks out, they'll join our enemies. They'll fight against us and leave the country."

So the Egyptians put slave drivers over the people of Israel. The slave drivers beat them down and made them work hard. The Israelites built the cities of Pithom and Rameses so Pharaoh could store things there.

But the more the slave drivers beat them down, the more the Israelites increased their numbers and spread out. So the Egyptians became afraid of them. They made them work hard. They didn't show them any pity. They made them suffer with hard labor. They forced them to work with bricks and mud. And they made them do all kinds of work in the fields. The Egyptians didn't show them any pity at all. They made them work very hard.

Then Pharaoh gave an order to all of his people. He said, "You must throw every baby boy into the Nile River. But let every baby girl live."

The Story of Moses

Exodus 2—6

Moses Is Born

A man and a woman from the tribe of Levi got married. She became pregnant and had a son by him. She saw that her baby was a fine child. So she hid him for three months.

After that, she couldn't hide him any longer. So she got a basket that was made out of the stems of tall grass. She coated it with tar. Then she placed the child in it. She put the basket in the tall grass that grew along the bank of the Nile River. The child's sister wasn't very far away. She wanted to see what would happen to him.

Pharaoh's daughter went down to the Nile River to take a bath. Her attendants were walking along the bank of the river. She saw the basket in the tall grass. So she sent her female slave to get it.

When she opened it, she saw the baby. He was crying. She felt sorry for him. "This is one of the Hebrew babies," she said.

Then his sister spoke to Pharaoh's daughter. She asked, "Do you want me to go and get one of the Hebrew women? She could nurse the baby for you."

"Yes. Go," she answered. So the girl went and got the baby's mother.

Pharaoh's daughter said to her, "Take this baby. Nurse him for me. I'll pay you." So the woman took the baby and nursed him.

When the child grew older, she took him to Pharaoh's daughter. And he became her son. She named him Moses. She said, "I pulled him out of the water."

Moses grew up. One day, he went out to where his own people were. He saw an Egyptian hitting a Hebrew man. Moses looked around and didn't see anyone. So he killed the Egyptian.

When Pharaoh heard about what had happened, he tried to kill Moses. But Moses escaped from Pharaoh and went to live with Midian.

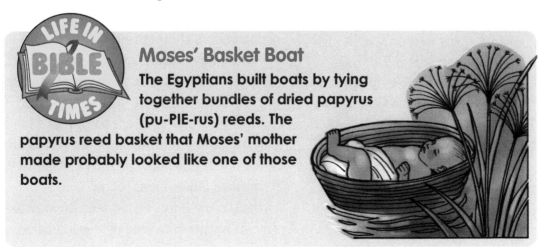

Moses' Basket Boat

The Egyptians built boats by tying together bundles of dried papyrus (pu-PIE-rus) reeds. The papyrus reed basket that Moses' mother made probably looked like one of those boats.

Moses agreed to stay with [a priest of Midian]. The man gave his daughter Zipporah to Moses to be his wife. Zipporah had a son by him. Moses named him Gershom. Moses said, "I'm an outsider in a strange land."

The LORD Sends Moses to Save His People

Moses was taking care of the flock of his father-in-law Jethro. Jethro was the priest of Midian. Moses led the flock to the western side of the desert. He came to Horeb. It was the mountain of God.

There the angel of the LORD appeared to him from inside a burning bush. Moses saw that the bush was on fire. But it didn't burn up. So Moses thought, "I'll go over and see this strange sight. Why doesn't the bush burn up?"

The LORD saw that Moses had gone over to look. So God spoke to him from inside the bush. He called out, "Moses! Moses!"

"Here I am," Moses said.

"Do not come any closer," God said. "Take off your sandals. The place you are standing on is holy ground." He continued, "I am the God of your father. I am the God of Abraham. I am the God of Isaac. And I am the God of Jacob."

When Moses heard that, he turned his face away. He was afraid to look at God.

The LORD said, "I have seen my people suffer in Egypt. I have heard them cry out because of their slave drivers. I am concerned about their suffering.

"So I have come down to save them from the Egyptians. I will bring them up out of that land. I will bring them into a good land. It has a lot of room. It is a land that has plenty of milk and honey. It is the home of the Canaanites, Hittites, Amorites, Perizzites, Hivites and Jebusites.

PEOPLE IN BIBLE TIMES

Moses

Moses was a Hebrew. That is another name for Israelite. He was rescued and raised by an Egyptian princess. Moses was afraid that he couldn't do what God had asked him to do. But God chose Moses to rescue the people of Israel. The people of Israel were slaves to the Egyptians.

"And now Israel's cry for help has reached me. I have seen the way the Egyptians are beating them down. So now, go. I am sending you to Pharaoh. I want you to bring the Israelites out of Egypt. They are my people."

But Moses spoke to God. "Who am I that I should go to Pharaoh?" he said. "Who am I that I should bring the Israelites out of Egypt?"

God said, "I will be with you. I will give you a miraculous sign. It will prove that I have sent you. When you have brought the people out of Egypt, all of you will worship me on this mountain."

Miraculous Signs for Moses to Do

Moses answered, "What if the elders of Israel won't believe me? What if they won't listen to me? Suppose they say, 'The LORD didn't appear to you.' Then what should I do?"

The LORD said to him, "What do you have in your hand?"

"A wooden staff," he said.

The LORD said, "Throw it on the ground."

So Moses threw it on the ground. It turned into a snake. He ran away from it. Then the LORD said to Moses, "Reach your hand out. Take the snake by the tail." So he reached out and grabbed hold of the snake. It turned back into a staff in his hand.

The LORD said, "When they see this miraculous sign, they will believe that I appeared to you. I am the God of their fathers. I am the God of Abraham. I am the God of Isaac. And I am the God of Jacob."

Don't Give Up

Sarah was seven. All of her friends rode bicycles. But when Sarah got on a bike, she was afraid. She didn't push the pedals hard. She stopped trying. And the bike fell over. "I'm just no good," Sarah thought. "I can't do it."

When God was speaking to Moses, Moses said, "Who am I?" His words mean the same thing as Sarah's "I'm just no good." Read the second paragraph on this page. Can you find a promise that God gave to Moses? It has five words in it. When Moses thought of this promise it helped him not to give up. How could this promise help Sarah? How could it help you when you feel like giving up?

Draw a picture from this Bible story. Write the five-word promise on your poster. Read it every day. Remember that God is always with you.

Then the LORD said, "Put your hand inside your coat." So Moses put his hand inside his coat. When he took it out, it was as white as snow. It was covered with a skin disease.

"Now put it back into your coat," the LORD said. So Moses put his hand back into his coat. When he took it out, the skin was healthy again. His hand was like the rest of his skin.

Then the LORD said, "Suppose they do not believe you or pay attention to the first miracle. Then maybe they will believe the second one.

"But suppose they do not believe either miracle. Suppose they will not listen to you. Then get some water from the Nile River. Pour it on the dry ground. The water you take from the river will turn to blood on the ground."

Moses spoke to the LORD. He said, "Lord, I've never been a good speaker. And I haven't gotten any better since you spoke to me. I don't speak very well at all."

The LORD said to him, "Who makes a man able to talk? Who makes him unable to hear or speak? Who makes him able to see? Who makes him blind? It is I, the LORD. Now go. I will help you speak. I will teach you what to say."

WORDS TO TREASURE

I will help you speak. I will teach you what to say.

Exodus 4:12

Pharaoh Makes the Israelites Work Even Harder

Later on, Moses and [his brother] Aaron went to Pharaoh. They said, "The LORD is the God of Israel. He says, 'Let my people go. Then they will be able to hold a feast in my honor in the desert.'"

Pharaoh said, "Who is the LORD? Why should I obey him? Why should I let Israel go? I don't even know the LORD. And I won't let Israel go."

Then Moses and Aaron said, "The God of the Hebrews has met with us. Now let us take a journey that lasts about three days. We want to go into the desert to offer sacrifices to the LORD our God. If we don't, he might strike us with plagues. Or he might let us be killed with swords."

But the king of Egypt said, "Moses and Aaron, why are you taking the people away from their work? Get back to work!" Pharaoh continued, "There are large numbers of your people in the land. But you are stopping them from working."

That same day Pharaoh gave orders to the slave drivers and the others who were in charge of the people. He said, "Don't give the people any more straw to make bricks. Let them go and get their own straw. But require them to make the same number of bricks as before. Don't lower the number they have to make. They don't want to work. That's why they are crying out, 'Let us go. We want to offer sacrifices to our God.' Make them work harder. Then they will be too busy to pay attention to lies."

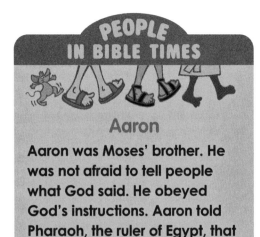

PEOPLE IN BIBLE TIMES

Aaron

Aaron was Moses' brother. He was not afraid to tell people what God said. He obeyed God's instructions. Aaron told Pharaoh, the ruler of Egypt, that he should let the people of Israel go. Aaron was the first high priest of the people of Israel.

Then the LORD spoke to Moses. He said, "Now you will see what I will do to Pharaoh. Because of my powerful hand, he will let the people of Israel go. Because of my mighty hand, he will drive them out of his country."

God continued, "I am the LORD. I appeared to Abraham, Isaac and Jacob as the Mighty God. But I did not show them the full meaning of my name, The LORD.

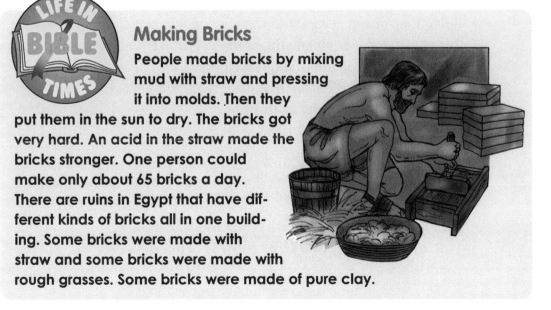

LIFE IN BIBLE TIMES

Making Bricks

People made bricks by mixing mud with straw and pressing it into molds. Then they put them in the sun to dry. The bricks got very hard. An acid in the straw made the bricks stronger. One person could make only about 65 bricks a day. There are ruins in Egypt that have different kinds of bricks all in one building. Some bricks were made with straw and some bricks were made with rough grasses. Some bricks were made of pure clay.

"I also made my covenant with them. I promised to give them the land of Canaan. That is where they lived as outsiders. Also, I have heard the groans of the Israelites. The Egyptians are keeping them as slaves. But I have remembered my covenant.

"So tell the people of Israel, 'I am the LORD. I will throw off the heavy load the Egyptians have put on your shoulders. I will set you free from being slaves to them. I will reach out my arm and save you with mighty acts when I judge Egypt.

"'I will take you to be my own people. I will be your God. You will know that I am the LORD your God when I throw off the load the Egyptians have put on your shoulders.

"'I will bring you to the land I promised with an oath to give to Abraham, Isaac and Jacob. I lifted up my hand and promised it to them. The land will belong to you. I am the LORD.'"

The Ten Plagues on Egypt

Exodus 7—12

So Moses and Aaron went to Pharaoh. They did exactly as the LORD had commanded them. Aaron threw his staff down in front of Pharaoh and his officials. It turned into a snake.

Then Pharaoh sent for wise men and those who do evil magic. By doing their magic tricks, the Egyptian magicians did the same things Aaron had done. Each one threw his staff down. Each staff turned into a snake. But Aaron's staff swallowed theirs up.

In spite of that, Pharaoh's heart became stubborn. He wouldn't listen to them, just as the LORD had said.

The Nile River Turns Into Blood

Then the LORD said to Moses, "Pharaoh's heart is very stubborn. He refuses to let the people go. In the morning Pharaoh will go down to the water. Go and wait on the bank of the Nile River to meet him. Take in your hand the wooden staff that turned into a snake.

"Say to Pharaoh, 'The LORD, the God of the Hebrews, has sent me to you. He says, "Let my people go. Then they will be able to worship me in the desert. But up to now you have not listened."

"'The Lord says, "Here is how you will know that I am the Lord. I will strike the water of the Nile River with the staff that is in my hand. The river will turn into blood. The fish in the river will die. The river will stink. The Egyptians will not be able to drink its water."'"

The Lord said to Moses, "Tell Aaron, 'Get your staff. Reach your hand out over the waters of Egypt. The streams, waterways, ponds and all of the lakes will turn into blood. There will be blood everywhere in Egypt. It will even be in the wooden buckets and stone jars.'"

Moses and Aaron did exactly as the Lord had commanded them.

The fish in the Nile died. The river smelled so bad the Egyptians couldn't drink its water. There was blood everywhere in Egypt.

But the Egyptian magicians did the same things by doing their magic tricks. So Pharaoh's heart became stubborn. He wouldn't listen to Moses and Aaron, just as the Lord had said. Even that miracle didn't change Pharaoh's mind. In fact, he turned around and went into his palace.

All of the Egyptians dug holes near the Nile River to get drinking water. They couldn't drink water from the river.

The Plague of Frogs

Seven days passed after the Lord struck the Nile River.

Then the Lord said to Moses, "Go to Pharaoh. Tell him, 'The Lord says, "Let my people go. Then they will be able to worship me.

"'"If you refuse to let them go, I will plague your whole country with frogs. The Nile River will be full of frogs. They will come up into your palace. You will have frogs in your bedroom and on your bed. They will be in the homes of your officials and your people. They will be in your ovens and in your bread pans. The frogs will be on you, your people and all of your officials."'"

Then the Lord spoke to Moses. He said, "Tell Aaron, 'Reach your hand out. Hold your staff over the streams, waterways and ponds. Make frogs come up on the land of Egypt.'"

So Aaron reached his hand out over the waters of Egypt. The frogs came up and covered the land. But the magicians did the same things by doing their magic tricks. They also made frogs come up on the land of Egypt.

The frogs died in the houses, courtyards and fields. The Egyptians piled them up. The land smelled very bad because of them.

But when Pharaoh saw that the frogs were dead, his heart became stubborn. He wouldn't listen to Moses and Aaron, just as the LORD had said.

The Plague of Gnats

Then the LORD spoke to Moses. He said, "Tell Aaron, 'Reach your wooden staff out. Strike the dust on the ground with it.' Then all over the land of Egypt the dust will turn into gnats."

So they did it. Aaron reached out the staff that was in his hand. He struck the dust on the ground with it. The dust all over the land of Egypt turned into gnats. They landed on people and animals alike.

The magicians tried to produce gnats by doing their magic tricks. But they couldn't. The gnats stayed on people and animals alike.

The magicians said to Pharaoh, "God's powerful finger has done this." But Pharaoh's heart was stubborn. He wouldn't listen, just as the LORD had said.

The Plague of Flies

Then the LORD spoke to Moses. He said, "Get up early in the morning. Talk to Pharaoh as he goes down to the river. Say to him, 'The LORD says, "Let my people go. Then they will be able to worship me. If you do not let my people go, I will send large numbers of flies. I will send them on you and your officials. I will send them on your people and into your

When Things Go Wrong

Read Exodus 5:1–21. Now answer these questions.
1. Moses did what God said. Did something good happen right away?
2. Did the people blame someone when they were told to work harder?
3. When Moses obeyed God, the slaves had more trouble. How did this make Moses feel?

Sometimes things get worse before they get better. But the people finally were free. Moses led them out of Egypt.

Think about some sad things that have happened to you. Now think about some happy things. Keep obeying God. He has many wonderful plans for you.

homes. The houses of the Egyptians will be full of flies. Even the area where they live will be full of flies.

So the LORD did it. Huge numbers of flies poured into Pharaoh's palace. They came into the homes of his officials. All over Egypt the flies destroyed the land.

Then Pharaoh sent for Moses and Aaron.

Pharaoh said, "I will let you and your people go to offer sacrifices. You can offer them to the LORD your God in the desert. But you must not go very far. And pray for me."

Moses replied, "As soon as I leave you, I will pray to the LORD. Tomorrow the flies will leave you. They will also leave your officials and your people. Just be sure you don't try to trick us again. Let the people go to offer sacrifices to the LORD."

Then Moses left Pharaoh and prayed to the LORD. And the LORD did what Moses asked. The flies left Pharaoh, his officials and his people. Not one fly remained. But Pharaoh's heart became stubborn that time also. He wouldn't let the people go.

The Plague on Livestock

Then the LORD spoke to Moses. He said, "Go to Pharaoh. Tell him, 'The LORD, the God of the Hebrews, says, "Let my people go. Then they will be able to worship me. Do not refuse to let them go. Do not keep holding them back.

"'"If you refuse, my powerful hand will bring a terrible plague on you. I will strike your livestock in the fields. I will strike your horses, donkeys, camels, cattle, sheep and goats. But I will treat Israel's livestock differently from yours. No animal that belongs to the people of Israel will die." ' "

The LORD set a time for the plague. He said, "Tomorrow I will send it on the land." So the next day the LORD sent it. All of the livestock of the Egyptians died. But not one animal that belonged to the Israelites died.

Pharaoh sent people to find out what had happened. They discovered that not even one animal that belonged to the Israelites had died. But his heart was still very stubborn. He wouldn't let the people go.

The Plague of Boils

Then the LORD spoke to Moses and Aaron. He said, "Take handfuls of ashes from a furnace. Have Moses toss them into the air in front of Pharaoh. The ashes will turn into fine dust all over the whole land of Egypt. Then boils will break out on people and animals all over the land. Their bodies will be covered with them."

So Moses and Aaron took ashes from a furnace and stood in front of Pharaoh. Moses tossed them into the air. Then boils broke out on people and animals alike. The bodies of all of the Egyptians were covered with boils. The magicians couldn't stand in front of Moses because of the boils that were all over them.

But the LORD made Pharaoh's heart stubborn. Pharaoh wouldn't listen to Moses and Aaron, just as the LORD had said to Moses.

The Plague of Hail

Then the LORD spoke to Moses. He said, "Reach your hand out toward the sky. Then hail will fall all over Egypt. It will beat down on people and animals alike. It will strike everything that is growing in the fields of Egypt."

What are God's "mighty acts"?

The ten terrible plagues God brought on Egypt are his "mighty acts." They are also called "miraculous signs and wonders." Each plague was worse than any other in Egypt's history. Each one came and went at Moses' command. Each one showed God's power to Pharaoh.

Moses reached his wooden staff out toward the sky. Then the LORD sent thunder and hail. Lightning flashed down to the ground. The LORD rained hail on the land of Egypt. Hail fell and lightning flashed back and forth. It was the worst storm in Egypt's entire history.

All over Egypt hail struck everything in the fields. It fell on people and animals alike. It beat down everything that was growing in the fields. It tore all of the leaves off the trees.

The only place it didn't hail was in the area of Goshen. That's where the people of Israel were.

Then Pharaoh sent for Moses and Aaron. "This time I've sinned," he said to them. "The LORD has done what is right. I and my people have done what is wrong. Pray to the LORD, because we've had enough thunder and hail. I'll let you and your people go. You don't have to stay here any longer."

Pharaoh saw that the rain, hail and thunder had stopped. So he sinned again. He and his officials made their hearts stubborn. So Pharaoh's heart was stubborn. He wouldn't let the people of Israel go, just as the LORD had said through Moses.

The Plague of Locusts

So Moses and Aaron went to Pharaoh. They said to him, "The LORD, the God of the Hebrews, says, 'How long will you refuse to obey me? Let my people go. Then they will be able to worship me.

"'If you refuse to let them go, I will bring locusts into your country tomorrow. They will cover the ground so that it can't be seen. They will eat what little you have left after the hail. That includes every tree that is growing in your fields. They will fill your houses. They will be in the homes of all of your officials and your people. Your parents and your people before them have never seen anything like it as long as they have lived here.'" Then Moses turned around and left Pharaoh.

So Moses reached his wooden staff out over Egypt. Then the LORD made an east wind blow across the land. It blew all that day and all that

Hard Heart, Soft Heart

Someone who is stubborn has a hard heart. This person will not do what God says. What do you think made Pharaoh stubborn?

Try this. On a warm, sunny day take two small bowls. Put a marshmallow in one bowl. Put an ice cube in the other bowl. Put both bowls in the sun. Wait for one hour. Look at the ice cube. Look at the marshmallow. What happened to them?

The hot sun is like God's Word. It melts an ice cube. But the marshmallow turns hard in the sun. The ice cube is like the heart of people who trust God. The marshmallow is like the heart of Pharaoh. Remember to keep your heart soft. Obey God's Word.

night. By morning the wind had brought the locusts. They came into every part of Egypt. They settled down in every area of the country in large numbers. There had never been a plague of locusts like it before. And there will never be one like it again.

The locusts covered the ground until it was black. They ate up everything that was left after the hail. They ate up everything that was growing in the fields. They ate up the fruit on the trees. There was nothing green left on any tree or plant in the whole land of Egypt.

Pharaoh quickly sent for Moses and Aaron. He said, "I have sinned against the LORD your God. I've also sinned against you. Now forgive my sin one more time. Pray to the LORD your God to take this deadly plague away from me."

After Moses left Pharaoh, he prayed to the LORD. The LORD changed the wind to a very strong west wind. The wind picked up the locusts. It blew them into the Red Sea. Not even one locust was left anywhere in Egypt.

But the LORD made Pharaoh's heart stubborn. And Pharaoh wouldn't let the people of Israel go.

The Plague of Darkness

The LORD spoke to Moses. He said, "Reach out your hand toward the sky. Darkness will spread over Egypt. It will be so dark that people can feel it."

So Moses reached out his hand toward the sky. Then complete darkness covered Egypt for three days. No one could see anyone else or go

Pharaoh on His Throne

When Pharaoh called for Moses, he probably sat on a big, fancy throne. He wore a crown and held a decorated pole called a scepter (SEP-ter). His crown and scepter showed that he was powerful. Pharaoh was the ruler of all Egypt. But he couldn't do anything against the power of God.

anywhere for three days. But all of the people of Israel had light where they lived.

But the Lord made Pharaoh's heart stubborn. So he wouldn't let the people go.

Pharaoh said to Moses, "Get out of my sight! Make sure you don't come to see me again! If you do, you will die."

"I'll do just as you say," Moses replied. "I will never come to see you again."

The Lord Announces the Tenth Plague

The Lord had spoken to Moses. He had said, "I will bring one more plague on Pharaoh and on Egypt. After that, he will let you and your people go. When he does, he will drive you completely away. Tell the men and women alike to ask their neighbors for articles made out of silver and gold."

The Lord caused the Egyptians to treat the Israelites in a kind way. Pharaoh's officials and the people had great respect for Moses.

Moses said, "The Lord says, 'About midnight I will go through every part of Egypt. Every oldest son in Egypt will die. The oldest son of Pharaoh, who sits on the throne, will die. The oldest son of the female slave, who works at her hand mill, will die. All of the male animals that were born first to their mothers among the cattle will also die. There will be loud crying all over Egypt. It will be worse than it's ever been before. And nothing like it will ever be heard again.'"

The First Passover Sacrifice

Then Moses sent for all of the elders of Israel. He said to them, "Go at once. Choose the animals for your families. Each family must kill a Passover lamb. Get a branch of a hyssop plant. Dip it into the blood in the bowl. Put some of the blood on the top and on both sides of the doorframe. None of you can go out the door of your house until morning.

"The Lord will go through the land to strike the Egyptians down. He'll see the blood on the top and sides of the doorframe. He will pass over that house. He won't let the destroying angel enter your homes to kill you.

"Obey all of these directions. It's a law for you and your children after you for all time to come. The Lord will give you the land, just as he promised. When you enter it, keep this holy day.

"Your children will ask you, 'What does this holy day mean to you?' Tell them, 'It's the Passover sacrifice in honor of the LORD. He passed over the houses of the people of Israel in Egypt. He spared our homes when he struck the Egyptians down.'"

Then the people of Israel bowed down and worshiped. They did just what the LORD commanded Moses and Aaron.

At midnight the LORD struck down every oldest son in Egypt. He killed the oldest son of Pharaoh, who sat on the throne. He killed all of the oldest sons of prisoners, who were in prison. He also killed all of the male animals that were born first to their mothers among the livestock.

Pharaoh and all of his officials got up during the night. So did all of the Egyptians. There was loud crying in Egypt because someone had died in every home.

What is the Passover?

One night God killed the oldest sons of the Egyptians. That night is called the Passover. God "passed over" the Israelite families. Their oldest sons did not die. God told the people of Israel to hold a special meal that night and each year on that date. This meal helps them remember that God saved his people when they were slaves in Egypt.

The People of Israel Leave Egypt

During the night, Pharaoh sent for Moses and Aaron. He said to them, "Get out of here! You and the Israelites, leave my people! Go. Worship the LORD, just as you have asked. Go. Take your flocks and herds, just as you have said. And also give me your blessing."

The Egyptians begged the people of Israel to hurry up and leave the country. "If you don't," they said, "we'll all die!"

The people of Israel lived in Egypt for 430 years. At the end of the 430 years, to the very day, all of the LORD's people marched out of Egypt like an army.

The Desert Journey Begins

Exodus 13—16

Israel Goes Through the Red Sea

Pharaoh let the people go. The shortest road from Goshen to Canaan went through the Philistine country. But God didn't lead them that way. God said, "If they have to go into battle, they might change their minds. They might return to Egypt."

So God led the people toward the Red Sea by taking them on a road through the desert. The Israelites were prepared for battle when they went up out of Egypt.

Moses took the bones of Joseph along with him. Joseph had made the sons of Israel take an oath and make a promise. He had said, "I'm sure that God will come to help you. When he does, you must carry my bones up from this place with you." *(Genesis 50:25)*

By day the LORD went ahead of them in a pillar of cloud. It guided them on their way. At night he led them with a pillar of fire. It gave them light. So they could travel by day or at night. The pillar of cloud didn't leave its place in front of the people during the day. And the pillar of fire didn't leave its place at night.

Then Pharaoh and his officials changed their minds about them. They said, "What have we done? We've let the people of Israel go! We've lost our slaves and all of the work they used to do for us!"

So he had his chariot made ready. He took his army with him. He took 600 of the best chariots in Egypt. He also took along all of the other chariots. Officers were in charge of all of them.

The LORD made the heart of Pharaoh, the king of Egypt, stubborn. So he chased the Israelites, who were marching out boldly. The Egyptians went after the Israelites. All of Pharaoh's horses and chariots and horsemen and troops went after them.

As Pharaoh approached, the people of Israel looked up. There were the Egyptians marching after them! The Israelites were terrified. They cried out to the LORD.

They said to Moses, "Why did you bring us to the desert to die? Weren't there any graves in Egypt? What have you done to us by bringing us out of Egypt? We told you in Egypt, 'Leave us alone. Let us serve the Egyptians.' It would have been better for us to serve the Egyptians than to die here in the desert!"

Moses answered the people. He said, "Don't be afraid. Stand firm. You will see how the LORD will save you today. Do you see those Egyptians? You will never see them again. The LORD will fight for you. Just be still."

Then the LORD spoke to Moses. He said, "Why are you crying out to me? Tell the people of Israel to move on. Hold your wooden staff out. Reach your hand out over the Red Sea to part the water. Then the people can go through the sea on dry ground."

Sand and Sea

Here's a fun game you can play. Ask a grown-up to help you. Mark off a small part of your yard. Call this part "sand." Mark off the rest of your yard. Call this part "sea." Have some of your friends be the people of Israel. Have some other friends be the soldiers of Egypt. Let the soldiers try to capture the people of Israel before time runs out. Follow these rules:

1. Decide how many seconds each turn will last. Ring a bell or give a shout when time runs out.
2. Everyone must walk. No one may run.
3. The people of Israel get to start first. They can walk into the "sea" for three seconds before anyone can go after them.
4. The soldiers must tag the people in the "sea" to capture them. Then they must walk slowly back to the "sand." If one of the people of Israel gets all the way back to the "sand," that person is out of the game.
5. A soldier caught in the "sea" when time runs out has "drowned." That soldier is out of the game. The people of Israel cannot "drown" in the "sea" when time runs out.
6. The team will lose if all of its members are captured or drowned.

After you play the game, talk about the story of Moses and his people crossing the Red Sea. Do you see how God took care of his people? How many people of Israel were captured? How many soldiers drowned?

The angel of God had been traveling in front of Israel's army. Now he moved back and went behind them. The pillar of cloud also moved away from in front of them. Now it stood behind them. It came between the armies of Egypt and Israel. All through the night the cloud brought darkness to one side and light to the other. Neither army went near the other all night long.

Then Moses reached his hand out over the Red Sea. All that night the LORD pushed the sea back with a strong east wind. He turned the sea into dry land. The waters were parted. The people of Israel went through the sea on dry ground. There was a wall of water on their right side and on their left.

The Egyptians chased them. All of Pharaoh's horses and chariots and horsemen followed them into the sea.

Near the end of the night the LORD looked down from the pillar of fire and cloud. He saw the Egyptian army and threw it into a panic. He kept their chariot wheels from turning freely. That made the chariots hard to drive.

The Egyptians said, "Let's get away from the Israelites! The LORD is fighting for Israel against Egypt."

Then the LORD spoke to Moses. He said, "Reach your hand out over the sea. The waters will flow back over the Egyptians and their chariots and horsemen." So Moses reached his hand out over the sea. At sunrise the sea went back to its place. The Egyptians tried to run away from the sea. But the LORD swept them into it. The water flowed back and covered the chariots and horsemen. It covered the entire army of Pharaoh that had followed the people of Israel into the sea. Not one of the Egyptians was left.

That day the LORD saved Israel from the power of Egypt. Israel saw the Egyptians lying dead on the shore. The Israelites saw the great power the LORD showed against the Egyptians. So they had respect for the LORD. They put their trust in him and in his servant Moses.

At the Waters of Marah and Elim

Then Moses led Israel away from the Red Sea. They went into the Desert of Shur. For three days they traveled in the desert. They didn't find any water there. When they came to Marah, they couldn't drink its water. It was bitter. That's why the place is named Marah. The people told Moses they weren't happy with him. They said, "What are we supposed to drink?"

Then Moses cried out to the LORD. The LORD showed him a stick. Moses threw it into the water. The water became sweet.

There the LORD made a rule and a law for the people. And there he put them to the test. He said, "I am the LORD your God. Listen carefully to my voice. Do what is right in my eyes. Pay attention to my commands. Obey all of my rules. If you do, I will not send on you any of the sicknesses I sent on the Egyptians. I am the LORD who heals you."

The people came to Elim. It had 12 springs and 70 palm trees. They camped there near the water.

The LORD Gives Israel Food Every Day

The whole community of Israel started out from Elim. They came to the Desert of Sin. It was between Elim and Sinai. They arrived there on the 15th day of the second month after they had come out of Egypt.

In the desert the whole community told Moses and Aaron they weren't happy with them. The Israelites said to them, "We wish the LORD had put us to death in Egypt. There we sat around pots of meat. We ate all of the food we wanted. But you have brought us out into this desert. You must want this entire community to die of hunger."

Then the LORD spoke to Moses. He said, "I will rain down bread from heaven for you. The people must go out each day. Have them gather enough bread for that day. Here is how I will put them to the test. I will see if they will follow my directions.

"On the sixth day they must prepare what they bring in. On that day they must gather twice as much as on the other days."

So Moses and Aaron spoke to all of the people of Israel. They said, "In the evening you will know that the LORD brought you out of Egypt. And in the morning you will see the glory of the LORD. He has heard you say you aren't happy with him. Who are we? Why are you telling us you aren't happy with us?"

Moses also said, "You will know that the LORD has heard you speak against him. He will give you meat to eat in the evening. He'll give you all of the bread you want in the morning. But who are we? You aren't speaking against us. You are speaking against the LORD."

Then Moses told Aaron, "Talk to the whole community of Israel. Say to them, 'Come to the LORD. He has heard you speak against him.'"

While Aaron was talking to the whole community of Israel, they looked toward the desert. There was the glory of the LORD appearing in the cloud!

The LORD said to Moses, "I have heard the people of Israel talking about how unhappy they are. Tell them, 'When the sun goes down, you will eat meat. In the morning you will be filled with bread. Then you will know that I am the LORD your God.'"

That evening quail came and covered the camp. In the morning the ground around the camp was covered with dew. When the dew was gone, thin flakes appeared on the desert floor. They looked like frost on the ground. The people of Israel saw the flakes. They asked each other, "What's that?" They didn't know what it was.

Moses said to them, "It's the bread the LORD has given you to eat. Here is what the LORD has commanded. He has said, 'Each one of you should gather as much as you need. Take two quarts for each person who lives in your tent.'"

The people of Israel did as they were told. Some gathered a lot, and some gathered a little. When they measured it out, those who gathered a lot didn't have too much. And those who gathered a little had enough. All of them gathered only what they needed.

The people of Israel called the bread manna. It was white like coriander seeds. It tasted like wafers that were made with honey.

Manna

Manna was a special food that God gave his people, the Israelites. The people gathered the manna from the ground. God gave it to them every day they were in the desert, except for on the Sabbath. The Hebrew meaning for the word *manna* was probably "What is it?" The Israelites didn't know exactly what manna was when they first saw it. But they soon found out that it tasted good and that it was good for them. Best of all, God had given it to them.

Moses said, "Here is what the LORD has commanded. He has said, 'Get two quarts of manna. Keep it for all time to come. Then those who live after you will see the bread I gave you to eat in the desert. I gave it to you when I brought you out of Egypt.'"

So Moses said to Aaron, "Get a jar. Put two quarts of manna in it. Then place it in front of the LORD. Keep it there for all time to come."

Aaron did exactly as the LORD had commanded Moses. He put the manna in front of the tablets of the covenant. He put it there so it would be kept for all time to come.

The people of Israel ate manna for 40 years. They ate it until they came to a land that was settled. They ate it until they reached the border of Canaan.

God Gives Moses the Ten Commandments

Exodus 19—20; 24; 26

Israel Comes to Mount Sinai

Exactly three months after the people of Israel left Egypt, they came to the Desert of Sinai. After they started out from Rephidim, they entered the Desert of Sinai. They camped there in the desert in front of the mountain.

Daily Bread

Moses led the people of Israel through the desert. There were about two million people. God gave them a special kind of food. It was called manna.

Every day God gave enough manna for the whole day. On the sixth day of the week God gave them enough manna for two days. This way they could rest on the Sabbath. The people could trust God to give them enough food every day.

Are you ready to trust God each day to supply everything you need for just that one day? Try this for one week. Pray about one thing each day (a test, a piano lesson, a safe ride on a field trip, or whatever). Don't worry about tomorrow. Keep track of how God answers these daily prayers.

Then Moses went up to God. The LORD called out to him from the mountain. He said, "Here is what I want you to say to my people, who came from Jacob's family. Tell the Israelites, 'You have seen for yourselves what I did to Egypt. You saw how I carried you on the wings of eagles and brought you to myself.

"'Now obey me completely. Keep my covenant. If you do, then out of all of the nations you will be my special treasure. The whole earth is mine. But you will be a kingdom of priests to serve me. You will be my holy nation.' That is what you must tell the Israelites."

So Moses went back. He sent for the elders of the people. He explained to them everything the LORD had commanded him to say. All of the people answered together. They said, "We will do everything the LORD has said."

So Moses brought their answer back to the LORD.

The LORD spoke to Moses. He said, "I am going to come to you in a thick cloud. The people will hear me speaking with you. They will always put their trust in you." Then Moses told the LORD what the people had said.

On the morning of the third day there was thunder and lightning. A thick cloud covered the mountain. A trumpet gave out a very loud blast. Everyone in the camp trembled with fear.

Then Moses led the people out of the camp to meet with God. They stood at the foot of the mountain.

Smoke covered Mount Sinai, because the LORD came down on it in fire. The smoke rose up from it like smoke from a furnace. The whole mountain trembled and shook. The sound of the trumpet got louder and louder. Then Moses spoke. And the voice of God answered him.

The LORD came down to the top of Mount Sinai. He told Moses to come to the top of the mountain. So Moses went up.

God Gives His People the Ten Commandments

Here are all of the words God spoke. He said,

"Do not put any other gods in place of me.

"Do not make statues of gods that look like anything in the sky or on the earth or in the waters. Do not bow down to them or worship them. I, the LORD your God, am a jealous God. I punish the children for the sin of their parents. I punish the grandchildren and great-grandchildren of those who hate me. But for all time to come I show love to all those who love me and keep my commandments.

"Do not misuse the name of the LORD your God. The LORD will find guilty anyone who misuses his name.

"Remember to keep the Sabbath day holy. Do all of your work in six days. But the seventh day is a Sabbath in honor of the LORD your God. Do not do any work on that day. The same command applies to your sons and daughters, your male and female servants, and your animals. It also applies to any outsiders who live in your cities. In six days I made the heavens and the earth. I made the oceans and everything in them. But I rested on the seventh day. So I blessed the Sabbath day and made it holy.

"Honor your father and mother. Then you will live a long time in the land the LORD your God is giving you.

"Do not commit murder.

"Do not commit adultery.

"Do not steal.

"Do not give false witness against your neighbor.

"Do not long for anything that belongs to your neighbor. Do not long for your neighbor's house, wife, male or female servant, ox or donkey."

The people saw the thunder and lightning. They heard the trumpet. They saw the mountain covered with smoke. They trembled with fear and stayed a long way off.

The Blood of the Covenant

The LORD said to Moses, "You and Aaron, Nadab and Abihu, and 70 of the elders of Israel must come up to me. Do not come close when you worship. Only Moses can come close to me. The others must not come near. And the people may not go up with him."

Moses went and told the people all of the LORD's words and laws. They answered with one voice. They said, "We will do everything the LORD has told us to do." Then Moses wrote down everything the LORD had said.

Ten Commandments

The Ten Commandments show us how to love God. They show us how to love people too. Here is a list of the commandments. Look at what each one means. See how you can obey these commandments each day.

The Commandment	*Meaning*	*I Obey It by:*
1. Put no gods in place of me.	Trust God only.	Praying about my needs.
2. Do not make statues of gods.	Worship God only.	Thanking and praising God.
3. Don't misuse God's name.	Use God's name respectfully.	Not saying bad words or using God's name like a bad word.
4. Keep the Sabbath holy.	Rest and think about God.	Going to church school.
5. Honor your father and mother.	Respect parents.	Obeying my mom and dad.
6. Do not murder.	Take care of human life.	Helping others not to get hurt.
7. Do not commit adultery.	Be true to husband or wife.	Keeping promises I make to others.
8. Do not steal.	Don't take what belongs to others.	Not taking things that belong to others.
9. Do not give false witness.	Don't lie about others.	Being truthful and not saying bad things about other people.
10. Do not long for what belongs to others.	Don't want what others have.	Being content with what I have.

Moses got up early the next morning. He built an altar at the foot of the mountain. He set up 12 stone pillars. They stood for the 12 tribes of Israel.

Then he sent young Israelite men to offer burnt offerings. They also sacrificed young bulls as friendship offerings to the LORD. Moses took half of the blood and put it in bowls. He sprinkled the other half on the altar.

Then he took the Scroll of the Covenant and read it to the people.

They answered, "We will do everything the LORD has told us to do. We will obey him."

Then Moses took the blood and sprinkled it on the people. He said, "This is the blood that puts the covenant into effect. The LORD has made this covenant with you in keeping with all of these words."

WORDS TO TREASURE

We will do everything the LORD has told us to do. We will obey him.

Exodus 24:7

Moses and Aaron, Nadab and Abihu, and the 70 elders of Israel went up. They saw the God of Israel. Under his feet was something like a street made out of sapphire. It was as clear as the sky itself. But God didn't raise his hand against those leaders of the people of Israel. They saw God. And they ate and drank.

The LORD said to Moses, "Come up to me on the mountain. Stay here. I will give you the stone tablets. They contain the law and commands I have written to teach the people."

Then Moses and Joshua, his helper, started out. Moses went up on the mountain of God. He said to the elders, "Wait for us here until we come back to you. Aaron and Hur are with you. Anyone who has a problem can go to them."

Moses went up on the mountain. Then the cloud covered it. The glory of the LORD settled on Mount Sinai. The cloud covered the mountain for six days.

On the seventh day the LORD called out to Moses from inside the cloud. The people of Israel saw the glory of the LORD. It looked like a fire burning on top of the mountain. Moses entered the cloud as he went on up the mountain. He stayed on the mountain for 40 days and 40 nights.

The Holy Tent

[The LORD said to Moses,] "Make ten curtains out of finely twisted linen for the holy tent. Make them with blue, purple and bright red yarn. Have a skilled worker sew cherubim into the pattern. Make all of the curtains the same size. They must be 42 feet long and six feet wide.

"Join five of the curtains together. Do the same thing with the other five. Make loops out of blue strips of cloth along the edge of the end curtain in one set. Do the same thing with the end curtain in the other set. Make 50 loops on the end curtain of the one set. Do the same thing on the end curtain of the other set. Put the loops across from each other. Make 50 gold hooks. Use them to join the curtains together so that the holy tent is all one piece.

"Make a total of 11 curtains out of goat hair to put over the holy tent. Make all 11 curtains the same size. They must be 45 feet long and six feet wide.

"Join five of the curtains together into one set. Do the same thing with the other six. Fold the sixth curtain in half at the front of the tent. Make 50 loops along the edge of the end curtain in the one set. Do the same thing with the other set. Then make 50 bronze hooks. Put them in the loops to join the tent together all in one piece.

"Let the extra half curtain hang down at the rear of the holy tent. The tent curtains will be one foot six inches longer on both sides. What is left over will hang over the sides of the holy tent and cover it.

"Make a covering for the tent. Make it out of ram skins that are dyed red. Put a covering of the hides of sea cows over that.

"Make frames out of acacia wood for the holy tent. Make each frame 15 feet long and two feet three inches wide. Add two small wooden pins to each frame. Make the pins stick out so that they are even with each other. Make all of the frames for the holy tent in the same way.

"Make 20 frames for the south side of the holy tent. And make 40 silver bases to go under them. Make two bases for each frame. Put one under each pin that sticks out.

"For the north side of the holy tent make 20 frames and 40 silver bases. Put two bases under each frame.

"Make six frames for the west end of the holy tent. Make two frames for the corners at the far end. At those two corners the frames must be double from top to bottom. They must be fitted into a single ring. Make both of them the same. There will be eight frames and 16 silver bases. There will be two bases under each frame.

"Also make crossbars out of acacia wood. Make five for the frames on one side of the holy tent. Make five for the frames on the other side. And make five for the frames on the west, at the far end of the holy tent. The center crossbar must reach from end to end at the middle of the frames.

"Cover the frames with gold. Make gold rings to hold the crossbars. Also cover the crossbars with gold.

"Set up the holy tent in keeping with the plan I showed you on the mountain.

"Make a curtain out of blue, purple and bright red yarn and finely twisted linen. Have a skilled worker sew cherubim into the pattern. Hang the curtain with gold hooks on four posts that are made out of acacia wood. Cover the posts with gold. Stand them on four silver bases. Hang the curtain from the hooks.

"Place the ark of the covenant behind the curtain. The curtain will separate the Holy Room from the Most Holy Room. Put the cover on the

The Ark of the Covenant

The ark of the covenant was the most important thing in the holy tent. It was placed in the Most Holy Place.

Once a year, on the day when sin was paid for, a priest went into the Most Holy Place. Then he poured the blood of a sacrifice on the cover. The cover of the ark was made of pure gold and had two angels called cherubim carved on it. They faced each other with their wings spread upward. There were three things in the ark. These things were the two tablets of the law that God had given to Moses, a jar of manna, and Aaron's rod that had produced buds and flowers and almonds.

ark of the covenant in the Most Holy Room. The cover will be the place where sin is paid for.

"Place the table outside the curtain on the north side of the holy tent. And put the lampstand across from it on the south side.

"For the entrance to the tent make a curtain out of blue, purple and bright red yarn and finely twisted linen. Have a person who sews skillfully make it. Make gold hooks for the curtain. Make five posts out of acacia wood. Cover them with gold. And make five bronze bases for them.

The Golden Calf

Exodus 32

Israel Worships a Golden Calf

The people saw that Moses took a long time to come down from the mountain. So they gathered around Aaron. They said to him, "Come. Make us a god that will lead us. This fellow Moses brought us up out of Egypt. But we don't know what has happened to him."

Aaron answered them, "Take the gold earrings off your wives, your sons and your daughters. Bring the earrings to me."

So all of the people took off their earrings. They brought them to Aaron. He took what they gave him and made it into a metal statue of a god. It looked like a calf. He shaped it with a tool.

Then the people said, "Israel, here is your god who brought you up out of Egypt."

When Aaron saw it, he built an altar in front of the calf. He said, "Tomorrow will be a feast day in the LORD's honor."

So the next day the people got up early. They sacrificed burnt offerings and brought friendship offerings. They sat down to eat and drink. Then they got up to dance wildly in front of their god.

The LORD spoke to Moses. He said, "Go down. Your people you brought up out of Egypt have become very sinful. They have quickly turned away from what I commanded them. They have made themselves a statue of a god that looks like a calf. They have bowed down and sacrificed to it. And they have said, 'Israel, here is your god who brought you up out of Egypt.'

"I have seen those people," the LORD said to Moses. "They are stubborn. Now leave me alone. My anger will burn against them. I will destroy them. Then I will make you into a great nation."

But Moses asked the LORD his God to show favor to the people. "LORD," he said, "why should your anger burn against your people? You used your great power and mighty hand to bring them out of Egypt. Why should the Egyptians say, 'He brought them out to hurt them. He wanted to kill them in the mountains. He wanted to wipe them off the face of the earth'? Turn away from your burning anger. Please take pity on your people. Don't destroy them!

"Remember your servants Abraham, Isaac and Israel. You made a promise. You took an oath in your name. You said, 'I will make your children after you as many as the stars in the sky. I will give them all of this land I promised them. It will belong to them forever.'"

Then the LORD took pity on his people. He didn't destroy them as he had said he would.

Moses turned and went down the mountain. He had the two tablets of the covenant in his hands. Words were written on both sides of the tablets, front and back. The tablets were the work of God. The words had been written by God. They had been carved on the tablets.

Joshua heard the noise of the people shouting. So he said to Moses, "It sounds like war in the camp."

The Golden Calf

Moses had been up on the mountain a long time. The people didn't know what had happened to him. They asked Aaron to make a god for them. So Aaron made a golden calf at Mount Sinai. He took the gold jewelry that the people gave him. He made it into a statue for the people to worship. The statues of gods that people worshiped often looked like a calf or a bull.

Moses replied,

"It's not the sound of winning.
 It's not the sound of losing.
 It's the sound of singing that I hear."

As Moses approached the camp, he saw the calf. He also saw the people dancing. So he burned with anger. He threw the tablets out of his hands. They broke into pieces at the foot of the mountain.

He took the calf the people had made. He burned it in the fire. Then he ground it into powder. He scattered it on the water. And he made the people of Israel drink it.

He said to Aaron, "What did these people do to you? How did they make you lead them into such terrible sin?"

"Please don't be angry," Aaron answered. "You know how these people like to do what is evil. They said to me, 'Make us a god that will lead us. This fellow Moses brought us up out of Egypt. But we don't know what has happened to him.'

"So I told them, 'Anyone who has any gold jewelry, take it off.' They gave me the gold. I threw it into the fire. And out came this calf!"

The LORD struck the people with a plague. That's because of what they did with the calf Aaron had made.

Moses Sets Up God's "Church"
Exodus 40

Moses Sets Up the Holy Tent

Then the LORD said to Moses, "Set up the holy tent, the Tent of Meeting. Set it up on the first day of the first month.

"Place in it the ark where the tablets of the covenant are kept. Screen the ark with the curtain. Bring in the table for the holy bread. Arrange the loaves of bread on it. Then bring in the lampstand. Set up its lamps. Place the gold altar for burning incense in front of the ark where the tablets of the covenant are kept. Put up the curtain at the entrance to the holy tent.

"Place the altar for burnt offerings in front of the entrance to the holy tent, the Tent of Meeting. Place the large bowl between the Tent of Meeting and the altar. Put water in the bowl.

"Set up the courtyard around the holy tent. Put the curtain at the entrance to the courtyard.

"Get the anointing oil. Anoint the holy tent and everything that is in it. Set apart the holy tent and everything that belongs to it. Then it will be holy. Anoint the altar for burnt offerings and all of its tools. Set the altar apart. Then it will be a very holy place. Anoint the large bowl and its stand. Set them apart.

"Bring Aaron and his sons to the entrance to the Tent of Meeting. Wash them with water. Dress Aaron in the sacred clothes. Anoint him and set him apart. Then he will be able to serve me as priest.

"Bring his sons and dress them in their inner robes. Anoint them just as you anointed their father. Then they will be able to serve me as priests. They will be anointed to do the work of priests. That work will last for all time to come."

Moses did everything just as the LORD had commanded him.

So the holy tent was set up. It was the first day of the first month in the second year. Moses set up the holy tent. He put the bases in place. He put the frames in them. He put in the crossbars. He set up the posts. He spread the holy tent over the frames. Then he put the coverings over the tent. Moses did it as the LORD had commanded him.

He got the tablets of the covenant. He placed them in the ark. He put the poles through its rings. And he put the cover on it. The cover was the place where sin is paid for. Moses brought the ark into the holy tent. He hung the curtain to screen the ark where the tablets of the covenant are kept. Moses did it as the LORD had commanded him.

He placed the table for the holy bread in the Tent of Meeting. It was on the north side of the holy tent outside the curtain. He arranged the loaves of bread on it in the sight of the LORD. Moses did it as the LORD had commanded him.

He placed the lampstand in the Tent of Meeting. It stood across from the table on the south side of the holy tent. He set up the lamps in the sight of the LORD. Moses did it as the LORD had commanded him.

He placed the gold altar for burning incense in the Tent of Meeting.

He placed it in front of the curtain. He burned sweet-smelling incense on it. Moses did it as the LORD had commanded him.

Then he put up the curtain at the entrance to the holy tent.

He set the altar for burnt offerings near the entrance to the holy tent, the Tent of Meeting. He sacrificed burnt offerings and grain offerings on it. Moses did it as the LORD had commanded him.

He placed the large bowl between the Tent of Meeting and the altar. He put water in the bowl for washing. Moses and Aaron and his sons used it to wash their hands and feet. They washed when they entered the Tent of Meeting or approached the altar. They did it as the LORD had commanded Moses.

Then Moses set up the courtyard around the holy tent and altar. He put up the curtain at the entrance to the courtyard. And so Moses completed the work.

The Glory of the LORD

Then the cloud covered the Tent of Meeting. The glory of the LORD filled the holy tent. Moses couldn't enter the Tent of Meeting because the cloud had settled on it. The glory of the LORD filled the holy tent.

The Holy Tent

The holy tent was the place where Israel worshiped God. It was called the "Tent of Meeting." It was where God met his chosen people. The holy tent had many parts. But it was built so it could be moved when Israel moved around in the desert. The courtyard of the tent had only one door. This was to remind the people that there is only one way to come to God. The holy tent had two rooms. They were called the Holy Place and the Most Holy Place.

The people of Israel continued their travels. When the cloud lifted from above the holy tent, they started out. But if the cloud didn't lift, they did not start out. They stayed until the day it lifted.

So the cloud of the LORD was above the holy tent during the day. Fire was in the cloud at night. The whole community of Israel could see the cloud during all of their travels.

The Israelites Get Closer to the Promised Land

Numbers 13—14

Some Men Check Out the Land of Canaan

The LORD spoke to Moses. He said, "Send some men to check out the land of Canaan. I am giving it to the people of Israel. Send one leader from each of Israel's tribes."

So Moses sent them out from the Desert of Paran. He sent them as the LORD had commanded. All of them were leaders of the people of Israel.

Moses sent them to check out Canaan. He said, "Go up through the Negev Desert. Go on into the central hill country. See what the land is like. See whether the people who live there are strong or weak. See whether they are few or many.

"What kind of land do they live in? Is it good or bad? What kind of towns do they live in? Do the towns have high walls around them or not? How is the soil? Is it rich land or poor land? Are there trees on it or not? Do your best to bring back some of the fruit of the land." It was the season for the first ripe grapes.

So the men went up and checked out the land.

The men came to the Valley of Eshcol. There they cut off a branch that had a single bunch of grapes on it. Two of them carried it on a pole between them. They carried some pomegranates and figs along with it. That place was called the Valley of Eshcol. That's because the men of Israel cut off a bunch of grapes there.

At the end of 40 days, the men returned from checking out the land.

The Men Report on What They Found

The men came back to Moses, Aaron and the whole community of Israel. The people were at Kadesh in the Desert of Paran. There the men reported to Moses and Aaron and all of the people. They showed them the fruit of the land.

They gave Moses their report. They said, "We went into the land you sent us to. It really does have plenty of milk and honey! Here's some fruit from the land.

"But the people who live there are powerful. Their cities have high walls around them and are very large. We even saw members of the family line of Anak there. The Amalekites live in the Negev Desert. The Hittites, Jebusites and Amorites live in the central hill country. The Canaanites live near the Mediterranean Sea. They also live along the Jordan River."

Then Caleb interrupted the men who were speaking to Moses. He said, "We should go up and take the land. We can certainly do it."

But the men who had gone up with him spoke. They said, "We can't attack those people. They are stronger than we are." The men spread a bad report about the land among the people of Israel. They said, "The land we checked out destroys those who live in it. All of the people we saw there are very big and tall."

The People Refuse to Obey the LORD

That night all of the people in the community raised their voices. They sobbed out loud.

The people of Israel spoke against Moses and Aaron. The whole community said to them, "We wish we had died in Egypt or even in this desert. Why is the LORD bringing us to this land? We're going to be killed with swords. Our enemies will capture our wives and children. Wouldn't it be better for us to go back to Egypt?"

They said to one another, "We should choose another leader. We should go back to Egypt."

Then Moses and Aaron fell with their faces to the ground. They did it in front of the whole community of Israel that was gathered there.

Joshua, the son of Nun, tore his clothes. So did Caleb, the son of Jephunneh. Joshua and Caleb were two of the men who had checked out the land. They spoke to the whole community of Israel. They said, "We passed through the land and checked it out. It's very good. If the LORD is pleased with us, he'll lead us into that land. It's a land that has plenty of milk and honey. He'll give it to us.

"But don't refuse to obey him. And don't be afraid of the people of the land. We will swallow them up. The LORD is with us. So nothing can save them. Don't be afraid of them."

Then the glory of the LORD appeared at the Tent of Meeting. All of the people of Israel saw it. The LORD spoke to Moses. He said, "How long will these people make fun of me? How long will they refuse to believe in me? They refuse even though I have done many miraculous signs among them. So I will strike them down with a plague. I will destroy them. But I will make you into a greater and stronger nation than they are."

Moses said to the LORD, "Then the Egyptians will hear about it. You used your power to bring these people up from among them.

"And the Egyptians will tell the people who live in Canaan about it. LORD, they have already heard a lot about you. They've heard that you are with these people. They've heard that you have been seen face to face. They've been told that your cloud stays over them. They've heard

The Results of Disobeying

God forgave his people when they did not obey him. But they were punished. They had to live in the desert for 40 years. All the adults who disobeyed died.

When God forgives us, he is not angry with us anymore. But we may still be punished for what we did. Read this story. What do you think this dad should do?

Dad told Andy, "Don't bounce your ball off the side of the house." But later Andy felt bored. He threw his ball at the side of the house. Crash! The ball went through the window. "Andy!" Dad called. "Come in here!"

What do you think Andy's dad should do? Punish him? Forgive him and then punish him? Make Andy pay for the window? Forgive Andy and make him pay for the window? Just forgive Andy? Tell your parents this story. Talk about what you think Andy's dad should do.

that you go in front of them in a pillar of cloud by day. They've been told that you go in front of them in a pillar of fire at night.

"Suppose you put these people to death all at one time. Then the nations who have heard those things about you will talk. They'll say, 'The LORD took an oath. He promised to give these people the land of Canaan. But he wasn't able to bring them into it. So he killed them in the desert.'

"Now, Lord, show your strength. You have said, 'I am the LORD. I am slow to get angry. I am full of love. I forgive those who sin. I forgive those who refuse to obey. But I do not let guilty people go without punishing them. I punish the children, grandchildren and great-grandchildren for the sin of their parents.'

"LORD, your love is great. So forgive the sin of these people. Forgive them just as you have done from the time they left Egypt until now."

The LORD replied, "I have forgiven them, just as you asked. You can be sure that I live. You can be sure that my glory fills the whole earth.

"And you can be just as sure that these men will not see the land I promised to give them. They have seen my glory. They have seen the miraculous signs I did in Egypt. And they have seen what I did in the desert. But they did not obey me. And they have put me to the test ten times. So not even one of them will ever see the land I promised with an oath to give to their people of long ago."

A Bronze Snake

Numbers 21

Moses Makes a Bronze Snake

The people of Israel traveled from Mount Hor along the way to the Red Sea. They wanted to go around Edom. But they grew tired on the way. So they spoke against God. They also spoke against Moses. They said to them, "Why have

DID YOU KNOW?

How is the bronze snake like Jesus?

God wanted the people of Israel to trust him. They were supposed to obey him. They were supposed to look at the bronze snake. Then they would be saved from the poisonous snakes. People today should trust God and obey him. They are to look to Jesus to forgive them. Then they are saved from their sins.

you brought us up out of Egypt? Do you want us to die here in the desert? We don't have any bread! We don't have any water! And we hate this awful food!"

Then the LORD sent poisonous snakes among the people of Israel. The snakes bit them. Many of the people died. The others came to Moses. They said, "We sinned when we spoke against the LORD and against you. Pray that the LORD will take the snakes away from us." So Moses prayed for the people.

The LORD said to Moses, "Make a snake. Put it up on a pole. Then anyone who is bitten can look at it and remain alive." So Moses made a bronze snake. He put it up on a pole. Then anyone who was bitten by a snake and looked at the bronze snake remained alive.

Balaam and His Donkey

Numbers 22

Balak Sends For Balaam

Then the people of Israel traveled to the flatlands of Moab. They camped along the Jordan River across from Jericho.

Balak was the son of Zippor. The people of Moab were terrified because there were so many Israelites. In fact, Moab was filled with panic because of the people of Israel.

The Moabites spoke to the elders of Midian. They said, "This huge mob is going to lick up everything around us. They'll lick it up as an ox licks up all of the grass in the fields."

Balak, the son of Zippor, was the king of Moab at that time. He sent messengers to get Balaam. Balaam was the son of Beor. Balaam was at the city of Pethor near the Euphrates River. Pethor was in the land where Balaam had been born. Balak told the messengers to say to Balaam,

"A nation has come out of Egypt. They are covering the face of the land. They've settled down next to me. So come and put a curse on those people. They are too powerful for me. Maybe I'll be able to win the battle over them. Maybe I'll be able to drive them out of the country. I know that those you bless will be blessed. And I know that those you put a curse on will be cursed."

Balaam's Donkey

Balaam got up in the morning. He put a saddle on his donkey. Then he went with the princes of Moab.

But God was very angry when Balaam went. So the angel of the LORD stood in the road to oppose him. Balaam was riding on his donkey. His two servants were with him. The donkey saw the angel of the LORD standing in the road. The angel was holding a sword. He was ready for battle. So the donkey left the road and went into a field. Balaam hit the donkey. He wanted to get it back on the road.

Then the angel of the LORD stood in a narrow path. The path went between two vineyards. There were walls on both sides. The donkey saw the angel of the LORD. So it moved close to the wall. It crushed Balaam's foot against the wall. He hit the donkey again.

Then the angel of the LORD moved on ahead. He stood in a narrow place. There was no room to turn, either right or left. The donkey saw the angel of the LORD. So it lay down under Balaam. That made him angry. He hit the donkey with his walking stick.

Then the LORD opened the donkey's mouth. It said to Balaam, "What have I done to you? Why did you hit me those three times?"

Balaam answered the donkey. He said, "You have made me look foolish! I wish I had a sword in my hand. If I did, I'd kill you right now."

Who Is in Control?

Read this story about Balaam. King Balak wanted him to curse the people of Israel. Balak wanted bad things to happen to them. Then the people of Israel would not be able to conquer his land.

But Balaam would not curse the people of Israel. He obeyed God instead. He would only say what God told him to say. He said good things about God and his people.

Does God control what you say? At your next mealtime listen to what each person says. Was it a good thing to say or not? Ask God to help you say good and helpful things.

The donkey said to Balaam, "I'm your own donkey. I'm the one you have always ridden. Haven't you been riding me to this very day? Have I ever made you look foolish before?"

"No," he said.

Then the LORD opened Balaam's eyes. He saw the angel of the LORD standing in the road. He saw that the angel was holding a sword. The angel was ready for battle. So Balaam bowed down. He fell with his face to the ground.

The angel of the LORD spoke to him. He asked him, "Why have you hit your donkey three times? I have come here to oppose you. What you are doing is foolish. The donkey saw me. It turned away from me three times. Suppose it had not turned away. Then I would certainly have killed you by now. But I would have spared the donkey."

Balaam spoke to the angel of the LORD. He said, "I have sinned. I didn't realize you were standing in the road to oppose me. Tell me whether you are pleased with me. If you aren't, I'll go back."

The angel of the LORD spoke to Balaam. He said, "Go with the men. But say only what I tell you to say." So Balaam went with the princes of Balak.

Donkeys

In Bible times, even important people rode on small donkeys. When a king rode a donkey into a nation or city, it meant he was coming in peace. A king who was going to war rode a horse. The most important person to ever ride a donkey was Jesus. He rode a donkey into Jerusalem to show he came in peace. The people who were in Jerusalem that day praised God. They threw branches and their coats on the road in front of Jesus.

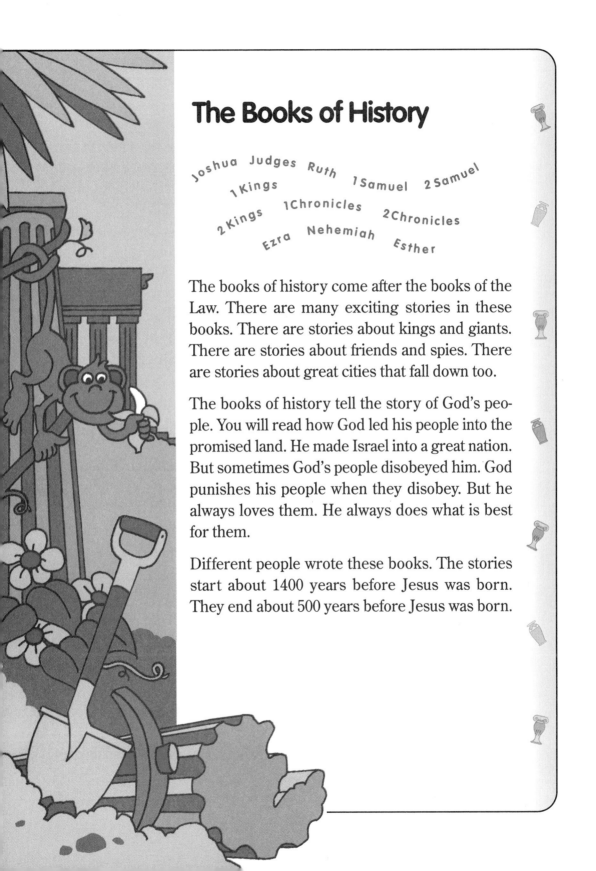

The Books of History

Joshua Judges Ruth 1 Samuel 2 Samuel
1 Kings
2 Kings 1 Chronicles 2 Chronicles
Ezra Nehemiah Esther

The books of history come after the books of the Law. There are many exciting stories in these books. There are stories about kings and giants. There are stories about friends and spies. There are stories about great cities that fall down too.

The books of history tell the story of God's people. You will read how God led his people into the promised land. He made Israel into a great nation. But sometimes God's people disobeyed him. God punishes his people when they disobey. But he always loves them. He always does what is best for them.

Different people wrote these books. The stories start about 1400 years before Jesus was born. They end about 500 years before Jesus was born.

Joshua Becomes Israel's Leader

Numbers 27; Deuteronomy 34; Joshua 1—2

Joshua Becomes Israel's New Leader

Then the LORD spoke to Moses. He said, "Go up this mountain in the Abarim range. See the land I have given the people of Israel. After you have seen it, you too will join the members of your family who have already died. You will die, just as your brother Aaron did.

"The community refused to obey me at the waters of Meribah Kadesh. At that time, you and Aaron did not obey my command. You did not honor me in front of them as the holy God." Meribah Kadesh is in the Desert of Zin.

Moses spoke to the LORD. He said, "LORD, you are the God who creates the spirits of all people. Please appoint a man to lead this community. Put him in charge of them. Tell him to take care of them. Then your people won't be like sheep that don't have a shepherd."

So the LORD said to Moses, "Joshua, the son of Nun, has the ability to be a wise leader. Get him and place your hand on him. Have him stand in front of the priest Eleazar and the whole community. Put him in charge while everyone is watching. Give him some of your authority. Then the whole community of Israel will obey him.

"Joshua will stand in front of the priest Eleazar. Eleazar will help him make decisions. Eleazar will get help from me by using the Urim. Joshua and the whole community of Israel must not make any move at all unless I command them to."

Moses did just as the LORD commanded him. He got Joshua and had him stand in front of the priest Eleazar and the whole community. Then Moses placed his hands on Joshua. And he put him in charge of the people. He did just as the LORD had directed through Moses.

Moses Dies

Moses climbed Mount Nebo. He went up from the flatlands of Moab to the highest slopes of Pisgah. It's across from Jericho.

At Pisgah the LORD showed him the whole land from Gilead all the way to Dan. Moses saw the whole land of Naphtali. He saw the territory of Ephraim and Manasseh. The LORD showed him the whole land of

Judah all the way to the Mediterranean Sea. Moses saw the Negev Desert. He saw the whole area from the Valley of Jericho all the way to Zoar. Jericho was also known as The City of Palm Trees.

Then the LORD spoke to Moses. He said, "This is the land I promised with an oath to Abraham, Isaac and Jacob. I told them, 'I will give this land to your children and their children.' Moses, I have let you see it with your own eyes. But you will not go across the Jordan River to enter it."

Moses, the servant of the LORD, died there in Moab, just as the LORD had said. The LORD buried the body of Moses in Moab. His grave is in the valley across from Beth Peor. But to this day no one knows where it is. Moses was 120 years old when he died. But his eyes were not weak. He was still very strong.

The people of Israel sobbed over Moses on the flatlands of Moab for 30 days. They did it until their time for sobbing and crying was over.

Joshua, the son of Nun, was filled with wisdom. That's because Moses had placed his hands on him. So the Israelites listened to Joshua. They did what the LORD had commanded Moses.

Since then, Israel has never had a prophet like Moses. The LORD knew him

PEOPLE IN BIBLE TIMES

Joshua

Joshua was a strong, brave man. He was one of the spies that Moses sent into Canaan. Joshua led the people of Israel after Moses died. He was a fair and wise ruler. Joshua obeyed God and won many battles.

face to face. Moses did many miraculous signs and wonders. The LORD had sent him to do them in Egypt. Moses did them against Pharaoh, against all of his officials and against his whole land. No one has ever had the mighty power Moses had. No one has ever done the wonderful acts he did in the sight of all of the people of Israel.

The LORD Gives Commands to Joshua

Moses, the servant of the LORD, died. After that, the LORD spoke to Joshua, the son of Nun. Joshua was Moses' helper. The LORD said to Joshua, "My servant Moses is dead. Now then, I want you and all of these people to get ready to go across the Jordan River. I want all of you to go into the land I am about to give to the people of Israel.

"Joshua, no one will be able to stand up against you as long as you live. I will be with you, just as I was with Moses. I will never leave you. I will never desert you.

"Be strong and brave. You will lead these people, and they will take the land as their very own. It is the land I promised with an oath to give their people long ago."

Joshua Gives Commands to the People

So Joshua gave orders to the officers of the people. He said, "Go through the camp. Tell the people, 'Get your supplies ready. Three days from now you will go across the Jordan River right here. You will go in and take over the land. The LORD your God is giving it to you as your very own.'"

Joshua also spoke to the tribes of Reuben and Gad and half of the tribe of Manasseh. He said to them, "Remember what Moses, the servant of the LORD, commanded you. He said, 'The LORD your God is giving you this land. It's a place where you can settle down and live in peace and rest.'

"Your wives, children and livestock can stay here east of the Jordan River. Moses gave you this land. But all of your fighting men must get ready for battle. They must go across ahead of the other tribes. You must help them until the LORD gives them rest. In the same way, he has already given you rest. You must help them until they also have taken over their land. It's the land the LORD your God is giving them. After that, you can come back here. Then you can live in your own land. It's the land that Moses, the servant of the LORD, gave you east of the Jordan River. It's toward the sunrise."

Then the tribes of Reuben and Gad and half of the tribe of Manasseh answered Joshua. They said, "We'll do what you have commanded us to do. We'll go where you send us. We obeyed Moses completely. And we'll obey you just as completely. But may the LORD your God be with you, just as he was with Moses."

Rahab Helps the Spies

Joshua, the son of Nun, sent two spies from Shittim. He sent them in secret. He said to them, "Go. Look the land over. Most of all, check out Jericho."

So they went to Jericho. They stayed at the house of a prostitute. Her name was Rahab.

The king of Jericho was told, "Look! Some of the people of Israel have come here tonight. They've come to check out the land."

So the king sent a message to Rahab. It said, "Bring out the men who came into your house. They've come to check out the whole land."

But the woman had hidden the two men. She said, "It's true that the men came here. But I didn't know where they had come from. They left at sunset, when it was time to close the city gate. I don't know which way they went. Go after them quickly. You might catch up with them."

But in fact she had taken them up on the roof. There she had hidden them under some flax she had piled up.

The king's men left to hunt down the spies. They took the road that leads to where the Jordan River can be crossed. As soon as they had gone out of the city, the gate was shut.

Rahab went up on the roof before the spies settled down for the night. She said to them, "I know that the LORD has given this land to you. We are very much afraid of you. Everyone who lives in this country is weak with fear because of you.

PEOPLE IN BIBLE TIMES

Rahab

Rahab lived in the city of Jericho. She lived among Israel's enemies who didn't worship God. She believed in God and was a brave woman. Rahab hid Joshua's spies to keep them safe. God saved Rahab and her family during a battle.

LIFE IN BIBLE TIMES

Drying Flax

The houses of Canaan had flat roofs. The rooftops were used for many things. Flax plants were piled on rooftops to dry. Stringy fibers taken from dried flax plants were woven to make linen cloth. In Jericho the Israelite spies hid under piles of drying flax plants.

"The LORD your God is the God who rules over heaven above and earth below.

"Now then, please take an oath. Promise me in the name of the LORD that you will be kind to my family. I've been kind to you. Promise me that you will spare the lives of my father and mother. Spare my brothers and sisters. Also spare everyone in their families. Promise that you won't put any of us to death."

So the men made a promise to her. "We'll give up our lives to save yours," they said. "But don't tell anyone what we're doing. Then we'll be kind and faithful to you when the LORD gives us the land."

The house Rahab lived in was part of the city wall. So she let the spies down by a rope through the window. She had said to them, "Go up into the hills. The men who are chasing you won't be able to find you. Hide yourselves there for three days until they return. Then you can go on your way."

The men said to her, "You made us take an oath and make a promise. But we won't keep it unless you do what we say. When we enter the land, you must tie this bright red rope in the window. Tie it in the window you let us down through.

Faith Like Rahab's

Rahab was a woman who lived in Jericho. She believed in the God of Israel. She protected God's spies. Joshua 2 tells the story of Rahab. It says that Rahab put a red cord in her window to save her own life and the lives of her family. When the people of Israel attacked Jericho, they found Rahab's house by looking for the red cord. They took her family to a safe place.

Rahab trusted God. She was willing to help others. You can too. Make a "Rahab cord" as a reminder. Ask for help if you need it. Take nine pieces of red yarn. Make each one about 18 inches long. Tie a knot at one end. Divide the yarn into three groups of three strands of yarn each. Braid the sections together. Tie the end. Hang the cord inside your window. Every time you look at it, let it remind you to be like Rahab by trusting God and helping others.

"Bring your father and mother into your house. Also bring your brothers and everyone else in your family into your house. None of you must go out into the street. If you do, anything that happens to you will be your own fault. Don't hold us accountable."

"I agree," Rahab replied. "I'll do as you say." So she sent them away, and they left. Then she tied the bright red rope in the window.

When the spies left, they went up into the hills. They stayed there for three days. By that time the men who were chasing them had searched all along the road. They couldn't find them. So they returned.

Then the two spies started back. They went down out of the hills. They went across the Jordan River. They came to Joshua, the son of Nun. They told him everything that had happened to them. They said, "We're sure the LORD has given the whole land over to us. All of the people there are weak with fear because of us."

The Israelites Enter the Promised Land

Joshua 3—4

Israel Goes Across the Jordan River

Joshua spoke to the people of Israel. He said, "Come here. Listen to what the LORD your God is saying. You will soon know that the living God is among you. You can be sure that he'll drive out the people who are now living in the land. He'll do it to make room for you.

"The ark will go into the Jordan River ahead of you. It's the ark of the covenant of the Lord of the whole earth.

"Choose 12 men from the tribes of Israel. Choose one from each tribe.

"The priests will carry the ark of the LORD. He's the Lord of the whole earth. As soon as the priests step into the Jordan, it will stop flowing. The water that's coming down the river will pile up in one place. That's how you will know that the living God is among you."

So the people took their tents down. They prepared to go across the Jordan River. The priests who were carrying the ark of the covenant went ahead of them.

The water of the Jordan was going over its banks. It always does that at the time the crops are being gathered. The priests came to the river. Their feet touched the water's edge. Right away the water that was coming down the river stopped flowing. It piled up far away at a town called Adam near Zarethan. The water that was flowing down to the Dead Sea was completely cut off. So the people went across the Jordan River opposite Jericho.

The priests carried the ark of the covenant of the LORD. They stood firm on dry ground in the middle of the river. They stayed there until the whole nation of Israel had gone across on dry ground.

After the whole nation had gone across the Jordan River, the LORD spoke to Joshua. He said, "Choose 12 men from among the people. Choose one from each tribe. Tell them to get 12 stones from the middle of the river. They must pick them up from right where the priests stood. They must carry the stones over with all of you. And they must put them down at the place where you will stay tonight."

So Joshua called together the 12 men he had appointed from among the people of Israel. There was one man from each tribe. He said to them, "Go back to the middle of the Jordan River. Go to where the ark of the LORD your God is. Each one of you must pick up a stone. You must carry it on your shoulder. There will be as many stones as there are tribes in Israel.

LIFE IN BIBLE TIMES

Memorials

The Israelites crossed the Jordan River into the promised land. God made a dry path through the water so the people could walk safely across. Then Joshua told one man from each of the 12 tribes of Israel to pick up a stone. He told the men to carry the stones to the other side. Joshua piled up the stones for a "memorial," or special reminder. The stones reminded God's people how God parted the waters and let the Israelites cross the river on dry ground.

"The stones will serve as a reminder to you. In days to come, your children will ask you, 'What do these stones mean?' Tell them that the LORD cut off the flow of water in the Jordan River. Tell them its water stopped flowing when the ark of the covenant of the LORD went across. The stones will always remind the Israelites of what happened there."

So the people of Israel did as Joshua commanded them. They took 12 stones from the middle of the Jordan River. There was one stone for each of the tribes of Israel. It was just as the LORD had told Joshua. The people carried the stones with them to their camp. There they put them down.

Joshua piled up the 12 stones that had been in the middle of the river. They had been right where the priests who carried the ark of the covenant had stood. And they are still there to this very day.

That day the LORD honored Joshua in the eyes of all of the people of Israel. They had respect for Joshua as long as he lived. They respected him just as much as they had respected Moses.

Then the priests came up out of the river. They were carrying the ark of the covenant of the LORD. As soon as they stepped out on dry ground, the water of the Jordan began to flow again. It went over its banks, just as it had done before.

Then [Joshua] spoke to the people of Israel. He said, "In days to come, your children after you will ask their parents, 'What do these stones mean?' Their parents must tell them, 'Israel went across the Jordan River on dry ground.' The LORD your God dried up the Jordan for you until you had gone across it. He did to the Jordan River the same thing he had done to the Red Sea. He dried up the Red Sea ahead of us until we had gone across it. He did it so that all of the nations on earth would know that he is powerful. He did it so that you would always have respect for the LORD your God."

The Fall of Jericho

Joshua 5—6

Israel Captures Jericho

When Joshua was near Jericho, he looked up and saw a man standing in front of him. The man was holding a sword. He was ready for battle. Joshua went up to him. He asked, "Are you on our side? Or are you on the side of our enemies?"

"I am not on either side," he replied. "I have come as the commander of the LORD's army." Then Joshua fell with his face to the ground. He asked the man, "What message does my Lord have for me?"

The commander of the LORD's army replied, "Take off your sandals. The place you are standing on is holy ground." So Joshua took them off.

The gates of Jericho were shut tight and guarded closely because of the people of Israel. No one went out. No one came in.

Then the LORD spoke to Joshua. He said, "I have handed Jericho over to you. I have also handed its king and its fighting men over to you.

"March around the city once with all of your fighting men. In fact, do it for six days. Have seven priests get trumpets that are made out of rams' horns. They must carry them in front of the ark. On the seventh day, march around the city seven times. Have the priests blow the trumpets as you march.

"You will hear them blow a long blast on the trumpets. When you do, have all of the men give a loud shout. The wall of the city will fall down. Then the whole army will go up to the city. Every man will go straight in." [Joshua did as the LORD commanded].

On the seventh day, they got up at sunrise. They marched around the city, just as they had done before. But on that day they went around it seven times.

A Dumb Thing to Do?

God told the people of Israel to destroy the city of Jericho. But they weren't to do it the usual way. They were told to just march around the city while the priests blew trumpets! They didn't know why God told them to do this. How silly they must have looked to the people of Jericho. But the people of Israel obeyed God. And they won!

You may not understand everything that your parents tell you to do. But it is not dumb to obey them. They love you and want what's best for you. Will you obey them?

On the seventh time around, the priests blew a long blast on the trumpets.

Then Joshua gave a command to the men. He said, "Shout! The LORD has given you the city! The city and everything that is in it must be set apart to the LORD in a special way to be destroyed. But the prostitute Rahab and all those who are with her in her house must be spared. That's because she hid the spies we sent.

"But keep away from the things that have been set apart to the LORD. If you take any of them, you will be destroyed. And you will bring trouble on the camp of Israel. You will cause it to be destroyed. All of the silver and gold is holy. It is set apart to the LORD. So are all of the articles that are made out of bronze and iron. All of those things must be added to the treasures that are kept in the LORD's house."

The priests blew the trumpets. As soon as the fighting men heard the sound, they gave a loud shout. Then the wall fell down. Every man charged straight in. So they took the city.

Then Joshua spoke to the two men who had gone in to check out the land. He said, "Go into the prostitute's house. Bring her out. Also bring out everyone who is with her. That's what you promised her you would do when you took an oath."

Jericho's Wall

Jericho was not a huge city, but it sat high up on a hill. Its walls were high and thick—so thick that people built their houses in them! The Israelite soldiers probably looked at Jericho and wondered how they would ever be able to scramble up that hill and then go over such huge walls. But God had an answer for the high walls of Jericho.

So the young men who had checked out the land went into Rahab's house. They brought her out along with her parents and brothers. They brought out everyone else who was there with her. They put them in a place that was outside the camp of Israel.

Then they burned the whole city and everything that was in it. But they added the silver and gold to the treasures that were kept in the LORD's house. They also put there the articles that were made out of bronze and iron.

So the LORD was with Joshua. And Joshua became famous everywhere in the land.

Joshua Says Good-by

Joshua 23—24

Joshua Says Good-by to the Leaders

A long time had passed. The LORD had given Israel peace and rest from all of their enemies who were around them. By that time Joshua was very old. So he sent for all of the elders, leaders, judges and officials of Israel. He said to them, "I'm very old. You yourselves have seen everything the LORD your God has done. You have seen what he's done to all of those nations because of you. The LORD your God fought for you.

"Remember how I've given you all of the land of the nations that remain here. I've given each of your tribes a share of it. It's the land of

Choosing to Serve God

When Joshua was old, he called all the people of Israel together. What did he ask them to do? Read the next page to find out. Joshua 24:15 is a very special verse. It says, "As for me and my family, we will serve the LORD." Have you decided to serve the Lord? Ask your mom and dad when they chose to serve the Lord. Ask them why they decided to serve him. Now talk about ways that you can serve the Lord as a family.

the nations I won the battle over. It's between the Jordan River and the Mediterranean Sea in the west. The LORD your God himself will drive those nations out of your way. He will push them out to make room for you. You will take over their land, just as the LORD your God promised you.

"Be very strong. Be careful to obey everything that is written in the Scroll of the Law of Moses. Don't turn away from it to the right or the left.

"Don't have anything to do with the nations that remain among you. Don't use the names of their gods for any reason at all. Don't take oaths and make promises in their names. You must not serve them. You must not bow down to them. You must remain true to the LORD your God, just as you have done until now.

"The LORD has driven out great and powerful nations to make room for you. To this very day no one has been able to fight against you and win. One of you can chase a thousand away. That's because the LORD your God fights for you, just as he promised he would. So be very careful to love the LORD your God.

"But suppose you turn away from him. You mix with the people who are left alive in the nations that remain among you. Later, you and they get married to each other. And you do other kinds of things with them. Then you can be sure of what the LORD your God will do. He won't drive out those nations to make room for you anymore. Instead, they will become traps and snares for you. They will be like whips on your backs. They will be like thorns in your eyes. All of that will continue until you are destroyed. It will continue until you are removed from this good land. It's the land the LORD your God has given you. But as for me and my family, we will serve the LORD.

WORDS TO TREASURE

As for me and my family, we will serve the LORD.
Joshua 24:15

"Now I'm about to die, just as everyone else on earth does. The LORD your God has kept all of the good promises he gave you. Every one of them has come true. Not one has failed to come true. And you know that with all your heart and soul.

"Every good promise of the LORD your God has come true. So you know that the LORD will bring on you all of the evil things he has warned you about. He'll do it until he has destroyed you. He'll do it until he has removed you from this good land. It's the land he has given you.

"Suppose you break the covenant the LORD your God made with you. He commanded you to obey it. But suppose you go and serve other gods. And you bow down to them. Then the LORD's anger will burn against you. You will quickly be destroyed. You will be removed from the good land he has given you."

Joshua Dies

Then Joshua, the servant of the LORD, died. He was the son of Nun. He was 110 years old when he died. His people buried his body at Timnath Serah on his own property. It's north of Mount Gaash in the hill country of Ephraim.

Israel served the LORD as long as Joshua lived. They also served him as long as the elders lived. Those were the elders who lived longer than Joshua did. They had seen for themselves everything the LORD had done for Israel.

The people of Israel had brought Joseph's bones up from Egypt. They buried his bones at Shechem in the piece of land Jacob had bought. He had bought it from the sons of Hamor. He had paid 100 pieces of silver for it. Hamor was the father of Shechem. That piece of land became the share that belonged to Joseph's children after him.

The People Forget God

Judges 2

The People Turn Away From the LORD

The people served the LORD as long as Joshua lived. They also served him as long as the elders lived. Those were the elders who lived longer than Joshua did. They had seen all of the great things the LORD had done for Israel.

All of the people of Joshua's time joined the members of their families who had already died. Then those who were born after them grew up. They didn't know the LORD. They didn't know what he had done for Israel.

The people of Israel did what was evil in the sight of the LORD. They served the gods that were named after Baal. They deserted the LORD, the God of their people. He had brought them out of Egypt. But now the people of Israel followed other gods and worshiped them. They served the gods of the nations that were around them. They made the LORD angry because they deserted him. They served Baal. They also served the goddesses that were named after Ashtoreth.

DID YOU KNOW?

Why was God angry with the people of Israel?

The people of Israel were told to worship only God. They were not to worship other people's false gods. But the people disobeyed God. They worshiped other gods. This made God angry.

The LORD became angry with Israel. So he handed them over to robbers. The robbers stole everything from them. He gave them over to their enemies who were all around them. Israel wasn't able to fight against them anymore and win. When Israel went out to fight, the LORD's power was against them. He let their enemies win the battle over them. The LORD had warned them with an oath that it would happen. And now they were suffering terribly.

Then the LORD gave them leaders. The leaders saved them from the power of those robbers. But the people wouldn't listen to their leaders.

Canaanite War Chariots

The Canaanites used heavy chariots covered with iron to fight battles. These chariots were the tanks of ancient armies. War chariots could only be used on flat ground, not on rocky hillsides. The Israelites had no iron chariots.

They weren't faithful to the LORD. They joined themselves to other gods and worshiped them. They didn't obey the LORD's commands as their people before them had done. They quickly turned away from the path their people had taken.

When the LORD gave them a leader, he was with that leader. He saved the people from the power of their enemies. He did it as long as the leader lived. He was very sorry for the people. They groaned because of what their enemies did to them. The enemies beat them down. They treated them badly.

But when the leader died, the people returned to their evil ways. The things they did were even more sinful than the things their people before them had done. They followed other gods. They served them. They worshiped them. They refused to give up their evil practices. They wouldn't change their stubborn ways.

So the LORD's anger burned against the people of Israel. He said, "This nation has broken my covenant. I made it with their people of long ago. But this nation has not listened to me. Joshua left some nations in the land when he died. I will not drive those nations out to make room for you anymore. I will use them to put Israel to the test. I will see whether Israel will live the way I want them to. I will see whether they will follow my path, just as their people did long ago."

The LORD had let those nations remain in the land. He didn't drive them out right away.

A Family History

Are the members of your family Christians? If so, make a scrapbook to help you remember what God means to your family. Ask your parents to get you a scrapbook. Then get pictures of your relatives. Ask each one to write you a letter about his or her life. Ask them to write what God has meant to them. Put the pictures and letters in the album. Look at it often. Then you will never forget what God has done for your family.

It really is important to remember God.

The Story of Deborah

Judges 4

Deborah

Deborah was a prophet. She was the wife of Lappidoth. Under The Palm Tree of Deborah she served the people as their judge. That place was between Ramah and Bethel in the hill country of Ephraim. The people of Israel came to her there. They came to have her decide cases for them. She settled matters between them.

Deborah sent for Barak. He was the son of Abinoam. Barak was from Kedesh in the land of Naphtali. Deborah said to Barak, "The LORD, the God of Israel, is giving you a command. He says, 'Go! Take 10,000 men from the tribes of Naphtali and Zebulun with you. Then lead the way to Mount Tabor. I will draw Sisera into a trap. He is the commander of Jabin's army. I will bring him, his chariots and his troops to the Kishon River. There I will hand him over to you.'"

PEOPLE IN BIBLE TIMES

Deborah

Deborah was a wise, brave woman. She was one of the rulers of Israel. She helped the people of Israel with their problems. Deborah also helped the people win an important battle.

Barak said to her, "If you go with me, I'll go. But if you don't go with me, I won't go."

"All right," Deborah said. "I'll go with you. But because of the way you are doing this, you won't receive any honor. The LORD will hand Sisera over to a woman."

So Deborah went to Kedesh with Barak. There he sent for Zebulun and Naphtali. And 10,000 men followed him. Deborah also went with him.

Then Deborah said to Barak, "Go! Today the LORD will hand Sisera over to you. Hasn't the LORD gone ahead of you?"

As Barak's men marched out, the LORD drove Sisera away from the field of battle. He scattered all of Sisera's chariots. Barak's men struck down Sisera's army with their swords. Sisera left his chariot behind. He ran away on foot.

But Barak chased Sisera's chariots and army. He chased them all the way to Harosheth Haggoyim. All of Sisera's men were killed with swords. Not even one was left.

The Story of Gideon

Judges 6—8

Gideon

Once again the people of Israel did what was evil in the sight of the LORD. So for seven years he handed them over to the people of Midian.

The Midianites treated the people of Israel very badly. That's why they made hiding places for themselves. They hid in holes in the mountains. They also hid in caves and in other safe places.

Each year the people planted their crops. When they did, the Midianites came into the country and attacked it. So did the Amalekites and other tribes from the east. They camped on the land. They destroyed the crops all the way to Gaza. They didn't spare any living thing for Israel. They didn't spare sheep or cattle or donkeys.

The Midianites came up with their livestock and tents. They came like huge numbers of locusts. It was impossible to count all of those men and their camels. They came into the land to destroy it.

Midian made the people of Israel very poor. So they cried out to the LORD for help.

They cried out to the LORD because of what Midian had done. So he sent a prophet to them. The prophet said, "The LORD is the God of Israel. He says, 'I brought you up out of Egypt. That is the land where you were slaves. I saved you from the power of Egypt. I saved you from all those who were beating you down. I drove the people of Canaan out to make room for you. I gave you their land.

"'I said to you, "I am the LORD your God. You are now living in the land of the Amorites. Do not worship their gods." But you have not listened to me.'"

PEOPLE IN BIBLE TIMES

Gideon

Gideon was a strong fighter. He was a great leader too. Sometimes Gideon was afraid. But he trusted and obeyed God. His army of only 300 men went to war with their enemies. Gideon won a great battle against the army of Midian.

The angel of the LORD came. He sat down under an oak tree in Ophrah. The tree belonged to Joash. He was from the family line of Abiezer.

Gideon was threshing wheat in a winepress at Ophrah. He was the son of Joash. Gideon was threshing in a winepress to hide the wheat from the Midianites.

The angel of the LORD appeared to Gideon. He said, "Mighty warrior, the LORD is with you."

"But sir," Gideon replied, "you say the LORD is with us. Then why has all of this happened to us? Where are all of the wonderful things he has done? Our parents told us about them. They said, 'Didn't the LORD bring us up out of Egypt?' But now the LORD has deserted us. He has handed us over to Midian."

The LORD turned to Gideon. He said to him, "You are strong. Go and save Israel from the power of Midian. I am sending you."

"But Lord," Gideon asked, "how can I possibly save Israel? My family group is the weakest in the tribe of Manasseh. And I'm the least important member of my family."

The LORD answered, "I will be with you. So you will strike down the men of Midian all at one time."

All of the Midianites and Amalekites gathered their armies together. Other tribes from the east joined them. All of them went across the Jordan River. They camped in the Valley of Jezreel.

Then the Spirit of the LORD came on Gideon. So Gideon blew the trumpet to send for the men of Abiezer. He told them to follow him. He sent messengers all through Manasseh. He called for the men of Manasseh to fight. He also sent messengers to the men of Asher, Zebulun and Naphtali. So all of those men went up to join the others.

Gideon said to God, "You promised you would use me to save Israel. Please do something for me. I'll put a piece of wool on the threshing floor. Suppose dew is only on the wool tomorrow morning. And suppose the ground all around it is dry. Then I will know that you will use me to save Israel. I'll know that your promise will come true."

And that's what happened. Gideon got up early the next day. He squeezed the dew out of the wool. The water filled a bowl.

Then Gideon said to God, "Don't let your anger burn against me. Let me ask you for just one more thing. Let me use the wool for one more test. This time make the wool dry. And cover the ground with dew."

So that night God did it. Only the wool was dry. The ground all around it was covered with dew.

The LORD spoke to Gideon. He said, "With the help of [300 men] I will save you. I will hand the Midianites over to you."

Gideon separated the 300 men into three companies. He put a trum-

Scared, but Willing

Gideon was the leader of God's army. He had many soldiers. But God told him he would conquer his enemy with just 300 men. Gideon was afraid, but he trusted God. So he told his men to do what God had told him to do. His men followed his example. They stood around the camp of the enemy and made lots of noise. The enemy ran away in fear.

Is there someone who is a good example for you? Someone who helps you trust God? Tell them so. Then try to be like them as you grow up.

pet and an empty jar into the hands of each man. And he put a torch inside each jar. "Watch me," he told them. Do what I do. I'll go to the edge of the enemy camp. Then do exactly as I do."

Gideon and the 100 men who were with him reached the edge of the enemy camp. It was about ten o'clock at night. It was just after the guard had been changed. Gideon and his men blew their trumpets. They broke the jars that were in their hands.

The three companies blew their trumpets. They smashed their jars. They held their torches in their left hands. They held in their right hands the trumpets they were going to blow. Then they shouted the battle cry, "A sword for the LORD and for Gideon!"

Each man stayed in his position around the camp. But all of the Midianites ran away in fear. They were crying out as they ran.

Gideon Refuses to Be Israel's Ruler

The people of Israel spoke to Gideon. They said, "Rule over us. We want you, your son and your grandson to be our rulers. You have saved us from the power of Midian."

But Gideon told them, "I will not rule over you. My son won't rule over you either. The LORD will rule over you."

Gideon Dies

Israel brought Midian under their control. Midian wasn't able to attack Israel anymore. So the land was at peace for 40 years. The peace lasted as long as Gideon was living.

Baal and Asherah

The statue called Baal was the chief Canaanite god in Old Testament times. Asherah was the chief goddess. Her sign was a tall wooden pole. Gideon destroyed the altar of Baal and cut down the Asherah pole. Then he built the right kind of altar to use in worshiping the true God instead of these false gods.

As soon as Gideon had died, the people of Israel joined themselves to the gods that were named after Baal. Israel wasn't faithful to the LORD. They worshiped Baal-Berith as their god. They forgot what the LORD their God had done for them. He had saved them from the power of their enemies who were all around them.

The Story of Samson

Judges 13; 16

Samson Is Born

Once again the people of Israel did what was evil in the sight of the LORD. So the LORD handed them over to the Philistines for 40 years.

A certain man from Zorah was named Manoah. He was from the tribe of Dan. Manoah had a wife who wasn't able to have children.

The angel of the LORD appeared to Manoah's wife. He said, "You are not able to have children. But you are going to become pregnant. You will have a baby boy. Make sure you do not drink any kind of wine. Also make sure you do not eat anything that is 'unclean.'

"You will become pregnant. You will have a son. He must not use a razor on his head. He must not cut his hair. That is because the boy will be a Nazirite. He will be set apart to God from the day he is born. He will begin to save Israel from the power of the Philistines."

Later, the woman had a baby boy. She named him Samson. As he grew up, the LORD blessed him. The Spirit of the LORD began to work in his life.

Giving Children to the Lord

This story tells about Samson. He was a Nazirite. He was set apart for God by a special promise. What special things did Samson's parents do to give their son to God?

Many parents dedicate their children to the Lord or have them baptized when they are babies. Did your parents do this for you? Ask them. How are your parents helping you live for God now?

Samson and Delilah

Some time later, Samson fell in love. The woman lived in the Valley of Sorek. Her name was Delilah.

The rulers of the Philistines went to her. They said, "See if you can get him to tell you the secret of why he's so strong. Find out how we can overpower him. Then we can tie him up. We can bring him under our control. Each of us will give you 28 pounds of silver."

So Delilah spoke to Samson. She said, "Tell me the secret of why you are so strong. Tell me how you can be tied up and controlled."

PEOPLE IN BIBLE TIMES

Samson

Samson was a leader of Israel. God made him very strong. Sometimes Samson made bad choices. He did not always obey God. Because of his disobedience Samson could not help the people of Israel escape from their enemies.

Samson answered her, "Let someone tie me up with seven new leather straps. They must be straps that aren't completely dry. Then I'll become as weak as any other man."

So the Philistine rulers brought seven new leather straps to her. They weren't completely dry. Delilah tied Samson up with them.

Men were hiding in the room. She called out to him. She said, "Samson! The Philistines are attacking you!" But he snapped the leather straps easily. They were like pieces of string that had come too close to a flame. So the secret of why he was so strong wasn't discovered.

Delilah spoke to Samson again. "You have made me look foolish," she said. "You told me a lie. Come on. Tell me how you can be tied up."

Samson said, "Let someone tie me tightly with new ropes. They must be ropes that have never been used. Then I'll become as weak as any other man."

So Delilah got some new ropes. She tied him up with them. Men were hiding in the room. She called out to him. She said, "Samson! The Philistines are attacking you!" But he snapped the ropes off his arms. They fell off just as if they were threads.

Delilah spoke to Samson again. "Until now, you have been making me look foolish," she said. "You have been telling me lies. This time really tell me how you can be tied up."

He replied, "Weave the seven braids of my hair into the cloth on a loom. Then pin my hair to the loom. If you do, I'll become as weak as any other man."

So while Samson was sleeping, Delilah took hold of the seven braids of his hair. She wove them into the cloth on a loom. Then she pinned his hair to the loom.

Again she called out to him. She said, "Samson! The Philistines are attacking you!" He woke up from his sleep. He pulled up the pin and the loom, together with the cloth.

Then she said to him, "How can you say, 'I love you'? You won't even share your secret with me. This is the third time you have made me look foolish. And you still haven't told me the secret of why you are so strong."

She continued to pester him day after day. She nagged him until he was sick and tired of it.

So he told her everything. "I've never used a razor on my head," he said. "I've never cut my hair. That's because I've been a Nazirite since the day I was born. A Nazirite is set apart to God. If you shave my head, I won't be strong anymore. I'll become as weak as any other man."

Delilah realized he had told her everything. So she sent a message to the Philistine rulers. She said, "Come back one more time. He has told me everything." So the rulers returned. They brought the silver with them.

Delilah got Samson to go to sleep on her lap. Then she called for a man to shave off the seven braids of his hair. That's how she began to bring him under her control. And he wasn't strong anymore.

She called out, "Samson! The Philistines are attacking you!"

Old Testament Houses

Houses in Bible times were often made of stone. They had straw or brush roofs. Most houses had only four or five small rooms. Usually six to eight people lived in a house. The ceilings of these houses were very low, but the people of those times were much shorter than people are today.

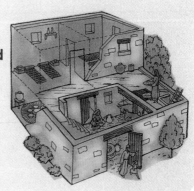

He woke up from his sleep. He thought, "I'll go out just as I did before. I'll shake myself free." But he didn't know that the LORD had left him.

Then the Philistines grabbed hold of him. They poked his eyes out. They took him down to Gaza. They put bronze chains around him. Then they made him grind grain in the prison. His head had been shaved. But the hair on it began to grow again.

Samson Dies

The rulers of the Philistines gathered together. They were going to offer a great sacrifice to their god Dagon. They were going to celebrate. They said, "Our god has handed our enemy Samson over to us."

When the people saw Samson, they praised their god. They said,

"Our god has handed our enemy over to us.
　　Our enemy has destroyed our land.
　　He has killed large numbers of our people."

After they had drunk a lot of wine, they shouted, "Bring Samson out. Let him put on a show for us." So they called Samson out of the prison. He put on a show for them.

They had him stand near the temple pillars. Then he spoke to the servant who was holding his hand. He said, "Put me where I can feel the pillars. I'm talking about the ones that hold the temple up. I want to lean against them."

The temple was crowded with men and women. All of the Philistine rulers were there. About 3,000 men and women were on the roof. They were watching Samson put on a show.

The Strongest Man in the World?

Samson was very strong on the outside. But he was weak on the inside. He did something that he knew was wrong.

Have you ever wanted to do something that you knew was wrong? If you did the right thing instead, you are stronger than Samson! Ask your mom or dad to put a gold star on your calendar every time you make a right choice.

Then he prayed to the LORD. He said, "LORD and King, show me that you still have concern for me. God, please make me strong just one more time. Let me pay the Philistines back for what they did to my two eyes. Let me do it with only one blow."

Then Samson reached toward the two pillars that were in the middle of the temple. They held the temple up. He put his right hand on one of them. He put his left hand on the other. He leaned hard against them.

Samson said, "Let me die together with the Philistines!" Then he pushed with all his might. The temple came down on the rulers. It fell on all of the people who were in it. So Samson killed many more Philistines when he died than he did while he lived.

The Story of Ruth

Ruth 1—4

Ruth Goes to Bethlehem With Naomi

There was a time when Israel didn't have kings to rule over them. But they had leaders to help them. This is a story about some things that happened during that time.

There wasn't enough food in the land of Judah. So a man went to live in the country of Moab for a while. He was from Bethlehem in Judah. His wife and two sons went with him.

The man's name was Elimelech. His wife's name was Naomi. The names of his two sons were Mahlon and Kilion. They were Ephrathites from Bethlehem in Judah. They went to Moab and lived there.

Naomi's husband Elimelech died. So she was left with her two sons. They got married to women from Moab. One was named Orpah. The other was named Ruth. Naomi's family lived in Moab for about ten years. Then Mahlon and Kilion also died. So Naomi was left without her two sons and her husband.

While Naomi was in Moab, she heard that the LORD had helped his people. He had begun to provide food for them again. So Naomi and her daughters-in-law prepared to go from Moab back to her home. She left the place where she had been living. Her two daughters-in-law went with her. They started out on the road that would take them back to the land of Judah.

Naomi said, "Go home, my daughters. Why would you want to come with me? Am I going to have any more sons who could become your husbands?

"Go home, my daughters. I'm too old to have another husband. Suppose I thought there was still some hope for me. Suppose I got married to a man tonight. And later I had sons by him. Would you wait until they grew up? Would you stay single until you could get married to them? No, my daughters. My life is more bitter than yours. The LORD's powerful hand has been against me!"

When they heard that, they broke down and sobbed again. Then Orpah kissed her mother-in-law good-by. But Ruth held on to her.

"Look," said Naomi. "Your sister-in-law is going back to her people and her gods. Go back with her."

But Ruth replied, "Don't try to make me leave you and go back. Where you go I'll go. Where you stay I'll stay. Your people will be my people. Your God will be my God. Where you die I'll die. And there my body will be buried. I won't let anything except death separate you from me. If I do, may the LORD punish me greatly."

Naomi realized that Ruth had made up her mind to go with her. So she stopped trying to make her go back.

So Naomi returned from Moab. Ruth, her daughter-in-law from Moab, came with her. They arrived in Bethlehem just when people were beginning to harvest the barley.

PEOPLE IN BIBLE TIMES

Naomi

There was no food in Israel. So Naomi and her family moved to Moab. But Naomi was sad and lonely when her husband and two sons died. She went back to Israel. Her daughter-in-law, Ruth, went with her.

PEOPLE IN BIBLE TIMES

Ruth

Ruth was a kind, caring woman. She loved her mother-in-law, Naomi. Ruth's husband died. She promised to stay with Naomi for as long as she lived. Ruth and Naomi went back to Israel. And Ruth married a kind man there named Boaz.

Ruth Meets Boaz

Naomi had a relative on her husband's side of the family. Her husband's name was Elimelech. The relative's name was Boaz. He was a very important man.

Ruth, who was from Moab, spoke to Naomi. She said, "Let me go out to the fields. I'll pick up the grain that has been left. I'll do it behind anyone who is pleased with me."

Naomi said to her, "My daughter, go ahead."

So Ruth went out and began to pick up grain. She worked in the fields behind those who were cutting and gathering the grain. As it turned out, she was working in a field that belonged to Boaz. He was from the family of Elimelech.

Just then Boaz arrived from Bethlehem. He greeted those who were cutting and gathering the grain. He said, "May the LORD be with you!"

"And may the LORD bless you!" they replied.

Boaz spoke to the man who was in charge of his workers. He asked, "Who is that young woman?"

Choose Friends Wisely

Make a friendship list. Write down the names of two or three close friends. Now write some things that a good friend does or does not do. Here are some ideas. A good friend takes turns. A good friend isn't bossy. A good friend helps you and won't leave you when you're in trouble.

Ruth was a good friend to Naomi. When they both lost someone they loved, Ruth stayed with Naomi. She made her home with Naomi and kept her company.

Keep looking at your friendship list. Let it help you to choose your friends wisely.

The man replied, "She's from Moab. She came back from there with Naomi. She said, 'Please let me walk behind the workers. Let me pick up the grain that is left.' Then she went into the field. She has kept on working there from morning until now. She took only one short rest in the shade."

So Boaz said to Ruth, "Dear woman, listen to me. Don't pick up grain in any other field. Don't go anywhere else. Stay here with my female servants. Keep your eye on the field where the men are cutting grain. Walk behind the women who are gathering it. Pick up the grain that is left. When you are thirsty, go and get a drink. Take water from the jars the men have filled."

When Ruth heard that, she bowed down with her face to the ground. She asked, "Why are you being so kind to me? In fact, why are you even noticing me? I'm from another country."

Boaz replied, "I've been told all about you. I've heard about everything you have done for your mother-in-law since your husband died. I know that you left your father and mother. I know that you left your country. You came to live with people you didn't know before.

"May the LORD reward you for what you have done. May the God of Israel bless you richly. You have come to him to find safety under his care."

So Ruth picked up grain in the field until evening. Then she separated the barley from the straw. It amounted to more than half a bushel. She carried it back to town. Her mother-in-law saw how much she had gathered. Ruth also brought out the food that was left over from the lunch Boaz had given her. She gave it to Naomi.

So Ruth stayed close to the female servants of Boaz as she picked up grain. She worked until the time when all of the barley and wheat had been harvested. And she lived with her mother-in-law.

Ruth Goes to Boaz At the Threshing Floor

One day Ruth's mother-in-law Naomi spoke to her. She said, "My daughter, shouldn't I try to find a secure place for you? Shouldn't you have peace and rest? Shouldn't I find a home where things will go well with you? You have been with the female servants of Boaz. He's a relative of ours. Tonight he'll be separating the straw from his barley on the threshing floor.

"So wash yourself. Put on some perfume. And put on your best clothes. Then go down to the threshing floor. But don't let Boaz know you are there. Wait until he has finished eating and drinking. Notice where he lies down. Then go over and uncover his feet. Lie down there. He'll tell you what to do."

"I'll do everything you say," Ruth answered. So she went down to the threshing floor. She did everything her mother-in-law had told her to do.

When Boaz had finished eating and drinking, he was in a good mood. He went over to lie down at the far end of the grain pile. Then Ruth approached quietly. She uncovered his feet and lay down there.

In the middle of the night, something surprised Boaz and woke him up. He turned and found a woman lying there at his feet.

"Who are you?" he asked.

"I'm Ruth," she said. "You are my family protector. So take good care of me by making me your wife."

"Dear woman, may the LORD bless you," he replied. "You are showing even more kindness now than you did earlier. You didn't run after the younger men, whether they were rich or poor. Dear woman, don't be afraid. I'll do for you everything you ask. All of the people of my town know that you are a noble woman."

So Boaz got married to Ruth. She became his wife. The LORD blessed her so that she became pregnant. And she had a son.

Rich Rewards

The people in Bethlehem saw how loving Ruth was to Naomi. They praised Ruth. Even Boaz praised her. He said, "May the LORD reward you for what you have done. May the God of Israel bless you richly." Later Boaz married Ruth. Their great-grandson David would become king of Israel. Someday Jesus would be born into their family line too.

It's good to treat our friends with kindness and to show them that they are important to us. Ask if you can have a friendship party for two or three friends. Serve a good treat. Buy little presents with your own money. Make a card for each guest. Write down why you're glad they are your friends.

The women said to Naomi, "We praise the LORD. Today he has provided a family protector for you. May this child become famous all over Israel! He will make your life new again. He'll take care of you when you are old. He's the son of your very own daughter-in-law. She loves you. She is better to you than seven sons."

Then Naomi put the child on her lap and took care of him. The women who were living there said, "Naomi has a son." They named him Obed. He was the father of Jesse. Jesse was the father of David.

The Story of Samuel

1 Samuel 1—3; 7—8

Samuel Is Born

A certain man from Ramathaim in the hill country of Ephraim was named Elkanah. He was the son of Jeroham. Jeroham was the son of Elihu. Elihu was the son of Tohu. Tohu was the son of Zuph. Elkanah belonged to the family line of Zuph. Elkanah lived in the territory of Ephraim.

Elkanah had two wives. One was named Hannah. The other was named Peninnah. Peninnah had children, but Hannah didn't.

Every time the day came for Elkanah to offer a sacrifice, he would give a share of the meat to his wife Peninnah. He would also give a share to each of her sons and daughters. But he would give two shares of meat to Hannah. That's because he loved her. He also gave her two shares because the LORD had kept her from having children.

Peninnah teased Hannah to make her angry. She did it because the LORD had kept Hannah from having children. Peninnah teased Hannah year after year. Every time Hannah would go up to the house of

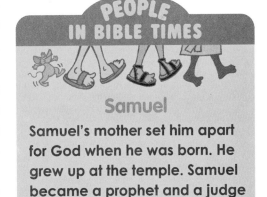

PEOPLE IN BIBLE TIMES

Samuel

Samuel's mother set him apart for God when he was born. He grew up at the temple. Samuel became a prophet and a judge in Israel. God told Samuel to anoint Saul as the first king of Israel. And later Samuel anointed David as king.

the LORD, Elkanah's other wife would tease her. She would keep doing it until Hannah cried and wouldn't eat.

Her husband Elkanah would speak to her. He would say, "Hannah, why are you crying? Why don't you eat? Why are you so angry and unhappy? Don't I mean more to you than ten sons?"

One time when they had finished eating and drinking in Shiloh, Hannah stood up. The priest Eli was sitting on a chair by the doorpost of the LORD's house. Hannah was very bitter. She sobbed and sobbed. She prayed to the LORD. She made a promise to him. She said, "LORD, you rule over all. Please see how I'm suffering! Show concern for me! Don't forget about me! Please give me a son! If you do, I'll give him back to you. Then he will serve you all the days of his life. He'll never use a razor on his head. He'll never cut his hair."

As Hannah kept on praying to the LORD, Eli watched her lips. She was praying in her heart. Her lips were moving. But she wasn't making a sound.

Eli thought Hannah was drunk. He said to her, "How long will you keep on getting drunk? Get rid of your wine."

"That's not true, sir," Hannah replied. "I'm a woman who is deeply troubled. I haven't been drinking wine or beer. I was telling the LORD all of my troubles. Don't think of me as an evil woman. I've been praying here because I'm very sad. My pain is so great."

Eli answered, "Go in peace. May the God of Israel give you what you have asked him for."

And the LORD showed concern for her. After some time, Hannah became pregnant. She had a baby boy. She said, "I asked the LORD for him." So she named him Samuel.

A Gift to and From God

Mothers often pray for their unborn children. Ask your mom if she did this for you. Ask her what she prayed. Ask if she prays for you now.

Hannah asked God to give her a child. She promised to give him back to God. Was anything in Hannah's prayer like your mother's prayers for you?

Hannah Gives Samuel to the LORD

Elkanah went up to Shiloh to offer the yearly sacrifice to the LORD. He also went there to keep a promise he had made. His whole family went with him.

But Hannah didn't go. She said to her husband, "When the boy doesn't need me to nurse him anymore, I'll take him to the LORD's house. I'll give him to the LORD there. He'll stay there for the rest of his life."

So Hannah stayed home. She nursed her son until he didn't need her milk anymore.

When the boy didn't need her to nurse him anymore, she took him with her to Shiloh. She took him there even though he was still very young. She brought him to the LORD's house. She brought along a bull that was three years old. She brought more than half a bushel of flour. She also brought a bottle of wine. The bottle was made out of animal skin.

After the bull was killed, Elkanah and Hannah brought the boy to Eli. Hannah said to Eli, "Sir, I'm the woman who stood here beside you praying to the LORD. And that's just as sure as you are alive. I prayed for this child. The LORD has given me what I asked him for. So now I'm giving him to the LORD. As long as he lives he'll be given to the LORD." And all of them worshiped the LORD there.

The boy Samuel served the LORD. He wore a sacred linen apron. Each year his mother made him a little robe. She took it to him when she went up to Shiloh with her husband. She did it when her husband went to offer the yearly sacrifice.

Eli would bless Elkanah and his wife. He would say, "May the LORD give you children by this woman. May they take the place of the boy she prayed for and gave to him." Then they would go home.

The LORD was gracious to Hannah. She became pregnant. Over a period of years she had three more sons and two daughters. During that whole time the boy Samuel grew up serving the LORD.

The LORD Calls Out to Samuel

The boy Samuel served the LORD under the direction of Eli. In those days the LORD didn't give many messages to his people. He didn't give them many visions.

One night Eli was lying down in his usual place. His eyes were becoming so weak he couldn't see very well. Samuel was lying down in the Lord's house. That's where the ark of God was kept. The lamp of God was still burning. The Lord called out to Samuel.

Samuel answered, "Here I am." He ran over to Eli. He said, "Here I am. You called out to me."

But Eli said, "I didn't call you. Go back and lie down." So he went and lay down.

Again the Lord called out, "Samuel!" Samuel got up and went to Eli. He said, "Here I am. You called out to me."

How old was Samuel when God called him in the night?

Samuel was about 12 years old when God spoke to him. You don't have to be an adult to listen to God. You can be a child and obey God too.

"My son," Eli said, "I didn't call you. Go back and lie down."

Samuel didn't know the Lord yet. That's because the Lord still hadn't given him a message.

The Lord called out to Samuel for the third time. Samuel got up and went to Eli. He said, "Here I am. You called out to me."

Then Eli realized that the Lord was calling the boy. So Eli told Samuel, "Go and lie down. If someone calls out to you again, say, 'Speak, Lord. I'm listening.'" So Samuel went and lay down in his place.

The Lord came and stood there. He called out, just as he had done the other times. He said, "Samuel! Samuel!"

Then Samuel replied, "Speak. I'm listening."

The Lord said to Samuel, "Pay attention! I am about to do something terrible in Israel. It will make the ears of everyone who hears about it ring.

"At that time I will do everything to Eli and his family that I said I would. I will finish what I have started. I told Eli I would punish his family forever. He knew his sons were sinning. He knew they were making fun of me. In spite of that, he failed to stop them.

"So I took an oath and made a promise to the family of Eli. I said, 'The sins of Eli's family will never be paid for by bringing sacrifices or offerings.'"

Samuel lay down until morning. Then he opened the doors of the

LORD's house. He was afraid to tell Eli about the vision he had received. But Eli called out to him. He said, "Samuel, my son."

Samuel answered, "Here I am."

"What did the LORD say to you?" Eli asked. "Don't hide from me anything he told you. If you do, may God punish you greatly."

So Samuel told him everything. He didn't hide anything from him.

Then Eli said, "He is the LORD. Let him do what he thinks is best."

Samuel Brings the Philistines Under Israel's Control

Samuel continued to lead Israel all the days of his life. From year to year he traveled from Bethel to Gilgal to Mizpah. He served Israel as judge in all of those places. But he always went back to Ramah. That's where his home was. He served Israel as judge there too. And he built an altar there to honor the LORD.

Israel Asks Samuel for a King

When Samuel became old, he appointed his sons to serve as judges for Israel. The name of his oldest son was Joel. The name of his second son was Abijah. They served as judges at Beersheba. But his sons didn't live as he did. They were only interested in making money. They accepted money from people who wanted special favors. They made things that were wrong appear to be right.

So all of the elders of Israel gathered together. They came to Samuel at Ramah. They said to him, "You are old. Your sons don't live as you do. So appoint a king to lead us. We want a king just like the kings all of the other nations have."

DID YOU KNOW?

How did the people of Israel defeat the Philistines?

Many people of Israel worshiped false gods. Samuel told them to serve the true God. The people obeyed. When they worshiped only God, he gave them victory and kept them safe from the Philistines.

Samuel wasn't pleased when they said, "Give us a king to lead us." So he prayed to the LORD.

The LORD told him, "Listen to everything the people are saying to you. You are not the one they have turned their backs on. I am the one they do not want as their king. They are doing just as they have always done. They have deserted me and served other gods. They have done that from the time I brought them up out of Egypt until this very day. Now they are deserting you too.

"Let them have what they want. But give them a strong warning. Let them know what the king who rules over them will do."

Samuel told the people who were asking him for a king everything the LORD had said. Samuel told them, "Here's what the king who rules over you will do. He will take your sons. He'll make them serve with his chariots and horses. They will run in front of his chariots. He'll choose some of your sons to be commanders of thousands of men. Some will be commanders of fifties. Others will have to plow his fields and gather his crops. Still others will have to make weapons of war and parts for his chariots.

"He'll also take your daughters. Some will have to make perfume. Others will be forced to cook and bake.

"He will take away your best fields and vineyards and olive groves. He'll give them to his attendants. He will take a tenth of your grain and a tenth of your grapes. He'll give it to his officials and attendants. He will also take your male and female servants. He'll take your best cattle and donkeys. He'll use all of them any way he wants to.

"He will take a tenth of your sheep and goats. You yourselves will become his slaves.

Why did the people of Israel want a king?

The people of Israel wanted to be like other nations. But Israel was not like other nations. God was the king and leader of Israel. It was not wrong to have a king. But Israel wanted a king for the wrong reason.

"When that time comes, you will cry out for help because of the king you have chosen. But the LORD won't answer you at that time."

In spite of what Samuel said, the people refused to listen to him. "No!" they said. "We want a king to rule over us. Then we'll be like all of the other nations. We'll have a king to lead us. He'll go out at the head of our armies and fight our battles."

Samuel heard everything the people said. He told the LORD about it. The LORD answered, "Listen to them. Give them a king."

The Story of King Saul

1 Samuel 9—10; 12; 13; 15

There was a man named Kish from the tribe of Benjamin. Kish was a very important person. Kish had a son named Saul. Saul was a handsome young man. There wasn't anyone like him among the people of Israel. He was a head taller than any of them.

The donkeys that belonged to Saul's father Kish were lost. So Kish spoke to his son Saul. He said, "Go and look for the donkeys. Take one of the servants with you."

Saul and his servant went through the hill country of Ephraim. They also went through the area around Shalisha. But they didn't find the donkeys. So they went on into the area of Shaalim. But the donkeys weren't there either. Then Saul went through the territory of Benjamin. But they still didn't find the donkeys.

When Saul and the servant who was with him reached the area of Zuph, Saul spoke to him. He said, "Come on. Let's go back. If we don't, my father will stop thinking about the donkeys and start worrying about us."

But the servant replied, "There's a man of God here in Ramah. People have a lot of respect for him. Everything he says comes true. So let's go and see him now. Perhaps he'll tell us which way to go."

Saul said to his servant, "That's a good idea. Come on. Let's go and ask the seer." So they started out for the town where the man of God lived.

They went up to the town. As they were entering it, they saw Samuel. He was coming toward them. He was on his way up to the high place.

The LORD had spoken to Samuel the day before Saul came. He had said, "About this time tomorrow I will send you a man. He is from the land of Benjamin. Anoint him to be the leader of my people Israel. He will save them from the powerful hand of the Philistines. I have seen how much my people are suffering. Their cry for help has reached me."

When Samuel saw a man coming toward him, the LORD spoke to Samuel again. He said, "He is the man I told you about. His name is Saul. He will govern my people."

Who was Israel's first king?

Saul was Israel's first king. People looked up to Saul because he was handsome and tall. At first Saul was a good king. He trusted God. He showed good judgment. But later Saul forgot God and disobeyed him.

Saul approached Samuel at the gate of the town. He asked Samuel, "Can you please show me the house where the seer is staying?"

"I'm the seer," Samuel replied. "Go on up to the high place ahead of me. I want you and your servant to eat with me today. Tomorrow morning I'll tell you what's on your mind. Then I'll let you go. Don't worry about the donkeys you lost three days ago. They've already been found. But who are all of the people of Israel longing for? You and your father's whole family!"

Then Samuel took a bottle of olive oil. He poured it on Saul's head and kissed him. He said, "The LORD has anointed you to be the leader of his people. When you leave me today, you will meet two men. They will be near Rachel's tomb at Zelzah on the border of Benjamin. They'll say to you, 'The donkeys you have been looking for have been found. Now your father has stopped thinking about them. Instead, he's worried about you. He's asking, "What can I do to find my son?"'

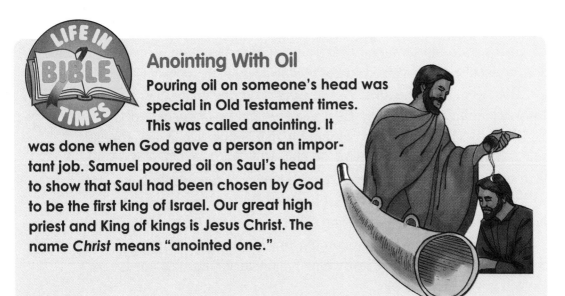

Anointing With Oil

Pouring oil on someone's head was special in Old Testament times. This was called anointing. It was done when God gave a person an important job. Samuel poured oil on Saul's head to show that Saul had been chosen by God to be the first king of Israel. Our great high priest and King of kings is Jesus Christ. The name *Christ* means "anointed one."

As Saul turned to leave Samuel, God changed Saul's heart. When Saul and his servant arrived at Gibeah, a group of prophets met Saul. then the Spirit of God came on him with power. He prophesied along with them. Those who had known Saul before asked one another, "What has happened to the son of Kish? Is Saul also one of the prophets?"

A man who lived in Gibeah answered, "Yes, he is. In fact, he's their leader." That's why people say, "Is Saul also one of the prophets?"

After Saul stopped prophesying, he went to the high place to worship.

Later, Saul's uncle spoke to him and his servant. He asked, "Where have you been?"

"Looking for the donkeys," he said. "But we couldn't find them. So we went to Samuel."

Saul's uncle said, "Tell me what Samuel said to you."

Saul replied, "He told us the donkeys had been found." But Saul didn't tell his uncle that Samuel had said he would become king.

Samuel sent a message to the people of Israel. He told them to meet with the LORD at Mizpah. He said to them, "The LORD is the God of Israel. He says, 'Israel, I brought you up out of Egypt. I saved you from their powerful hand. I also saved you from the powerful hand of all of the kingdoms that had beaten you down.'

Acting Foolishly

Eric's dad was supposed to come home to take him fishing. But Eric got tired of waiting. He took his fishing pole, dug a few worms and rode his bike to the river. He fished all by himself.

Later Eric's dad found him. He said, "Eric, why didn't you wait? Mr. Carson was planning to take us out in his boat. It was a special surprise for you. But Mr. Carson has already left. Now it's too late. You should have waited."

Saul didn't wait either. He didn't obey God. So God chose a new leader for the people of Israel.

Eric and Saul did not wait. They both disobeyed. They lost something special because they couldn't wait.

DID YOU KNOW?

Why couldn't a king help the people of Israel?

The best things the people could do were to worship and obey God. God took care of them when they obeyed him. A king would not be a better leader than God.

"But now you have turned your backs on your God. He saves you out of all of your trouble and suffering. In spite of that, you have said, 'We refuse to listen. Place a king over us.'

"So now gather together to meet with the LORD. Do it tribe by tribe and family group by family group."

Then Samuel had each tribe of Israel come forward. The tribe of Benjamin was chosen. Next he had the tribe of Benjamin come forward, family group by family group. Matri's group was chosen. Finally Saul, the son of Kish, was chosen. But when people looked for him, they realized he wasn't there. They needed more help from the LORD. So they asked him, "Has the man come here yet?"

The LORD said, "Yes. He has hidden himself among the supplies."

So they ran over there and brought him out. When he stood up, the people saw that he was a head taller than any of them.

Samuel spoke to all of the people. He said, "Look at the man the LORD has chosen! There isn't anyone like him among all of the people."

Then the people shouted, "May the king live a long time!"

Samuel Tells Israel to Serve the LORD

Samuel spoke to all of the people of Israel. He said, "I've done everything you asked me to do. I've placed a king over you. Now you have a king as your leader. But I'm old. My hair is gray. My sons are here with you. I've been your leader from the time I was young until this very day.

"You must have respect for the LORD. You must serve him and obey him. You must not say no to his commands. Both you and the king who rules over you must follow the LORD your God. If you do, that's good. But you must not disobey him. You must not say no to his commands. If you do, his powerful hand will punish you. That's what happened to your people who lived before you.

"So stand still. Watch the great thing the LORD is about to do right here in front of you! It's time to gather in the wheat, isn't it? I'll call out to the Lord to send thunder and rain. Then you will realize what an evil thing you did in the sight of the Lord. You shouldn't have asked for a king."

Samuel called out to the Lord. That same day the Lord sent thunder and rain. So all of the people had great respect for the Lord and for Samuel.

Saul was 30 years old when he became king. He ruled over Israel for 42 years.

The Lord Is Sorry He Has Made Saul King

Then the Lord gave Samuel a message. He said, "I am very sorry I have made Saul king. He has turned away from me. He has not done what I directed him to do."

When Samuel heard that, he was troubled. He cried out to the Lord during that whole night.

The Story of King David

1 Samuel 16—18; 20; 2 Samuel 2—5; 9; 11; 26; 1 Chronicles 22

Samuel Anoints David to Be Israel's King

The Lord said to Samuel, "How long will you be filled with sorrow because of Saul? I have refused to have him as king over Israel. Fill your animal horn with olive oil. I am sending you to Jesse in Bethlehem. I have chosen one of his sons to be king."

Jesse sent for his [youngest] son. His skin was tanned. He had a fine appearance and handsome features.

Then the Lord said, "Get up and anoint him. He is the one."

From that day on, the Spirit of the Lord came on David with power.

David Kills Goliath

The Philistine army was camped on one hill. Israel's army was on another. The valley was between them.

A mighty hero named Goliath came out of the Philistine camp. He was from Gath. He was more than nine feet tall. He had a bronze helmet on his head. He wore a coat of bronze armor. It weighed 125 pounds. On his legs he wore bronze guards. He carried a bronze javelin on his back. His spear was as big as a weaver's rod. Its iron point weighed 15 pounds. The man who carried his shield walked along in front of him.

Goliath stood and shouted to the soldiers of Israel. He said, "Why do you come out and line up for battle? I'm a Philistine. You are servants of Saul. Choose one of your men. Have him come down and face me. If he's able to fight and kill me, we'll become your slaves. But if I win and kill him, you will become our slaves and serve us." Goliath continued, "This very day I dare the soldiers of Israel to send a man down to fight against me."

Every morning and evening Goliath came forward and stood there. He did it for 40 days.

David said to Saul, "Don't let anyone lose hope because of that Philistine. I'll go out and fight him.

The Saul dressed David in his own military clothes. He put a coat of armor on him. He put a bronze helmet on his head. David put on Saul's sword over his clothes. He walked around for awhile in all of that armor because he wasn't used to it.

"I can't go out there in all of this armor," he said to Saul. I'm not used to it." So he took it off.

Then David picked up his wooden staff. He went down to a stream and chose five smooth stones. He put them in the pocket of his shepherd's bag. Then he took his sling in his hand and approached Goliath.

At that same time, the Philistine kept coming closer to David. The man who was carrying Goliath's shield walked along in front of him.

Goliath looked David over. He saw how young he was. He also saw

The Bible Story Everybody Knows

Do you know the story of David and Goliath? Do you think everyone else knows the story too? Just for fun, ask five of your friends if they know the story. Read it in the Bible first. Try to remember every part.

What is important about this story? It tells us that Goliath was a giant. He was Israel's enemy. But David was not afraid of him. David trusted God. He knew that God could help him.

how tanned and handsome he was. And he hated him. He said to David, "Why are you coming at me with sticks? Do you think I'm only a dog?" The Philistine called down curses on David in the name of his god. "Come over here," he said. "I'll feed your body to the birds of the air! I'll feed it to the wild animals!"

David said to Goliath, "You are coming to fight against me with a sword, a spear and a javelin. But I'm coming against you in the name of the LORD who rules over all. He is the God of the armies of Israel. He's the one you have dared to fight against.

"This very day the LORD will hand you over to me. I'll strike you down. I'll cut your head off. This very day I'll feed the bodies of the Philistine army to the birds of the air. I'll feed them to the wild animals. Then the whole world will know there is a God in Israel."

As the Philistine moved closer to attack him, David ran quickly to the battle line to meet him. He reached into his bag. He took out a stone. He put it in his sling. He slung it at Goliath. The stone hit him on the forehead and sank into it. He fell to the ground on his face.

So David won the fight against Goliath with a sling and a stone. He struck the Philistine down and killed him. He did it without even using a sword.

David ran and stood over him. He took hold of Goliath's sword and pulled it out. After he killed him, he cut off his head with the sword.

The Philistines saw that their hero was dead. So they turned around and ran away.

Saul Becomes Jealous of David

From that time on, Saul kept David with him. He didn't let him return to his father's home.

Jonathan made a covenant with David because [they became close friends. Jonathan] loved him just as he loved himself. Jonathan took off the robe he was wearing and gave it to David. He also gave him his military clothes. He even gave him his sword, his bow and his belt.

David did everything Saul sent him to do. He did it so well that Saul gave him a high rank in the army. That pleased Saul's whole army, including his officers.

After David had killed Goliath, the men of Israel returned home. The

David was a good leader of the army. He won all his battles. He was a hero. The people praised David more than they praised Saul. That made Saul angry. Saul was afraid of David too. Saul had disobeyed God. Saul knew that God didn't want him to be king anymore. He also knew that David obeyed God. Saul knew that David always won because God was with him.

women came out of all of the towns of Israel to meet King Saul. They danced and sang joyful songs. They played lutes and tambourines. As they danced, they sang,

"Saul has killed thousands of men.
    David has killed tens of
    thousands."

That song made Saul very angry. It really upset him. He said to himself, "They are saying David has killed tens of thousands of men. But they are saying I've killed only thousands. The only thing left for him to get is the kingdom itself." From that time on, Saul became very jealous of David. He remained David's enemy as long as he was king.

Jonathan Helps David Get Away

David was in Naioth at Ramah. He ran away from there to where Jonathan was. He asked him, "What have I done? What crime have I committed? I haven't done anything to harm your father. So why is he trying to kill me?"

"Come on," Jonathan said. "Let's go out to the field." So they went there together.

Then Jonathan spoke to David. He said, "I promise you that I'll find out what my father is planning to do. I'll find out by this time the day after tomorrow. The LORD, the God of Israel, is my witness. Suppose my father feels kind toward you. Then I'll send you a message and let you know. But suppose he wants to harm you. And I don't let you know about it. I don't help you get away safely. Then may the LORD punish me greatly. May he be with you, just as he has been with my father.

"I'll shoot three arrows to one side of the stone. I'll pretend I'm practicing my shooting. Then I'll send a boy out there. I'll tell him, 'Go and find the arrows.' Suppose I say to him, 'The arrows are on this side of you. Bring them here.' Then come. That will mean you are safe. You won't be in any danger. And that's just as sure as the LORD is alive. But suppose I tell the boy, 'The arrows are far beyond you.' Then go. That will mean the LORD is sending you away."

So David hid in the field. When the time for the New Moon Feast came, the king sat down to eat. He sat in his usual place by the wall. Jonathan sat across from him. Abner sat next to Saul. But David's place was empty.

The next day, David's place was empty again. It was the second day of the month.

Finally, Saul spoke to his son Jonathan. He said, "Why hasn't the son of Jesse come to the meal? He hasn't been here yesterday or today."

Jonathan replied, "David begged me to let him go to Bethlehem. He said, 'Let me go. Our family is offering a sacrifice in the town. My brother has ordered me to be there. Are you pleased with me? If you are, let me go and see my brothers.' That's why he hasn't come to eat at your table."

Saul burned with anger against Jonathan. He said to him, "You are an evil son. You have refused to obey me. I know that you are on the side of Jesse's son. You should be ashamed of that. And your mother should be ashamed of having a son like you. You will never be king as long as Jesse's son lives on this earth. And you will never have a kingdom either. So send for the son of Jesse. Bring him to me. He must die!"

So Jonathan got up from the table. He was burning with anger. On that second day of the month, he refused to eat. He was very sad that his father was treating David so badly.

The next morning Jonathan went out to the field to meet David. He took a young boy with him. He said to the boy, "Run and find the arrows I shoot." As the boy ran, Jonathan shot an arrow far beyond him. The boy came to the place where Jonathan's arrow had fallen.

Showing Friendship

David and Jonathan were special friends. Jonathan helped David a lot. He listened to David's problems. He loved David.

Make a picture for your room. Draw three ways you can help your friends. Write this Bible verse on your poster: "A friend loves at all times" (Proverbs 17:17). Remember to be a good friend like Jonathan was.

Then Jonathan shouted to him, "The arrow went far beyond you, didn't it?" He continued, "Hurry up! Run fast! Don't stop!"

The boy picked up the arrow and returned to his master. The boy didn't know what was going on. Only Jonathan and David knew. Jonathan gave his weapons to the boy. He told him, "Go back to town. Take the weapons with you."

After the boy had gone, David got up from the south side of the stone. He bowed down in front of Jonathan with his face to the ground. He did it three times. Then they kissed each other and cried. But David cried more than Jonathan did.

Jonathan said to David, "Go in peace. In the name of the LORD we have taken an oath. We've promised to be friends. We've said, 'The LORD is a witness between you and me. He's a witness between your children and my children forever.'"

Then David left, and Jonathan went back to the town.

That day David ran away from Saul.

David Spares Saul's Life

David stayed in the desert. He saw that Saul had followed him there. [David] went to the place where Saul had camped. [The soldier] Abishai went with him. They found Saul lying asleep inside the camp. His spear was stuck in the ground near his head. David said, "Don't destroy him! No one can lay a hand on the LORD's anointed king. The LORD himself will strike Saul down."

Saul Takes His Own Life

The Philistines fought against Israel. The Philistines kept chasing Saul and his sons. They killed his sons. The fighting was heavy around Saul. Men caught up with him. They shot their arrows at him and wounded him badly.

Saul spoke to the man who was carrying his armor. He said, "Pull out your sword. Stick it through me. If you don't, they'll stick their swords through me and hurt me badly."

But the man wouldn't do it. So Saul took his own sword and fell on it.

David Is Anointed to Be King Over Judah

Then the men of Judah came to Hebron. There they anointed David to be king over the people of Judah.

David was told that the men of Jabesh Gilead had buried Saul's body. So he sent messengers to them to speak for him.

The messengers said, "You were kind to bury the body of your master Saul. May the LORD bless you for that. And may he now be kind and faithful to you. David will treat you well for being kind to Saul's body. Now then, be strong and brave. Your master Saul is dead. And the people of Judah have anointed David to be king over them."

The Armies of David and Saul Fight Each Other

Abner, the son of Ner, was commander of Saul's army. He had brought Saul's son Ish-Bosheth to Mahanaim. There he made him king over Gilead, Ashuri and Jezreel. He also made him king over Ephraim, Benjamin and other areas of Israel.

Ish-Bosheth was 40 years old when he became king over Israel. He ruled for two years. But the people of Judah followed David. David was king in Hebron over the people of Judah for seven and a half years.

Abner, the son of Ner, left Mahanaim and went to Gibeon. The men of Ish-Bosheth, the son of Saul, went with him. Joab, the son of Zeruiah, and David's men also went out. All of them met at the pool in Gibeon. One group sat down on one side of the pool. The other group sat on the other side.

Then Abner said to Joab, "Let's have some of the young men get up and fight. Let's tell them to fight hand to hand in front of us."

"All right. Let them do it," Joab said.

So the young men stood up and were counted off. There were 12 on the side of Benjamin and Saul's son Ish-Bosheth. And there were 12 on David's side. Each man grabbed one of his enemies by the head. Each one stuck his dagger into the other man's side. And all of them fell down together and died. So that place in Gibeon was named Helkath Hazzurim.

The fighting that day was very heavy. Abner and the men of Israel lost the battle to David's men.

The three sons of Zeruiah were there. Their names were Joab, Abishai and Asahel. Asahel was as quick on his feet as a wild antelope. He chased Abner. He didn't turn to the right or the left as he chased him. Abner looked behind him. He asked, "Asahel, is that you?"

"It is," he answered.

Then Abner said to him, "Turn to the right or the left. Fight one of the young men. Take his weapons away from him." But Asahel wouldn't stop chasing him.

Again Abner warned Asahel, "Stop chasing me! If you don't, I'll strike you down. Then how could I look your brother Joab in the face?"

But Asahel refused to give up the chase. So Abner drove the dull end of his spear into Asahel's stomach. The spear came out of his back. He fell and died right there on the spot. Every man stopped when he came to the place where Asahel had fallen and died.

But Joab and Abishai chased Abner. As the sun was going down, they came to the hill of Ammah. It was near Giah on the way to the dry and empty land close to Gibeon. The men of Benjamin gathered in a group around Abner. They took their stand on top of a hill.

Abner called out to Joab, "Do you want our swords to keep on killing us off? Don't you know that all of this fighting will end in bitter feelings? How long will it be before you order your men to stop chasing their fellow Israelites?"

Joab answered, "It's a good thing you spoke up. If you hadn't, the men would have kept on chasing their fellow Israelites until morning. And that's just as sure as God is alive."

So Joab blew a trumpet. All of the men stopped. They didn't chase Israel anymore. They didn't fight anymore either.

All that night Abner and his men marched through the Arabah Valley. They went across the Jordan River. They kept on going through the whole Bithron. Finally, they came to Mahanaim.

Then Joab returned from chasing Abner. He gathered all of his men together. Besides Asahel, only 19 of David's men were missing. But David's men had killed 360 men from Benjamin who were with Abner. They got Asahel's body and buried it in his father's tomb at Bethlehem. Then Joab and his men marched all night. They arrived at Hebron at sunrise.

The war between Saul's royal house and David's royal house lasted a long time. David grew stronger and stronger. But the royal house of Saul grew weaker and weaker.

Jonathan, the son of Saul, had a son named Mephibosheth. Both of Mephibosheth's feet were hurt. He was five years old when the news that Saul and Jonathan had died came from Jezreel. His nurse picked him up and ran. But as she hurried to get away, he fell down. That's how his feet were hurt.

David Becomes King Over Israel

[Saul's son Ish-Bosheth was killed while he slept.] All of the tribes of Israel came to see David at Hebron. They said, "We are your own flesh and blood. In the past, Saul was our king. But you led the men of Israel on their military campaigns. And the LORD said to you, 'You will be the shepherd over my people Israel. You will become their ruler.'"

All of the elders of Israel came to see King David at Hebron. There the king made a covenant with them in the sight of the LORD. They anointed David as king over Israel.

David was 30 years old when he became king. He ruled for 40 years. In Hebron he ruled over Judah for seven and a half years. In Jerusalem he ruled over all of Israel and Judah for 33 years.

David Captures Jerusalem

The king and his men marched to Jerusalem. They went to attack the Jebusites who lived there.

The Jebusites said to David, "You won't get in here. Even blind people and those who are disabled can keep you from coming in." They thought, "David can't get in here."

But David captured the fort of Zion. It became known as the City of David.

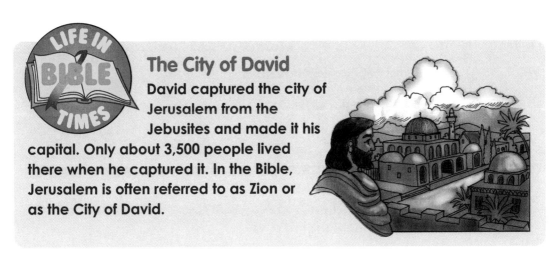

The City of David

David captured the city of Jerusalem from the Jebusites and made it his capital. Only about 3,500 people lived there when he captured it. In the Bible, Jerusalem is often referred to as Zion or as the City of David.

David asked, "Is anyone left from the royal house of Saul? If there is, I want to be kind to him because of Jonathan."

Ziba was a servant in Saul's family. David sent for him to come and see him. The king said to him, "Are you Ziba?"

"I'm ready to serve you," he replied.

The king asked, "Isn't anyone left from the royal house of Saul? God has been very kind to me. I would like to be kind to someone in the same way."

Ziba answered the king, "A son of Jonathan is still living. Both of his feet were hurt."

"Where is he?" the king asked.

Ziba answered, "He's in the town of Lo Debar. He's staying at the house of Makir, the son of Ammiel."

So King David had Mephibosheth brought from Makir's house in Lo Debar.

Mephibosheth came to David. He was the son of Jonathan, the son of Saul. Mephibosheth bowed down to David to show him respect.

David said, "Mephibosheth!"

"I'm ready to serve you," he replied.

"Don't be afraid," David told him. "You can be sure that I will be kind to you because of your father Jonathan. I'll give back to you all of the land that belonged to your grandfather Saul. And I'll always provide what you need."

Showing Kindness

This story is about Mephibosheth (Meh-FIB-o-sheth). He was the only son of Jonathan who was still alive. He was crippled in both feet. David was kind to him. David treated him like his own son. That is because he was the son of David's best friend Jonathan.

Do you know any children who are crippled or who look different from most children? They need special kindness from you. You can talk to them and find ways to play with them. Or send a card. Let them know you are praying for them.

Mephibosheth bowed down to David. He said, "Who am I? Why should you pay attention to me? I'm nothing but a dead dog."

Then the king sent for Saul's servant Ziba. He said to him, "I'm giving your master's grandson everything that belonged to Saul and his family. You and your sons and your servants must farm the land for him. You must bring in the crops. Then he'll be taken care of. I'll always provide what he needs." Ziba had 15 sons and 20 servants.

Then Ziba said to the king, "I'll do anything you command me to do. You are my king and master." So David provided what Mephibosheth needed. He treated him like one of the king's sons.

Mephibosheth had a young son named Mica. All of the members of Ziba's family became servants of Mephibosheth. Mephibosheth lived in Jerusalem. The king always provided what he needed. Both of his feet were hurt.

David and Bathsheba

It was spring. It was the time when kings go off to war. So David sent Joab out with the king's special troops and the whole army of Israel. They destroyed the Ammonites. They went to the city of Rabbah. They surrounded it and got ready to attack it. But David remained in Jerusalem.

One evening David got up from his bed. He walked around on the roof of his palace. From the roof he saw a woman taking a bath. She was very beautiful.

David sent a messenger to find out who she was. The messenger returned and said, "She is Bathsheba. She's the daughter of Eliam. She's the wife of Uriah. He's a Hittite."

Then David sent messengers to get her. She came to him. Later, Bathsheba found out she was pregnant. She sent a message to David. It said, "I'm pregnant."

So David sent a message to Joab. It said, "Send me Uriah, the Hittite." Joab sent him to David.

Uriah came to David. David asked him how Joab and the soldiers were doing. He also asked him how the war was going.

David said to Uriah, "Go home and enjoy some time with your wife." So Uriah left the palace. Then the king sent him a gift.

But Uriah didn't go home. Instead, he slept at the entrance to the palace. He stayed there with all of his master's servants.

Did David ever sin?

Yes. David did a terrible thing. He took another man's wife. He had the man killed. But David said he was sorry for his sin. And God forgave him.

David was told, "Uriah didn't go home." So he sent for Uriah. He said to him, "You have been away for a long time. Why didn't you go home?"

Uriah said to David, "The ark and the army of Israel and Judah are out there in tents. My master Joab and your special troops are camped in the open fields. How could I go to my house to eat and drink? I could never do a thing like that. And that's just as sure as you are alive!"

The next morning David wrote a letter to Joab. He sent it along with Uriah. In it he wrote, "Put Uriah on the front lines. That's where the fighting is the heaviest. Then pull your men back from him. When you do, the Ammonites will strike him down and kill him."

So Joab attacked the city. He put Uriah at a place where he knew the strongest enemy fighters were. The troops came out of the city. They fought against Joab. Some of the men in David's army were killed. Uriah, the Hittite, also died.

Uriah's wife heard that her husband was dead. She sobbed over him. When her time of sadness was over, David had her brought to his house. She became his wife. And she had a son by him. But the LORD wasn't pleased with what David had done.

David Makes Plans for Building the Temple

David gave orders to bring together the outsiders who were living in Israel. He appointed some of them to cut stones. He wanted them to prepare blocks of stone for building the house of God.

David provided a large amount of iron to make nails. They were for the doors of the gates and for the fittings. He provided more bronze than anyone could weigh. He also provided more cedar logs than anyone could count. The people of Sidon and Tyre brought large numbers of logs to David.

David said, "My son Solomon is young. He's never done anything like this before. The house that will be built for the LORD should be very grand and wonderful. It should be famous and beautiful in the eyes of all of the nations. I'll get things ready for it." So David got many things ready before he died.

Then he sent for his son Solomon. He told him to build a house for the LORD, the God of Israel.

David said to Solomon, "My son, with all my heart I wanted to build a house for the LORD my God. That's where his Name will be. But a message from the LORD came to me. It said, 'You have spilled the blood of many people. You have fought many wars. You are not the one who will build a house for my Name. That is because I have seen you spill the blood of many people on the earth.

"'But you are going to have a son. He will be a man of peace. And I will give him peace and rest from all of his enemies on every side. His name will be Solomon. I will give Israel peace and quiet while he is king. He will build a house for my Name. He will be my son. And I will be his father. I will make his kingdom secure over Israel. It will last forever.'

"My son, may the LORD be with you. May you have success. May you build the house of the LORD your God, just as he said you would. May the LORD give you good sense. May he give you understanding when he makes you king over Israel. Then you will keep the law of the LORD your God.

"Be careful to obey the rules and laws the LORD gave Moses for Israel. Then you will have success. Be strong and brave. Don't be afraid. Don't lose hope.

"I've tried very hard to provide for the LORD's temple. I've provided 3,750 tons of gold and 37,500 tons of silver. I've provided more bronze and iron than anyone can weigh. I've also given plenty of wood and stone. You can add to it.

"You have a lot of workers. You have people who can cut stones and people who can lay the stones. You have people who can work with wood. You also have people who are skilled in every other kind of work. Some of them can work with gold and silver. Others can work with bronze and iron. There are more workers than anyone can count. So begin the work. May the LORD be with you."

Then David ordered all of Israel's leaders to help his son Solomon. He said to them, "The LORD your God is with you. He's given you peace and rest on every side. He's handed the people who are living in the land over to me. The land has been brought under the control of the LORD and his people.

"So look to the LORD your God with all your heart and soul. Start building the temple of the LORD God. Then bring the ark of the covenant of the LORD into it. Also bring in the sacred articles that belong to God. The temple will be built for the Name of the LORD."

Look to the Lord your God with all your heart and soul.
1 Chronicles 22:19

King Solomon
1 Kings 2—4; 6—8

David Gives Orders to Solomon

Do everything the LORD your God requires. Live the way he wants you to. Obey his orders and commands. Keep his laws and rules.
1 Kings 2:3

The time came near for David to die. So he gave orders to his son Solomon. He said,

"I'm about to die, just as everyone else on earth does. So be strong. Show how brave you are. Do everything the LORD your God requires. Live the way he wants you to. Obey his orders and commands. Keep his laws and rules. Do everything that is written in the Law of Moses. Then you will have success in everything you do. You will succeed everywhere you go.

"The LORD will keep the promise he made to me. He said, 'Your sons must be careful about how they live. They must be

faithful to me with all their heart and soul. Then you will always have a man sitting on the throne of Israel.'"

David joined the members of his family who had already died. His body was buried in the City of David. He had ruled over Israel for 40 years. He ruled for seven years in Hebron. Then he ruled for 33 years in Jerusalem.

So Solomon sat on the throne of his father David. His position as king was made secure.

Solomon Asks God for Wisdom

Solomon and Pharaoh, the king of Egypt, agreed to help each other. So Solomon got married to Pharaoh's daughter. He brought her to the City of David. She stayed there until he finished building his palace, the LORD's temple, and the wall that was around Jerusalem.

But the people continued to offer sacrifices at the high places where they worshiped. That's because a temple hadn't been built yet where the LORD would put his Name.

Solomon showed his love for the LORD. He did it by obeying the laws his father David had taught him. But Solomon offered sacrifices at the high places. He also burned incense there.

The LORD appeared to Solomon at Gibeon. He spoke to him in a dream during the night. God said, "Ask for anything you want me to give you."

Solomon answered, "You have been very kind to my father David, your servant. That's because he was faithful to you. He did what was right. His heart was honest. And you have continued to be very kind to him. You have given him a son to sit on his throne this very day.

"LORD my God, you have now made me king. You have put me in the place of my father David. But I'm only a little child. I don't know how to carry out my duties. I'm here among the people you have chosen. They are a great nation. They are more than anyone can count. So give me a heart that understands. Then I can rule over your people. I can tell the difference between what is right and what is wrong. Who can possibly rule over this great nation of yours?"

The Lord was pleased that Solomon had asked for that. So God said to him, "You have not asked to live for a long time. You have not asked to be wealthy. You have not even asked to have your enemies killed. Instead, you have asked for understanding. You want to do what is right and fair when you judge people. Because that is what you have asked for, I will give it to you. I will give you a wise and understanding heart. So here is what will be true of you. There has never been anyone like you. And there never will be.

"And that is not all. I will give you what you have not asked for. I will give you riches and honor. As long as you live, no other king will be as great as you are. Live the way I want you to. Obey my laws and commands, just as your father David did. Then I will let you live for a long time."

Four Prayers God Will Answer

God hears all of your prayers. But he doesn't always answer the way we think he will. Sometimes God says yes, but sometimes he says no, or wait. Here are four prayers that God will always say yes to. Find the words below that best complete each prayer.

1. God, at church help me to _____.
2. God, help me to _____ my parents.
3. God, help me to _____ to my brothers and sisters.
4. God, help me to _____ when I play with my friends.

a) obey; b) be kind; c) listen; d) take turns.

Write each prayer on a small piece of paper. Each day choose one thing to pray about.

Solomon ruled over all of the kingdoms that were west of the Euphrates River. He ruled from Tiphsah all the way to Gaza. And he had peace and rest on every side.

While Solomon was king, Judah and Israel lived in safety. They were secure from Dan all the way to Beersheba. Each man had his own vine and fig tree.

Solomon had 4,000 spaces where he kept his chariot horses. He had a total of 12,000 horses.

God Makes Solomon Very Wise

God made Solomon very wise. His understanding couldn't even be measured. It was like the sand on the seashore. People can't measure that either.

Solomon's wisdom was greater than the wisdom of all of the people of the east. It was greater than all of the wisdom of Egypt. Solomon was wiser than any other man. He was wiser than Ethan, the Ezrahite. He was wiser than Heman, Calcol and Darda. They were the sons of Mahol. Solomon became famous in all of the nations that were around him.

He spoke 3,000 proverbs. He wrote 1,005 songs. He explained all about plants. He knew everything about them, from the cedar trees in Lebanon to the hyssop plants that grow out of walls. He taught about animals and birds. He also taught about reptiles and fish.

The kings of all of the world's nations heard about how wise Solomon was. So they sent their people to listen to him.

How wise was Solomon?

Solomon was very wise. He wrote many sayings in the book of Proverbs (page 228). He studied plants and animals. He built great buildings. He kept Israel at peace all 40 years of his rule. Solomon wrote the book of Ecclesiastes (ee-KLEE-zee-as-tees; see page 237). That book tells us that knowing God and pleasing God are more important than being wise.

Solomon Builds the Temple

Solomon began to build the temple of the LORD. It was 480 years after the people of Israel had come out of Egypt. It was in the fourth year of Solomon's rule over Israel. He started in the second month.

The temple King Solomon built for the LORD was 90 feet long. It was 30 feet wide. And it was 45 feet high. The temple had a porch in front of the main hall. The porch was as wide as the temple itself. It was 30 feet wide. It came out 15 feet from the front of the temple. Solomon made narrow windows high up in the temple walls.

He built side rooms around the temple. They were built against the walls of the main hall and the Most Holy Room. On the first floor the side rooms were seven and a half feet wide. On the second floor they were nine feet wide. And on the third floor they were ten and a half feet wide. Solomon made the walls of the temple thinner as they went up floor by floor. The result was ledges along the walls. So the floor beams of the side rooms rested on the ledges. The beams didn't go into the temple walls.

All of the stones that were used for building the temple were shaped where they were cut. So hammers, chisels and other iron tools couldn't be heard where the temple was being built.

The entrance to the first floor was on the south side of the temple. A stairway led up to the second floor. From there it went on up to the third floor.

So Solomon built the temple and finished it. He made its roof out of beams and cedar boards. He built side rooms all along the temple. Each room was seven and a half feet high. They were joined to the temple by cedar beams.

A message came to Solomon from the LORD. The LORD said, "You are now building this temple. Follow my orders. Keep my rules. Obey all of my commands. Then I will make the promise I gave your father David come true. I will do it through you. I will live among my people Israel. I will not desert them."

So Solomon built the temple and finished it. He put cedar boards on its inside walls. He covered them from floor to ceiling. He covered the temple floor with pine boards. He put up a wall 30 feet from the back of the temple. He made it with cedar boards from floor to ceiling. That formed a room inside the temple. It was the Most Holy Room. The main hall in front of the room was 60 feet long. The inside of the temple was covered with cedar wood. Gourds and open flowers were carved on the wood. Everything was cedar. There wasn't any stone showing anywhere.

Solomon prepared the Most Holy Room inside the temple. That's where the ark of the covenant of the LORD would be placed. The Most Holy Room was 30 feet long. It was 30 feet wide. And it was 30 feet high. Solomon covered the inside of it with pure gold. He prepared the cedar altar for burning incense. He covered it with gold. Solomon covered the inside of the main hall with pure gold. He placed gold chains across the front of the Most Holy Room. That room was covered with gold. So Solomon covered the inside of the whole temple with gold. He also covered the altar for burning incense with gold. It was right in front of the Most Holy Room.

For the Most Holy Room Solomon made a pair of cherubim. He made them out of olive wood. Each cherub was 15 feet high. One wing of the first cherub was seven and a half feet long. The other wing was also seven and a half feet long. So the wings measured 15 feet from tip to tip. The second cherub's wings also measured 15 feet from tip to tip. The two cherubim had the same size and shape. Each cherub was 15 feet high.

Solomon placed the cherubim inside the Most Holy Room in the temple. Their wings were spread out. The wing tip of one cherub touched one wall. The wing tip of the other touched the other wall. The tips of their wings touched each other in the middle of the room. Solomon covered the cherubim with gold.

On the walls that were all around the temple he carved cherubim, palm trees and open flowers. He carved them on the walls of the Most Holy Room and the main hall. He also covered the floors of those two rooms with gold.

For the entrance to the Most Holy Room he made two doors out of olive wood. Each doorpost had five sides. On the two olive wood doors he carved cherubim, palm trees and open flowers. He covered the cherubim and palm trees with hammered gold.

In the same way he made olive wood doorposts for the entrance to the main hall. Each doorpost had four sides. He also made two pine doors. Each door had two parts. They turned in bases that were shaped like cups. He carved cherubim, palm trees and open flowers on the doors. He covered the doors with gold. He hammered the gold evenly over the carvings.

He used blocks of stone to build a wall around the inside courtyard. The first three layers of the wall were made out of stone. The top layer was made out of beautiful cedar wood.

Everything was finished just as the plans required. Solomon had spent seven years building the temple.

King Solomon finished all of the work for the LORD's temple. Then he brought in the things his father David had set apart for the LORD. They included the silver and gold and all of the articles for the LORD's temple. Solomon placed them with the other treasures that were there.

Solomon Brings the Ark to the Temple

Then King Solomon sent for the elders of Israel. He told them to come to him in Jerusalem. They included all of the leaders of the tribes. They also included the chiefs of the families of Israel. Solomon wanted them to bring up the ark of the LORD's covenant from Zion. Zion was the City of David. All of the men of Israel came together to where King

Solomon's Temple

Solomon built the temple in Jerusalem. It was very beautiful. He used stone, carved wood and a lot of gold. Because the temple was the house of God, all loud hammering and chiseling had to be done away from the place where the temple would stand. No noisy iron tools were used near the temple. God promised to live among the Israelites if Solomon would obey and build the temple as God told him to.

Solomon was. It was at the time of the Feast of Booths. The feast was held in the month of Ethanim. That's the seventh month.

All of the elders of Israel arrived. Then the priests picked up the ark and carried it. They brought up the ark of the LORD. They also brought up the Tent of Meeting and all of the sacred articles that were in the tent. The priests and Levites carried everything up.

The entire community of Israel had gathered around King Solomon. All of them were in front of the ark. They sacrificed huge numbers of sheep and cattle. There were so many that they couldn't be recorded. In fact, they couldn't even be counted.

The priests brought the ark of the LORD's covenant to its place in the Most Holy Room of the temple. They put it under the wings of the cherubim. The cherubim's wings were spread out over the place where the ark was. They covered the ark. They also covered the poles that were used to carry it. The poles were so long that their ends could be seen from the Holy Room in front of the Most Holy Room. But they couldn't be seen from outside the Holy Room. They are still there to this very day.

There wasn't anything in the ark except the two stone tablets. Moses had placed them in it at Mount Horeb. That's where the LORD had made a covenant with the Israelites. He made it after they came out of Egypt.

The priests left the Holy Room. Then the cloud filled the temple of the LORD. The priests couldn't do their work because of it. That's because the glory of the LORD filled his temple.

Remembering Answered Prayers

King Solomon prayed when he dedicated the great temple in Jerusalem to God. What kinds of things do you pray for? Can you remember how God has answered your prayers?

Get a small notebook. Ask your mom or dad to start writing down the things you pray about. Leave space for writing down the way that God answers your prayers. Look at your notebook together once in a while. It will help you see that God cares about you. He hears your prayers. Remember to praise God for his answers.

Then Solomon said, "LORD, you have said you would live in a dark cloud. As you can see, I've built a beautiful temple for you. You can live in it forever."

The whole community of Israel was standing there. The king turned around and gave them his blessing.

Solomon finished all of those prayers. He finished asking the LORD to show his favor to his people. Then he got up from in front of the LORD's altar. He had been down on his knees with his hands spread out toward heaven. He stood in front of the whole community of Israel. He blessed them with a loud voice.

The Bad Kings

1 Kings 14—16

Rehoboam, the King of Judah

Rehoboam was king in Judah. He was the son of Solomon. Rehoboam was 41 years old when he became king. He ruled for 17 years in Jerusalem. It was the city the LORD had chosen out of all of the cities in the tribes of Israel. He wanted to put his Name there. Rehoboam's mother was Naamah from Ammon.

The people of Judah did what was evil in the sight of the LORD. The sins they had committed stirred up his jealous anger. They did more to make him angry than their people who lived before them had done.

Judah also set up for themselves high places for worship. They set up sacred stones. They set up poles that were used to worship the goddess Asherah. They did it on every high hill and under every green tree.

There were even male prostitutes at the temples in the land. The people took part in all of the practices of other nations. The LORD hated those practices. He had driven those nations out to make room for the people of Israel.

[Rehoboam died.] His son Abijah became the next king after him.

Abijah Becomes King of Judah

Abijah became king of Judah. It was in the 18th year of Jeroboam's rule over Israel. Jeroboam was the son of Nebat. Abijah ruled in

Jerusalem for three years. His mother's name was Maacah. She was Abishalom's daughter.

Abijah committed all of the sins his father had committed before him. Abijah didn't follow the LORD his God with all his heart. He didn't do what King David had done.

But the LORD still kept the lamp of Abijah's kingdom burning brightly in Jerusalem. He did it by giving him a son to be the next king after him. He also did it by making Jerusalem strong. The LORD did those things because of David. David had done what was right in the eyes of the LORD. He had kept all of the LORD's commands. He had obeyed them all the days of his life. But he hadn't obeyed the LORD in the case of Uriah, the Hittite.

There was war between Jeroboam and Abijah's father Rehoboam. The war continued all through Abijah's life. The other events of Abijah's rule are written down. Everything he did is written down. All of those things are written in the official records of the kings of Judah. There was war between Abijah and Jeroboam.

Abijah joined the members of his family who had already died. His body was buried in the City of David. His son Asa became the next king after him.

What were Israel and Judah?

When Solomon died, his kingdom was broken in two pieces. The land in the south became a nation called Judah. The land in the north became a nation called Israel. The first king of Judah was Rehoboam. The first king of Israel was Jeroboam. In the rest of the books of 1 Kings and in 2 Kings, Israel and Judah are the names of these two nations.

Ahab Becomes King of Israel

Ahab became king of Israel. It was in the 38th year that Asa was king of Judah. Ahab ruled over Israel in Samaria for 22 years. He was the son of Omri. Ahab, the son of Omri, did what was evil in the sight of the LORD. He did more evil things than any of the kings who had ruled before him. He thought it was only a small thing to commit the sins Jeroboam, the son of Nebat, had committed.

Ahab also got married to Jezebel. She was Ethbaal's daughter. Ethbaal was king of the people of Sidon. Ahab began to serve the god Baal

How many good kings did Israel have?

Not one king of Israel worshiped God. They all did "what was evil in the sight of the LORD." Many evil kings of Israel are listed in 1 Kings chapters 15 and 16. The worst king of all was Ahab. He was the enemy of Elijah the prophet.

and worship him. He set up an altar to honor Baal. He set it up in the temple of Baal that he built in Samaria. Ahab also made a pole that was used to worship the goddess Asherah.

He made the LORD very angry. He did more to make him angry than all of the kings of Israel had done before him. The LORD is the God of Israel.

In Ahab's time, Hiel from Bethel rebuilt Jericho. When he laid its foundations, it cost him the life of his oldest son Abiram. When he set up its gates, it cost him the life of his youngest son Segub. That's what the LORD had said would happen. He had spoken it through Joshua, the son of Nun.

PEOPLE IN BIBLE TIMES

Elijah

Elijah was a prophet. He spoke for God. He loved and obeyed God. He was not afraid of evil King Ahab. He was not afraid of Ahab's wicked wife, Jezebel. God gave Elijah great power. Elijah could do wonderful things for God.

The Story of Elijah

1 Kings 17—19; 21; 2 Kings 2

Elijah Is Fed by Ravens

Elijah was from Tishbe in the land of Gilead. He said to Ahab, "I serve the LORD. He is the God of Israel. You can be sure that he lives. And you can be just as sure that there won't be any dew or rain on the whole land. There won't be any during the next few years. It won't come until I say so."

Then a message from the LORD came to Elijah. It said, "Leave this place. Go east and hide in the Kerith Valley. It is east of the Jordan River. You will drink water from the brook. I have ordered some ravens to feed you there."

So Elijah did what the LORD had told him to do. He went to the Kerith Valley. It was east of the Jordan River. He stayed there. The ravens brought him bread and meat in the morning. They also brought him bread and meat in the evening. He drank water from the brook.

Elijah Visits a Widow at Zarephath

Some time later the brook dried up. It hadn't rained in the land for quite a while. A message came to Elijah from the LORD. He said, "Go right away to Zarephath in the territory of Sidon. Stay there. I have commanded a widow in that place to supply you with food."

So Elijah went to Zarephath. He came to the town gate. A widow was there gathering sticks. He called out to her. He asked, "Would you bring me a little water in a jar? I need a drink."

She went to get the water.

Then he called out to her, "Please bring me a piece of bread too."

"I don't have any bread," she replied. "And that's just as sure as the LORD your God is alive. All I have is a small amount of flour in a jar and a little olive oil in a jug. I'm gathering a few sticks to take home. I'll make one last meal for myself and my son. We'll eat it. After that, we'll die."

Elijah said to her, "Don't be afraid. Go home. Do what you have said. But first make a little bread for me. Make it out of what you have. Bring it to me. Then make some for yourself and your son.

"The LORD is the God of Israel. He says, 'The jar of flour will not be used up. The jug will always have oil in it. You will have flour and oil until the day the LORD sends rain on the land.'"

God's Care

God uses many ways to take care of the people he loves. How did God take care of Elijah?

Usually God takes care of children through their parents. He helps their mom or dad find a job. Then there is money for food and other things a family needs.

Sometimes one family can help out another family. Can you think of some ways that God could use you to help someone? Do you know an older person who has trouble raking leaves? You could help them. Do you have clothes in your closet that don't fit anymore? Maybe there's a family in your town who had a house fire. They could probably use some clothes.

She went away and did what Elijah had told her to do. So Elijah had food every day. There was also food for the woman and her family. The jar of flour wasn't used up. The jug always had oil in it. That's what the LORD had said would happen. He had spoken that message through Elijah.

Some time later the son of the woman who owned the house became sick. He got worse and worse. Finally he stopped breathing.

Then Elijah cried out to the LORD. He said, "LORD my God, I'm staying with this widow. Have you brought pain and sorrow to her? Have you caused her son to die?"

Then he lay down on the boy three times. He cried out to the LORD. He said, "LORD my God, give this boy's life back to him!"

The LORD answered Elijah's prayer. He gave the boy's life back to him. So the boy lived. Elijah picked up the boy. He carried him down from the upstairs room into the house. He gave him to his mother. He said, "Look! Your son is alive!"

Then the woman said to Elijah, "Now I know that you are a man of God. I know that the message you have brought from the LORD is true."

It was now three years since it had rained. A message came to Elijah from the LORD. He said, "Go. Speak to Ahab. Then I will send rain on the land."

So Elijah went to speak to Ahab.

The LORD Answers Elijah's Prayer on Mount Carmel

When [Ahab] saw Elijah, he said to him, "Is that you? You are always stirring up trouble in Israel."

"I haven't made trouble for Israel," Elijah replied. "But you and your father's family have. You have turned away from the LORD's commands. You have followed the gods that are named after Baal.

"Now send for people from all over Israel. Tell them to meet me on Mount Carmel. And bring the 450 prophets of the god Baal. Also bring the 400 prophets of the goddess Asherah. All of them eat at Jezebel's table."

So Ahab sent that message all through Israel. He gathered the prophets together on Mount Carmel.

Elijah went there and stood in front of the people. He said, "How long will it take you to make up your minds? If the LORD is the one and only God, follow him. But if Baal is the one and only God, follow him."

The people didn't say anything.

Then Elijah said to them, "I'm the only one of the LORD's prophets left. But Baal has 450 prophets. Get two bulls for us. Let Baal's prophets choose one for themselves. Let them cut it into pieces. Then let them put it on the wood. But don't let them set fire to it. I'll prepare the other bull. I'll put it on the wood. But I won't set fire to it. Then you pray to your god. And I'll pray to the LORD. The god who answers by sending fire down is the one and only God."

Then all of the people said, "What you are saying is good."

[The prophets] prayed to Baal from morning until noon. "Baal! Answer us!" they shouted. But there wasn't any reply. No one answered. Then they danced around the altar they had made.

At noon Elijah began to tease them. "Shout louder!" he said. "I'm sure Baal is a god! Perhaps he has too much to think about. Or maybe he has gone to the toilet. Or perhaps he's away on a trip. Maybe he's sleeping. You might have to wake him up."

So they shouted louder. They cut themselves with swords and spears until their blood flowed. That's what they usually did when things really looked hopeless. It was now past noon. The prophets of Baal continued to prophesy with all their might. They did it until the time came to offer the evening sacrifice. But there wasn't any reply. No one answered. No one paid any attention.

Then Elijah said to all of the people, "Come here to me." So they went to him. He rebuilt the altar of the LORD. It had been

Why did the prophets of Baal cut themselves?

Some people in Bible times cut themselves with knives to show how sad they were. But that's not why the prophets of Baal cut themselves. They cut themselves because they thought it would make their god notice them.

destroyed. Elijah got 12 stones. There was one for each tribe in the family line of Jacob. The LORD's message had come to Jacob. It had said, "Your name will be Israel." Elijah used the stones to build an altar in honor of the LORD. He dug a ditch around it. The ditch was large enough to hold 13 quarts of seeds. He arranged the wood for the fire. He cut the bull into pieces. He placed the pieces on the wood.

Then he said to some of the people, "Fill four large jars with water. Pour it on the offering and the wood." So they did.

"Do it again," he said. So they did it again.

"Do it a third time," he ordered. And they did it the third time. The water ran down around the altar. It even filled the ditch.

When it was time to offer the evening sacrifice, the prophet Elijah stepped forward. He prayed, "LORD, you are the God of Abraham, Isaac and Israel. Today let everyone know that you are God in Israel. Let them know I'm your servant. Let them know I've done all of these things because you commanded me to. Answer me. LORD, answer me. Then these people will know that you are the one and only God. They'll know that you are turning their hearts back to you again."

The fire of the LORD came down. It burned up the sacrifice. It burned up the wood and the stones and the soil. It even licked up the water in the ditch.

All of the people saw it. Then they fell down flat with their faces toward the ground. They cried out, "The LORD is the one and only God! The LORD is the one and only God!"

So they grabbed [the prophets of Baal.] Elijah had them brought down to the Kishon Valley. There he had them put to death.

So Jezebel sent a message to Elijah. She said, "You can be sure that I will kill you, just as I killed the other prophets. I'll do it by this time tomorrow."

Elijah was afraid. So he ran for his life. He kept going until he arrived at Horeb. It was the mountain of God. He went into a cave and spent the night.

The LORD Appears to Elijah

A message came to Elijah from the LORD. He said, "Elijah, what are you doing here?"

He replied, "LORD God who rules over all, I've been very committed to you. The people of Israel have turned their backs on your covenant. They have torn down your altars. They've put your prophets to death with their swords. I'm the only one left. And they are trying to kill me."

The LORD said, "Go out. Stand on the mountain in front of me. I am going to pass by."

As the LORD approached, a very powerful wind tore the mountains apart. It broke up the rocks. But the LORD wasn't in the wind.

After the wind there was an earthquake. But the LORD wasn't in the earthquake.

After the earthquake a fire came. But the LORD wasn't in the fire.

And after the fire there was only a gentle whisper. When Elijah heard it, he pulled his coat over his face. He went out and stood at the entrance to the cave.

Ahab Takes Over Naboth's Vineyard

Some time later King Ahab wanted a certain vineyard. It belonged to Naboth from Jezreel. The vineyard was in Jezreel. It was close to the palace of Ahab, the king of Samaria.

Ahab said to Naboth, "Let me have your vineyard. It's close to my palace. I want to use it for a vegetable garden. I'll trade you a better vineyard for it. Or, if you prefer, I'll pay you what it's worth."

But Naboth replied, "May the LORD keep me from giving you the land my family handed down to me."

So Ahab went home. He was angry. He was in a bad mood because of what Naboth from Jezreel had said. He had told him, "I won't give you the land my family handed down to me."

So Ahab lay on his bed. He was in a very bad mood. He wouldn't even eat anything.

His wife Jezebel came in. She asked him, "Why are you in such a bad mood? Why won't you eat anything?"

He answered her, "Because I spoke to Naboth from Jezreel. I said,

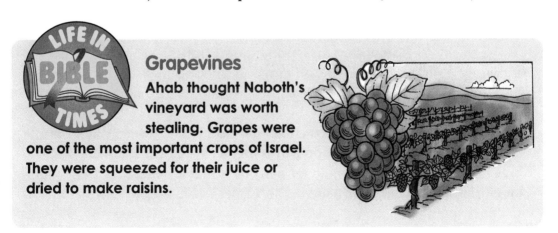

Grapevines
Ahab thought Naboth's vineyard was worth stealing. Grapes were one of the most important crops of Israel. They were squeezed for their juice or dried to make raisins.

'Sell me your vineyard. Or, if you prefer, I'll give you another vineyard in its place.' But he said, 'I won't sell you my vineyard.'"

His wife Jezebel said, "Is this how the king of Israel acts? Get up! Eat something! Cheer up. I'll get you the vineyard of Naboth from Jezreel."

So she wrote some letters in Ahab's name. She stamped them with his seal. Then she sent them to the elders and nobles who lived in the city where Naboth lived. In those letters she wrote,

> "Announce a day when people are supposed to go without eating. Have Naboth sit in an important place among the people. But put two worthless and evil men in seats across from him. Have them witness to the fact that he has called down curses on God and the king. Then take him out of the city. Kill him by throwing stones at him."

So the elders and nobles who lived in that city did what Jezebel wanted.

Jezebel heard that Naboth had been killed. As soon as she heard it, she said to Ahab, "Get up. Take over the vineyard of Naboth from Jezreel. It's the one he wouldn't sell to you. He isn't alive anymore. He's dead."

Ahab heard that Naboth was dead. So he got up. He went down to take over Naboth's vineyard.

Wanting Something Too Much

Sometimes we really want something that someone else has. But God says this is wrong. One of God's laws says, "Do not long for anything that belongs to your neighbor" (Exodus 20:17; see page 62). In this Bible story, King Ahab longed for a field of grapevines that belonged to a man named Naboth.

Wanting what others have can make us unhappy. We might even do bad things to get what others have. God wants us to be happy with what he has given us.

Here are some things that can help you stop wanting what other people have. Think about all of the good things that you have. Choose a favorite toy to play with. Invite a friend over and share that favorite toy. Thank God for all of the good things you have. Then other things you want won't seem so important.

Then a message from the LORD came to Elijah, who was from Tishbe. It said, "Go down to see Ahab, the king of Israel. He rules in Samaria. You will find him in Naboth's vineyard. He has gone there to take it over. Tell him, 'The LORD says, "Haven't you murdered a man? Haven't you taken over his property?"' Then tell him, 'The LORD says, "Dogs licked up Naboth's blood. In that same place dogs will lick up your blood. Yes, I said your blood!"'"

Ahab said to Elijah, "My enemy! You have found me!"

"I have found you," he answered. "That's because you gave yourself over to do evil things. You did what was evil in the sight of the LORD. So the LORD says, 'I am going to bring horrible trouble on you.'

"The LORD also says, 'Dogs will eat up Jezebel near the wall of Jezreel.'"

There was never anyone like Ahab. He gave himself over to do what was evil in the sight of the LORD. His wife Jezebel talked him into it. He acted in the most evil way. He worshiped statues of gods. He was like the Amorites. The LORD drove them out to make room for Israel.

Elijah Is Taken Up to Heaven

Elijah and [his assistant] Elisha were on their way from Gilgal. The LORD was going to use a strong wind to take Elijah up to heaven. Elijah said to Elisha, "Stay here. The LORD has sent me to Bethel."

But Elisha said, "I won't leave you. And that's just as sure as the LORD and you are alive."

Elijah spoke to Elisha. He said, "Tell me. What can I do for you before I'm taken away from you?"

"Please give me a double share of your spirit," Elisha replied.

"You have asked me for something I can't give you," Elijah said. "Only the LORD can give it. But suppose you see me when I'm taken away from you. Then you will receive what you have asked for. If you don't see me, you won't receive it."

They kept walking along and talking together. Suddenly a chariot and horses appeared. Fire was all around them. The

DID YOU KNOW?

How many people have gone to heaven without dying first?

Two people went to heaven without dying. Genesis 5:24 tells us about Enoch. The other person was Elijah. He went to heaven in a chariot pulled by horses.

chariot and horses came between the two men. Then Elijah went up to heaven in a strong wind. Elisha saw it. He cried out to Elijah, "My father! You are like a father to me! You are the true chariots and horsemen of Israel!" Elisha didn't see Elijah anymore. Then Elisha took hold of his own clothes and tore them apart.

He picked up the coat that had fallen from Elijah. He went back and stood on the banks of the Jordan River. Then he struck the water with Elijah's coat. When Elisha struck the water, it parted to the right and to the left. He went across the river.

The Story of Elisha

2 Kings 4—5

The Son of a Woman From Shunem Is Brought Back to Life

One day Elisha went to the town of Shunem. A rich woman lived there. She begged him to stay and have a meal. So every time he came by, he stopped there to eat.

The woman said to her husband, "That man often comes by here. I know that he is a holy man of God. Let's make a small room for him on the roof. We'll put a bed and a table in it. We'll also put a chair and a lamp in it. Then he can stay there when he comes to visit us."

One day Elisha came. He went up to his room. He lay down there. He said to his servant Gehazi, "Go and get the Shunammite woman." So he did. She stood in front of Elisha.

He said to Gehazi, "Tell her, 'You have gone to a lot of trouble for us. Now what can we do for you? Can we speak to the king for you? Or can we speak to the commander of the army for you?'"

She replied, "I live among my own people. I have everything I need here."

After she left, Elisha asked Gehazi, "What can we do for her?"

Gehazi said, "Well, she doesn't have a son. And her husband is old."

Then Elisha said, "Bring her here again." So he did. She stood in the doorway. "You will hold a son in your arms," Elisha said. "It will be about this time next year."

"No, my master!" she objected. "You are a man of God. Don't lie to me!"

But the woman became pregnant. She had a baby boy. It happened the next year about that same time. That's exactly what Elisha had told her would happen.

The child grew. One day he went out to get his father. His father was with those who were gathering the crops.

The boy said to his father, "My head hurts! It really hurts!"

His father told a servant, "Carry him to his mother." The servant lifted the boy up. He carried him to his mother.

The boy sat on her lap until noon. Then he died. She went up to the room on the roof. There she laid him on the bed of the man of God. Then she shut the door and went out.

She sent for her husband. She said, "Please send me one of the servants and a donkey. Then I can go quickly to the man of God and return."

When she was still a long way off, [Elisha] saw her coming.

She came to the man of God at the mountain. Then she took hold of his feet.

"My master, did I ask you for a son?" she said. "Didn't I tell you, 'Don't get my hopes up'?" So Elisha got up and followed her.

Elisha arrived at the house. The boy was dead. He was lying on Elisha's bed.

Elisha went into the room. He shut the door. He was alone with the boy. He prayed to the Lord.

Then he got on the bed. He lay down on the boy. His mouth touched the boy's mouth. His eyes touched the boy's eyes. And his hands touched the boy's hands. As Elisha lay on the boy, the boy's body grew warm.

Elisha turned away. He walked back and forth in the room. Then he got on the bed again. He lay down on the boy once more. The boy sneezed seven times. After that, he opened his eyes.

Elisha sent for Gehazi. He said to him, "Go and get the Shunammite woman." So he did. When she came, Elisha said, "Take your son."

She came in. She fell at Elisha's feet. She bowed down with her face toward the ground. Then she took her son and went out.

Naaman Is Healed of a Skin Disease

Naaman was commander of the army of the king of Aram. He was a very important man in the eyes of his master. And he was highly respected. That's because the Lord had helped him win the battle over

Aram's enemies. He was a brave soldier. But he had a skin disease.

Companies of soldiers from Aram had marched out. They had captured a young girl from Israel. She became a servant of Naaman's wife. She spoke to the woman she was serving. She said, "I wish my master would go and see the prophet who is in Samaria. He would heal my master of his skin disease."

Naaman went to see his own master. He told him what the girl from Israel had said.

"I think you should go," the king of Aram replied.

So Naaman went to see Elisha. He took his horses and chariots with him. He stopped at the door of Elisha's house.

Elisha sent a messenger out to him. The messenger said, "Go. Wash yourself in the Jordan River seven times. Then your skin will be healed. You will be pure and clean again."

But Naaman went away angry. He said, "I was sure he would come out to me. I thought he would stand there and pray to the LORD his God. I thought he would wave his hand over my skin. Then I would be healed."

Naaman's servants went over to him. They said, "You are like a father to us. What if the prophet Elisha had told you to do some great thing? Wouldn't you have done it? But he only said, 'Wash yourself. Then you will be pure and clean.' You should be even more willing to do that!"

So Naaman went down to the Jordan River. He dipped himself in it seven times. He did exactly what the man of God had told him to do. Then his skin was made pure again. It became clean like the skin of a young boy.

Telling the Good News

This story tells about a girl from Israel who was close to your age. She was a servant for the wife of Naaman. Naaman was an army commander for the king of Aram. But he had a terrible skin disease. The servant girl wanted to help him. She wanted him to know the power of God. So she told him about Elisha. He was a prophet in Samaria who could help him.

Who do you know who can help your friends with their problems? That's right. Jesus! Don't be afraid to tell your friends what you know about Jesus.

Israel Is Forced to Go Away

2 Kings 17

Hoshea Becomes the Last King of Israel

Hoshea became king of Israel in Samaria. Hoshea did what was evil in the sight of the LORD. But he wasn't as evil as the kings of Israel who ruled before him.

Shalmaneser was king of Assyria. He had been Hoshea's master. But the king of Assyria found out that Hoshea had turned against him. Hoshea had sent messengers to So, the king of Egypt. Hoshea didn't send gifts to the king of Assyria anymore. He had been sending them every year. So Shalmaneser grabbed hold of him and put him in prison.

The king of Assyria marched into the whole land of Israel. He marched to Samaria and surrounded it for three years. From time to time he attacked it. Finally, the king of Assyria captured Samaria. It was in the ninth year of Hoshea. The king of Assyria took the people of Israel away from their own land. He sent them off to Assyria. He settled some of them in Halah. He settled others in Gozan on the Habor River. And he settled still others in the towns of the Medes.

Israel Is Forced to Go Away to Assyria

All of that took place because the people of Israel had committed sins against the LORD their God. He had brought them up out of Egypt. He had brought them out from under the power of Pharaoh, the king of Egypt. But they worshiped other gods.

The LORD had driven out other nations to make room for them. But they followed the evil practices of those nations.

The LORD warned Israel and Judah through all of his prophets and seers. He said, "Turn from your evil ways. Keep my commands and rules. Obey every part of my Law. I commanded your people who lived long ago to obey it. And I gave it to you through my servants the prophets."

But the people wouldn't listen. They were as stubborn as their people of long ago had been. Those people didn't trust in the LORD their God. They refused to obey his rules. They broke the covenant he had made with them. They didn't pay any attention to the warnings he had given them. They worshiped worthless statues of gods. Then they them-

Punishment

Did you ever do something wrong, even though you knew you shouldn't? God wanted the people of Israel to worship only him. He taught them right from wrong. But the people worshiped other gods. This made God angry. He told them to stop. When they refused, he punished them.

Show your parents this story. Ask them to tell you about a time when they were punished as children. Talk about the times you have been punished too. Have your parents followed God's example? Do they teach, warn and then punish?

selves became worthless. They followed the example of the nations that were around them. They did it even though the LORD had ordered them not to. He had said, "Do not do as they do."

So the LORD was filled with anger against Israel. He removed them from his land. Only the tribe of Judah was left. And even Judah didn't obey the commands of the LORD their God. They followed the practices Israel had started.

So the LORD turned his back on all of the people of Israel. He made them suffer. He handed them over to people who stole everything they had. And finally he threw them out of his land. They were forced to go to Assyria.

A Very Young King

2 Chronicles 24

Joash Repairs the Temple

Joash was seven years old when he became king. He ruled in Jerusalem for 40 years. His mother's name was Zibiah. She was from Beersheba.

Joash did what was right in the eyes of the LORD. He lived that way as long as the priest Jehoiada was alive. Jehoiada chose two wives for

Joash. They had sons and daughters by Joash.

Some time later Joash decided to make the LORD's temple look like new again. He called together the priests and Levites. He said to them, "Go to the towns of Judah. Collect the money that the nation of Israel owes every year. Use it to repair the temple of your God. Do it now." But the Levites didn't do it right away.

King Joash commanded that a wooden chest be made. It was placed outside near the gate of the LORD's temple. Then a message went out in Judah and Jerusalem. It said that the people should bring the tax to the LORD. God's servant Moses had required Israel to pay that tax when they were in the desert.

All of the officials and people gladly brought their money. They dropped it into the chest until it was full.

The chest was brought in by the Levites to the king's officials. Every time the officials saw there was a large amount of money in the chest, it was emptied out. The royal secretary and the officer of the chief priest came and emptied it. Then they carried it back to its place. They did it regularly. They collected a great amount of money.

DID YOU KNOW?

What kind of king was Joash?

Joash was weak. But Jehoiada helped Joash. Jehoiada was the priest. Joash did well when he listened to the priest. But when the priest died, Joash listened to others. Then Joash became very wicked.

Good King Hezekiah

2 Kings 18, 20; 2 Chronicles 29—31

Hezekiah Becomes King of Judah

Hezekiah began to rule as king over Judah. It was in the third year that Hoshea was king of Israel. Hezekiah was 25 years old when he became king. He ruled in Jerusalem for 29 years.

Hezekiah did what was right in the eyes of the LORD, just as King David had done. Hezekiah removed the high places. He smashed the

Hezekiah

Hezekiah was a good king of Judah (the two southern tribes after Israel divided). He was 25 years old when he became king. He trusted and obeyed God. So God made him successful. The people of Assyria destroyed Israel. Then they tried to destroy Judah. But they could not do it.

sacred stones. He cut down the poles that were used to worship the goddess Asherah. He broke into pieces the bronze snake Moses had made. Up to that time the people of Israel had been burning incense to it. They called it Nehushtan.

Hezekiah trusted in the LORD, the God of Israel. There was no one like him among all of the kings of Judah. There was no king like him either before him or after him. Hezekiah remained true to the LORD. He didn't stop following him. He obeyed the commands the LORD had given Moses.

The LORD was with Hezekiah. He was successful in everything he did. He refused to remain under the control of the king of Assyria. He didn't serve him. He won the war against the Philistines. He won battles at their lookout towers. He won battles at their cities that had high walls around them. He won battles against the Philistines all the way to Gaza and its territory.

Hezekiah Purifies the Temple

In the first month of Hezekiah's first year as king, he opened the doors of the LORD's temple. He repaired them. He brought the priests and Levites in. He gathered them together in the open area on the east side of the temple.

He said, "Levites, listen to me! Set yourselves apart to the LORD. Set apart the temple of the LORD. He's the God of your people. Remove anything that is 'unclean' from the temple. Our people weren't faithful. They did what was evil in the sight of the LORD our God. They deserted him. They turned their faces away from the place where he lives. They turned their backs on him. They also shut the doors of the temple porch. They put the lamps out. They didn't burn incense at the temple. They didn't sacrifice burnt offerings to the God of Israel there.

"So the LORD has become angry with Judah and Jerusalem. He has made them look so bad that everyone is shocked when they see them.

They laugh at them. You can see it with your own eyes. That's why our people have been killed with swords. That's why our sons and daughters and wives have become prisoners."

[The Levites] set themselves apart to the LORD. Then they went in to purify the LORD's temple. That's what the king had ordered them to do. They did what the LORD told them to. The priests went into the LORD's temple to make it pure. They brought out to the temple courtyard everything that was "unclean." They had found "unclean" things in the LORD's temple. The Levites took them and carried them out to the Kidron Valley.

On the first day of the first month they began to set everything in the temple apart to the LORD. By the eighth day of the month they reached the LORD's porch. For eight more days they set the LORD's temple itself apart to him. They finished on the 16th day of the first month.

Then they went to King Hezekiah. They reported, "We've purified the whole temple of the LORD. That includes the altar for burnt offerings and all of its tools. It also includes the table for the holy bread and all of its articles. We've prepared all of the articles King Ahaz had removed. We've set them apart to the LORD. Ahaz had removed them while he was king. He wasn't faithful to the LORD. The articles are now in front of the LORD's altar."

Early the next morning King Hezekiah gathered the city officials together. They went up to the LORD's temple. They brought seven bulls, seven rams, seven male lambs and seven male goats with them. They sacrificed the animals as a sin offering for the kingdom, for the temple and for Judah. The king commanded the priests to offer them on the LORD's altar. The priests were from the family line of Aaron.

He stationed the Levites in the LORD's temple. They had cymbals, harps and lyres. They did everything in the way King David, his prophet Gad, and the prophet Nathan had required. The LORD had given commands about all of those things through his prophets. So the Levites stood ready with David's musical instruments. And the priests had their trumpets ready.

Hezekiah gave the order to sacrifice the burnt offering on the altar. The offering began. Singing to the LORD also began. The singing was accompanied by the trumpets and by the instruments of David. He had

DID YOU KNOW?

What shows that Hezekiah was a godly king?

Hezekiah showed that he loved God. He fixed up God's temple. He promised to obey God. He kept the Passover. He smashed the people's false gods. He did many good things.

been king of Israel. The whole community bowed down. They worshiped the LORD. At the same time the singers sang. The priests blew their trumpets. All of that continued until the burnt offering had been sacrificed.

So the offerings were finished. King Hezekiah got down on his knees. He worshiped the LORD. So did everyone who was with him.

The king and his officials ordered the Levites to praise the LORD. They used the words of David and the prophet Asaph. They sang praises with joy. They bowed their heads and worshiped the LORD.

Then Hezekiah said, "You have set yourselves apart to the LORD. Come and bring sacrifices and thank offerings to his temple."

So the whole community brought sacrifices and thank offerings. Everyone who wanted to brought burnt offerings.

So the service of the LORD's temple was started up again. Hezekiah and all of the people were filled with joy. That's because everything had been done so quickly. God had provided for his people in a wonderful way.

Hezekiah Celebrates the Passover Feast

Hezekiah sent a message to all of the people of Israel and Judah. He also wrote letters to the tribes of Ephraim and Manasseh. He invited everyone to come to the LORD's temple in Jerusalem. He wanted them to celebrate the Passover Feast in honor of the LORD. He is the God of Israel.

The king, his officials and the whole community in Jerusalem decided to celebrate the Passover in the second month. They hadn't been able to celebrate it at the regular time. That's because there weren't enough priests who had set themselves apart to the LORD. Also, the people hadn't gathered together in Jerusalem.

The plan seemed good to the king and the whole community. They decided to send a message all through Israel. It was sent out from Beersheba all the way to Dan. The message invited the people to come to

Jerusalem. It invited them to celebrate the Passover in honor of the LORD, the God of Israel.

The Passover hadn't been celebrated by large numbers of people for a long time. It hadn't been done in keeping with what was written in the law.

Messengers went all through Israel and Judah. They carried letters from the king and his officials.

A very large crowd of people gathered together in Jerusalem. They went there to celebrate the Feast of Unleavened Bread. It took place in the second month. They removed the altars in Jerusalem. They cleared away the altars for burning incense. They threw all of the altars into the Kidron Valley.

They killed the Passover lamb on the 14th day of the second month. The priests and Levites were filled with shame. They set themselves apart to the LORD. They brought burnt offerings to his temple. Then they went to their regular positions. They did it just as the Law of Moses, the man of God, required. The Levites gave the blood of the animals to the priests. The priests sprinkled it on the altar.

Many people came from Ephraim, Manasseh, Issachar and Zebulun. Most of them hadn't made themselves pure and clean. But they still ate the Passover meal. That was against what was written in the law. But Hezekiah prayed for them. He said, "The LORD is good. May he forgive everyone who wants to worship God with all his heart. God is the LORD, the God of their people. May God forgive them even if they aren't 'clean' in keeping with the rules of the temple."

The LORD answered Hezekiah's prayer. He healed the people.

The people of Israel who were in Jerusalem celebrated the Feast of Unleavened Bread. They celebrated for seven days with great joy.

The Levites and priests sang to the LORD every day. Their singing was accompanied by musical instruments. The instruments were used to praise the LORD.

Hezekiah spoke words that gave hope to all of the Levites. They understood how to serve the LORD well. For the seven days of the Feast they ate the share that was given to them. They also sacrificed friendship offerings. They praised the LORD, the God of their people.

The entire community of Judah was filled with joy. So were the priests and Levites. And so were all of the people who had gathered together from Israel. That included the outsiders who had come from Israel. It also included those who lived in Judah.

There was great joy in Jerusalem. There hadn't been anything like it in Israel since the days of Solomon, the son of David. Solomon had been king of Israel.

The priests and Levites gave their blessing to the people. God heard them. Their prayer reached all the way to heaven.

Hezekiah did what was good and right. He was faithful to the LORD his God. He looked to his God. He worked for him with all his heart. That's the way he worked in everything he did to serve God's temple. He obeyed the law. He followed the LORD's commands. So he had success.

Hezekiah Becomes Sick

In those days Hezekiah became very sick. He knew he was about to die.

The prophet Isaiah, the son of Amoz, went to him. Isaiah told Hezekiah, "The LORD says, 'Put everything in order. Make out your will. You are going to die soon. You will not get well again.'"

Hezekiah turned his face toward the wall. He prayed to the LORD. He said, "LORD, please remember how faithful I've been to you. I've lived

Pray When You Are Sick

Have you ever been sick and asked God to make you well? King Hezekiah had a large, red boil. It made him so sick that he knew he was about to die. He asked God to heal him. Hezekiah's prayer touched God's heart. God healed Hezekiah.

Draw a picture of Hezekiah. Draw a large, red sore somewhere on him. Now get a bandage and put it on the picture of the sore. Write Psalm 30:2 on your picture: "LORD my God, I called out to you for help. And you healed me."

Put your picture in your family's first aid kit. Let it remind you to pray when someone gets sick.

the way you wanted me to. I've served you with all my heart. I've done what is good in your sight." And Hezekiah cried bitterly.

Isaiah was leaving the middle courtyard. Before he had left it, a message came to him from the LORD. He said, "Go back and speak to Hezekiah. He is the leader of my people. Tell him, 'The LORD, the God of King David, says, "I have heard your prayer. I have seen your tears. And I will heal you. On the third day from now you will go up to my temple. I will add 15 years to your life. And I will save you and this city from the powerful hand of the king of Assyria. I will guard this city. I will do it for myself. And I will do it for my servant David."'"

The other events of the rule of Hezekiah are written down. Everything he accomplished is written down. That includes how he made the pool and the tunnel. He used them to bring water into Jerusalem. All of those things are written in the official records of the kings of Judah.

Hezekiah joined the members of his family who had already died. His son Manasseh became the next king after him.

Judah Is Destroyed

2 Chronicles 36

The people and the leaders of the priests became more and more unfaithful. They followed all of the practices of the nations. The LORD hated those practices. The people and leaders made the LORD's temple "unclean." The LORD had set the temple in Jerusalem apart in a special way for himself.

Nebuchadnezzar Destroys Jerusalem

The LORD, the God of Israel, sent word to his people through his messengers. He sent it to them again and again. He took pity on his people. He also took pity on the temple where he lived.

But God's people made fun of his messengers. They hated his words. They laughed at his prophets. Finally the LORD's burning anger was stirred up against his people. Nothing could save them.

The LORD brought the king of Babylonia against them. The Babylonian army killed their young people with their swords at the temple.

DID YOU KNOW?

When was the city of Jerusalem destroyed?

People from Babylon destroyed Jerusalem. They destroyed it about 600 years before Jesus was born. They burned the city. They took all of the things from the temple. They took thousands of people away from their homes.

They didn't spare young men or women. They didn't spare the old people either. God handed all of them over to Nebuchadnezzar.

Nebuchadnezzar carried off to Babylon all of the articles from God's temple. Some of the articles were large. Others were small. He carried off the treasures of the temple. He also carried off the treasures that belonged to the king and his officials.

The Babylonians set God's temple on fire. They broke down the wall of Jerusalem. They burned all of the palaces. They destroyed everything of value there.

Nebuchadnezzar took the rest of the people to Babylon as prisoners. They had escaped from being killed with swords. They served him and his sons. That lasted until the kingdom of Persia became stronger than Babylonia.

The land of Israel enjoyed its sabbath years. It rested. That deserted land wasn't farmed for a full 70 years. What the LORD had spoken through Jeremiah came true.

The People Return to Judah and Rebuild the Temple

Ezra 1—3; Nehemiah 7—8; Ezra 4

Cyrus Helps the Jews Build the LORD's Temple

It was the first year of the rule of Cyrus. He was king of Persia. The LORD stirred him up to send a message all through his kingdom. It happened so that what the LORD had spoken through Jeremiah would come true. The message was written down. It said,

"Cyrus, the king of Persia, says,

"'The Lord is the God of heaven. He has given me all of the kingdoms on earth. He has appointed me to build a temple for him at Jerusalem in Judah.

"'Any one of his people among you can go up to Jerusalem. And may your God be with you. You can build the Lord's temple. He is the God of Israel. He is the God who is in Jerusalem.

"'The people who are still left alive in every place must bring him gifts. They must provide him with silver and gold. They must bring goods and livestock. They should also bring any offerings they choose to. All of those gifts will be for God's temple in Jerusalem.'"

Then everyone God had stirred up got ready to go. They wanted to go up to Jerusalem and build the Lord's temple there. They included the family leaders of Judah and Benjamin. They also included the priests and Levites.

All of their neighbors helped them. They gave them silver and gold articles. They gave them goods and livestock. And they gave them gifts of great value. All of those things were added to the other offerings the people chose to give.

King Cyrus also brought out the articles that belonged to the Lord's temple. Nebuchadnezzar had carried them off from Jerusalem. He had

Leaving Home

It's not easy to move away from your home where everything is familiar. The people of Israel were now called Jews. They had been in Babylon for about 60 years. They were taken there as prisoners. Babylon had become their home. Only the old people could remember their homeland of Judah. Now they are told they can move back to Judah. But only some of the Jews want to move.

Have you ever had to move to a new home? There are some things you can do to make it easier. Find out about the new area you will be living in. What is special about it? Draw pictures of how you would like to fix up your new room. Ask God for a special new friend when you get to your new home.

put them in the temple of his own god. Cyrus, the king of Persia, told Mithredath to bring them out. Mithredath was in charge of the temple treasures. He counted the articles. Then he gave them to Sheshbazzar, the prince of Judah. Sheshbazzar took all of them with him to Jerusalem. He brought them along when the Jews who had been forced to leave Judah came back from Babylon.

People Who Returned to Judah

Nebuchadnezzar had taken many Jews away from the land of Judah. He had forced them to go to Babylonia as prisoners. Now they returned to Jerusalem and Judah. All of them went back to their own towns. Nebuchadnezzar was king of Babylonia.

All of the people arrived at the LORD's temple in Jerusalem. Then some of the leaders of the families brought offerings they chose to give. They would be used for rebuilding the house of God. It would stand in the same place it had been before. The people gave money for the work. It was based on how much they had. They gave 1,100 pounds of gold. They also gave three tons of silver. And they gave 100 sets of clothes for the priests. All of that was added to the temple treasure.

The priests and Levites settled in their own towns. So did the singers, the men who guarded the gates, and the temple servants. The rest of the people of Israel also settled in their own towns.

The People Begin to Rebuild the Temple

The people gave money to those who worked with stone and those who worked with wool. They gave food and drink and olive oil to the people of Sidon and Tyre. Then those people brought cedar logs down from Lebanon to the Mediterranean Sea. They floated them down to Joppa. Cyrus, the king of Persia, authorized them to do it.

It was the second month of the second year after they had arrived at the house of God in Jerusalem. Zerubbabel, the son of Shealtiel, began the work. Jeshua, the son of Jehozadak, helped him. So did everyone else. That included the priests and Levites. It also included the rest of those who had returned to Jerusalem. They had been prisoners in Babylonia. Levites who were 20 years old or more were appointed to be in charge of building the LORD's house.

Those who joined together to direct the work included Jeshua and his sons and brothers. They also included Kadmiel and his sons. And they included the sons of Henadad and all of their sons and brothers. All of those men were Levites. Kadmiel and his sons were members of the family line of Hodaviah.

The builders laid the foundation of the LORD's temple. Then the priests came. They were wearing their special clothes. They brought their trumpets with them. The Levites who belonged to the family line of Asaph also came. They brought their cymbals with them. The priests and Levites took their places to praise the LORD. They did everything just as King David had required them to. They sang to the LORD. They praised him. They gave thanks to him. They said,

"The LORD is good.
His faithful love to Israel continues forever."

All of the people gave a loud shout. They praised the LORD. They were glad because the foundation of the LORD's temple had been laid.

But many of the older priests and Levites and family leaders sobbed out loud. They had seen the first temple. So when they saw the foundation of the second temple being laid, they sobbed. Others shouted with joy.

No one could tell the difference between the shouts of joy and the sounds of sobbing. That's because the people made so much noise. The sound was heard far away.

Enemies Oppose the Rebuilding of the Temple

The nations that were around Judah tried to make its people lose hope. They wanted to make them afraid to go on building. So they hired advisers to work against them. They wanted their plans to fail.

DID YOU KNOW?

Who were the enemies of God's people?

Many years before, the king of Assyria had sent God's people to Assyria. Then he let other people live in their land. These people did not worship God. But they thought that God owned Israel, so they started to worship him. But they still worshiped their old gods too. Later they offered to help God's people rebuild the temple. God's people did not want them to help. This made the other people angry. They tried to stop God's people from doing their work.

Later Enemies Also Oppose the Jews

The enemies of the Jews brought charges against the people of Judah and Jerusalem. It happened when Xerxes began to rule over Persia.

Then Artaxerxes became king of Persia. During his rule, Bishlam, Mithredath, Tabeel and their friends wrote a letter to him. It was written in the Aramaic language. And it used the Aramaic alphabet.

Rehum and Shimshai also wrote a letter to King Artaxerxes. Rehum was the commanding officer. Shimshai was the secretary. Their letter was against the people of Jerusalem.

Here is a copy of the letter that was sent to Artaxerxes.

We want you to know that the Jews who left you and came up to us have gone to Jerusalem. They are rebuilding that evil city. It has caused trouble for a long time. The Jews are making its walls like new again. They are repairing the foundations.

Here is something else we want you to know. Suppose this city is rebuilt. And suppose its walls are made like new again. Then no more taxes, gifts or fees will be collected. And there will be less money for you.

We owe a lot to you. We don't want to see dishonor brought on you. So we're sending this letter to tell you what is going on. Then you can have a search made in the official records. Have someone check the records of the kings who ruled before you.

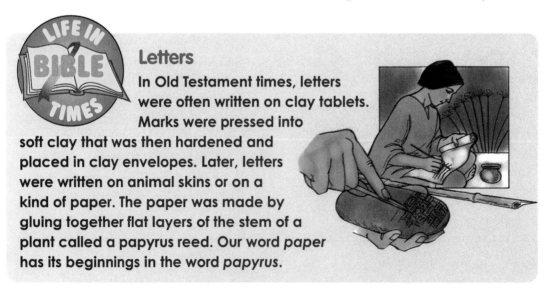

Letters

In Old Testament times, letters were often written on clay tablets. Marks were pressed into soft clay that was then hardened and placed in clay envelopes. Later, letters were written on animal skins or on a kind of paper. The paper was made by gluing together flat layers of the stem of a plant called a papyrus reed. Our word *paper* has its beginnings in the word *papyrus*.

If you do, you will find out that Jerusalem is an evil city. It causes trouble for kings and countries. For a long time the city has refused to let anyone rule over it. That's why it was destroyed. We want you to know that this city shouldn't be rebuilt. Its walls shouldn't be made like new again. If that happens, you won't have anything left west of the Euphrates River.

The king replied,

The letter you sent us has been read to me. It has been explained to me in my language. I gave an order. I had a search made. We found out that Jerusalem has a long history of turning against the kings of the countries that have ruled over it. It has refused to remain under their control. It is always stirring up trouble. Jerusalem has had powerful kings. Some of them ruled over everything west of the Euphrates. Taxes, gifts and fees were paid to them.

So give an order to those men. Make them stop their work. Then the city won't be rebuilt until I give the order. Pay careful attention to this matter. Why should we let this danger grow? That would not be in our best interests.

And so the work on the house of God in Jerusalem came to an end. Nothing more was done on it until the second year that Darius was king of Persia.

Tattenai Sends a Letter to King Darius

Here is a copy of the letter that was sent to King Darius. It was from Tattenai, the governor of the land west of the Euphrates. Shethar-Bozenai joined him in writing it. So did their friends. They were officials of that land. The report they sent to the king said,

We want you to know that we went to the land of Judah. We went to the temple of the great God. The people are building it with large stones. They are putting wooden beams in the walls. The people are working hard. The work is moving ahead very quickly under the direction of the people.

We asked the elders some questions. We said to them, "Who authorized you to rebuild this temple? Who told you that you could make this building like new again?" We also asked them their names. We wanted to write down the names of their leaders for your information.

King Darius Sends a Reply to Tattenai

[King Darius wrote back,]

Tattenai, you are governor of the land west of the Euphrates River. I want you to stay away from the temple in Jerusalem. Shethar-Bozenai and the other officials of that area must also stay away from it. Don't try to stop the work on God's temple. Let the governor of the Jews and their elders rebuild the house of their God. Let them build it in the same place where it stood before.

Here is what I want you to do for the elders of the Jews. Here is how you must help the men who build the house of their God.

Pay all of their expenses from the royal treasures. Use the money you collect from the people who live west of the Euphrates. Don't let the work on the temple stop. Don't fail to give the priests in Jerusalem what they ask for each day. Give them what they need. Give them young bulls, rams and male lambs. The priests can use them to sacrifice burnt offerings to the God of heaven. Also give them wheat, salt, wine and olive oil. Give them those things so they can offer sacrifices that please the God of heaven. And I want them to pray that things will go well for me and my sons.

Don't change this order. If a man tries to change it, he must be put to death. A pole must be pulled from his house. The pole must be stuck through his body. Then it must be set up where people can see it. Because the man tried to change my royal order, his house must be broken to pieces. God has chosen to put his Name in the temple at Jerusalem. May he wipe out any king or nation that lifts a hand to change this order. May he also wipe out anyone who tries to destroy the temple in Jerusalem.

That's what I have ordered. I am King Darius. Make sure you carry out my order.

The governor Tattenai carried out the order King Darius had sent. So did Shethar-Bozenai and their friends.

The elders of the Jews continued to build the temple. They enjoyed great success because of the preaching of the prophets Haggai and Zechariah. Zechariah belonged to the family line of Iddo.

The people finished building the temple. That's what the God of Israel had commanded them to do. Cyrus and Darius had given orders allowing them to do it. Later, Artaxerxes supplied many things that were needed in the temple. Those three men were kings of Persia.

So the temple was completed in the sixth year that Darius was king.

When the house of God was set apart, the people of Israel celebrated with joy. The priests and Levites joined them. So did the rest of those who had returned from Babylonia.

The priests were appointed to their companies. And the Levites were appointed to their groups. All of them served God at Jerusalem. They served him in keeping with what is written in the Scroll of Moses.

The Story of Nehemiah

Nehemiah 1—2; 6—10; Ezra 5—6

These are the words of Nehemiah.

I was in the safest place in Susa. I was there in the 20th year that Artaxerxes was king. It was in the month of Kislev. At that time Hanani came from Judah with some other men. He was one of my brothers. I asked him and the other men about the Jews who were left alive in Judah. They had returned from Babylonia. I also asked him about Jerusalem.

He and the men who were with him said to me, "Some of the people who returned are still alive. They are back in the land of Judah. But they are having a hard time. People are making fun of them. The wall of Jerusalem is broken down. Its gates have been burned with fire."

When I heard about those things, I sat down and sobbed. For several days I was very sad. I didn't eat any food. And I prayed to the God of heaven. I said,

"LORD, you are the God of heaven. You are a great and wonderful God. You keep the covenant you made with those who love you and obey your commands. You show them your love.

"Please pay careful attention to my prayer. See how your people are suffering. Please listen to me. I'm praying to you day and night. I'm praying for the people of Israel. We Israelites have committed sins against you. All of us admit it. I and my family have also sinned against you. We've done some very evil things. We haven't obeyed the commands, rules and laws you gave your servant Moses.

"Remember what you told him. You said, 'If you people are not faithful, I will scatter you among the nations. But if you return to me, I will bring you back. If you obey my commands, I will gather you together again. I will bring you back from the farthest places on earth. I will bring you to the special place where I have chosen to put my Name.'

"LORD, they are your people. They serve you. You used your great strength and mighty hand to set them free from Egypt. Lord, please pay careful attention to my prayer. Listen to the prayers of all of us. We take delight in bringing honor to your name. Give me success today. Help King Artaxerxes show me his favor."

I was the king's wine taster.

Artaxerxes Sends Nehemiah to Jerusalem

Wine was brought in for King Artaxerxes. It was the month of Nisan in the 20th year of his rule. I got the wine and gave it to him. I hadn't been sad in front of him before. But now I was. So the king asked me, "Why are you looking so sad? You aren't sick. You must be feeling sad deep down inside."

PEOPLE IN BIBLE TIMES

Wine Taster

The wine taster was a very important servant to a king in Bible times. It was an honor to fill the king's cup when he ate, and to taste the king's food and wine to be sure it was not poisoned. Ordinary people drank out of shallow clay cups, but kings drank out of cups made of gold and silver.

I was really afraid. But I said to the king, "May you live forever! Why shouldn't I look sad? The city where my people of long ago are buried has been destroyed. And fire has burned up its gates."

The king said to me, "What do you want?"

I prayed to the God of heaven. Then I answered the king, "Are you pleased with me, King Artaxerxes? If it pleases you, send me to Judah. Let me go to the city of Jerusalem. That's where my people are buried. I want to rebuild it."

The queen was sitting beside the king. He turned and asked me, "How long will your journey take? When will you get back?" It pleased the king to send me. So I chose a certain time.

I also said to him, "If it pleases you, may I take some letters with me? I want to give them to the governors of the land west of the Euphrates River. Then they'll help me travel safely through their territory until I arrive in Judah.

"May I also have a letter to Asaph? He takes care of your forest. I want him to give me some logs so I can make beams out of them. I want to use them for the gates of the fort that is by the temple. Some of the logs will be used in the city wall. And I'll need some for the house I'm going to live in." The gracious hand of my God helped me. So the king gave me what I asked for.

Fast, Silent Prayer

In Bible times, some kings would kill anyone who upset them. In this story, the king asked Nehemiah why he looked sad. Nehemiah was afraid that he had made the king upset. So what did Nehemiah do? He quickly prayed before he answered the king.

We don't know just what words Nehemiah prayed. But it must have been a fast, silent prayer. He answered the king's question right away.

Are there times when you might want to say a fast, silent prayer? If you get lost in a store, you might quickly pray, "God, help my mother find me." Can you think of other times when you might pray this way? God hears your fast, silent prayers just as well as your long ones.

Then I went to the governors of the land west of the Euphrates. I gave them the king's letters. He had also sent army officers and horsemen along with me.

Sanballat and Tobiah heard about what was happening. They were very upset that someone had come to work for the good of Israel's people. Sanballat was a Horonite. Tobiah was an official from Ammon.

Nehemiah Checks Out the Walls of Jerusalem

I went to Jerusalem. I stayed there for three days. Then at night I took a few men with me to check out the walls. I hadn't told anyone what my God wanted me to do for Jerusalem. There weren't any donkeys with me except the one I was riding on.

That night I went out through the Valley Gate. I went toward the Jackal Well and the Dung Gate. I checked out the walls of Jerusalem. They had been broken down. I also checked the city gates. Fire had burned them up. I moved on toward the Fountain Gate and the King's Pool. But there wasn't enough room for my donkey to get through. It was still night. I went up the Kidron Valley. I kept checking the wall. Finally, I turned back. I went back in through the Valley Gate.

The officials didn't know where I had gone. They didn't know what I had done either. That's because I hadn't said anything to anyone yet. I hadn't told the priests or nobles or officials. And I hadn't spoken to any others who would be rebuilding the wall.

I said to them, "You can see the trouble we're in. Jerusalem has been destroyed. Fire has burned up its gates. Come on. Let's rebuild the wall of Jerusalem. Then people won't make fun of us anymore." I also told them how the gracious hand of my God was helping me. And I told them what the king had said to me.

They replied, "Let's start rebuilding." So they began that good work.

The City Wall Is Completed

So the city wall was completed in 52 days. All of our enemies heard about it. All of the nations that were around us became afraid. They weren't sure of themselves anymore. They realized that our God had helped us finish the work.

In those days the nobles of Judah sent many letters to Tobiah. And replies from Tobiah came back to them. Tobiah's friends kept reporting to me the good things he did. They also kept telling him what I said. And Tobiah himself sent letters to scare me.

The wall had been rebuilt. I had put up the gates at the main entrances to the city. Those who guarded the gates were appointed to their positions. So were the singers and Levites. I put my brother Hanani in charge of Jerusalem. Hananiah helped him. Hananiah was commander of the fort that was by the temple. Hanani was an honest man. He had more respect for God than most people do.

I said to Hanani and Hananiah, "Don't open the gates of Jerusalem until the hottest time of the day. Tell the men who guard the gates to shut them before they go off duty. Make sure they lock them up tight. Also appoint as guards some people who live in Jerusalem. Station some of them at their appointed places. Station others near their own homes."

Jerusalem was large. It had a lot of room. But only a few people lived there. The houses hadn't been rebuilt yet. So my God stirred me up to gather the people together.

Ezra Reads the Law to the People

The people of Israel had settled down in their towns. In the seventh month, all of them gathered together. They went to the open area in front of the Water Gate. They told Ezra to bring out the Scroll of the Law of Moses. The LORD had given Israel that law so they would obey him. Ezra was a teacher of the law.

The priest Ezra brought the Law out to the whole community. It was the first day of the seventh month. The group was made up of men and women and everyone who was old enough to understand what Ezra was going to read.

DID YOU KNOW?

Why did Ezra have to tell the people what the law of God meant?

The Old Testament was written in Hebrew. God's people used to speak Hebrew. Now they spoke a new language. It was called Aramaic. The people did not understand the old Hebrew words. So Ezra had to tell them what the words meant.

He read the Law to them from sunrise until noon. He did it as he faced the open area in front of the Water Gate. He read it to the men, women and others who could understand. And all of the people paid careful attention as Ezra was reading the Scroll of the Law.

Ezra, the teacher, stood on a high wooden stage. It had been built for the occasion. Mattithiah, Shema and Anaiah stood at his right side. So did Uriah, Hilkiah and Maaseiah. Pedaiah, Mishael and Malkijah stood at his left side. So did Hashum, Hashbaddanah, Zechariah and Meshullam.

Ezra opened the scroll. All of the people could see him. That's because he was standing above them. As he opened the scroll, the people stood up. Ezra praised the LORD. He is the great God. All of the people lifted up their hands. They said, "Amen! Amen!" Then they bowed down. They turned their faces toward the ground. And they worshiped the LORD.

The Levites taught the Law to the people. They remained standing while the Levites taught them. The Levites who were there included Jeshua, Bani, Sherebiah, Jamin, Akkub, Shabbethai and Hodiah. They also included Maaseiah, Kelita, Azariah, Jozabad, Hanan and Pelaiah. All of those Levites read parts of the Scroll of the Law of God to the people. They made it clear to them. They told them what it meant. So the people were able to understand what was being read.

Then Nehemiah and Ezra spoke up. So did the Levites who were teaching the people. All of those men said to the people, "This day is set apart to honor the LORD your God. So don't sob. Don't be sad." All of the people had been sobbing as they listened to the words of the Law. Nehemiah was governor. Ezra was a priest and a teacher of the law.

Nehemiah said, "Go and enjoy some good food and sweet drinks.

Books

In Old Testament times, a book was a scroll. A strip of animal skin (called parchment) or paper (called papyrus) was rolled up on two sticks. One copy of the book of Isaiah, which was made 200 years before Jesus was born, is ten inches high and 24 feet long! It was about 100 years after Jesus was born that sheets of papyrus began to be stacked together into something like our books.

Send some of it to those who don't have any. This day is set apart to honor our Lord. So don't be sad. The joy of the LORD makes you strong."

The Levites calmed all of the people down. They said, "Be quiet. This is a sacred day. So don't be sad."

Then all of the people went away to eat and drink. They shared their food with others. They celebrated with great joy. Now they understood the words they had heard. That's because everything had been explained to them.

All of the family leaders gathered around Ezra, the teacher. So did the priests and Levites. All of them paid attention to the words of the Law. It was the second day of the month.

The LORD had given the Law through Moses. He wanted the people of Israel to obey it. It is written there that they were supposed to live in booths during the Feast of Booths. That Feast was celebrated in the seventh month. They were also supposed to spread the message all through their towns and in Jerusalem. They were supposed to announce, "Go out into the central hill country. Bring back some branches from olive and wild olive trees. Also bring some from myrtle, palm and shade trees. Use the branches to make booths."

So the people went out and brought some branches back. They built themselves booths on their own roofs. They made them in their courtyards. They put them up in the courtyards of the house of God. They

Celebration

The Jews celebrated the "Feast of Booths." They did something special to help them remember God's care for them. For seven days God's people lived in booths, or tents. They remembered how God had brought their families out of Egypt long ago. They remembered how the families had lived in tents in the desert.

Have you ever had a party to remember a special event? Maybe you could have your own Feast of Booths. Put up a tent in your yard. Spend some time inside of it. Think of how God has taken care of your family and has given you a home to live in. Even without a tent, you can still remember all of the good things God has given you.

built them in the open area in front of the Water Gate. And they built them in the open area in front of the Gate of Ephraim.

All those who had returned from Babylonia made booths. They lived in them during the Feast of Booths. They hadn't celebrated the Feast with so much joy for a long time. In fact, they had never celebrated it like that from the days of Joshua, the son of Nun, until that very day. So their joy was very great.

Day after day, Ezra read parts of the Scroll of the Law of God to them. He read it out loud from the first day to the last. They celebrated the Feast of Booths for seven days. On the eighth day they gathered together. They followed the required rules for celebrating the Feast.

The People of Israel Pray to the Lord

The people of Israel gathered together again. They stood and admitted they had sinned.

They listened while the Levites read parts of the Scroll of the Law of the Lord their God. They listened for a fourth of the day. They spent another fourth of the day admitting their sins.

The People Agree to Obey God's Law

[The people said,] "We are making a firm agreement. We're writing it down. Our leaders are stamping it with their seals. And so are our Levites and priests."

The people gathered together. They included the priests, the Levites and the men who guarded the gates. They included the

A "Do Good" Plan

Do you feel sorry when you do something wrong? The people of Judah had told God they were sorry for their sins. Then they promised God that they would do better. They even wrote down their promises.

God wants us to tell him we're sorry when we sin. He wants us to plan to do good.

How can you plan to do good? Say a prayer to God. Tell him you promise to try to please him. Think of three ways you can do good. Try to do them all this week!

singers and temple servants. They also included all those who separated themselves from the surrounding nations to obey the Law of God. All of those men brought their wives with them. And they brought all of their sons and daughters who were old enough to understand what was being agreed to. All of the men joined the nobles of their people. They made a firm agreement. They put themselves under a curse and took an oath. They promised to follow the Law of God. It had been given through Moses, the servant of God. They promised to obey carefully all of the commands, rules and laws of the LORD our Lord.

Esther Becomes Queen and Saves Her People

Esther 1—5; 7—9

Vashti Is Removed From Her Position as Queen

King Xerxes ruled over the 127 territories in his kingdom. They reached from India all the way to Cush. Here is what happened during the time Xerxes ruled over the whole Persian kingdom. He was ruling from his royal throne in the safest place in Susa.

In the third year of his rule King Xerxes gave a big dinner. It was for all of his nobles and officials. The military leaders of Persia and Media were there. So were the princes and the nobles of the territories he ruled over. Every day for 180 days he showed his guests the great wealth of his kingdom. He also showed them how glorious his kingdom was.

When those days were over, the king gave another big dinner. It lasted for seven days. It was held in the garden of the king's courtyard. It was for all of the people who lived in the safest place in Susa. Everyone from the least important person to the most important was invited.

The garden was decorated with white and blue linen banners. They hung from ropes that were made out of white linen and purple cloth. The ropes were connected to silver rings on marble pillars. There were gold and silver couches in the garden. They were placed on a floor that was made out of small stones. The floor had purple crystal, marble, mother-of-pearl and other stones of great value.

Royal wine was served in gold cups. Each cup was different from all of the others. There was plenty of wine. The king always provided as much as his guests wanted. He commanded that they should be allowed to drink as much or as little as they wished. He directed all of his servants to give them what they asked for.

Queen Vashti also gave a big dinner. Only women were invited. It was held in the royal palace of King Xerxes.

[The king told his attendants] to bring Queen Vashti to him. He wanted her to come wearing her royal crown. He wanted to show off her beauty to the people and nobles. She was lovely to look at.

The attendants told Queen Vashti what the king had ordered her to do. But she refused to come. So the king became very angry. In fact, he burned with anger.

Esther Becomes Queen of Persia

Later, the anger of King Xerxes calmed down. Then he remembered Vashti and what she had done. He also remembered the royal order he had sent out concerning her.

At that time the king's personal attendants made a suggestion. They said, "King Xerxes, let a search be made for some beautiful young virgins for you. Appoint some officials in every territory in your kingdom. Have them bring all of those beautiful virgins into the safest place in Susa. Put them in the special place where the virgins stay. Then put Hegai in charge of them. He's the eunuch who serves you. He's in charge of the virgins. Let beauty care be given to the new group of virgins. Then let the one who pleases you the most become queen in Vashti's place."

The king liked that advice. So he followed it.

There was a Jew living in the safest place in Susa. He was from the tribe of Benjamin. His name was Mordecai. He was the son of Jair. Jair was the son of Shimei. Shimei was the son of Kish. Nebuchadnezzar had forced Mordecai to leave Jerusalem. He was among the prisoners who were carried off along with Jehoiachin. Jehoiachin had been king of Judah. Nebuchadnezzar was king of Babylonia.

Mordecai had a cousin named Hadassah. He had brought her up in his own home. She didn't have a father or mother. Hadassah was also called Esther. She was very beautiful. Mordecai had adopted her as his own daughter. He had done it when her father and mother died.

After the king's order and law were announced, many virgins were brought to the safest place in Susa. Hegai was put in charge of them. Esther was also taken to the king's palace. She was put under the control of Hegai. He was in charge of the place where the virgins stayed.

Esther pleased him. He showed her his favor. Right away he provided her with her beauty care and special food. He appointed seven female attendants to help her. They were chosen from the king's palace. He moved her and her attendants into the best part of the place where the virgins stayed.

Esther hadn't told anyone who her people were. She hadn't talked about her family. That's because Mordecai had told her not to.

Mordecai tried to find out how Esther was getting along. He wanted to know what was happening to her. So he walked back and forth near the courtyard by the place where the virgins stayed. He did it every day.

Nobody Special

Do some of your friends run faster than you do? Or do they have more friends than you do? Do you feel like you aren't very special? Read about Esther.

Esther's parents had died. Her cousin raised her. Nothing seemed extra special about her. But when she grew up, the king chose her to be the new queen! God had a very special plan for her life, didn't he?

God has a plan for your life too. Jeremiah 29:11 says, "I know the plans I have for you. I want you to enjoy success. I do not plan to harm you. I will give you hope for the years to come." Remember this verse. Now you can never say that you aren't special.

Mordecai had adopted Esther. She had been the daughter of his uncle Abihail. Her turn came to go in to the king. She only asked for what Hegai suggested. He was the king's eunuch who was in charge of the place where the virgins stayed. Everyone who saw Esther was pleased with her. She was taken to King Xerxes in the royal house. It was now the tenth month. That was the month of Tebeth. It was the seventh year of the rule of Xerxes.

The king liked Esther more than he liked any of the other women. She pleased him more than any of the other virgins. So he put a royal crown on her head. He made her queen in Vashti's place.

Then the king gave a big dinner. It was in honor of Esther. All of his nobles and officials were invited. He announced a holiday all through the territories he ruled over. He freely gave many gifts in keeping with his royal wealth.

Haman Plans to Destroy the Jews

After those events, King Xerxes honored Haman. Haman was the son of Hammedatha. He was from the family line of Agag. The king gave Haman a higher position than he had before. He gave him a seat of honor. It was higher than the positions any of the other nobles had. All of the royal officials at the palace gate got down on their knees. They gave honor to Haman. That's because the king had commanded them to do it.

But Mordecai refused to get down on his knees. He wouldn't give Haman any honor at all.

The royal officials at the palace gate asked Mordecai a question. They said, "Why don't you obey the king's command?" Day after day they spoke to him. But he still refused to obey. So they told Haman about it. They wanted to see whether he would let Mordecai get away with what he was doing. Mordecai had told them he was a Jew.

Haman noticed that Mordecai wouldn't get down on his knees. He wouldn't give Haman any honor. So Haman burned with anger. But he had found out who Mordecai's people were. So he decided not to kill just Mordecai. He also looked for a way to destroy all of Mordecai's people. They were Jews. He wanted to kill all of them everywhere in the kingdom of Xerxes.

The lot was cast in front of Haman. That was done to choose a day and a month. It was the 12th year that Xerxes was king. It was in the first month. The lot chose the 12th month. The lot was also called *pur*.

Then Haman said to King Xerxes, "Certain people are scattered among the nations. They live in all of the territories in your kingdom. Their practices are different from the practices of all other people. They don't obey your laws. It really isn't good for you to put up with them.

"If it pleases you, give the order to destroy them. I'll even add 375 tons of silver to the royal treasures. You can use it to pay the men who take care of the matter."

What does it mean to "cast lots"?

People used to cast lots to learn what would happen in the future. This was something like flipping a coin. We're not sure how they did this. But Haman cast lots to find a good day to ask the king to destroy God's people.

So the king took his ring off his finger. The ring had his royal seal on it. He gave the ring to Haman. Haman was the son of Hammedatha, the Agagite. He was the enemy of the Jews.

"Keep the money," the king said to Haman. "Do what you want to with those people."

Mordecai Talks Esther Into Helping the Jews

Mordecai found out about everything that had been done. So he tore his clothes. He put on black clothes. He sat down in ashes. Then he went out into the city. He sobbed out loud. He cried bitter tears. But he only went as far as the palace gate. That's because no one who was dressed in black clothes was allowed to go through it.

All of the Jews were very sad. They didn't eat anything. They sobbed and cried. Many of them put on black clothes. They were lying down in ashes. They did all of those things in every territory where the king's order and law had been sent.

Esther's eunuchs and female attendants came to her. They told her about Mordecai. So she became very troubled.

Mordecai told [Esther's servant] to show the order to Esther. He told him to try and get her to go to the king. He wanted her to beg for mercy.

Then Esther sent a reply to Mordecai. She said, "Go. Gather together all of the Jews who are in Susa. And fast for my benefit. Don't eat or drink

WORDS TO TREASURE

I'll go to the king. I'll do it even though it's against the law. And if I have to die, I'll die.

Esther 4:16

anything for three days. Don't do it night or day. I and my attendants will fast just as you do. Then I'll go to the king. I'll do it even though it's against the law. And if I have to die, I'll die."

So Mordecai went away. He carried out all of Esther's directions.

Esther Invites the King and Haman to a Big Dinner

On the third day Esther put her royal robes on. She stood in the inner courtyard of the palace. It was in front of the king's hall.

The king was sitting on his royal throne in the hall. He was facing the entrance. He saw Queen Esther standing in the courtyard. He was pleased with her. So he reached out toward her the gold rod that was in his hand. Then Esther approached him. She touched the tip of the rod.

The king asked, "What is it, Queen Esther? What do you want? I'll give it to you. I'll even give you up to half of my kingdom."

Esther replied, "King Xerxes, if it pleases you, come to a big dinner today. I've prepared it for you. Please have Haman come with you."

"Bring Haman at once," the king said to his servants. "Then we'll do what Esther asks."

So the king and Haman went to the big dinner Esther had prepared. As they were drinking wine, the king asked Esther the same question again. He said, "What do you want? I'll give it to you. What do you want me to do for you? I'll even give you up to half of my kingdom."

Esther replied, "Here is what I want. Here is my appeal to you. I hope you will show me your favor. I hope you will be pleased to give me what I want. And I hope you will be pleased to listen to my appeal. If you are, I'd like you and Haman to come tomorrow to the big dinner I'll prepare for you. Then I'll answer your question."

Haman Is Put to Death

So the king and Haman went to dine with Queen Esther. They were drinking wine on the second day. The king again asked, "What do you want, Queen Esther? I'll give it to you. What do you want me to do for you? I'll even give you up to half of my kingdom."

Then Queen Esther answered, "King Xerxes, I hope you will show me your favor. I hope you will be pleased to let me live. That's what I want. Please spare my people. That's my appeal to you.

"My people and I have been sold to be destroyed. We've been sold to be killed and wiped out. Suppose we had only been sold as male and female slaves. Then I wouldn't have said anything. That kind of suffering wouldn't be a good enough reason to bother you."

King Xerxes asked Queen Esther, "Who is the man who has dared to do such a thing? And where is he?"

Esther said, "The man hates us! He's our enemy! He's this evil Haman!"

Then Haman was terrified in front of the king and queen.

The king got up. He was burning with anger. He left his wine and went out into the palace garden.

But Haman realized that the king had already decided what he was going to do to him.

Then Harbona said, "There's a pole standing near Haman's house. He has gotten it ready for Mordecai. Mordecai is the one who spoke up to help you. Haman had planned to have him put to death. He was going to have the pole stuck through his body. Then he was going to set it up at a place where it would be 75 feet above the ground." Harbona was one of the officials who attended the king.

The king said to his men, "Put Haman to death! Stick the pole through his body! Set it up where everyone can see it!" So they did. And they used the pole Haman had gotten ready for Mordecai. Then the king's anger calmed down.

The King Allows the Jews to Fight for Their Lives

That same day King Xerxes gave Queen Esther everything Haman had owned. Haman had been the enemy of the Jews.

Esther had told the king that Mordecai was her cousin. So Mordecai came to see the king. The king took his ring off. It had his royal seal on it. He had taken it back from Haman. Now he gave it to Mordecai. And Esther put Mordecai in charge of everything Haman had owned.

Esther made another appeal to the king. She fell at his feet and sobbed. She begged him to put an end to the evil plan of Haman, the Agagite. He had decided to kill the Jews.

The king reached out his gold rod toward Esther. She got up and stood in front of him.

"King Xerxes, I hope you will show me your favor," she said. "I hope you will think that what I'm asking is the right thing to do. I hope you are pleased with me. If you are, and if it pleases you, let an order be written. Let it take the place of the messages Haman wrote. Haman was the son of Hammedatha, the Agagite. He planned to kill the Jews. He wrote orders to destroy us in all of your territories. I couldn't stand by and see the horrible trouble that would fall on my people! I couldn't stand to see my family destroyed!"

Right away the king [wrote the order.] The Jews in every city could now gather together and fight for their lives. The king's order gave them that right. But what if soldiers from any nation or territory attacked them? What if they attacked their women and children? Then the Jews could destroy, kill and wipe out those soldiers. They could also take the goods that belonged to their enemies. A day was appointed for the Jews to do that in all of the king's territories. It was the 13th day of the 12th month. That was the month of Adar.

A copy of the order was sent out as law in every territory. It was announced to the people of every nation. So the Jews would be ready on that day. They could pay their enemies back.

The King's Signet Ring

People in Bible times did not sign important papers. Instead they pressed their signet ring into a bit of clay that was pressed onto papers that had been tied together. When the king gave Mordecai his signet ring, it meant Mordecai could write any orders he wanted in the king's name.

The king's order had to be carried out on the 13th day of the 12th month. That was the month of Adar. On that day the enemies of the Jews had hoped to win the battle over them. But now everything had changed. The Jews had gained the advantage over those who hated them.

The Jews gathered together in their cities. They gathered in all of the territories King Xerxes ruled over. They came together to attack those who were trying to destroy them. No one could stand up against them. The people from all of the other nations were afraid of them.

A report was brought to the king that same day. He was told how many men had been killed in the safest place in Susa. He said to Queen Esther, "The Jews have killed 500 men. They destroyed them in the safest place in Susa. They also killed the ten sons of Haman there. What have they done in the rest of my territories? Now what do you want? I'll give it to you. What do you want me to do for you? I'll do that too."

"If it pleases you," Esther answered, "let the Jews in Susa carry out today's order tomorrow also. Stick poles through the dead bodies of Haman's ten sons. Set them up where everyone can see them."

So the king commanded that it be done. An order was sent out in Susa. And the king's men did to the bodies of Haman's sons everything they were told to do. The Jews in Susa came together on the 14th day of the month of Adar. They put 300 men to death in Susa. But they didn't take anything that belonged to those men.

During that time, the rest of the Jews also gathered together. They lived in the king's territories. They came together to fight for their lives. They didn't want their enemies to bother them anymore. They wanted to get some peace and rest. So they killed 75,000 of their enemies. But they didn't take anything that belonged to them. It happened on the 13th of Adar. On the 14th day they rested. They made it a day to celebrate with great joy. And they enjoyed good food.

The Books of Poetry

Job   Psalms

Ecclesiastes   Song of Songs   Proverbs

The books of poetry are found in the middle of the Old Testament of the Bible. These books were written by wise men. The writers were thinking out loud about God and about life. The writers were writing down what they felt about God. The books of poetry will not give you facts. The books of poetry will help you say what you feel about God. They will help you talk to God.

The book of Job is very old. It asks questions about God and about life. Why do people suffer? Where is God when bad things happen? The psalms are songs written to praise God. The writers tell God how they feel. King David wrote many of these songs. The book of Proverbs is a book of wise sayings. They teach us how to live in ways that please God. King Solomon wrote most of the proverbs. Many people think that Solomon wrote Ecclesiastes and the Song of Songs too.

The Story of Job

Job 1—5; 8; 11; 27; 38; 40; 42

The Story Begins

There was a man who lived in the land of Uz. His name was Job. He was honest. He did what was right. He had respect for God and avoided evil.

Job had seven sons and three daughters. He owned 7,000 sheep and 3,000 camels. He owned 500 pairs of oxen and 500 donkeys. He also had a large number of servants. He was the most important man among all of the people in the east.

His sons used to take turns giving big dinners in their homes. They would invite their three sisters to eat and drink with them.

When the time for enjoying good food was over, Job would have his children made pure and clean. He would sacrifice a burnt offering for each of them. He would do it early in the morning. He would think, "Perhaps my children have sinned. Maybe they have spoken evil things against God in their hearts."

That's what Job always did for his children when he felt they had sinned.

Job Is Put to the Test

One day angels came to the LORD. Satan also came with them. The LORD said to Satan, "Where have you come from?"

Satan answered, "From traveling all around the earth. I've been going from one end of it to the other."

Then the LORD said to Satan, "Have you thought about my servant Job? There isn't anyone on earth like him. He is honest. He does what is right. He has respect for me and avoids evil."

"You always give Job everything he needs," Satan replied. "That's why he has respect for you. Haven't you guarded him and his family? Haven't you taken care of everything he has? You have blessed everything he does. His flocks and herds are spread all through the land.

"But reach out your hand and strike down everything he has. Then I'm sure he will speak evil things against you. In fact, he'll do it right in front of you."

The LORD said to Satan, "All right. I am handing everything he has over to you. But do not touch the man himself."

Then Satan left the LORD and went on his way.

One day Job's sons and daughters were at their oldest brother's house. They were enjoying good food and drinking wine.

During that time a messenger came to Job. He said, "The oxen were plowing. The donkeys were eating grass near them. Then the Sabeans attacked us and carried the animals off. They killed some of the servants with their swords. I'm the only one who has escaped to tell you!"

While he was still speaking, a second messenger came. He said, "God sent lightning from the sky. It struck the sheep and killed them. It burned up some of the servants. I'm the only one who has escaped to tell you!"

While he was still speaking, a third messenger came. He said, "The Chaldeans separated themselves into three groups. They attacked your camels and carried them off. They killed the rest of the servants with their swords. I'm the only one who has escaped to tell you!"

While he was still speaking, a fourth messenger came. He said, "Your sons and daughters were at their oldest brother's house. They were enjoying good food and drinking wine. Suddenly a strong wind blew in from the desert. It struck the four corners of the house. The house fell down on your children. Now all of them are dead. I'm the only one who has escaped to tell you!"

After Job heard all of those reports, he got up and tore his robe. He shaved his head. Then he fell to the ground and worshiped the LORD. He said,

Bad Things Happen to Good People

Sometimes bad things happen to good people. Job was a very good person. Even so, some terrible things happened to him.

How do you feel when bad things happen to you—like getting sick and having to stay in bed all day?

Don't think of it as a punishment from God. It's not. We just don't live in a perfect world. But God does have wonderful blessings planned for you!

"I was born naked.
    And I'll leave here naked.
You have given, and you have taken away.
    May your name be praised."

In spite of everything, Job didn't sin by blaming God for doing anything wrong.

Job Is Put to the Test Again

On another day angels came to the LORD. Satan also came to him along with them. The LORD said to Satan, "Where have you come from?"

Satan answered, "From traveling all around the earth. I've been going from one end of it to the other."

Then the LORD said to Satan, "Have you thought about my servant Job? There isn't anyone on earth like him. He is honest. He does what is right. He has respect for me and avoids evil. You tried to turn me against him. You wanted me to destroy him without any reason. But he still continues to be faithful."

Satan replied, "A man will give everything he has to save himself. So Job is willing to give up the lives of his family to save his own life.

"But reach out your hand and strike his flesh and bones. Then I'm sure he will speak evil things against you. In fact, he'll do it right in front of you."

The LORD said to Satan, "All right. I am handing him over to you. But you must spare his life."

Then Satan left the LORD and went on his way. He sent painful sores on Job. They covered him from the bottom of his feet to the top of his head. He got part of a broken pot. He used it to scrape his skin. He did it while he was sitting in ashes.

His wife said to him, "Are you still continuing to be faithful to the LORD? Speak evil things against him and die!"

We accept good things from God. So we should also accept trouble when he sends it.
Job 2:10

Job replied, "You are talking like a foolish woman. We accept good things from God. So we should also accept trouble when he sends it."

In spite of everything, Job didn't say anything that was sinful.

Job's Three Friends Come to Comfort Him

Job had three friends named Eliphaz the Temanite, Bildad the Shuhite, and Zophar the Naamathite. They heard about all of the troubles that had come to Job. So they started out from their homes. They had agreed to meet together. They wanted to go and show their concern for Job. They wanted to comfort him.

When they got closer to where he lived, they could see him. But they could hardly recognize him. They began to sob out loud. They tore their robes and sprinkled dust on their heads.

Then they sat down on the ground with him for seven days and seven nights. No one said a word to him. That's because they saw how much he was suffering.

Job Wishes He Had Never Been Born

After a while, Job opened his mouth to speak. He called down a curse on the day he had been born.

Then Eliphaz the Temanite replied,

How sad did Job feel?

So many terrible things had happened to Job. He was so sad that he said he wished he had never been born.

Showing Sadness

In Bible times, people showed their sadness so everyone could see how bad they felt. When something sad happened to them or to someone they loved, they would often cry loudly, tear their clothing, sit on the bare ground, and sprinkle dust or ashes on their heads. Job's friends were very upset because of all that had happened to him. For seven days and nights they showed their grief in all of these ways.

"Blessed is the person God corrects.
So don't hate the Mighty One's training.
He wounds. But he also bandages up those he wounds.
He harms. But his hands also heal those he harms."

The First Speech of Bildad

Then Bildad the Shuhite said,

"Job, how long will you talk like that?
Your words don't have any
meaning.
Does God ever treat people unfairly?
Does the Mighty One make what
is wrong
appear to be right?
Your children sinned against him.
So he punished them for their sin.
But look to God.
Make your appeal to the Mighty One.
Be pure and honest.
And he will rise up and help you now.
He'll return you to the place where you belong.
In the past, things went well with you.
But in days to come, things will get even better."

DID YOU KNOW?

What happens to people who forget God?

People who forget God are like plants without water. They die. People who forget God have no hope.

The First Speech of Zophar

Then Zophar the Naamathite [said to Job,]

"Don't all of your words require an answer?
I'm sure that what you are saying can't be right.
Your useless talk won't keep us quiet.
Someone has to correct you when you make fun of truth.
You say to God, 'My beliefs are perfect.
I'm pure in your sight.'
I wish God would speak.
I wish he'd answer you.

I wish he'd show you the secrets of wisdom.
    After all, true wisdom has two sides.
Here's what I want you to know.
    God has forgotten some of your sins.

"So commit yourself to God completely.
    Reach out your hands to him for help.
Get rid of all of the sin you have."

Job's Reply

Job replied,

"God hasn't treated me fairly.
    The Mighty One has made my spirit bitter.
You can be sure that God lives.
    And here's something else you can be sure of.
As long as I have life
    and God gives me breath,
my mouth won't say evil things.
    My lips won't tell lies.
I'll never admit you people are right.
    Until I die, I'll say I'm telling the truth.
I'll continue to say I'm right.
    I'll never let go of that.
    I won't blame myself as long as I live."

The First Speech of the Lord

The Lord spoke to Job out of a storm. He said,

"Who do you think you are to disagree with my plans?
    You do not know what you are talking about.
Get ready to stand up for yourself.
    I will ask you some questions.
    Then I want you to answer me.

"Where were you when I laid the earth's foundation?
    Tell me, if you know.
Who measured it? I am sure you know!
    Who stretched a measuring line across it?

What was it built on?
    Who laid its most important stone?
When it happened, the morning stars sang together.
    All of the angels shouted with joy."

The LORD continued,

"I am the Mighty One.
    Will the man who argues with me correct me?
    Let him who brings charges against me answer me!"

Job's Reply

Job replied to the LORD,

"I'm not worthy. How can I reply to you?
    I'm putting my hand over my mouth. I'll stop talking.
I spoke once. But I really don't have any answer.
    I spoke twice. But I won't say anything else."

The Second Speech of the LORD

Then the LORD spoke to Job out of the storm. He said,

"Get ready to stand up for yourself.
    I will ask you some more questions.
    Then I want you to answer me.

"Would you dare to claim that I am
            not being fair?
    Would you judge me in order to
            make yourself seem right?
Is your arm as powerful as mine is?"

Job replied to the LORD,

"I know that you can do anything.
    No one can keep you from doing
            what you plan to do.
You asked me, 'Who do you think you
            are to disagree with my
            plans?

What did God say to Job?

God told Job to think hard. God said that Job didn't know how great God is. Job didn't even understand the things God does in nature. So how could Job understand what God was doing in his life?

You do not know what you are talking about.'
I spoke about things I didn't completely understand.
    I talked about things that were too wonderful for me to know.

"You said, 'Listen now, and I will speak.
    I will ask you some questions.
    Then I want you to answer me.'
My ears had heard about you.
    But now my own eyes have seen you.
So I hate myself.
    I'm really sorry for what I said about you.
    That's why I'm sitting in dust and ashes."

The Story Ends

After the LORD finished speaking to Job, he spoke to Eliphaz the Temanite. He said, "I am angry with you and your two friends. You have not said what is true about me, as my servant Job has.

"So now get seven bulls and seven rams. Go to my servant Job. Then sacrifice a burnt offering for yourselves. My servant Job will pray for you. And I will accept his prayer. I will not punish you for saying the foolish things you said. You have not said what is true about me, as my servant Job has."

So Eliphaz the Temanite, Bildad the Shuhite, and Zophar the Naamathite did what the LORD told them to do. And the LORD accepted Job's prayer.

After Job had prayed for his friends, the LORD made him successful again. He gave him twice as much as he had before. All of his brothers and sisters and everyone who had known him before came to see him. They ate with him in his house. They showed their concern for him. They comforted him because of all of the troubles the LORD had brought on him. Each one gave him a piece of silver and a gold ring.

DID YOU KNOW?

What happened to Job?

God healed Job. God gave Job a lot of money and success. He also gave Job a new family. Job had tried hard to understand God. Job had tried to be honest with God. God was pleased with Job.

The LORD blessed the last part of Job's life even more than the first part. He gave Job 14,000 sheep and 6,000 camels. He gave him 1,000 pairs of oxen and 1,000 donkeys.

Job also had seven sons and three daughters. He named the first daughter Jemimah. He named the second Keziah. And he named the third Keren-Happuch. Job's daughters were more beautiful than any other women in the whole land. Their father gave them a share of property along with their brothers.

After all of that happened, Job lived for 140 years. He saw his children, his grandchildren and his great-grandchildren. And so he died. He had lived for a very long time.

Praises and Singing

Psalms 47, 81, 92, 96, 100, 113, 136, 150

Psalm 47

For the director of music. A psalm of the Sons of Korah.

Clap your hands, all you nations.
    Shout to God with cries of joy.
How wonderful is the LORD Most High!
    He is the great King over the whole earth.
He brought nations under our control.
    He made them fall under us.
He chose our land for us.
    The people of Jacob are proud of their land,
    and God loves them.   *Selah*

God went up to his throne while his
    people were shouting with joy.
    The LORD went up while trumpets were playing.
Sing praises to God. Sing praises.
    Sing praises to our King. Sing praises.

God is the King of the whole earth.

Sing a psalm of praise to him.
God rules over the nations.
He is seated on his holy throne.
The nobles of the nations come together.
They are now part of the people of the God of Abraham.
The kings of the earth belong to God.
He is greatly honored.

Psalm 81

For the director of music. For *gittith*.
A psalm of Asaph.

Sing joyfully to God! He gives us strength.
Give a loud shout to the God of Jacob!
Let the music begin. Play the tambourines.
Play sweet music on harps and lyres.

Blow the ram's horn on the day of the New Moon Feast.
Blow it again when the moon is full and the Feast of Booths begins.
This is an order given to Israel.
It is a law of the God of Jacob.
He gave it as a covenant law for the people of Joseph
when God went out to punish Egypt.
There we heard language we didn't understand.

God said, "I removed the load from your shoulders.
I set your hands free from carrying heavy baskets.
You called out when you were in trouble, and I saved you.
I answered you out of a thundercloud.
I put you to the test at the waters of Meribah.   *Selah*

"My people, listen and I will warn you.
Israel, I wish you would listen to me!
Don't have anything to do with the gods of other nations.
Don't bow down and worship strange gods.

I am the LORD your God.
> I brought you up out of Egypt.
> Open your mouth wide, and I will fill it with good things.

Psalm 92

A psalm. A song for the Sabbath day.

LORD, it is good to praise you.
> Most High God, it is good to make
> > music to honor you.

It is good to sing every morning about your love.
> It is good to sing every night about
> > how faithful you are.

I sing about it to the music of the lyre
> > that has ten strings.
> I sing about it to the music of the
> > harp.

LORD, you make me glad by what you
> > have done.
> I sing with joy about the works of
> > your hands.

LORD, how great are the things you do!
> How wise your thoughts are!

WORDS TO TREASURE

LORD, it is good to praise you.
Most High God, it is good to
make music to honor you.
Psalm 92:1

Here is something a man who isn't wise doesn't know.
> Here is what a foolish person doesn't understand.

Those who are evil spring up like grass.
> Those who do wrong succeed.
> But they will be destroyed forever.

But LORD, you are honored forever.

LORD, your enemies will certainly die.
> All those who do evil will be scattered.

You have made me as strong as a wild ox.
> You have poured the finest olive oil on me.

I've seen my evil enemies destroyed.
> I've heard that they have lost the battle.

Those who do what is right will grow like a palm tree.

They will grow strong like a cedar tree in Lebanon.

Their roots will be firm in the house of the LORD.

They will grow strong and healthy in the courtyards of our
God.

When they get old, they will still bear fruit.

Like young trees they will stay fresh and strong.

They will say to everyone, "The LORD is honest.

He is my Rock. There is no evil in him."

Psalm 96

Sing a new song to the LORD.

All you people of the earth, sing to the LORD.

Sing to the LORD. Praise him.

Day after day tell about how he saves us.

Tell the nations about his glory.

Tell all people about the wonderful things he has done.

The LORD is great. He is really worthy of praise.

People should have respect for him as the greatest God of all.

All of the gods of the nations are like their statues.

They can't do anything.

But the LORD made the heavens.

Glory and majesty are all around him.

Strength and glory can be seen in his temple.

Praise the LORD, all you nations.

Praise the LORD for his glory and strength.

Praise the LORD for the glory that belongs to him.

Bring an offering and come into the courtyards of his temple.

Worship the LORD because of his beauty and holiness.

All you people of the earth, tremble when you are with him.

Say to the nations, "The LORD rules."

The world is firmly set in place. It can't be moved.

The LORD will judge the people of the world fairly.

Let the heavens be full of joy. Let the earth be glad.

Let the ocean and everything in it roar.

Let the fields and everything in them be glad.
Then all of the trees in the forest will sing with joy.
    They will sing to the LORD,
        because he is coming to judge the earth.
He will judge the people of the world
        in keeping with what is right and true.

Psalm 100

A psalm for giving thanks.

Shout to the LORD with joy, everyone on
                earth.
    Worship the LORD with gladness.
    Come to him with songs of joy.
I want you to realize that the LORD is God.
    He made us, and we belong to him.
We are his people.
    We are the sheep belonging to his
        flock.

Give thanks as you enter the gates of
        his temple.
    Give praise as you enter its
        courtyards.
    Give thanks to him and praise his name.
The LORD is good. His faithful love continues forever.
    It will last for all time to come.

Shout to the LORD with joy,
everyone on earth. Worship
the LORD with gladness. Come
to him with songs of joy.
Psalm 100:1–2

Psalm 113

Praise the LORD.

Praise him, you who serve the LORD.
    Praise the name of the LORD.
Let us praise the name of the LORD,
    both now and forever.
From the sunrise in the east to the sunset in the west,
    may the name of the LORD be praised.

The LORD is honored over all of the nations.
His glory reaches to the highest heavens.
Who is like the LORD our God?
He sits on his throne in heaven.
He bends down to look
at the heavens and the earth.

He raises poor people up from the trash pile.
He lifts needy people out of the ashes.
He lets them sit with princes.
He lets them sit with the princes of their own people.
He gives children to the woman who doesn't have any children.
He makes her a happy mother in her own home.

Praise the LORD.

Psalm 136

Give thanks to the LORD, because he is good.
His faithful love continues forever.
Give thanks to the greatest God of all.
His faithful love continues forever.
Give thanks to the most powerful Lord of all.
His faithful love continues forever.

Give thanks to the only one who can do great miracles.
His faithful love continues forever.
By his understanding he made the heavens.
His faithful love continues forever.

He spread out the earth on the waters.
His faithful love continues forever.
He made the great lights in the sky.
His faithful love continues forever.
He made the sun to rule over the day.
His faithful love continues forever.
He made the moon and stars to rule over the night.
His faithful love continues forever.

Give thanks to the One who killed the oldest son of each family
in Egypt.
His faithful love continues forever.
He brought the people of Israel out of Egypt.
His faithful love continues forever.
He did it by reaching out his mighty hand and powerful arm.
His faithful love continues forever.

Give thanks to the One who parted the Red Sea.
His faithful love continues forever.
He brought Israel through the middle of it.
His faithful love continues forever.
But he swept Pharaoh and his army into the Red Sea.
His faithful love continues forever.

Give thanks to the One who led his people through the desert.
His faithful love continues forever.
He killed great kings.
His faithful love continues forever.
He struck down mighty kings.
His faithful love continues forever.
He killed Sihon, the king of the Amorites.
His faithful love continues forever.
He killed Og, the king of Bashan.
His faithful love continues forever.
He gave their land as a gift.
His faithful love continues forever.
He gave it as a gift to his servant Israel.
His faithful love continues forever.

Give thanks to the One who remembered us when things were
    going badly for us.

                His faithful love continues forever.

He set us free from our enemies.

                His faithful love continues forever.

He gives food to every creature.

                His faithful love continues forever.

Give thanks to the God of heaven.

                His faithful love continues forever.

Psalm 150

Praise the LORD.

Praise God in his holy temple.
    Praise him in his mighty heavens.
Praise him for his powerful acts.
    Praise him because he is greater than anything else.
Praise him by blowing trumpets.
    Praise him with harps and lyres.
Praise him with tambourines and dancing.
    Praise him with stringed instruments and flutes.
Praise him with clashing cymbals.
    Praise him with clanging cymbals.

Let everything that has breath praise the LORD.

Praise the LORD.

Nature

Psalms 8, 19, 93

Psalm 8

For the director of music. For *gittith*. A psalm of David.

LORD, our Lord,
    how majestic is your name in the whole earth!

You have made your glory
　　higher than the heavens.
You have made sure that children
　　and infants praise you.
You have done it because of your
　　enemies.
　　　You have done it to put a stop to
　　　their talk.

I think about the heavens.
　　I think about what your fingers
　　have created.
I think about the moon and stars
　　that you have set in place.
What is a human being that you think about him?
　　What is a son of man that you take care of him?
You made him a little lower than the heavenly beings.
　　You placed on him a crown of glory and honor.

You made human beings the rulers over all that your hands
　　　have created.
　　You put everything under their control.
They rule over all flocks and herds
　　and over the wild animals.
They rule over the birds of the air
　　and over the fish in the ocean.

Look at the Heavens

As a boy, David cared for his father's sheep. Many nights he stayed outside all night. He watched the moon and stars. They made him think about God. He wrote songs about his thoughts.

On some clear night, go outside and look at the stars. Without a telescope you can see just over 1,000 stars. But with today's big telescopes you can see millions of stars! As you look at the stars, think about how great God is.

They rule over everything that swims in the oceans.

LORD, our Lord,
how majestic is your name in the whole earth!

Psalm 19

For the director of music. A psalm of David.

The heavens tell about the glory of God.
The skies show that his hands created them.
Day after day they speak about it.
Night after night they make it known.
But they don't speak or use words.
No sound is heard from them.
At the same time, their voice goes out into the whole earth.
Their words go out from one end of the world to the other.

God has set up a tent in the heavens for the sun.
The sun is like a groom coming out of the room where he
spent his wedding night.
The sun is like a great runner who takes delight in running
a race.
It rises at one end of the heavens.
Then it moves across to the other end.
Nothing can hide from its heat.

The law of the LORD is perfect.
It gives us new strength.
The laws of the LORD can be trusted.
They make childish people wise.
The rules of the LORD are right.
They give joy to our hearts.
The commands of the LORD shine brightly.
They give light to our minds.
The law that brings respect for the LORD is pure.
It lasts forever.
The directions the LORD gives are true.
All of them are completely right.
They are more priceless than gold.

In Control

Did you ever watch a sunset and think about who made it? God did, of course! He makes sure the sun rises and sets every day. He placed the earth just far enough from the sun so it could give us light and warmth. He makes the earth turn so that the light and warmth can reach everywhere.

Cut a round circle in the center of a piece of blue paper. Over the hole, tape a piece of yellow tissue paper. Hang the paper in your bedroom window. When the sun shines through the hole, remember that God is in control. He cares about the sun. He cares about you too.

They have greater value than huge amounts of pure gold.
They are sweeter than honey
    that is taken from the honeycomb.
I am warned by them.
    When I obey them, I am greatly rewarded.

Can I know my mistakes?
    Forgive my hidden faults.
Keep me also from the sins I want to commit.
    May they not be my master.
Then I will be without blame.
    I will not be guilty of any great sin against your law.

LORD, may the words of my mouth and the thoughts of my heart
    be pleasing in your eyes.
    You are my Rock and my Redeemer.

Psalm 93

The LORD rules.
    He puts on majesty as if it were clothes.
    The LORD puts on majesty and strength.
The world is firmly set in place.
    It can't be moved.
LORD, you began to rule a long time ago.

You have always existed.

Lord, the seas have lifted up their voice.
　　They have lifted up their pounding waves.
But Lord, you are more powerful than the roar of the ocean.
　　You are stronger than the waves of the sea.
　　Lord, you are powerful in heaven.

Your laws do not change.
　　Lord, your temple will be holy
　　for all time to come.

God Is My Teacher and Guide

Psalms 1, 23, 37, 101, 119, 128, 145

Psalm 1

Blessed is the one who obeys the law of the Lord.
　　He doesn't follow the advice of evil people.
　　　　　　He doesn't make a habit of doing what
　　　　　　　　sinners do.
　　　　　　He doesn't join those who make fun
　　　　　　　　of the Lord and his law.
　　　　　　Instead, he takes delight in the law of
　　　　　　　　the Lord.
　　　　　　He thinks about his law day and night.
　　　　　He is like a tree that is planted near a
　　　　　　　stream of water.
　　　　　　It always bears its fruit at the right
　　　　　　　　time.
　　　　Its leaves don't dry up.
　　　　　　Everything godly people do turns
　　　　　　　out well.

Sinful people are not like that at all.
　　They are like straw
　　that the wind blows away.

WORDS TO TREASURE

Blessed is the one who obeys the law of the Lord. He doesn't follow the advice of evil people. He doesn't make a habit of doing what sinners do. He doesn't join those who make fun of the Lord and his law.

Psalm 1:1

When the LORD judges them, their life will come to an end.
    Sinners won't have any place among those who are godly.

The LORD watches over the lives of those who are godly.
    But the lives of sinful people will lead to their death.

Psalm 23

A psalm of David.

The LORD is my shepherd. He gives me everything I need.
    He lets me lie down in fields of green grass.
He leads me beside quiet waters.
    He gives me new strength.
He guides me in the right paths
    for the honor of his name.
Even though I walk
    through the darkest valley,
I will not be afraid.
    You are with me.
Your shepherd's rod and staff
    comfort me.

You prepare a feast for me
    right in front of my enemies.
You pour oil on my head.

What God Is Like

Psalm 23 says that God is like a shepherd. A shepherd loves and cares for his sheep. He watches them closely, protects them from danger, and makes sure they have enough to eat and drink. To say that God is our shepherd means that he watches over us and will show us what is best for us.

God Is My Shepherd

A shepherd is someone who takes care of sheep. He watches over them. He makes sure they get food and water. He makes sure no harm comes to them. If even one gets lost, he looks until he finds it.

God is like a shepherd. There is not a minute that he does not watch over you. He makes sure you have everything you need. Nothing happens to you that he does not see.

Make a Psalm 23 picture. On a large poster board glue strips of green paper for grass. Use aluminum foil for the quiet water and cotton balls for sheep. Draw a shepherd and glue a twig in his hand for a shepherd's staff. Ask where you can hang your poster so that the whole family is reminded of God's care.

My cup runs over.
I am sure that your goodness and love will follow me
    all the days of my life.
And I will live in the house of the LORD
    forever.

Psalm 37

A psalm of David.

Don't be upset because of sinful people.
    Don't be jealous of those who do wrong.
Like grass, they will soon dry up.
    Like green plants, they will soon die.

Trust in the LORD and do good.
    Then you will live in the land and enjoy its food.
Find your delight in the LORD.
    Then he will give you everything your heart really wants.

Commit your life to the LORD.
    Here is what he will do if you trust in him.
He will make your godly ways shine like the dawn.

He will make your honest life shine like the sun at noon.

Be still. Be patient. Wait for the LORD to
     act.
  Don't be upset when other people
     succeed.
  Don't be upset when they carry out
     their evil plans.

Keep from being angry. Turn away
     from anger.
  Don't be upset. That only leads to
     evil.
Sinful people will be cut off from the
     land.
  But it will be given to those who put
     their hope in the LORD.

In a little while, there won't be any
     more sinners.
  Even if you look for them, you won't be able to find them.
But those who are free of pride will be given the land.
  They will enjoy great peace.

Sinful people make plans to harm those who do what is right.
  They grind their teeth at them.
But the Lord laughs at those who do evil.
  He knows the day is coming when he will judge them.

Sinners pull out their swords.
  They bend their bows.
They want to kill poor and needy people.
  They plan to murder those who lead honest lives.
But they will be killed with their own swords.
  Their own bows will be broken.

Those who do what is right may have very little.
  But it's better than the wealth of many sinners.
The power of those who are evil will be broken.

But the LORD takes good care of those who do what is right.

Every day the LORD watches over those who are without blame.
  What he has given them will last forever.
When trouble comes to them, they will have what they need.
  When there is little food in the land, they will still have plenty.

But sinful people will die.
  The LORD's enemies will be like flowers in the field.
  They will disappear like smoke.

Sinful people borrow and don't pay back.
  But those who are godly give freely to others.
The LORD will give the land to those he blesses.
  But he will cut off those he puts a curse on.

If the LORD is pleased with the way a man lives,
  he makes his steps secure.
Even if the man trips, he won't fall.
  The LORD's hand takes good care of him.

I once was young, and now I'm old.
  But I've never seen godly people deserted.
  I've never seen their children begging for bread.
The godly are always giving and lending freely.
  Their children will be blessed.

Turn away from evil and do good.
  Then you will live in the land forever.
The LORD loves those who are honest.
  He will not desert those who are faithful to him.

They will be kept safe forever.
  But the children of sinners will be cut off from the land.
Those who do what is right will be given the land.
  They will live in it forever.

The mouths of those who do what is right speak words of wisdom.
  They say what is honest.
God's law is in their hearts.
  Their feet do not slip.

Those who are evil hide and wait for godly people.
  They are trying to kill them.
But the LORD will not leave the godly in their powe
  He will not let them be found guilty when they
  court.

Wait for the LORD to act.
  Live as he wants you to.
He will honor you by giving you the land.
  When sinners are cut off from it, you will see it.

I saw a mean and sinful person.
  He was doing well, like a green tree in its own soil.
But he soon passed away and was gone.
  Even though I looked for him, I couldn't find him.

Think about those who are without blame. Look at those who are
  honest.
  A man who loves peace will have a tomorrow.
But all sinners will be destroyed.
  Those who are evil won't have a tomorrow.
  They will be cut off from the land.

The LORD saves those who do what is right.
  He is their place of safety when trouble comes.
The LORD helps them and saves them.
  He saves them from sinful people
  because they go to him for safety.

Psalm 101

A psalm of David.

I will sing about your love and
  fairness.
  LORD, I will sing praise to you.
I will be careful to lead a life
  that is without blame.
  When will you come and help me?

WORDS TO TREASURE

I will be careful to lead a life
that is without blame.
Psalm 101:2

ll lead a life
  that is without blame in my house.
  I won't look at anything that is evil.

I hate the acts of people who aren't faithful to you.
  I don't even want people like that around me.
I will stay away from those whose hearts are twisted.
  I don't want to have anything to do with evil.

I will get rid of anyone
  who tells lies about his neighbor in secret.
I won't put up with anyone
  whose eyes and heart are proud.

I will look with favor on the faithful people in the land.
  They will live with me.
  Those whose lives are without blame will serve me.

No one who lies and cheats
  will live in my house.
No one who tells lies
  will serve me.

Every morning I will get rid of
  all the sinful people in the land.
I will remove from the city of the Lord
  everyone who does what is evil.

Psalm 119

א Aleph

Blessed are those who live without blame.
  They live in keeping with the law of the Lord.
Blessed are those who obey his covenant laws.
  They trust in him with all their hearts.
They don't do anything wrong.
  They live as he wants them to live.
You have given me rules
  that I must obey completely.

I hope I will always stand firm
in following your orders.
Then I won't be put to shame
when I think about all of your commands.
I will praise you with an honest heart
as I learn about how fair your decisions are.
I will obey your orders.
Please don't leave me all alone.

ב Beth

How can a young person keep his life pure?
By living in keeping with your word.
I trust in you with all my heart.
Don't let me wander away from your commands.
I have hidden your word in my heart
so that I won't sin against you.
LORD, I give praise to you.
Teach me your orders.
With my lips I talk about
all of the decisions you have made.
Following your covenant laws gives me joy
just as great riches give joy to others.

Memorize Scripture

Psalm 119, verse 11 says, "I have hidden your word in my heart." That means learning a verse and doing what it says. Here are fun ways to learn Bible verses with a friend:

1. Read the verse out loud, leaving out one word. Have your friend try to remember the missing word. Take turns reading the verse. Leave out a different word each time.

2. Each time you read the verse, leave out one more word. Have your friend try to fill in the missing words.

3. Write the verse on two cards. For each card, cut out each word and scramble them. See who can put the words in the right order first.

I spend time thinking about your rules.
    I consider how you want me to live.
I take delight in your orders.
    I won't fail to obey your word.

ח Heth

LORD, you are everything I need.
    I have promised to obey your words.
I have looked to you with all my heart.
    Be kind to me as you have promised.
I have thought about the way I live.
    And I have decided to follow your covenant laws.
I won't waste any time.
    I will be quick to obey your commands.
Evil people may tie me up with ropes.
    But I won't forget to obey your law.
At midnight I get up to give you thanks
    because your decisions are very fair.
I'm a friend to everyone who has respect for you.
    I'm a friend to everyone who follows your rules.
LORD, the earth is filled with your love.
    Teach me your orders.

ט Teth

WORDS TO TREASURE

You are good, and what you do is good.
Psalm 119:68

LORD, be good to me
    as you have promised.
Increase my knowledge and give me
    good sense,
    because I believe in your commands.
Before I went through suffering, I went
        down the wrong path.
    But now I obey your word.
You are good, and what you do is good.

Teach me your orders.
Proud people have spread lies about me and have taken away my
good name.
But I follow your rules with all my heart.
Their hearts are hard and stubborn. They don't feel anything.
But I take delight in your law.
It was good for me to suffer.
That's what helped me to understand your orders.
The law you gave is worth more to me
than thousands of pieces of silver and gold.

׳ Yodh

You made me and formed me with your own hands.
Give me understanding so that I can learn your commands.
May those who have respect for you be filled with joy when they
see me.
I have put my hope in your word.
LORD, I know that your laws are right.
You were faithful to your promise when you made me suffer.
May your faithful love comfort me
as you have promised me.
Show me your tender love so that I can live.
I take delight in your law.
Proud people have treated me badly without any reason. May they
be put to shame.
I will spend time thinking about your rules.
May those who have respect for you come to me.
Then I can teach them your covenant laws.
May my heart be without blame as I follow your orders.
Then I won't be put to shame.

כ Kaph

I deeply long for you to save me.
I have put my hope in your word.
My eyes grow tired looking for what you have promised.

I say, "When will you comfort me?"
I'm as useless as a wineskin that smoke has dried up.
But I don't forget to follow your orders.
How long do I have to wait?
When will you punish those who attack me?
Proud people do what is against your law.
They dig pits for me to fall into.
All of your commands can be trusted.
Help me, because people attack me without any reason.
They almost wiped me off the face of the earth.
But I have not turned away from your rules.
Keep me alive, because you love me.
Then I will obey the covenant laws you have given.

ל Lamedh

LORD, your word lasts forever.
It stands firm in the heavens.
You will be faithful for all time to come.
You made the earth, and it continues to exist.
Your laws continue to this very day,
because all things serve you.
If I had not taken delight in your law,
I would have died because of my suffering.
I will never forget your rules.
You have kept me alive, because I obey them.
Save me, because I belong to you.
I've tried to obey your rules.
Sinful people are waiting to destroy me.
But I will spend time thinking about your covenant laws.
I've learned that everything has its limits.
But your commands are perfect. They are always there when I need them.

What God Is Like

Psalm 119:97 says God is the lawgiver. He gives us rules to live by, to keep us from doing wrong. God is good, and he shows us how to do good. The writer of this psalm loved God's rules, thought about them all day long, and obeyed them.

מ Mem

LORD, I really love your law!
  All day long I spend time thinking about it.
Your commands make me wiser than my enemies,
  because your commands are always in my heart.
I know more than all of my teachers do,
  because I spend time thinking about your covenant laws.
I understand more than the elders do,
  because I obey your rules.
I've kept my feet from every path that sinners take
  so that I might obey your word.
I haven't turned away from your laws,
  because you yourself have taught me.
Your words are very sweet to my taste!
  They are sweeter than honey to me.
I gain understanding from your rules.
  So I hate every path that sinners take.

Psalm 128

A song for those who go up to Jerusalem to worship the LORD.

Blessed are all those who have respect for the LORD.
  They live as he wants them to live.

Your work will give you what you need.
> Blessings and good things will come
> to you.
As a vine bears a lot of fruit,
> so your wife will have many children
> by you.
They will sit around your table
> like young olive trees.
Only a man who has respect for the LORD
> will be blessed like that.

May the LORD bless you from Zion.
> May you enjoy the good things that
> come to Jerusalem
all the days of your life.

May you live to see your grandchildren.

May Israel enjoy peace.

Psalm 145

A psalm of praise. A psalm of David.

I will honor you, my God the King.
> I will praise your name for ever and ever.
Every day I will praise you.
> I will praise your name for ever and ever.

LORD, you are great. You are really worthy of praise.
> No one can completely understand how great you are.
Parents will praise your works to their children.
> They will tell about your mighty acts.
They will speak about your glorious majesty.
> I will spend time thinking about your miracles.
They will speak about the powerful and wonderful things you do.
> I will talk about the great things you have done.
They will celebrate your great goodness.
> They will sing with joy about your holy acts.

The LORD is gracious. He is kind and tender.
    He is slow to get angry. He is full of love.
The LORD is good to all.
    He shows deep concern for everything he has made.
LORD, every living thing you have made will praise you.
    Your faithful people will praise you.
They will tell about your glorious kingdom.
    They will speak about your power.
Then all people will know about the mighty things you have done.
    They will know about the glorious majesty of your kingdom.
Your kingdom is a kingdom that will last forever.
    Your rule will continue for all time to come.

The LORD is faithful and will keep all of his promises.
    He is loving toward everything he has made.
The LORD takes good care of all those
                who fall.
    He lifts up all those who feel
                helpless.
Every living thing looks to you for food.
    You give it to them exactly when
                they need it.
You open your hand
    and satisfy the needs of every
                living creature.

WORDS TO TREASURE

The LORD is good to all.
Psalm 145:9

The LORD is right in everything he does.
    He is loving toward everything he has made.
The LORD is ready to help all those who call out to him.
    He helps those who really mean it when they call out to him.
He satisfies the needs of those who have respect for him.
    He hears their cry and saves them.
The LORD watches over all those who love him.
    But he will destroy all sinful people.

I will praise the LORD with my mouth.
    Let every creature praise his holy name
    for ever and ever.

God Helps Me

Psalms 51, 55, 67, 95, 121, 139

Psalm 51

For the director of music. A psalm of David when the
prophet Nathan came to him after David had
committed adultery with Bathsheba.

WORDS TO TREASURE

Wash away all of the evil
things I've done. Make me
pure from my sin.

Psalm 51:2

God, show me your favor
in keeping with your faithful love.
Because your love is so tender and kind,
wipe out my lawless acts.
Wash away all of the evil things I've
done.
Make me pure from my sin.

I know the lawless acts I've committed.
I can't forget my sin.
You are the one I've really sinned
against.
I've done what is evil in your sight.
So you are right when you sentence me.
You are fair when you judge me.
I know I've been a sinner ever since I was born.
I've been a sinner ever since my mother became pregnant with
me.
I know that you want truth to be in my heart.
You teach me wisdom deep down inside me.

Make me pure by sprinkling me with hyssop plant. Then I will be
clean.
Wash me. Then I will be whiter than snow.
Let me hear you say, "Your sins are forgiven."
That will bring me joy and gladness.
Let the body you have broken be glad.
Take away all of my sins.
Wipe away all of the evil things I've done.

God, create a pure heart in me.
 Give me a new spirit that is faithful to you.
Don't send me away from you.
 Don't take your Holy Spirit away from me.
Give me back the joy that comes from being saved by you.
 Give me a spirit that obeys you. That will keep me going.

Then I will teach your ways to those who commit lawless acts.
 And sinners will turn back to you.
You are the God who saves me.
 I have committed murder.
 Take away my guilt.
Then my tongue will sing about how right you are
 no matter what you do.
Lord, open my lips so that I can speak.
 Then my mouth will praise you.
You don't take delight in sacrifice.
 If you did, I would bring it.
 You don't take pleasure in burnt offerings.
The greatest sacrifice you want is a broken spirit.
 God, you will gladly accept a heart
 that is broken because of sadness over sin.

May you be pleased to give Zion success.
 Build up the walls of Jerusalem.
Then holy sacrifices will be offered in the right way.
 Whole burnt offerings will bring delight to you.
 And bulls will be offered on your altar.

Psalm 55

For the director of music. A *maskil* of David
to be played on stringed instruments.

God, listen to my prayer.
 Pay attention to my cry for help.
 Hear me and answer me.
My thoughts upset me. I'm very troubled.

I'm troubled by what my enemies say about me.
I'm upset because sinful people stare at me.
They cause me all kinds of suffering.
When they are angry, they attack me with their words.

I feel great pain deep down inside me.
The terrors of death are crushing me.
Fear and trembling have taken hold of me.
Panic has overpowered me.
I said, "I wish I had wings like a dove!
Then I would fly away and be at rest.
I would escape to a place far away.
I would stay out in the desert.   *Selah*
I would hurry to my place of safety.
It would be far away from the winds and storms I'm facing."

Lord, destroy the plans of sinners. Keep them from understanding
one another.
I see people destroying things and fighting in the city.
Day and night they prowl around on top of its walls.
The city is full of crime and trouble.
Forces that destroy are at work inside it.
Its streets are full of people who cheat others and take
advantage of them.

If an enemy were making fun of me,
I could stand it.
If he were looking down on me,
I could hide from him.
But it's you, someone like myself.
It's my companion, my close friend.
We used to enjoy good friendship
as we walked with the crowds at the house of God.

Let death take my enemies by surprise.
Let them be buried alive,
because their hearts and homes are full of evil.

But I call out to God.
    And the LORD saves me.
Evening, morning and noon
    I groan and cry out.
    And he hears my voice.
Even though many enemies are fighting
            against me,
    he brings me safely back from the
            battle.
God sits on his throne forever.
    He hears my prayers and makes
        my enemies suffer.   *Selah*
They never change their ways.
    They don't have any respect for God.

My companion attacks his friends.
    He breaks his promise.
His talk is as smooth as butter.
    But he has war in his heart.
His words flow like olive oil.
    But they are like swords ready for battle.

Turn your worries over to the LORD.
    He will keep you going.
    He will never let godly people fall.
God, you will bring sinners
    down to the grave.
Murderers and liars
    won't live out even half of their lives.

But I trust in you.

WORDS TO TREASURE

I call out to God. And
the LORD saves me.
Psalm 55:16

Psalm 67

For the director of music. A psalm. A song
to be played on stringed instruments.

God, show us your favor. Bless us.
    May you smile on us with your favor.   *Selah*

Then your ways will be known on earth.
　　All nations will see that you have the power to save.

God, may the nations praise you.
　　May all of the people on earth praise you.
May the nations be glad and sing with joy.
　　You rule the people of the earth fairly.
　　You guide the nations of the earth.　　　　　　*Selah*
God, may the nations praise you.
　　May all of the people on earth praise you.

Then the land will produce its crops.
　　God, our God, will bless us.
God will bless us.
　　People from one end of the earth to the other
　　will have respect for him.

Psalm 95

Come, let us sing with joy to the LORD.
　　Let us give a loud shout to the Rock who saves us.
Let us come to him and give him thanks.
　　Let us praise him with music and song.

The LORD is the great God.

He is the greatest King.
He rules over all of the gods.
He owns the deepest parts of the earth.
　　The mountain peaks belong to him.
The ocean is his, because he made it.
　　He formed the dry land with his
　　　　hands.

Come, let us bow down and worship
　　him.
　　Let us fall on our knees in front of
　　　　the LORD our Maker.
He is our God.

WORDS TO TREASURE

He is our God. We are
the sheep belonging to
his flock. We are the people
he takes good care of.

Psalm 95:7

We are the sheep belonging to his flock.
We are the people he takes good care of.

Listen to his voice today.
If you hear it, don't be stubborn as you were at Meribah.
Don't be stubborn as you were that day at Massah in the
desert.
There your people of long ago really put me to the test.
They did it even though they had seen what I had done for
them.
For 40 years I was angry with them.
I said, "Their hearts are always going down the wrong path.
They do not know how I want them to live."
So when I was angry, I took an oath.
I said, "They will never enjoy the rest I planned for them."

Psalm 121

A song for those who go up to Jerusalem to worship the LORD.

I look up to the hills.
Where does my help come from?
My help comes from the LORD.
He is the Maker of heaven and earth.

He won't let your foot slip.
He who watches over you won't get tired.
In fact, he who watches over Israel
won't get tired or go to sleep.

The LORD watches over you.
The LORD is like a shade tree at your right hand.
The sun won't harm you during the day.
The moon won't harm you during the night.

The LORD will keep you from every kind of harm.
He will watch over your life.
The LORD will watch over your life no matter where you go,
both now and forever.

Psalm 139

For the director of music. A psalm of David.

LORD, you have seen what is in my heart.
    You know all about me.
You know when I sit down and when I get up.
    You know what I'm thinking even though you are far away.
You know when I go out to work and when I come back home.
    You know exactly how I live.
LORD, even before I speak a word,
    you know all about it.

You are all around me. You are behind me and in front of me.
    You hold me in your power.
I'm amazed at how well you know me.
    It's more than I can understand.

How can I get away from your Spirit?
    Where can I go to escape from you?
If I go up to the heavens, you are there.
    If I lie down in the deepest parts of the earth, you are also
            there.
Suppose I were to rise with the sun in the east
    and then cross over to the west where it sinks into the ocean.
Your hand would always be there to guide me.
    Your right hand would still be holding me close.

Suppose I were to say, "I'm sure the darkness will hide me.
    The light around me will become as dark as night."
Even that darkness would not be dark to you.
    The night would shine like the day,
    because darkness is like light to you.

You created the deepest parts of my being.
    You put me together inside my mother's body.
How you made me is amazing and wonderful.
    I praise you for that.
What you have done is wonderful.

I know that very well.
None of my bones was hidden from you
    when you made me inside my mother's body.
    That place was as dark as the deepest parts of the earth.
When you were putting me together there,
    your eyes saw my body even before it was formed.
You planned how many days I would live.
    You wrote down the number of them in your book
    before I had lived through even one of them.

God, your thoughts about me are priceless.
    No one can possibly add them all up.
If I could count them,
    they would be more than the grains of sand.
If I were to fall asleep counting and then wake up,
    you would still be there with me.

God, I wish you would kill the people who are evil!
    I wish those murderers would get away from me!
They are your enemies. They misuse your name.
    They misuse it for their own evil purposes.
LORD, I really hate those who hate you!
    I really hate those who rise up against you!
I have nothing but hatred for them.
    I consider them to be my enemies.

What God Is Like

Psalm 139 says that God knew David even before David was born. God created David and loved him and watched him grow. God knew you and watched over you too, even before you were born. He still watches over you every minute. You are special to God because he made you.

God, see what is in my heart.
  Know what is there.
Put me to the test.
  Know what I'm thinking.
See if there's anything in my life you don't like.
  Help me live in the way that is always right.

Teaching About Wisdom

Proverbs 1—3; 15; 22; 24

Purpose

These are the proverbs of Solomon. He was the son of David and the king of Israel.

Proverbs teach you wisdom and train you.
  They help you understand wise sayings.
They provide you with training and help you live wisely.
  They lead to what is right and honest and fair.
They give understanding to childish people.
  They give knowledge and good sense to those who are young.
Let wise people listen and add to what they have learned.
  Let those who understand what is right get guidance.
What I'm teaching also helps you understand proverbs and stories.
  It helps you understand the sayings and riddles of those who
    are wise.

Main Point

If you really want to gain knowledge, you must begin by having
    respect for the LORD.
  But foolish people hate wisdom and training.

Think and Live Wisely
A Warning Against a Life of Crime

My son, listen to your father's advice.
  Don't turn away from your mother's teaching.

What they teach you will be like a beautiful crown on your head.
   It will be like a chain to decorate your neck.

Good Things Come From Wisdom

My son, accept my words.
   Store up my commands inside you.
Let your ears listen to wisdom.
   Apply your heart to understanding.
Call out for the ability to be wise.
   Cry out for understanding.
Look for it as you would look for silver.
   Search for it as you would search for hidden treasure.
Then you will understand how to have respect for the LORD.
   You will find out how to know God.
The LORD gives wisdom.
   Knowledge and understanding come from his mouth.
He stores up success for honest people.
   He is like a shield to those who live without blame. He keeps
      them safe.
He guards the path of those who are honest.
   He watches over the way of his faithful ones.

Think Before You Act

"Come on! Let's go get him!" Justin started running. Everyone followed. Everyone but Jason. He had read Proverbs 2:12. He knew that "wisdom will save you from the ways of evil men." Try what Jason did. It will help you think before you act. "Count to five" with these questions.

1. Is it right?
2. Is it good?
3. Is it helpful?
4. Would my parents be happy?
5. Would God be happy?

Stop counting if one of the answers is no. And go the other way!

You will understand what is right and honest and fair.
    You will understand the right way to live.
Your heart will become wise.
    Your mind will delight in knowledge.
Good sense will keep you safe.
    Understanding will guard you.

Wisdom will save you from the ways of evil men.
    It will save you from men who twist their words.
Men like that leave the straight paths
    to walk in dark ways.
They take delight in doing what is wrong.
    They take joy in twisting everything around.
Their paths are crooked.
    Their ways are not straight.

You will walk in the ways of good people.
    You will follow the paths of those who do right.
Honest people will live in the land.
    Those who are without blame will remain in it.
But sinners will be cut off from the land.
    Those who aren't faithful will be torn away from it.

More Good Things Come From Wisdom

My son, do not forget my teaching.
    Keep my commands in your heart.
They will help you live for many years.
    They will bring you success.

Don't let love and truth ever leave you.
    Tie them around your neck.
    Write them on the tablet of your heart.
Then you will find favor and a good name
    in the eyes of God and people.

Trust in the LORD with all your heart.
    Do not depend on your own understanding.
In all your ways remember him.

Then he will make your paths
    smooth and straight.

Don't be wise in your own eyes.
    Have respect for the LORD and
        avoid evil.
That will bring health to your body.
    It will make your bones strong.

Honor the LORD with your wealth.
    Give him the first share of all your
        crops.
Then your storerooms will be so full
        they can't hold everything.
    Your huge jars will spill over with
        fresh wine.

My son, do not hate the LORD's training.
    Do not object when he corrects you.
The LORD trains those he loves.
    He is like a father who trains the son he is pleased with.

Blessed is the one who finds wisdom.
    Blessed is the one who gains understanding.

By wisdom the LORD laid the earth's foundations.
    Through understanding he set the heavens in place.
By his knowledge the seas were separated,
    and the clouds dropped their dew.

My son, hold on to good sense and the understanding of what is
        right.
    Don't let them out of your sight.
They will be life for you.
    They will be like a gracious necklace around your neck.
Then you will go on your way in safety.
    You will not trip and fall.
When you lie down, you won't be afraid.
    When you lie down, you will sleep soundly.

Don't be terrified by sudden trouble.
Don't be afraid when sinners are destroyed.
The LORD is the one you will trust in.
He will keep your feet from being caught in a trap.

A gentle answer turns anger away.
But mean words stir up anger.

The eyes of the LORD are everywhere.
They watch those who are evil and those who are good.

A foolish person turns his back on how his father has trained him.
But anyone who accepts being corrected shows understanding.

The houses of those who do what is right hold great wealth.
But those who do what is wrong earn only trouble.

The lips of wise people spread knowledge.
But that's not true of the hearts of foolish people.

The LORD hates how sinners live.
But he loves those who run after what is right.

Anyone who makes fun of others doesn't like to be corrected.
He won't ask wise people for advice.

A happy heart makes a face look cheerful.
But a sad heart produces a broken spirit.

You should want a good name more than you want great riches.
To be highly respected is better than having silver or gold.

Have respect for the LORD and don't be proud.
That will bring you wealth and honor and life.

Thorns and traps lie in the paths of evil people.

WORDS TO TREASURE

A happy heart makes a face look cheerful. But a sad heart produces a broken spirit.
Proverbs 15:13

But those who guard themselves stay far away from them.

Train a child in the way he should go.
When he is old, he will not turn away from it.

Anyone who plants evil gathers a harvest of trouble.
His power to beat others down will be destroyed.

Anyone who gives freely will be blessed.
That's because he shares his food
with those who are poor.

If you drive away those who make fun of
others, fighting also goes away.
Arguing and unkind words will stop.

Have a pure and loving heart, and
speak kindly.
Then you will be a friend of the king.

A child is going to do foolish things.
But correcting him will drive his
foolishness far away from him.

Does anyone like being punished?

No one likes to get in trouble. But Proverbs 22:15 says that punishments can help us. They keep us from doing wrong and foolish things. And that makes life good.

Sayings of Those Who Are Wise

Pay attention and listen to the sayings of those who are wise.
Apply your heart to the sayings I teach.
It is pleasing when you keep them in your heart.
Have all of them ready on your lips.
You are the one I am teaching today.
I want you to trust in the LORD.
I have written 30 sayings for you.
They will give you knowledge and good advice.
I am teaching you words that are completely true.
Then you can give the right answers to the one who sent you.

1.

Don't take advantage of poor people just because they are poor.
Don't beat down those who are in need by taking them to court.

The LORD will stand up for them in court.
  He will take back the stolen goods from those who have
    robbed them.

2.

Don't be a friend with anyone who burns with anger.
  Don't go around with a person who gets angry easily.
You might learn his habits.
  And then you will be trapped by them.

3.

Don't agree to pay for
  what someone else owes.
Don't put up money for him.
  If you don't have the money to pay,
  your bed will be taken right out from under you!

4.

Don't move old boundary stones
  that your people set up long ago.

5.

Do you see a man who does good work?
  He will serve kings.
  He won't serve ordinary people.

19.

Do not want what evil men have.
  Don't long to be with them.
In their hearts they plan to hurt others.
  With their lips they talk about making trouble.

20.

By wisdom a house is built.
  Through understanding it is made secure.
Through knowledge its rooms are filled
  with priceless and beautiful things.

21.

A wise man has great power.
  A man who has knowledge increases his strength.
If you go to war, you need guidance.
  If you want to win, you need many good advisers.

22.

Wisdom is too high for anyone who is foolish.
  He has nothing to say when people meet at the city gate to
  conduct business.

23.

Anyone who thinks up sinful things to do
  will be known as one who plans evil.
Foolish plans are sinful.
  People hate those who make fun of others.

24.

If you grow weak when trouble comes,
  your strength is very small!

25.

Save those who are being led away to death.
  Hold back those who are about to be killed.
Don't say, "But we didn't know anything about this."
  The One who knows what you are thinking sees it.
The One who guards your life knows it.
  He will pay each person back for what he has done.

26.

Eat honey, my child. It is good.
  Honey from a honeycomb has a sweet taste.
I want you to know that wisdom is sweet to you.
  If you find it, there is hope for you tomorrow.
  So your hope will not be cut off.

Don't hide and wait like a burglar at a godly person's house.
    Don't rob his home.
Even if godly people fall down seven times, they always get up.
    But those who are evil are brought down by trouble.

Don't be happy when your enemy falls.
    When he trips, don't let your heart be glad.
The LORD will see it, but he won't be pleased.
    He might turn his anger away from your enemy.

Don't be upset because of evil people.
    Don't long for what sinners have.
Tomorrow evil people won't have any hope.
    The lamps of sinners will be blown out.

My son, have respect for the LORD and the king.
    Don't join those who disobey them.
The LORD and the king will suddenly destroy them.
    Who knows what trouble those two can bring?

Laughing at Others

Did you ever make a mistake and have someone laugh at you? Maybe you tripped on your shoe lace or got sand in your swimsuit. How did you feel when someone laughed at you?

Did you ever laugh at someone else? How do you think that person felt? The person who wrote this wise saying said we should not laugh at others. He said, "The LORD will see it, but he won't be pleased" (Proverbs 24:18). What will you do the next time you feel like laughing at someone?

What Has Meaning?

Ecclesiastes 2—3; 12

I, the Teacher, was king over Israel in Jerusalem.

I've seen what is done on this earth. It doesn't have any meaning.

Pleasure Doesn't Have Any Meaning

I said to myself, "Come on. I'll put pleasure to the test. I want to find out what is good." But that also proved to be meaningless.

I tried cheering myself up by drinking wine. I even tried living in a foolish way. But wisdom was still guiding my mind. I wanted to see what was really important for men to do on earth during the few days of their lives.

So I started some large projects. I built houses for myself. I planted vineyards. I made gardens and parks. I planted all kinds of fruit trees in them. I made lakes to water groves of healthy trees.

I bought male and female slaves. And I had other slaves who were born in my house. I also owned more herds and flocks than anyone in Jerusalem ever had before. I stored up silver and gold for myself. I gathered up the treasures of kings and their kingdoms. I got some male and female singers. I also got many women for myself.

I became far more important than anyone in Jerusalem had ever been before. And in spite of everything, I didn't lose my wisdom.

I gave myself everything my eyes wanted.

There wasn't any pleasure that I refused to give myself.

Gardens

Rich people planted vegetables, spices and fruit trees in walled gardens. They liked to relax in their gardens. In summertime many slept outdoors in their gardens.

I took delight in everything I did.

And that was what I got for all of my work.

But then I looked over everything my hands had done.

I saw what I had worked so hard to get.

And nothing had any meaning.

It was like chasing the wind.

Nothing was gained on this earth.

There Is a Time for Everything

There is a time for everything.

There's a time for everything that is done on earth.

There is a time for everything. There's a time for everything that is done on earth.

Ecclesiastes 3:1

There is a time to be born.

And there's a time to die.

There is a time to plant.

And there's a time to pull up what is planted.

There is a time to kill.

And there's a time to heal.

There is a time to tear down.

And there's a time to build up.

There is a time to cry.

And there's a time to laugh.

There is a time to be sad.

And there's a time to dance.

There is a time to scatter stones.

And there's a time to gather them.

There is a time to hug.

And there's a time not to hug.

There is a time to search.

And there's a time to stop searching.

There is a time to keep.

And there's a time to throw away.

There is a time to tear.

And there's a time to mend.

There is a time to be silent.

And there's a time to speak.

There is a time to love.
　　And there's a time to hate.
There is a time for war.
　　And there's a time for peace.

What does the worker get for his hard work? I've seen the heavy load God has put on men. He has made everything beautiful in its time. He has also given men a sense of what he's been doing down through the ages. But they can't completely figure out what he's done from the beginning to the end.

They should be happy and do good while they live. I know there's nothing better for them to do than that. Everyone should eat and drink. People should be satisfied with all of their hard work. That is God's gift to them.

I know that everything God does will last forever. Nothing can be added to it. And nothing can be taken from it. God does that so men will have respect for him.

Everything that now exists has already been.
　　And what is coming has existed before.
　　God will judge those who treat others badly.

Here's something else I saw on earth.

Where people should be treated right,
　　they are treated wrong.
Where people should be treated fairly,
　　they are treated unfairly.

I said to myself,

"God will judge
　　godly and sinful people alike.
He has a time for every act.
　　He has a time for everything that is done."

Remember the One who created you.
　　Remember him while you are still young.

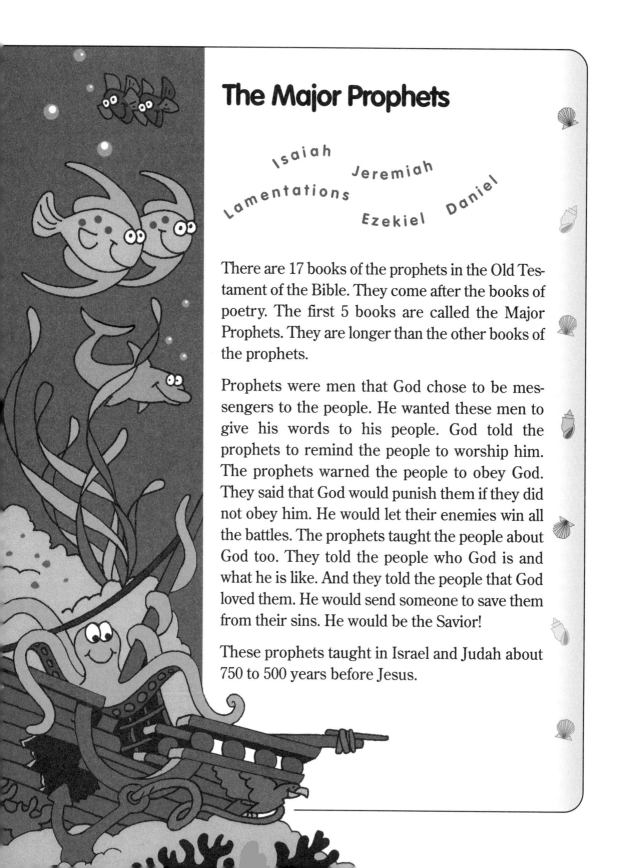

The Major Prophets

Isaiah

Jeremiah

Lamentations

Ezekiel   Daniel

There are 17 books of the prophets in the Old Testament of the Bible. They come after the books of poetry. The first 5 books are called the Major Prophets. They are longer than the other books of the prophets.

Prophets were men that God chose to be messengers to the people. He wanted these men to give his words to his people. God told the prophets to remind the people to worship him. The prophets warned the people to obey God. They said that God would punish them if they did not obey him. He would let their enemies win all the battles. The prophets taught the people about God too. They told the people who God is and what he is like. And they told the people that God loved them. He would send someone to save them from their sins. He would be the Savior!

These prophets taught in Israel and Judah about 750 to 500 years before Jesus.

Words From the Prophet Isaiah

Isaiah 6—7; 9; 11—12; 35; 40; 53; 60; 64

The Lord Appoints Isaiah to Speak for Him

In the year that King Uzziah died, I saw the Lord. He was seated on his throne. His long robe filled the temple. He was highly honored.

Above him were seraphs. Each of them had six wings. With two wings they covered their faces. With two wings they covered their feet. And with two wings they were flying. They were calling out to one another. They were saying,

> "Holy, holy, holy is the LORD who rules over all.
>   The whole earth is full of his glory."

The sound of their voices caused the stone doorframe to shake. The temple was filled with smoke.

"How terrible it is for me!" I cried out. "I'm about to be destroyed! My mouth speaks sinful words. And I live among people who speak sinful words. Now I have seen the King with my own eyes. He is the LORD who rules over all."

A seraph flew over to me. He was holding a hot coal. He had used tongs to take it from the altar. He touched my mouth with the coal. He said, "This has touched your lips. Your guilt has been taken away. Your sin has been paid for."

Called by God

A prophet is someone who tells people how God wants them to live, as well as what will happen in the future. That is what God wanted Isaiah to be. Do you think that Isaiah planned to be a prophet when he grew up?

What do you want to be when you grow up? A teacher? A ball player? A computer expert? Ask your mom or dad to write it down with today's date. Put the paper in your Bible. Look at it once in a while.

What's the most important thing you can be? It's to be what God wants you to be. And he'll let you know.

Then I heard the voice of the Lord. He said, "Who will I send? Who will go for us?"

I said, "Here I am. Send me!"

So he said, "Go and speak to these people. Tell them,

"'You will hear but never understand.
    You will see but never know what you are seeing.'
Make the hearts of these people stubborn.
    Plug up their ears.
    Close their eyes.
Otherwise they might see with their eyes.
    They might hear with their ears.
    They might understand with their hearts.
And they might turn to me and be healed."

Then I said, "Lord, how long will it be like that?"
He answered,

"It will last until the cities of Israel are destroyed
    and no one is living in them.
It will last until the houses are deserted.
    The fields will be completely destroyed.
It will last until I have sent everyone far away.
    The land will be totally deserted.
Even if a tenth of the people remain there,
    the land will be completely destroyed again.
But when oak trees and terebinth trees
    are cut down, stumps are left.
And my holy people will be like stumps
    that begin to grow again."

The Miraculous Sign of Immanuel

Then I said, "Listen, you members of the royal family of Ahaz! Isn't it enough for you to test the patience of men? Are you also going to test the patience of my God? The LORD himself will give you a miraculous sign. The virgin is going to have a baby. She will give birth to a son. And he will be called Immanuel.

"The time will come when he is old enough to decide between what is wrong and what is right. By that time he will have only butter and honey to eat. But even before that happens, the lands of the two kings you are afraid of will be completely destroyed.

"The LORD will also bring the king of Assyria against you. And he will bring him against your people and the whole royal family. That will be a time of trouble unlike any since the people of Ephraim broke away from Judah."

A Son Will Be Given to Us

But there won't be any more sadness for those who were suffering. In the past the LORD brought shame on the land of Zebulun. He also brought shame on the land of Naphtali. But in days to come he will honor Galilee, where people from other nations live. He will honor the land along the Mediterranean Sea. And he will honor the territory east of the Jordan River.

The people who are now living in darkness
> will see a great light.
They are now living in a very dark land.
> But a light will shine on them.
LORD, you will make our nation larger.
> You will increase their joy.
They will show you how glad they are.
> They will be as glad as people are at harvest time.
They will be as glad as soldiers are
> when they share the things they've taken after a battle.
You set Israel free from Midian long ago.
> In the same way, you will break
the heavy yoke that weighs Israel down.
> You will break the wooden beams that are on their shoulders.
> You will break the rods of those who strike them down.

Every fighting man's boot that is used in battle will be burned up.
So will every piece of clothes
that is covered with blood.
All of them will be thrown into the fire.

A child will be born to us.
A son will be given to us.
He will rule over us.
And he will be called
Wonderful Adviser and Mighty God.
He will also be called Father Who Lives
Forever
and Prince Who Brings Peace.
The authority of his rule will continue
to grow.
The peace he brings will never end.
He will rule on David's throne
and over his kingdom.
He will make the kingdom strong
and secure.

His rule will be based on what is fair and right.
It will last forever.
The LORD's great love will make sure that happens.
He rules over all.

DID YOU KNOW?

Does the Old Testament talk about Jesus?

There are many messages about Jesus in the Old Testament. These messages are called prophecies. A prophecy tells about something in the future. Isaiah chapter 9 and Isaiah chapter 11 are prophecies about Jesus.

A Branch Will Come From Jesse's Family Line

Jesse's family is like a tree that has been cut down.
A new little tree will grow from its stump.
From its roots a Branch will grow and produce fruit.
The Spirit of the LORD will rest on that Branch.
He will help him to be wise and understanding.
He will help him make wise plans and carry them out.
He will help him know the LORD and have respect for him.
The Branch will take delight
in respecting the LORD.

He will not judge things only by the way they look.
He won't make decisions based simply on what people say.

He will always do what is right
  when he judges those who are in need.
He'll be completely fair
  when he makes decisions about poor people.
When he commands that people be punished,
  it will happen.
When he orders that evil people be put to death,
  it will take place.
He will put godliness on as if it were his belt.
  He'll wear faithfulness around his waist.

Wolves will live with lambs.
  Leopards will lie down with goats.
Calves and lions will eat together.
  And little children will lead them around.
Cows will eat with bears.
  Their little ones will lie down together.
  . And lions will eat straw like oxen.
A baby will play near a hole where cobras live.
  A young child will put his hand into a nest
  where poisonous snakes live.
None of those animals will harm or destroy anything or anyone
  on my holy mountain of Zion.
The oceans are full of water.
  In the same way, the earth will be filled
  with the knowledge of the LORD.

A Perfect World

Have you ever seen a cat catch a mouse? Or a cat and a dog in a fight? Animals often fight and hurt each other. When Jesus returns, the world will be perfect. This Bible passage tells how animals will act in the new world. Did you ever think of having an animal parade? Have all your friends bring their pets. You will need leashes, cages, boxes and wagons. Form a parade through your neighborhood.

Two Songs of Praise

In days to come, the people of Israel will sing,

"LORD, we will praise you.
> You were angry with us.
But now your anger has turned away from us.
> And you have brought us comfort.
God, you are the one who saves us.
> We will trust in you.
> Then we won't be afraid.
LORD, you give us strength.
> We sing about you.
> LORD, you have saved us."
People of Israel, he will save you.
> That will bring you joy like water that is brought up from wells.

In days to come, the people of Israel will sing,

"Give thanks to the LORD. Worship him.
> Tell the nations what he has done.
> Announce how honored he is.
Sing to the LORD. He has done glorious
> things.
> Let it be known all over the world.
People of Zion, give a loud shout!
> Sing with joy!
The Holy One of Israel is among you.
> And he is great."

WORDS TO TREASURE

Give thanks to the LORD.
Worship him. Tell the nations
what he has done.

Isaiah 12:4

The LORD Will Set His People Free

The desert and the dry ground will be glad.
> The dry places will be full of joy.
> Flowers will grow there.
Like the first crocus in the spring,
> the desert will bloom with flowers.

It will be very glad and shout with joy.
The glorious beauty of Lebanon will be given to it.
    It will be as beautiful as the rich lands
    of Carmel and Sharon.
Everyone will see the glory of the LORD.
    They will see the beauty of our God.

Strengthen the hands of those who are
            weak.
    Help those whose knees give way.
Say to those whose hearts are afraid,
    "Be strong. Do not fear.
Your God will come.
    He will pay your enemies back.
    He will come to save you."

Then the eyes of those who are blind will be opened.
    The ears of those who can't hear will be unplugged.
Those who can't walk will leap like a deer.
    And those who can't speak will shout with joy.
Water will pour out in dry places.
    Streams will flow in the desert.
The burning sand will become a pool of water.
    The thirsty ground will become bubbling springs.
In the places where wild dogs once lay down,
    tall grass and papyrus will grow.

A wide road will go through the land.
    It will be called The Way of Holiness.
Only those who are pure and clean can travel on it.
    Only those who lead a holy life can use it.
    Evil and foolish people can't walk on it.
No lions will use it.
    No wild animals will be on it.
    None of them will be there.
Only people who have been set free will walk on it.
    Those the LORD has saved will return to their land.

They will sing as they enter the city of Zion.
Joy that lasts forever will be
like beautiful crowns on their heads.
They will be filled with gladness and joy.
Sorrow and sighing will be gone.

God Comforts His People

"Comfort my people," says your God.
"Comfort them.
Speak tenderly to the people of Jerusalem.
Announce to them
that their hard service has been completed.
Tell them that their sin has been paid for.
Tell them I have punished them enough
for all of their sins."

A messenger is calling out,
"In the desert prepare
the way for the LORD.
Make a straight road through it
for our God.
Every valley will be filled in.
Every mountain and hill will be made level.
The rough ground will be smoothed out.
The rocky places will be made flat.
Then the glory of the LORD will appear.
And everyone will see it.

The LORD has spoken."

Another messenger says, "Cry out."
And I said, "What should I cry?"

"Cry out, 'All people are like grass.
They don't last any longer than flowers in the field.
The grass dries up. The flowers fall to the ground.
That happens when the LORD makes his wind blow on them.
So people are just like grass.

The grass dries up. The flowers fall to the ground.
But what our God says will stand forever.'"

Zion, you are bringing good news to your people.
Go up on a high mountain and announce it.
Jerusalem, you are bringing good news to them.
Shout the message loudly.
Shout it out loud. Don't be afraid.
Say to the towns of Judah,
"Your God is coming!"
The LORD and King is coming with power.
His powerful arm will rule for him.
He has set his people free.
He is bringing them back as his reward.
He has won the battle over their enemies.
He takes care of his flock like a shepherd.
He gathers the lambs in his arms.
He carries them close to his heart.
He gently leads those that have little ones.

So who will you compare God to?
Is there any other god like him?
Will you compare him to a statue of a god?
Any skilled worker can make a statue.
Then another worker covers it with gold
and makes silver chains for it.
But someone who is too poor to bring that kind of offering
will choose some wood that won't rot.
Then he looks for a skilled worker.
He pays the worker to make a statue of a god that won't fall over.

Family of Jacob, why do you say,
"The LORD doesn't notice our condition"?
People of Israel, why do you say,
"Our God doesn't pay any attention to our rightful claims"?
Don't you know who made everything?
Haven't you heard about him?

Those who trust in the LORD will receive new strength. They will fly as high as eagles. They will run and not get tired. They will walk and not grow weak.
Isaiah 40:31

The LORD is the God who lives forever.
　He created everything on earth.
He won't become worn out or get tired.
　No one will ever know how great his
　　understanding is.
He gives strength to those who are tired.
　He gives power to those who are
　　weak.
Even young people become worn out and
　get tired.
　Even the best of them trip and fall.
But those who trust in the LORD
　will receive new strength.
They will fly as high as eagles.
　They will run and not get tired.
　They will walk and not grow weak.

The Suffering and Glory of the LORD's Servant

Who has believed what we've been saying?
　Who has seen the LORD's saving power?
His servant grew up like a tender young plant.
　He grew like a root coming up out of dry ground.
He didn't have any beauty or majesty that made us notice him.
　There wasn't anything special about the way he looked that
　　drew us to him.
Men looked down on him. They didn't accept him.
　He knew all about sorrow and suffering.
He was like someone people turn their faces away from.
　We looked down on him. We didn't have any respect for him.

He suffered the things we should have suffered.
　He took on himself the pain that should have been ours.
But we thought God was punishing him.
　We thought God was wounding him and making him suffer.
But the servant was pierced because we had sinned.
　He was crushed because we had done what was evil.

He was punished to make us whole again.
> His wounds have healed us.

All of us are like sheep. We have wandered away from God.
> All of us have turned to our own way.

And the Lord has placed on his servant
> the sins of all of us.

He was beaten down and made to suffer.
> But he didn't open his mouth.

He was led away like a sheep to be killed.
> Lambs are silent while their wool is being cut off.
> In the same way, he didn't open his mouth.

He was arrested and sentenced to death.
> Then he was taken away.
> He was cut off from this life.

He was punished for the sins of my people.
> Who among those who were living at that time
> could have understood those things?

He was given a grave with those who were evil.
> But his body was buried in the tomb of a rich man.

He was killed even though he hadn't harmed anyone.
> And he had never lied to anyone.

The Lord says, "It was my plan to crush him
> and cause him to suffer.
> I made his life a guilt offering to pay for sin.

But he will see all of his children after him.
> In fact, he will continue to live.
> My plan will be brought about through him.

After he suffers, he will see the light that leads to life.
> And he will be satisfied.

My godly servant will make many people godly
> because of what he will accomplish.
> He will be punished for their sins.

So I will give him a place of honor among those who are great.
> He will be rewarded just like others who win the battle.

That is because he was willing to give his life as a sacrifice.

He was counted among those who had committed crimes.
He took the sins of many people on himself.
And he gave his life for those who had done what is wrong."

Zion Will Be Glorious

"People of Jerusalem, get up.
Shine, because your light has come.
My glory will shine on you.
Darkness covers the earth.
Thick darkness spreads over the nations.
But I will rise and shine on you.
My glory will appear over you.
Nations will come to your light.
Kings will come to the brightness of your new day.

"People from other lands will rebuild your walls.
Their kings will serve you.
When I was angry with you, I struck you.
But now I will show you my tender love.
Your gates will always stand open.
They will never be shut, day or night.
Then people can bring you the wealth of the nations.
Their kings will come along with them.
The nation or kingdom that will not serve you will be destroyed.
It will be completely wiped out.

"Lebanon's glorious trees will be brought to you.
Its pines, firs and cypress trees will be brought.
They will be used to make my temple beautiful.
And I will bring glory to the place where my throne is.
The children of those who crush you will come and bow down to you.
All those who hate you will kneel down at your feet.
Jerusalem, they will call you The City of the LORD.
They will name you Zion, the City of the Holy One of Israel.

"You have been deserted and hated.
No one even travels through you.

But I will make you into something to be proud of forever.
    You will be a place of joy for all time to come.
You will get everything you need from kings and nations.
    You will be like children who are nursing
    at their mother's breasts.
Then you will know that I am the one who saves you.
    I am the LORD. I set you free.
    I am the Mighty One of Jacob.
Instead of bronze I will bring you gold.
    In place of iron I will give you silver.
Instead of wood I will bring you bronze.
    In place of stones I will give you iron.
I will make peace govern you.
    I will make godliness rule over you.
People will no longer harm one another in your land.
    They will not wipe out or destroy anything inside your borders.
You will call your walls Salvation.
    And you will name your gates Praise.
You will not need the light of the sun by day anymore.
    The bright light of the moon will no longer have to shine on you.
I will be your light forever.
    My glory will shine on you.
    I am the LORD your God.
Your sun will never set again.
    Your moon will never lose its light.
I will be your light forever.
    Your days of sorrow will come to an end.
Then all of your people will do what is right.
    The land will belong to them forever.
They will be like a young tree I have planted.
    My hands have created them.
    They will show how glorious I am.
The smallest family among you will become a tribe.
    The smallest tribe will become a mighty nation.
I am the LORD.
    When it is the right time, I will act quickly."

Isaiah Prays to the LORD

I wish you would open up your heavens
  and come down to us!
I wish the mountains would tremble
  when you show your power!
Be like a fire that causes twigs to burn.
  It also makes water boil.
So come down and make yourself known to your enemies.
  Cause the nations to shake with fear
  when they see your power!
Long ago you did some wonderful things we didn't expect.
  You came down, and the mountains trembled
  when you showed your power.
No one's ears have ever heard of a God like you.
  No one's eyes have ever seen a God who is greater than you.
No God but you acts for the good
  of those who trust in him.
You come to help those who enjoy doing what is right.
  You help those who thank you for teaching them how to live.
But when we continued to disobey you,
  you became angry with us.
  So how can we be saved?

All of us have become like someone
    who is "unclean."
  All of the good things we do are like
    polluted rags to you.
All of us are like leaves that have dried up.
  Our sins sweep us away like the wind.
No one prays to you.
  No one asks you for help.
You have turned your face away from us.
  You have let us waste away
  because we have sinned so much.

LORD, you are our Father.
  We are the clay. You are the potter.

WORDS TO TREASURE

Lord, you are our Father.
We are the clay. You are
the potter. Your hands
made all of us.

Isaiah 64:8

254

Your hands made all of us.
Don't be so angry with us, LORD.
    Don't remember our sins anymore.
Please show us your favor.
    All of us belong to you.

The Warning of the Prophet Jeremiah

Jeremiah 1; 24

These are the words Jeremiah received from the LORD. He was the son of Hilkiah. Jeremiah was one of the priests at Anathoth. That's a town in the territory of Benjamin. A message came to Jeremiah from the LORD. It came in the 13th year that Josiah was king over Judah. Josiah was the son of Amon.

The LORD's message also came to Jeremiah during the whole time Jehoiakim was king over Judah. Jehoiakim was the son of Josiah. The LORD continued to speak to Jeremiah until the fifth month of the 11th year that Zedekiah was king over Judah. That's when the people of Jerusalem were forced to leave their country. Zedekiah was the son of Josiah. Here is what Jeremiah said.

The LORD Chooses Jeremiah

A message came to me from the LORD. He said,

"Before I formed you in your mother's body I chose you.
    Before you were born I set you apart to serve me.
    I appointed you to be a prophet to the nations."

"You are my LORD and King," I said. "I don't know how to speak. I'm only a child."

But the LORD said to me, "Do not say, 'I'm only a child.' You must go to everyone I send you to. You must say everything I command you to say. Do not be afraid of the people I send you to. I am with you. I will save you," announces the LORD.

Then the LORD reached out his hand. He touched my mouth and spoke to me. He said, "I have put my words in your mouth. Today I am appointing you to speak to nations and kingdoms. I want you to pull

God Has a Plan for Your Life

Jeremiah was a very special person to God. Find the verses in Jeremiah chapter 1 that say the following things:

1. God knew Jeremiah even before he was born.
2. God planned work for Jeremiah to do even before he was born.
3. Jeremiah had to trust God and do his work.
4. God would help Jeremiah do his work.

You are just as special to God as Jeremiah was. Even though you are young, you can ask God what he wants you to do. He has a plan for you. He has a plan for now and a plan for when you grow up.

them up by the roots and tear them down. I want you to destroy them and crush them. But I also want you to build them up and plant them."

A message came to me from the LORD. He asked me, "What do you see, Jeremiah?"

"The branch of an almond tree," I replied.

The LORD said to me, "You have seen correctly. I am watching to see that my word comes true."

Another message came to me from the LORD. He asked me, "What do you see?"

"A pot that has boiling water in it," I answered. "It's leaning toward us from the north."

The LORD said to me, "Something very bad will be poured out on everyone who lives in this land. It will come from the north. I am about to send for all of the armies in the northern kingdoms," announces the LORD.

"Their kings will come to Jerusalem.
    They will set up their thrones at the very gates of the city.
They will attack all of the walls that surround the city.
    They will go to war against all of the towns of Judah.
I will judge my people.
    They have done many evil things.
    They have deserted me.

They have burned incense to other gods.
    They have worshiped the gods
    their own hands have made.

"So get ready! Stand up! Tell them everything I command you to. Do not let them terrify you. If you do, I will terrify you in front of them. Today I have made you like a city that has a high wall around it. I have made you like an iron pillar and a bronze wall. Now you can stand up against the whole land. You can stand against the kings and officials of Judah. You can stand against its priests and its people. They will fight against you. But they will not overcome you. I am with you. I will save you," announces the LORD.

Judah Is Like Two Baskets of Figs

King Jehoiachin was forced to leave Jerusalem. He was the son of Jehoiakim. Jehoiachin was taken to Babylon by Nebuchadnezzar, the king of Babylonia. The officials and all of the skilled workers were forced to leave with him.

After they left, the LORD showed me two baskets of figs. They were in front of his temple. One basket had very good figs in it. They were like figs that ripen early. The other basket had figs that weren't good at all. In fact, they were so bad they couldn't even be eaten.

Then the LORD asked me, "What do you see, Jeremiah?"

"Figs," I answered. "The good ones are very good. But the others are so bad they can't be eaten."

Then a message came to me from the LORD. He said, "I am the LORD, the God of Israel. I say, 'I consider the people who were forced to leave Judah to be like those good figs. I sent them away from this place. I forced them to go to Babylonia. My eyes will watch over them. I will be good to them. And I will bring them back to this land. I will build them up. I will not tear them down. I will plant them. I will not pull them up by the roots.

"'I will change their hearts. Then they will know that I am the LORD. They will be my people. And I will be their God. They will return to me with all their heart.

"'But there are also figs that are not very good. In fact, they are so bad they can't be eaten,' says the LORD. 'Zedekiah, the king of Judah, is like those bad figs. So are his officials and the people of Jerusalem who are still left alive. I will punish them whether they remain in this land or live in Egypt.

"'I will make all of the kingdoms on earth displeased with them. In fact, they will hate them a great deal. They will laugh and joke about them. They will call down curses on them. All of that will happen no matter where I force them to go. I will send war, hunger and plague against them. They will be destroyed from the land I gave them and their people of long ago.'"

A Song of Sadness About Egypt

Ezekiel 30

A message came to [Ezekiel] from the LORD. He said, "Son of man, prophesy. Say, 'The LORD and King says,

"'"Cry out,
    'A terrible day is coming!'
The day is near.
    The day of the LORD is coming.
It will be a cloudy day.
    The nations have been sentenced to die.
I will send Nebuchadnezzar's sword against Egypt.
    Cush will suffer terribly.
Many will die in Egypt.
    Then its wealth will be carried away.
    Its foundations will be torn down.

The people of Cush, Put, Lydia, Libya and the whole land of Arabia will be killed with swords. So will the Jews who live in Egypt. They went there from the covenant land of Israel. And the Egyptians will die too.'"'

The LORD says,

"Those who were going to help Egypt will die.
    The strength Egypt was so proud of will fail.
Its people will be killed with swords
    from Migdol all the way to Aswan,"
        announces the LORD and King.
"Egypt will be more empty than any other land.

Its cities will be completely destroyed.
I will set Egypt on fire.
All those who came to help it will be crushed.
Then they will know that I am the LORD."

The Fiery Furnace

Daniel 3

Daniel's Friends Are Thrown Into a Blazing Furnace

King Nebuchadnezzar made a statue that was covered with gold. It was 90 feet tall and 9 feet wide. He set it up on the flatlands of Dura near the city of Babylon.

At that time some people who studied the heavens came forward. They spoke against the Jews. They said, "King Nebuchadnezzar, may you live forever! You commanded everyone to fall down and worship the gold statue. You told them to do it when they heard the horns, flutes, zithers, lyres, harps, pipes and other musical instruments. If they didn't, they would be thrown into a blazing furnace. But you have appointed some Jews to help govern Babylon and the towns around it. Their names are Shadrach, Meshach and Abednego. They don't pay any attention to you, King Nebuchadnezzar. They don't serve your gods. And they refuse to worship the gold statue you have set up."

Nebuchadnezzar burned with anger. He sent for Shadrach, Meshach and Abednego. So they were brought to him.

The king said to them, "Shadrach, Meshach and Abednego, is what I heard about you true? Don't you serve my gods? Don't you worship the gold statue I set up? You will hear the horns, flutes, zithers, lyres, harps, pipes and other musical instruments. When you do, fall down and worship the statue I made. If you will, that's very good. But if you won't, you will be thrown at once into a blazing furnace. Then what god will be able to save you from my powerful hand?"

Shadrach, Meshach and Abednego replied to the king. They said, "King Nebuchadnezzar, we don't need to talk about this anymore. We might be thrown into the blazing furnace. But the God we serve is able to bring us out of it alive. He will save us from your powerful hand.

"But we want you to know this. Even if we knew that our God wouldn't save us, we still wouldn't serve your gods. We wouldn't worship the gold statue you set up."

Then Nebuchadnezzar's anger burned against Shadrach, Meshach and Abednego. The look on his face changed. And he ordered that the furnace be heated seven times hotter than usual. He also gave some of the strongest soldiers in his army a command. He ordered them to tie up Shadrach, Meshach and Abednego. Then he told his men to throw them into the blazing furnace. So they were tied up. Then they were thrown into the furnace. They were wearing their robes, pants, turbans and other clothes.

The king's command was carried out quickly. The furnace was so hot that its flames killed the soldiers who threw Shadrach, Meshach and Abednego into it. So the three men were firmly tied up. And they fell into the blazing furnace.

Then King Nebuchadnezzar leaped to his feet. He was so amazed he asked his advisers, "Didn't we tie three men up? Didn't we throw three men into the fire?"

"Yes, we did," they replied.

The king said, "Look! I see four men walking around in the fire. They aren't tied up. And the fire hasn't even harmed them. The fourth man looks like a son of the gods."

Trusting God When Things Look Bad

Three Jewish men refused to bow down to a statue that the king of Babylon had set up. The king ordered that they be thrown into a furnace. The men said, "The God we serve is able to bring us out of it alive" (Daniel 3:17). Things looked pretty hopeless. But God was with them. They didn't get burned. They didn't even smell like smoke! Sometimes things get pretty tough for kids too. Here's something you can make to help you through those times. Fold a sheet of paper in three sections so that two are like doors. Close the doors and draw flames on the outside. On the inside paste a picture of you and one of Jesus. Then remember that no matter how rough things get, God is there with you.

Then the king approached the opening of the blazing furnace. He shouted, "Shadrach, Meshach and Abednego, come out! You who serve the Most High God, come here!"

So they came out of the fire. The royal rulers, high officials, governors and advisers crowded around them. They saw that the fire hadn't harmed their bodies. Not one hair on their heads was burned. Their robes weren't burned either. And they didn't even smell like smoke.

Then Nebuchadnezzar said, "May the God of Shadrach, Meshach and Abednego be praised! He has sent his angel and saved his servants. They trusted in him. They refused to obey my command. They were willing to give up their lives. They would rather die than serve or worship any god except their own God.

"No other god can save people that way. So I'm giving an order. No one from any nation or language can say anything against the God of Shadrach, Meshach and Abednego. If they do, they'll be cut to pieces. And their houses will be turned into piles of trash."

Then the king honored Shadrach, Meshach and Abednego. He gave them higher positions in the city of Babylon and the towns around it.

The Writing on the Wall
Daniel 5

A Hand Writes on the Palace Wall

King Belshazzar gave a big dinner. He invited a thousand of his nobles to it. He drank wine with them.

While Belshazzar was drinking his wine, he gave orders to his servants. He commanded them to bring in some gold and silver cups. They were the cups his father Nebuchadnezzar had taken from the temple in Jerusalem. Belshazzar had them brought in so everyone could drink from them. That included the king himself, his nobles, his wives and his concubines.

So the servants brought in the gold cups that had been taken from God's temple in Jerusalem. The king and his nobles drank from them. So did his wives and concubines. As they drank the wine, they praised their gods. The statues of those gods were made out of gold, silver, bronze, iron, wood or stone.

Suddenly the fingers of a human hand appeared. They wrote something on the plaster of the palace wall. It happened near the lampstand.

The king watched the hand as it wrote. His face turned pale. He became so afraid that his knees knocked together. His legs couldn't hold him up any longer.

The king sent for those who try to figure things out by using magic. He also sent for those who study the heavens. All of them were wise men in Babylon. He ordered that they be brought to him. He said to them, "I want one of you to read this writing and tell me what it means. If you do, you will be dressed in purple clothes. A gold chain will be put around your neck. And you will be made the third highest ruler in the kingdom."

Then all of the king's wise men came in. But they couldn't read the writing. They couldn't tell him what it meant. So King Belshazzar became even more terrified. His face grew more pale. And his nobles were bewildered.

The queen heard the king and his nobles talking. So she came into the dining hall. "King Belshazzar, may you live forever!" she said. "Don't be afraid! Don't look so pale! I know a man in your kingdom who has the spirit of the holy gods in him. He has understanding and wisdom and good sense just like the gods. That was discovered when your father

Babylon

When Daniel came to Babylon, it was the richest and most famous city in the world. Its palm trees, hanging gardens and beautiful buildings made it special. The huge double wall that surrounded it was not just for protection but also for beauty. It had designs and figures carved into it. The city had 50 temples for statues of gods. If Babylon was still there today, it would be in the country of Iraq. However, there is only bare ground where this greatest city of ancient times used to be.

Nebuchadnezzar was king. Nebuchadnezzar appointed him chief of those who tried to figure things out by using magic. He also put him in charge of those who studied the heavens.

"The man's name is Daniel. Your father called him Belteshazzar. He has a clever mind and knowledge and understanding. He is also able to tell what dreams mean. He can explain riddles and solve hard problems. Send for him. He'll tell you what the writing means."

So Daniel was brought to the king. The king said to him, "Are you Daniel? Are you one of the prisoners my father the king brought here from Judah? I have heard that the spirit of the gods is in you. I've also heard that you have understanding and good sense and special wisdom.

"The wise men and those who practice magic were brought to me. They were asked to read this writing and tell me what it means. But they couldn't.

"I have heard that you are able to explain things and solve hard problems. I hope you can read this writing and tell me what it means. If you can, you will be dressed in purple clothes. A gold chain will be put around your neck. And you will be made the third highest ruler in the kingdom."

Then Daniel answered the king. He said, "You can keep your gifts for yourself. You can give your rewards to someone else. But I will read the writing for you. I'll tell you what it means.

"King Belshazzar, the Most High God was good to your father Nebuchadnezzar. He gave him authority and greatness and glory and honor. God gave him a high position. Then all of the people from every nation and language became afraid of the king. He put to death anyone he wanted to. He spared anyone he wanted to spare. He gave high positions to anyone he wanted to. And he brought down anyone he wanted to bring down.

"But his heart became very stubborn and proud. So he was removed from his royal throne. His glory was stripped away from him. He was driven away from people. He was given the mind of an animal. He lived like the wild donkeys. He ate grass just as cattle do. His body became wet with the dew of heaven. He stayed that way until he recognized that the Most High God rules over all of the kingdoms of men. He puts anyone he wants to in charge of them.

"But you knew all of that, Belshazzar. After all, you are Nebuchadnezzar's son. In spite of that, you are still proud. You have taken your stand against the Lord of heaven. You had your servants bring cups from his temple to you. You and your nobles drank wine from them. So did your wives and concubines. You praised your gods. The statues of those gods are made out of silver, gold, bronze, iron, wood or stone. They can't see or hear or understand anything. But you didn't honor the God who holds in his hand your very life and everything you do. So he sent the hand that wrote on the wall.

"Here is what was written.

MENE, MENE, TEKEL, PARSIN

"And here is what those words mean.

> *Mene* means that God has limited the time of your rule. He has brought it to an end.
> *Tekel* means that you have been weighed on scales. And you haven't measured up to God's standard.
> *Peres* means that your authority over your kingdom will be taken away from you. It will be given to the Medes and Persians."

Then Belshazzar commanded his servants to dress Daniel in purple clothes. So they did. They put a gold chain around his neck. And he was made the third highest ruler in the kingdom.

That very night Belshazzar, the king of Babylonia, was killed. His kingdom was given to Darius the Mede. Darius was 62 years old.

Daniel and the Lions' Den

Daniel 6

Daniel Is Thrown Into a Den of Lions

It pleased Darius to appoint 120 royal rulers over his entire kingdom. He placed three leaders over them. One of the leaders was Daniel. The royal rulers were made accountable to the three leaders. Then the king wouldn't lose any of his wealth. Daniel did a better job than the other two leaders or any of the royal rulers. He was an unusually good and able man. So the king planned to put him in charge of the whole kingdom.

But the other two leaders and the royal rulers heard about it. So they looked for a reason to bring charges against Daniel. They tried to find something wrong with the way he ran the government. But they weren't able to. They couldn't find any fault with his work. He could always be trusted. He never did anything wrong. And he always did what he was supposed to.

Finally those men said, "It's almost impossible for us to come up with a reason to bring charges against this man Daniel. If we do, it will have to be in connection with the law of his God."

So the two leaders and the royal rulers went as a group to the king. They said, "King Darius, may you live forever! All of the royal leaders, high officials, royal rulers, advisers and governors want to make a suggestion. We've agreed that you should give an order. And you should make sure it's obeyed. Here is the command you should give. King Darius, during the next 30 days don't let any of your people pray to any god or man except to you. If they do, throw them into the lions' den.

"Now give the order. Write it down in the laws of the Medes and Persians. Then it can't be changed." So King Darius put the order in writing.

Daniel found out that the king had signed the order. In spite of that, he did just as he had always done before. He went home to his upstairs room. Its windows opened toward Jerusalem. He went to his room three times a day to pray. He got down on his knees and gave thanks to his God.

Always Do What God Says

The king made a law that no one could pray to anyone but him for 30 days. But Daniel loved God. So what did he do? He prayed to God anyway. Read the rest of this exciting story.

Should Christians obey laws that the government makes? Yes, unless those laws are against something that God teaches us in the Bible.

Ask your mom or dad for a strip of cloth about 4 inches wide and 14 inches long. Find a picture of a lion. Trace its head on one end of the strip of cloth. Go over the lines with a marker to make them dark. Wrap the cloth around your arm so that the lion's head shows. Have your mom pin it snugly. When you play, it will remind you that God protects you when you do what is right.

Some of the other royal officials went to where Daniel was staying. They saw him praying and asking God for help. So they went to the king. They spoke to him about his royal order. They said, "King Darius, didn't you sign an official order? It said that for the next 30 days none of your people could pray to any god or man except to you. If they did, they would be thrown into the lions' den."

The king answered, "The order must still be obeyed. It's one of the laws of the Medes and Persians. So it can't be changed."

Then they spoke to the king again. They said, "Daniel is one of the prisoners from Judah. He doesn't pay any attention to you, King Darius. He doesn't obey the order you put in writing. He still prays to his God three times a day."

When the king heard that, he was very upset. He didn't want Daniel to be harmed in any way. Until sunset, he did everything he could to save him.

Then the men went as a group to the king. They said to him, "King Darius, remember that no order or law you make can be changed. That's what the laws of the Medes and Persians require."

So the king gave the order. Daniel was brought out and thrown into the lions' den. The king said to him, "You always serve your God faithfully. So may he save you!"

A stone was brought and placed over the opening of the den. The king sealed it with his own special ring. He also sealed it with the rings of his nobles. Then nothing could be done to help Daniel.

Prayer

People in the Bible prayed in many different places and positions. When Daniel prayed, he got down on his knees to show his respect for God. Back in the book of Exodus, Moses was so upset because of Israel's worship of the golden calf that he fell facedown before the Lord to pray. In the New Testament, the apostle Paul told believers to lift up their hands when they prayed.

The king returned to his palace. He didn't eat anything that night. He didn't ask for anything to be brought to him for his enjoyment. And he couldn't sleep.

As soon as the sun began to rise, the king got up. He hurried to the lions' den. When he got near it, he called out to Daniel. His voice was filled with great concern. He said, "Daniel! You serve the living God. You always serve him faithfully. So has he been able to save you from the lions?"

Daniel answered, "My king, may you live forever! My God sent his angel. And his angel shut the mouths of the lions. They haven't hurt me at all. That's because I haven't done anything wrong in God's sight. I've never done anything wrong to you either, my king."

The king was filled with joy. He ordered his servants to lift Daniel out of the den. So they did. They didn't see any wounds on him. That's because he had trusted in his God.

Then the king gave another order. The men who had said bad things about Daniel were brought in. They were thrown into the lions' den. So were their wives and children. Before they hit the bottom of the den, the lions attacked them. And the lions crushed all of their bones.

Then King Darius wrote to the people from every nation and language in the whole world. He said,

"May you have great success!

"I order people in every part of my kingdom to respect and honor Daniel's God.

"He is the living God.
    He will live forever.
His kingdom will not be destroyed.
    His rule will never end.
He sets people free and saves them.
    He does miraculous signs and wonders.
    He does them in the heavens and on the earth.
He has saved Daniel
    from the power of the lions."

So Daniel had success while Darius was king. Things went well with him during the rule of Cyrus, the Persian.

The Minor Prophets

Hosea   Joel   Jonah   Amos   Obadiah   Micah   Nahum   Habakkuk   Zephaniah   Haggai   Zechariah   Malachi

The books of the Minor Prophets are small books. But they have a big message. These prophets had to tell the people of Judah and Israel and some other nations some hard things. Sometimes the people wouldn't listen. The prophets promised that God would punish them if they did not obey. God was angry because the people were not worshiping him. They were not doing what is right or what is fair. The rich people were cheating the poor people.

These prophets have a message for everyone. God is holy. He will not put up with people who are not holy. But he will forgive everyone who comes to him and obeys him. He will forgive their sins and make them holy.

Warnings From the Prophet Hosea

Hosea 14

The LORD Blesses Those Who Turn Away From Sin

Israel, return to the LORD your God.
    Your sins have destroyed you!
Tell the LORD you are turning away from your sins.
    Return to him.
Say to him,
    "Forgive us for all of our sins.
Please be kind to us.
    Welcome us back to you.
    Then our lips will offer you our praise.
Assyria can't save us.
    We won't trust in our war horses.
Our own hands have made statues of gods.
    But we will never call them our gods again.
We are like children whose fathers have died.
    But you show us your tender love."

Then the LORD will answer,

"My people always wander away from me.
    But I will put an end to that.
My anger has turned away from them.
    Now I will love them freely.
I will be like the dew to Israel.
    They will bloom like a lily.
They will send their roots down deep
    like a cedar tree in Lebanon.
They will spread out like new branches.
    They will be as beautiful as an olive tree.
    They will smell as sweet as the cedar trees in Lebanon.
Once again my people will live
    in the safety of my shade.
    They will grow like grain.

They will bloom like vines.
And they will be as famous
as wine from Lebanon.
Ephraim will have nothing more to do
with other gods.
I will answer the prayers of my
people.
I will take good care of them.
I will be like a green pine tree to them.
All of the fruit they bear will come
from me."

If you are wise, you will realize
that what I've said is true.
If you have understanding,
you will know what it means.

The ways of the LORD are right.
People who are right with God live the way he wants them to.
But those who refuse to obey him trip and fall.

Warnings From the Prophet Amos

Amos 1; 8—9

These are the words of Amos. He was a shepherd from the town of Tekoa. Here is the vision he saw concerning Israel. It came to him two years before the earthquake. At that time Uzziah was king of Judah. Jeroboam was king of Israel. He was the son of Jehoash. Here are the words of Amos.

I said,

"The LORD roars like a lion from Jerusalem.
His voice sounds like thunder from Zion.
The grasslands of the shepherds turn brown.
The top of Mount Carmel dries up."

The LORD Gives Amos Another Vision

The LORD and King gave me a vision. He showed me a basket of ripe fruit. "What do you see, Amos?" he asked.

"A basket of ripe fruit," I replied.

Then the LORD said to me, "The time is ripe for my people Israel. I will no longer spare them.

"The time is coming when the songs in the temple will turn to crying," announces the LORD and King. "Many, many bodies will be thrown everywhere! So be quiet!"

What is a vision?

A vision is like a dream. But a dream happens when you sleep. A vision happens when you're awake. God used visions and dreams to speak to people in the Bible.

Listen to me, you who walk all over needy people.
    You crush those who are poor in the land.

You say,

"When will the New Moon Feast be over?
    Then we can sell our grain.
When will the Sabbath day come to an end?
    Then people can buy our wheat."
But you don't measure out the right amount.
    You raise your prices.
    You cheat others by using dishonest scales.
You buy poor people to make slaves out of them.
    You buy those who are in need for a mere pair of sandals.
    You even sell the worthless parts of your wheat.

People of Jacob, you are proud that the LORD is your God. But he has taken an oath in his own name. He says, "I will never forget anything Israel has done.

"The land will tremble because of what will happen.
    Everyone who lives in it will sob.
So the whole land will rise like the Nile River.
    It will be stirred up.

Sandals

People in Bible times wore sandals on their feet instead of shoes. Some of the rich people in Amos's time thought that using their money to buy a pair of fancy sandals was better than using it to help someone in need.

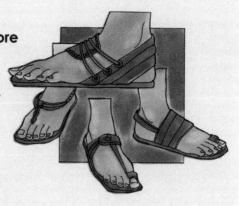

Then it will settle back down again
    like that river in Egypt."

Israel Will Be Made Like New Again

"The time will come when I will rebuild
    David's fallen tent.
I will repair its broken places.
    I will rebuild what was destroyed.
    I will make it what it used to be.
Then my people will take control of those
    who are left alive in Edom.
They will also possess all of the nations
    that belong to me,"

                                    announces the LORD.
He will do all of those things.

"A new day is coming," announces the LORD.

"At that time those who plow the land
    will catch up with those who harvest the crops.
Those who stomp on grapes
    will catch up with those who plant the vines.
Fresh wine will drip from the mountains.
    It will flow down from all of the hills.

I will bring my people Israel back home.

I will bless them with great success again.

They will rebuild the destroyed cities and live in them.

They will plant vineyards and drink the wine they produce.

They will make gardens and eat their fruit.

I will plant Israel in their own land.

They will never again be removed

from the land I have given them,"

says the LORD your God.

Jonah and the Fish

Jonah 1—3

Jonah Runs Away From the LORD

A message from the LORD came to Jonah. He was the son of Amittai. The LORD said, "Go to the great city of Nineveh. Preach against it. The sins of its people have come to my attention."

But Jonah ran away from the LORD. He headed for Tarshish. So he went down to the port of Joppa. There he found a ship that was going to Tarshish. He paid the fare and went on board. Then he sailed for Tarshish. He was running away from the LORD.

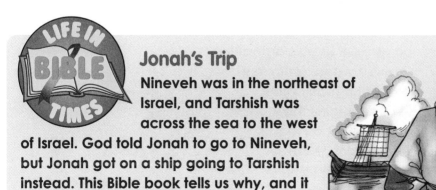

Jonah's Trip
Nineveh was in the northeast of Israel, and Tarshish was across the sea to the west of Israel. God told Jonah to go to Nineveh, but Jonah got on a ship going to Tarshish instead. This Bible book tells us why, and it tells us what happened to Jonah.

But the L ORD sent a strong wind over the Mediterranean Sea. A wild storm came up. It was so wild that the ship was in danger of breaking apart. All of the sailors were afraid. Each one cried out to his own god for help. They threw the ship's contents into the sea. They were trying to make the ship lighter.

But Jonah had gone below deck. There he lay down and fell into a deep sleep. The captain went down to him and said, "How can you sleep? Get up and call out to your god for help! Maybe he'll pay attention to what's happening to us. Then we won't die."

The sailors said to one another, "Come. Let's cast lots to find out who is to blame for getting us into all of this trouble." So they did. And Jonah was picked.

They asked him, "What terrible thing have you done to bring all of this trouble on us? Tell us. What do you do for a living? Where do you come from? What is your country? What people do you belong to?"

He answered, "I'm a Hebrew. I worship the L ORD. He is the God of heaven. He made the sea and the land."

They found out he was running away from the L ORD. That's because he had told them. Then they became terrified. So they asked him, "How could you do a thing like that?"

The sea was getting rougher and rougher. So they asked him, "What should we do to you to make the sea calm down?"

Cargo Ships

In ancient times cargo ships carried wood, grain, animals and many other things from one port to another. The crew of a ship lived and slept on the deck of their ship. When storms came they tried to find a sheltered harbor, because otherwise they might be swept overboard by the wind and waves.

"Pick me up and throw me into the sea," he replied. "Then it will become calm. I know it's my fault that this terrible storm has come on you."

Instead of doing what he said, the men did their best to row back to land. But they couldn't. The sea got even rougher than before.

Then they cried out to the LORD. They prayed, "LORD, please don't let us die for taking this man's life. After all, he might not be guilty of doing anything wrong. So don't hold us accountable for killing him. LORD, you always do what you want to." Then they took Jonah and threw him overboard. And the stormy sea became calm.

When the men saw what had happened, they began to have great respect for the LORD. They offered a sacrifice to him. And they made promises to him.

But the LORD sent a huge fish to swallow Jonah. And Jonah was inside the fish for three days and three nights.

Jonah Prays to the LORD

From inside the fish Jonah prayed to the LORD his God. He said,

"When I was in trouble, I called out to you.
　　And you answered me.
When I had almost drowned,
　　I called out for help.
　　And you listened to my cry."

The LORD gave the fish a command. And it spit Jonah up onto dry land.

Jonah Goes to Nineveh

A message came to Jonah from the LORD a second time. He said, "Go to the great city of Nineveh. Announce to its people the message I give you."

Jonah obeyed the LORD. He went to Nineveh. It was a very important city. In fact, it took about three days to see all of it. On the first day, Jonah started into the city. He announced, "In 40 days Nineveh will be destroyed."

The people of Nineveh believed God's warning. They decided not to eat any food for a while. All of them put on black clothes. That's what everyone from the least important of them to the most important did.

The news reached the king of Nineveh. He got up from his throne. He took his royal robes off and dressed himself in black clothes. He sat down in the dust. Then he sent out a message to the people of Nineveh. He said,

"I and my nobles give this order.

"Don't let any person or animal taste anything. That includes your herds and flocks. People and animals must not eat or drink anything. Let people and animals alike be covered with black cloth. All of you must call out to God with all your hearts. Stop doing what is evil. Don't harm others. Who knows? God might take pity on us. He might turn away from his burning anger. Then we won't die."

God saw what they did. They stopped doing what was evil. So he took pity on them. He didn't destroy them as he had said he would.

A Warning From Micah the Prophet

Micah 6

The LORD Brings Charges Against Israel

Israel, listen to the LORD's message. He says to me,

"Stand up in court.
    Let the mountains serve as witnesses.
    Let the hills hear what you have to say."

Hear the LORD's case, you mountains.
    Listen, you age-old foundations of the earth.
The LORD has a case against his people Israel.
    He is bringing charges against them.

The LORD says,

"My people, what have I done to you?
    Have I made things too hard for you? Answer me.
I brought your people up out of Egypt.

I set them free from the land
    where they were slaves.
I sent Moses to lead them.
    Aaron and Miriam helped him.
Remember how Balak, the king of Moab,
    planned to put a curse on your people.
But Balaam, the son of Beor,
    gave them a blessing instead.
Remember their journey from Shittim to Gilgal.
    I want you to know
    that I always do what is right."

The people of Israel say,

"What should we bring with us
    when we go to worship the LORD?
What should we offer the God of heaven
    when we bow down to him?
Should we take burnt offerings to him?
    Should we sacrifice calves
    that are a year old?
Will the LORD be pleased with thousands
        of rams?
    Will he take delight in 10,000 rivers of
        olive oil?
Should we offer our oldest sons
    for the wrong things we've done?
Should we sacrifice our own children
    to pay for our sins?"

The LORD has shown you what is good.
    He has told you what he requires
        of you.
You must treat people fairly.
    You must love others faithfully.
And you must be very careful to live
    the way your God wants you to.

WORDS TO TREASURE

The LORD has shown you what is good. He has told you what he requires of you. You must treat people fairly. You must love others faithfully. And you must be very careful to live the way your God wants you to.

Micah 6:8

A Warning From the Prophet Nahum

Nahum 1

Here is a message the LORD gave Nahum in a vision about Nineveh. It is written on a scroll. Nahum was from the town of Elkosh. Here is what he said.

The LORD Is Angry With Nineveh

The LORD is a jealous God who punishes people.
　　He pays them back for the evil things they do.
　　His anger burns against them.
The LORD punishes his enemies.
　　He holds his anger back
　　until the right time to use it.
The LORD is slow to get angry.
　　He is very powerful.
The LORD will not let guilty people go
　　without punishing them.

The Prophet Habakkuk

Habakkuk 3

Habakkuk Prays to the LORD

This is a prayer of the prophet Habakkuk. It is on *shigionoth*. Here is what he said.

LORD, I know how famous you are.
　　I have great respect for you
　　because of your mighty acts.
Do them again for us.
　　Make them known in our time.
When you are angry,
　　please show us your tender love.
When you stoop up,
　　the earth shook.

I listened and my heart pounded.

My lips trembled at the sound.
My bones seemed to rot.
And my legs shook.
But I will be patient.
I'll wait for the day of trouble to come on Babylonia.
It's the nation that is attacking us.
The fig trees might not bud.
The vines might not produce any grapes.
The olive crop might fail.
The fields might not produce any food.
There might not be any sheep in the pens.
There might not be any cattle in the barns.
But I will still be glad
because of what the LORD has done.
God my Savior fills me with joy.

The LORD and King gives me strength.
He makes my feet like the feet of a deer.
He helps me walk on the highest places.

The LORD and King gives me strength. He makes my feet like the feet of a deer.

Habakkuk 3:19

Mountain Goats

High mountain cliffs are dangerous places for people. But deer can walk there safely. This picture from nature teaches that God will keep his people safe, even in dangerous places.

The Prophet Zephaniah

Zephaniah 1—2

A message came to Zephaniah from the LORD. He was the son of Cushi. Cushi was the son of Gedaliah. Gedaliah was the son of Amariah. Amariah was the son of King Hezekiah. The LORD spoke to Zephaniah during the rule of Josiah. He was king of Judah and the son of Amon.

The Day of the LORD Is Coming

"The great day of the LORD is near.
In fact, it is coming quickly.
Listen! The cries on that day will be
bitter.
Even soldiers will cry out in
fear.
At that time I will pour out my
anger.
There will be great suffering
and pain.
It will be a day of horrible trouble.
It will be a time of darkness and
gloom.
It will be filled with the blackest clouds.
Trumpet blasts and battle cries will be heard.
Soldiers will attack cities
that have forts and corner towers."

So look to him, all of you people in the land
who worship him faithfully.
You always do what he commands you to do.
Continue to do what is right.
Don't be proud.
Then perhaps the LORD will keep you safe
on the day he pours out his anger on the world.

WORDS TO TREASURE

The great day of the
LORD is near.
Zephaniah 1:14

New Testament

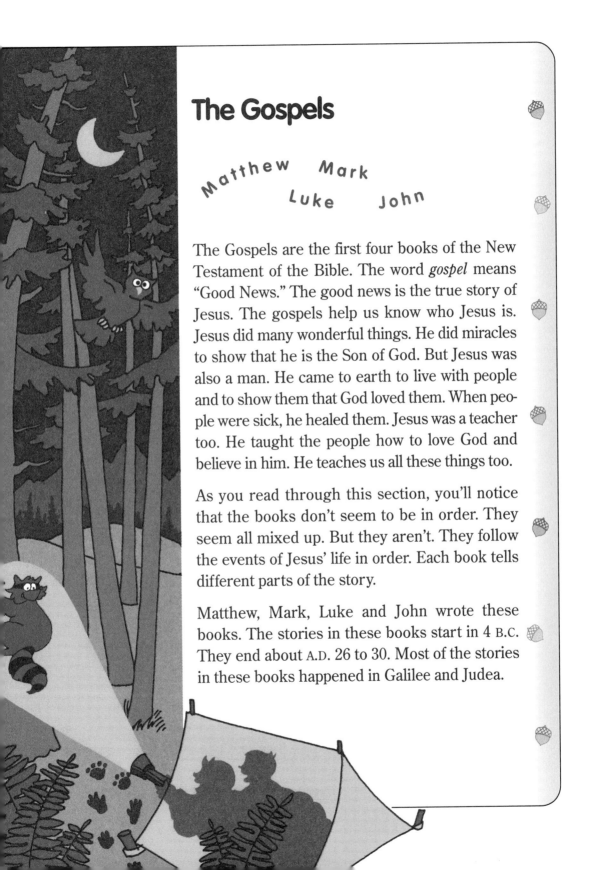

The Gospels

Matthew Mark
   Luke   John

The Gospels are the first four books of the New Testament of the Bible. The word *gospel* means "Good News." The good news is the true story of Jesus. The gospels help us know who Jesus is. Jesus did many wonderful things. He did miracles to show that he is the Son of God. But Jesus was also a man. He came to earth to live with people and to show them that God loved them. When people were sick, he healed them. Jesus was a teacher too. He taught the people how to love God and believe in him. He teaches us all these things too.

As you read through this section, you'll notice that the books don't seem to be in order. They seem all mixed up. But they aren't. They follow the events of Jesus' life in order. Each book tells different parts of the story.

Matthew, Mark, Luke and John wrote these books. The stories in these books start in 4 B.C. They end about A.D. 26 to 30. Most of the stories in these books happened in Galilee and Judea.

Angels Announce the Birth of Two Babies

Luke 1

Luke Writes an Orderly Report

Many people have attempted to write about the things that have taken place among us. Reports of these things were handed down to us. There were people who saw these things for themselves from the beginning and then passed the word on.

I myself have carefully looked into everything from the beginning. So it seemed good also to me to write down an orderly report of exactly what happened. I am doing this for you, most excellent Theophilus. I want you to know that the things you have been taught are true.

The Coming Birth of John the Baptist

Herod was king of Judea. During the time he was ruling, there was a priest named Zechariah. He belonged to a group of priests named after Abijah. His wife Elizabeth also came from the family line of Aaron. Both of them did what was right in God's eyes. They obeyed all the Lord's commandments and rules faithfully. But they had no children, because Elizabeth was not able to have any. And they were both very old.

One day Zechariah's group was on duty. He was serving as a priest in God's temple. He happened to be chosen, in the usual way, to go into the temple of the Lord. There he was supposed to burn incense. The time came for this to be done. All who had gathered to worship were praying outside.

Then an angel of the Lord appeared to Zechariah. The angel was standing at the right side of the incense altar. When Zechariah saw him, he was amazed and terrified.

But the angel said to him, "Do not be afraid, Zechariah. Your prayer has been heard. Your wife Elizabeth will have a child. It will be a boy,

PEOPLE IN BIBLE TIMES

Zechariah and Elizabeth

Mary was Jesus' mother. Elizabeth came from Mary's family. She was married to a priest. His name was Zechariah. They were both very old. They did not have any children. An angel told them that they would have a baby boy. The angel said to name the baby John. He is known as John the Baptist.

and you must name him John. He will be a joy and delight to you. His birth will make many people very glad. He will be important in the Lord's eyes.

"He must never use wine or other such drinks. He will be filled with the Holy Spirit from the time he is born. He will bring many of Israel's people back to the Lord their God. And he will prepare the way for the Lord. He will have the same spirit and power that Elijah had. He will teach parents how to love their children. He will also teach people who don't obey to be wise and do what is right. In this way, he will prepare a people who are ready for the Lord."

Zechariah asked the angel, "How can I be sure of this? I am an old man, and my wife is old too."

The angel answered, "I am Gabriel. I serve God. I have been sent to speak to you and to tell you this good news. And now you will have to be silent. You will not be able to speak until after John is born. That's because you did not believe my words. They will come true when the time is right."

During that time, the people were waiting for Zechariah to come out. They wondered why he stayed in the temple so long. When he came out, he could not speak to them. They realized he had seen a vision in the temple. They knew this because he kept motioning to them. He still could not speak.

When his time of service was over, he returned home. After that, his wife Elizabeth became pregnant. She stayed at home for five months. "The Lord has done this for me," she said. "In these days, he has been kind to me. He has taken away my shame among the people."

The Coming Birth of Jesus

In the sixth month after Elizabeth had become pregnant, God sent the angel Gabriel to Nazareth, a town in Galilee. He was sent to a virgin. The girl was engaged to a man named Joseph. He came from the family line of David. The virgin's name was Mary. The angel greeted her and said, "The Lord has given you special favor. He is with you."

Mary was very upset because of his words. She wondered what kind of greeting this could be. But the angel said to her, "Do not be afraid, Mary. God is very pleased with you. You will become pregnant and give

birth to a son. You must name him Jesus. He will be great and will be called the Son of the Most High God. The Lord God will make him a king like his father David of long ago. He will rule forever over his people, who came from Jacob's family. His kingdom will never end."

"How can this happen?" Mary asked the angel. "I am a virgin."

The angel answered, "The Holy Spirit will come to you. The power of the Most High God will cover you. So the holy one that is born will be called the Son of God. Your relative Elizabeth is old. And even she is going to have a child. People thought she could not have children. But she has been pregnant for six months now. Nothing is impossible with God."

"I serve the Lord," Mary answered. "May it happen to me just as you said it would." Then the angel left her.

Mary Visits Elizabeth

At that time Mary got ready and hurried to a town in Judea's hill country. There she entered Zechariah's home and greeted Elizabeth. When Elizabeth heard Mary's greeting, the baby inside her jumped. And Elizabeth was filled with the Holy Spirit. In a loud voice she called out, "God has blessed you more than other women. And blessed is the child you will have! But why is God so kind to me? Why has the mother of my Lord come to me? As soon as I heard the sound of your voice, the baby inside me jumped for joy. You are a woman God has blessed. You have believed that what the Lord has said to you will be done!"

Mary stayed with Elizabeth about three months. Then she returned home.

John the Baptist

Luke 1

John the Baptist Is Born

The time came for Elizabeth to have her baby. She gave birth to a son. Her neighbors and relatives heard that the Lord had been very kind to her. They shared her joy.

On the eighth day, they came to have the child circumcised. They were going to name him Zechariah, like his father. But his mother spoke up. "No!" she said. "He must be called John."

They said to her, "No one among your relatives has that name."

Then they motioned to his father. They wanted to find out what he would like to name the child. He asked for something to write on. Then he wrote, "His name is John." Everyone was amazed.

Right away Zechariah could speak again. His first words gave praise to God. The neighbors were all filled with fear and wonder. All through Judea's hill country, people were talking about all these things. Everyone who heard this wondered about it. And because the Lord was with John, they asked, "What is this child going to be?"

The child grew up, and his spirit became strong. He lived in the desert until he appeared openly to Israel.

Jesus Is Born

Luke 2; Matthew 2

In those days, Caesar Augustus made a law. It required that a list be made of everyone in the whole Roman world. It was the first time a list was made of the people while Quirinius was governor of Syria. All went to their own towns to be listed.

So Joseph went also. He went from the town of Nazareth in Galilee to Judea. That is where Bethlehem, the town of David, was. Joseph went there because he belonged to the family line of David. He went there with Mary to be listed. Mary was engaged to him. She was expecting a baby.

While Joseph and Mary were there, the time came for the child to be born. She gave birth to her first baby. It was a boy. She wrapped him in large strips of cloth. Then she placed him in a manger. There was no room for them in the inn.

Angels Appear to the Shepherds

There were shepherds living out in the fields nearby. It was night, and they were looking after their sheep. An angel of the Lord appeared to them. And the glory of the Lord shone around them. They were terrified.

But the angel said to them, "Do not be afraid. I bring you good news of great joy. It is for all the people. Today in the town of David a Savior has been born to you. He is Christ the Lord. Here is how you will know

The Stable

A stable was a place where animals were kept and fed. The stables in Bethlehem were usually caves instead of buildings. The stable where Jesus was born was probably one of these caves.

288

I am telling you the truth. You will find a baby wrapped in strips of cloth and lying in a manger."

Suddenly a large group of angels from heaven also appeared. They were praising God. They said,

"May glory be given to God in the highest heaven!
And may peace be given to those he is pleased with on earth!"

The angels left and went into heaven. Then the shepherds said to one another, "Let's go to Bethlehem. Let's see this thing that has happened, which the Lord has told us about."

So they hurried off and found Mary and Joseph and the baby. The baby was lying in the manger. After the shepherds had seen him, they told everyone. They reported what the angel had said about this child. All who heard it were amazed at what the shepherds said to them.

But Mary kept all these things like a secret treasure in her heart. She thought about them over and over.

PEOPLE IN BIBLE TIMES

Jesus

Jesus is the Son of God. God chose him to be the Christ. He is the Savior of his people. God called Jesus "my Son" (Matthew 3:17, page 294). That means that Jesus is truly God. The Bible also calls him the "Son of Man" (Mark 8:31). That tells us that Jesus was also a real human being.

A Jesus Baby Book

Did your mom or dad keep a baby book for you? Ask if you can look at it. It will have pictures of you as a baby. It will tell interesting things about when you were young and how you grew.

You can make a baby book for Jesus. On these pages you will learn many things about Jesus' birth. Draw pictures of these things on some pieces of paper. Write Bible verses that tell about each picture. Now stack the papers and punch two holes on one end. Thread a long piece of yarn through the holes. Tie the yarn to hold the papers together.

The shepherds returned. They gave glory and praise to God. Everything they had seen and heard was just as they had been told.

Joseph and Mary Take Jesus to the Temple

When the child was eight days old, he was circumcised. At the same time he was named Jesus. This was the name the angel had given him before his mother became pregnant.

The time for making them pure came as it is written in the Law of Moses. So Joseph and Mary took Jesus to Jerusalem. There they presented him to the Lord. In the Law of the Lord it says, "The first boy born in every family must be set apart for the Lord." *(Exodus 13:2,12)* They also offered a sacrifice. They did it in keeping with the Law, which says, "a pair of doves or two young pigeons." *(Leviticus 12:8)*

In Jerusalem there was a man named Simeon. He was a good and godly man. He was waiting for God's promise to Israel to happen. The Holy Spirit was with him. The Spirit had told Simeon that he would not die before he had seen the Lord's Christ. The Spirit led him into the temple courtyard.

Then Jesus' parents brought the child in. They came to do for him what the Law required.

Simeon took Jesus in his arms and praised God. He said,

"Lord, you are the King over all.
    Now let me, your servant, go in peace.
    That is what you promised.
My eyes have seen your salvation.

Two Pigeons
People who could afford it offered God a lamb when their first son was born. Joseph and Mary, however, gave two pigeons. God said this offering could be given by those who were poor.

You have prepared it in the sight of all people.
It is a light to be given to those who aren't Jews.
It will bring glory to your people Israel."

The child's father and mother were amazed at what was said about him. Then Simeon blessed them. He said to Mary, Jesus' mother, "This child is going to cause many people in Israel to fall and to rise. God has sent him. But many will speak against him. The thoughts of many hearts will be known. A sword will wound your own soul too."

Joseph and Mary did everything the Law of the Lord required. Then they returned to Galilee. They went to their own town of Nazareth. And the child grew and became strong. He was very wise. He was blessed by God's grace.

The Wise Men Visit Jesus

Jesus was born in Bethlehem in Judea. This happened while Herod was king of Judea.

After Jesus' birth, Wise Men from the east came to Jerusalem. They asked, "Where is the child who has been born to be king of the Jews? When we were in the east, we saw his star. Now we have come to worship him."

When King Herod heard about it, he was very upset. Everyone in Jerusalem was troubled too. So Herod called together all the chief priests of the people. He also called the teachers of the law. He asked them where the Christ was going to be born.

"In Bethlehem in Judea," they replied. "This is what the prophet has written. He said,

"'But you, Bethlehem, in the land of Judah,
    are certainly not the least important among the towns of Judah.
A ruler will come out of you.
    He will be the shepherd of my people Israel.'"   *(Micah 5:2)*

Then Herod called for the Wise Men secretly. He found out from them exactly when the star had appeared. He sent them to Bethlehem. He said, "Go! Make a careful search for the child. As soon as you find him, bring me a report. Then I can go and worship him too."

After the Wise Men had listened to the king, they went on their way. The star they had seen when they were in the east went ahead of them. It finally stopped over the place where the child was. When they saw the star, they were filled with joy.

The Wise Men went to the house. There they saw the child with his mother Mary. They bowed down and worshiped him. Then they opened their treasures. They gave him gold, incense and myrrh.

But God warned them in a dream not to go back to Herod. So they returned to their country on a different road.

Jesus at the Temple

Luke 2

The child grew and became strong. He was very wise. He was blessed by God's grace.

The Boy Jesus at the Temple

Every year Jesus' parents went to Jerusalem for the Passover Feast. When he was 12 years old, they went up to the Feast as usual.

After the Feast was over, his parents left to go back home. The boy Jesus stayed behind in Jerusalem. But they were not aware of it. They thought he was somewhere in their group. So they traveled on for a day.

Then they began to look for him among their relatives and friends. They did not find him. So they went back to Jerusalem to look for him. After three days they found him in the temple courtyard. He was sitting with the teachers. He was listening to them and asking them questions. Everyone who heard him was

DID YOU KNOW?

Why did Jesus go to the temple when he turned 12?

The Jews said a boy was an adult when he turned 12. He was old enough to keep God's law like an adult. The men went to Jerusalem on the Passover. They worshiped at the temple. Jesus was 12. So he went to Jerusalem. He worshiped at the temple too.

amazed at how much he understood. They also were amazed at his answers.

When his parents saw him, they were amazed. His mother said to him, "Son, why have you treated us like this? Your father and I have been worried about you. We have been looking for you everywhere."

"Why were you looking for me?" he asked. "Didn't you know I had to be in my Father's house?" But they did not understand what he meant by that.

Then he went back to Nazareth with them, and he obeyed them. But his mother kept all these things like a secret treasure in her heart. Jesus became wiser and stronger. He also became more and more pleasing to God and to people.

John Baptizes People

Matthew 3; Mark 1

John the Baptist Prepares the Way

In those days John the Baptist came and preached in the Desert of Judea. He said, "Turn away from your sins! The kingdom of heaven is near."

John is the one the prophet Isaiah had spoken about. He had said,

"A messenger is calling out in the desert,
'Prepare the way for the Lord.
Make straight paths for him.'"

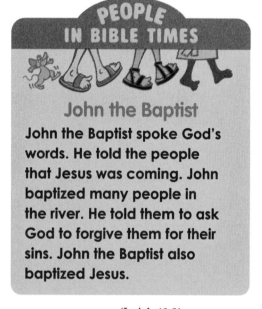

PEOPLE IN BIBLE TIMES

John the Baptist

John the Baptist spoke God's words. He told the people that Jesus was coming. John baptized many people in the river. He told them to ask God to forgive them for their sins. John the Baptist also baptized Jesus.

(Isaiah 40:3)

John's clothes were made out of camel's hair. He had a leather belt around his waist. His food was locusts and wild honey. People went out to him from Jerusalem and all of Judea. They also came from the whole area around the Jordan River. He preached that people should be baptized and turn away from their sins. Then God would forgive them. When they admitted they had sinned, John baptized them in the Jordan River.

Here is what John was preaching. "After me, one will come who is more powerful than I am. I'm not good enough to bend down and untie his sandals. I baptize you with water. But he will baptize you with the Holy Spirit."

John Baptizes Jesus

Matthew 3; John 1

Jesus Is Baptized

Jesus came from Galilee to the Jordan River. He wanted to be baptized by John. But John tried to stop him. He told Jesus, "I need to be baptized by you. So why do you come to me?"

Jesus replied, "Let it be this way for now. It is right for us to do this. It carries out God's holy plan." Then John agreed.

As soon as Jesus was baptized, he came up out of the water. At that moment heaven was opened. Jesus saw the Spirit of God coming down on him like a dove.

A voice from heaven said, "This is my Son, and I love him. I am very pleased with him."

Jesus Is the Lamb of God

John said, "Look! The Lamb of God! He takes away the sin of the world! This is the One I was talking about. I said, 'A man who comes after me is more important than I am. That's because he existed before I was born.' I did not know him. But God wants to make it clear to Israel who this person is. That's the reason I came baptizing with water."

WORDS TO TREASURE

This is my Son, and I love him. I am very pleased with him.

Matthew 3:17

DID YOU KNOW?

What does "Lamb of God" mean?

In Bible times, lambs were used as offerings. When a person sinned, that person killed a lamb and then offered the lamb to God. To call Jesus the Lamb of God means that he is our offering. Jesus would die to take away our sins.

Then John told them, "I saw the Holy Spirit come down from heaven like a dove. The Spirit remained on Jesus. I would not have known him. But the One who sent me to baptize with water told me, 'You will see the Spirit come down and remain on someone. He is the One who will baptize with the Holy Spirit.' I have seen it happen. I give witness that this is the Son of God."

Jesus Is Tempted in the Desert

Matthew 4

The Holy Spirit led Jesus into the desert. There the devil tempted him. After 40 days and 40 nights of going without eating, Jesus was hungry.

The tempter came to him. He said, "If you are the Son of God, tell these stones to become bread."

Jesus answered, "It is written, 'Man doesn't live only on bread. He also lives on every word that comes from the mouth of God.'" *(Deuteronomy 8:3)*

Then the devil took Jesus to the holy city. He had him stand on the highest point of the temple. "If you are the Son of God," he said, "throw yourself down. It is written,

What did Jesus do when he was tempted?

Jesus thought about what the Bible says. And he decided to obey God's Word. It's important for you to know the Bible too. It will help you when you're tempted.

"'The Lord will command his angels to take good care of you.
They will lift you up in their hands.
Then you won't trip over a stone.'" *(Psalm 91:11,12)*

Jesus answered him, "It is also written, 'Do not put the Lord your God to the test.'" *(Deuteronomy 6:16)*

Finally, the devil took Jesus to a very high mountain. He showed him all the kingdoms of the world and their glory. "If you bow down and worship me," he said, "I will give you all of this."

Doing What You Should Do

Did anyone ever try to get you to do something that you knew you shouldn't? If so, this person was trying to tempt you. Jesus was tempted too. He was tempted by the devil. What three words did Jesus say to Satan each time that he was tempted? He said, "It is written." He was talking about God's words in the Bible. Jesus fought temptation by obeying what God says in the Bible. You can do the same thing. Listen carefully when the Bible is being read. Learn what God wants you to do. Then when you are tempted to do something wrong, decide to obey God's Word instead.

Jesus said to him, "Get away from me, Satan! It is written, 'Worship the Lord your God. He is the only one you should serve.'" *(Deuteronomy 6:13)*

Then the devil left Jesus. Angels came and took care of him.

The First Disciples

Luke 5

Jesus Chooses the First Disciples

One day Jesus was standing by the Sea of Galilee. The people crowded around him and listened to the word of God. Jesus saw two boats at the edge of the water. They had been left there by the fishermen, who were washing their nets. He got into the boat that belonged to Simon. Jesus asked him to go out a little way from shore. Then he sat down in the boat and taught the people.

When he finished speaking, he turned to Simon. He said, "Go out into deep water. Let the nets down so you can catch some fish."

Simon answered, "Master, we've worked hard all night and haven't caught anything. But because you say so, I will let down the nets."

When they had done so, they caught a large number of fish. There were so many that their nets began to break. So they motioned to their partners in the other boat to come and help them. They came and filled both boats so full that they began to sink.

Fishing

When Jesus was alive, fishermen in boats worked on the Sea of Galilee. The fish they caught in their nets were salted or dried and then sold all through the Holy Land. Jesus told his first disciples to be fishers of people instead of fishers of fish.

When Simon Peter saw this, he fell at Jesus' knees. "Go away from me, Lord!" he said. "I am a sinful man!"

He and everyone with him were amazed at the number of fish they had caught. So were James and John, the sons of Zebedee, who worked with Simon.

Then Jesus said to Simon, "Don't be afraid. From now on you will catch people."

So they pulled their boats up on shore. Then they left everything and followed him.

People Jesus Chooses

Who would you ask to do a hard job? We learn four things about the men Jesus chose to be his disciples:
1. They worked hard.
2. They were respectful.
3. They did what they were told to do.
4. They worked well with other people as a team.

Each day for one week try to live as Jesus' followers did. Each day that you work hard, are respectful, do what you are told to do, or get along with others, put a check mark on your family's calendar.

Jesus Teaches Nicodemus

John 3

There was a Pharisee named Nicodemus. He was one of the Jewish rulers. He came to Jesus at night and said, "Rabbi, we know you are a teacher who has come from God. We know that God is with you. If he weren't, you couldn't do the miraculous signs you are doing."

Jesus replied, "What I'm about to tell you is true. No one can see God's kingdom without being born again."

"How can I be born when I am old?" Nicodemus asked. "I can't go back inside my mother! I can't be born a second time!"

Jesus answered, "What I'm about to tell you is true. No one can enter God's kingdom without being born through water and the Holy Spirit. People give birth to people. But the Spirit gives birth to spirit. You should not be surprised when I say, 'You must all be born again.'

"The wind blows where it wants to. You hear the sound it makes. But you can't tell where it comes from or where it is going. It is the same with everyone who is born through the Spirit."

"How can this be?" Nicodemus asked.

"You are Israel's teacher," said Jesus. "Don't you understand these things?

PEOPLE IN BIBLE TIMES

Nicodemus

Nicodemus was a ruler of the Jews. He came to Jesus at night. He had questions about God. Jesus told him about being born again. He told Nicodemus about eternal life too.

LET'S LIVE IT!

Born Again

When you were born, your body was alive. When you are "born again," your spirit lives forever with God. Your life in your body will someday end when you die. But when you are "born again," your spirit will not die. Your spirit will live forever with God in heaven.

How can you be born again? Memorize John 3:16 (on the next page). You must believe in Jesus as your Savior. Then you are born again and will have eternal life.

"What I'm about to tell you is true. We speak about what we know. We give witness to what we have seen. But still you people do not accept our witness. I have spoken to you about earthly things, and you do not believe. So how will you believe if I speak about heavenly things?

"No one has ever gone into heaven except the One who came from heaven. He is the Son of Man. Moses lifted up the snake in the desert. The Son of Man must be lifted up also. Then everyone who believes in him can live with God forever.

"God loved the world so much that he gave his one and only Son. Anyone who believes in him will not die but will have eternal life.

"God did not send his Son into the world to judge the world. He sent his Son to save the world through him. Anyone who believes in him is not judged. But anyone who does not believe is judged already. He has not believed in the name of God's one and only Son.

"Here is the judgment. Light has come into the world, but people loved darkness instead of light. They loved darkness because what they did was evil.

WORDS TO TREASURE

God loved the world so much that he gave his one and only Son. Anyone who believes in him will not die but will have eternal life.

John 3:16

"Everyone who does evil things hates the light. They will not come into the light. They are afraid that what they do will be seen. But anyone who lives by the truth comes into the light. He does this so that it will be easy to see that what he has done is with God's help."

Jesus Heals a Man With a Skin Disease

Luke 5

While Jesus was in one of the towns, a man came along. He had a skin disease all over his body. When he saw Jesus, he fell with his face to the ground. He begged him, "Lord, if you are willing to make me 'clean,' you can do it."

Jesus reached out his hand and touched the man. "I am willing to do it," he said. "Be 'clean'!" Right away the disease left him.

Then Jesus ordered him, "Don't tell anyone. Go and show yourself to the priest. Offer the sacrifices that Moses commanded. It will be a witness to the priest and the people that you are 'clean.'"

But the news about Jesus spread even more. So crowds of people came to hear him. They also came to be healed of their sicknesses. But Jesus often went away to be by himself and pray.

Jesus Heals a Man Who Could Not Walk

Mark 2

Jesus entered Capernaum again. The people heard that he had come home. So many people gathered that there was no room left. There was not even room outside the door. And Jesus preached the word to them.

Four of those who came were carrying a man who could not walk. But they could not get him close to Jesus because of the crowd. So they made a hole in the roof above Jesus. Then they lowered the man through it on a mat.

Jesus saw their faith. So he said to the man, "Son, your sins are forgiven."

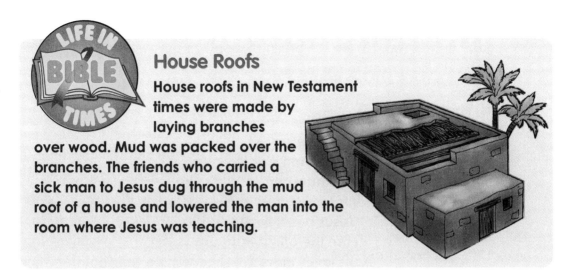
Some teachers of the law were sitting there. They were thinking, "Why is this fellow talking like that? He's saying a very evil thing! Only God can forgive sins!"

Right away Jesus knew what they were thinking. So he said to them, "Why are you thinking these things? Is it easier to say to this man, 'Your sins are forgiven'? Or to say, 'Get up, take your mat and walk'? I want you to know that the Son of Man has authority on earth to forgive sins."

Then Jesus spoke to the man who could not walk. "I tell you," he said, "get up. Take your mat and go home."

The man got up and took his mat. Then he walked away while everyone watched. All the people were amazed. They praised God and said, "We have never seen anything like this!"

Jesus Is Lord of the Sabbath Day

Luke 6

One Sabbath day Jesus was walking through the grainfields. His disciples began to break off some heads of grain. They rubbed them in their hands and ate them.

Some of the Pharisees said, "It is against the Law to do this on the Sabbath. Why are you doing it?"

Jesus answered them, "Haven't you ever read about what David did?

He and his men were hungry. He entered the house of God and took the holy bread. He ate the bread that only priests were allowed to eat. David also gave some to his men."

Who were the Pharisees?

They were religious men. They wanted to please God. They studied the Old Testament. But they did not really understand what they read. They tried to please God by being better than other people. Jesus showed them they were wrong. They hated him and became his enemies.

Then Jesus said to them, "The Son of Man is Lord of the Sabbath day."

On another Sabbath day, Jesus went into the synagogue and was teaching. A man whose right hand was weak and twisted was there. The Pharisees and the teachers of the law were trying to find fault with Jesus. So they watched him closely. They wanted to see if he would heal on the Sabbath.

But Jesus knew what they were thinking. He spoke to the man who had the weak and twisted hand. "Get up and stand in front of everyone," he said. So the man got up and stood there.

Then Jesus said to them, "What does the Law say we should do on the Sabbath day? Should we do good? Or should we do evil? Should we save life? Or should we destroy it?"

He looked around at all of them.

Then he said to the man, "Stretch out your hand."

He did, and his hand was as good as new.

But the Pharisees and the teachers of the law were very angry. They began to talk to each other about what they might do to Jesus.

The Twelve Disciples

Matthew 10

Jesus Sends Out the Twelve Disciples

Jesus called for his 12 disciples to come to him. He gave them authority to drive out evil spirits and to heal every illness and sickness.

Here are the names of the 12 apostles. First are Simon Peter and his brother Andrew. Then come James, son of Zebedee, and his brother

John. Next are Philip and Bartholomew, and also Thomas and Matthew the tax collector. Two more are James, son of Alphaeus, and Thaddaeus. The last are Simon the Zealot and Judas Iscariot. Judas is the one who was later going to hand Jesus over to his enemies.

Jesus sent these 12 out with the following orders. "Preach this message, 'The kingdom of heaven is near.' Heal those who are sick. Bring those who are dead back to life. Make those who have skin diseases 'clean' again. Drive out demons. You have received freely, so give freely.

"Do not take along any gold, silver or copper in your belts. Do not take a bag for the journey. Do not take extra clothes or sandals or walking sticks. A worker should be given what he needs.

What did Jesus' disciples do?

A disciple is a learner. A disciple does not lead. A disciple follows. Jesus trained his disciples to preach and teach. The disciples were common men. They weren't smarter than other people. They weren't better. But they loved Jesus. They learned by doing what Jesus did.

"Some people may not welcome you or listen to your words. If they don't, shake the dust off your feet when you leave that home or town. What I'm about to tell you is true. On judgment day it will be easier for Sodom and Gomorrah than for that town.

"I am sending you out like sheep among wolves. So be as wise as snakes and as harmless as doves.

"Aren't two sparrows sold for only a penny? But not one of them falls to the ground without your Father knowing it. He even counts every hair on your head! So don't be afraid. You are worth more than many sparrows.

"What about someone who says in front of others that he knows me? I will also say in front of my Father who is in heaven that I know him. But what about someone who says in front of others that he doesn't know me? I will say in front of my Father who is in heaven that I don't know him.

"Anyone who loves his father or mother more than me is not worthy of me. Anyone who loves his son or daughter more than me is not worthy of me. And anyone who does not pick up his cross and follow me is not worthy of me. If anyone finds his life, he will lose it. If anyone loses his life because of me, he will find it.

"Anyone who welcomes you welcomes me. And anyone who welcomes me welcomes the One who sent me. Suppose someone welcomes a prophet as a prophet. That one will receive a prophet's reward. And suppose someone welcomes a godly person as a godly person. That one will receive a godly person's reward. Suppose someone gives even a cup of cold water to a little one who follows me. What I'm about to tell you is true. That one will certainly be rewarded."

Jesus Teaches the People

Matthew 5—7

Jesus Gives Blessings

Jesus saw the crowds. So he went up on a mountainside and sat down. His disciples came to him. Then he began to teach them.

He said,

"Blessed are those who are spiritually needy.
    The kingdom of heaven belongs to them.
Blessed are those who are sad.
    They will be comforted.

Blessed are those who are hungry and thirsty for what is right. They will be filled.
Matthew 5:6

Blessed are those who are free of pride.
    They will be given the earth.
Blessed are those who are hungry and
        thirsty for what is right.
    They will be filled.
Blessed are those who show mercy.
    They will be shown mercy.
Blessed are those whose hearts are
            pure.
    They will see God.
Blessed are those who make peace.
    They will be called sons of God.

Blessed are those who suffer for
doing what is right.
The kingdom of heaven belongs
to them.

"Blessed are you when people make fun of you and hurt you because of me. You are also blessed when they tell all kinds of evil lies about you because of me. Be joyful and glad. Your reward in heaven is great. In the same way, people hurt the prophets who lived long ago.

Salt and Light

"You are the salt of the earth. But suppose the salt loses its saltiness. How can it be made salty again? It is no longer good for anything. It will be thrown out. People will walk all over it.

"You are the light of the world. A city on a hill can't be hidden. Also, people do not light a lamp and put it under a bowl. Instead, they put it on its stand. Then it gives light to everyone in the house.

"In the same way, let your light shine in front of others. Then they will see the good things you do. And they will praise your Father who is in heaven.

Jesus Gives Full Meaning to the Law

"Do not think I have come to get rid of what is written in the Law or in the Prophets. I have not come to do that. Instead, I have come to give full meaning to what is written. What I'm about to tell you is true. Heaven and earth will disappear before the smallest letter disappears from the Law. Not even the smallest stroke of a pen will disappear from the Law until everything is completed.

"Do not break even one of the least important commandments. And do not teach others to break them. If you do, you will be called the least important person in the kingdom of heaven. Instead, practice and teach these commands. Then you will be called important in the kingdom of heaven.

DID YOU KNOW?

What are these blessings?

These blessings are special sayings of Jesus. They explain how to be truly happy. Some people think that money will make them happy. Some people think that being strong will make them happy. Jesus wants people to know how to be truly happy.

"Here is what I tell you. You must be more godly than the Pharisees and the teachers of the law. If you are not, you will certainly not enter the kingdom of heaven.

Murder

"You have heard what was said to people who lived long ago. They were told, 'Do not commit murder. *(Exodus 20:13)* Anyone who murders will be judged for it.' But here is what I tell you. Do not be angry with your brother. Anyone who is angry with his brother will be judged. Again, anyone who says to his brother, 'Raca,' must stand trial in the Sanhedrin. But anyone who says, 'You fool!' will be in danger of the fire in hell.

"Suppose you are offering your gift at the altar. And you remember that your brother has something against you. Leave your gift in front of the altar. First go and make peace with your brother. Then come back and offer your gift.

"Suppose someone has a claim against you and is taking you to court. Settle the matter quickly. Do it while you are still with him on your way. If you don't, he may hand you over to the judge. The judge may hand you over to the officer. And you may be thrown into prison. What I'm about to tell you is true. You will not get out until you have paid the very last penny!

Oaths

"Again, you have heard what was said to your people long ago. They were told, 'Do not break the promises you make to the Lord. Keep the oaths you have made to him.' But here is what I tell you. Do not make any promises like that at all. Do not make them in the name of heaven. That is God's throne. Do not make them in the name of the earth. That is the stool for God's feet. Do not make them in the name of Jerusalem. That is the city of the Great King. And do not take an oath in the name of your head. You can't make even one hair white or black.

"Just let your 'Yes' mean 'Yes.' Let your 'No' mean 'No.' Anything more than this comes from the evil one.

Be Kind to Others

"You have heard that it was said, 'An eye must be put out for an eye. A tooth must be knocked out for a tooth.' *(Exodus 21:24; Leviticus 24:20; Deuteron-*

Being an Important Person

Do you know how to be really important? Jesus said that serving others is the way to be important. Here are two lists of things children may do. One tells about a child who likes to serve. The other tells about one who likes to be the boss. Can you tell which is which?

List #1
Always wants to be the leader in games.

Wants only the best players on his or her team.

Always insists "I'm right."

Never listens to others' ideas.

List #2
Takes turns being leader.

Wants friends on the team even if they're not the best.

Gives in to others sometimes.

Listens to others and shares ideas.

It's easy to pick the servant's list, isn't it? You can be a great Christian if you are willing to serve others.

omy 19:21) But here is what I tell you. Do not fight against an evil person.

"Suppose someone hits you on your right cheek. Turn your other cheek to him also. Suppose someone takes you to court to get your shirt. Let him have your coat also. Suppose someone forces you to go one mile. Go two miles with him.

"Give to the one who asks you for something. Don't turn away from the one who wants to borrow something from you.

Love your enemies. Pray for those who hurt you.
Matthew 5:44

Love Your Enemies

"You have heard that it was said, 'Love your neighbor. *(Leviticus 19:18)* Hate your enemy.' But here is what I tell you. Love your enemies. Pray for those who hurt you. Then you will be sons of your Father who is in heaven.

"He causes his sun to shine on evil people and good people. He sends rain on those who do right and those who don't.

"If you love those who love you, what reward will you get? Even the tax collectors do that. If you greet only your own people, what more are you doing than others? Even people who are ungodly do that. So be perfect, just as your Father in heaven is perfect.

Giving to Needy People

"Be careful not to do 'good works' in front of others. Don't do them to be seen by others. If you do, your Father in heaven will not reward you.

"When you give to needy people, do not announce it by having trumpets blown. Do not be like those who only pretend to be holy. They announce what they do in the synagogues and on the streets. They want to be honored by others. What I'm about to tell you is true. They have received their complete reward.

"When you give to the needy, don't let your left hand know what your right hand is doing. Then your giving will be done secretly. Your Father will reward you. He sees what you do secretly.

Prayer

"When you pray, do not be like those who only pretend to be holy. They love to stand and pray in the synagogues and on the street corners. They want to be seen by others. What I'm about to tell you is true. They have received their complete reward.

"When you pray, go into your room. Close the door and pray to your Father, who can't be seen. He will reward you. Your Father sees what is done secretly.

Giving to the Needy

The Jewish people believed that God would bless people who gave money to the poor. But God was not pleased with those who gave only when they were sure others would see them. These people cared more about what people thought of them than about God's blessing.

"When you pray, do not keep talking on and on the way ungodly people do. They think they will be heard because they talk a lot. Do not be like them. Your Father knows what you need even before you ask him.

"This is how you should pray.

"'Our Father in heaven,
may your name be honored.
May your kingdom come.
May what you want to happen be done
on earth as it is done in heaven.
Give us today our daily bread.
Forgive us our sins,
just as we also have forgiven those
who sin against us.
Keep us from falling into sin when we
are tempted.
Save us from the evil one.'

"Forgive people when they sin against you. If you do, your Father who is in heaven will also forgive you. But if you do not forgive people their sins, your Father will not forgive your sins.

Fasting

"When you go without eating, do not look gloomy like those who only pretend to be holy. They make their faces very sad. They want to show people they are fasting. What I'm about to tell you is true. They have received their complete reward.

"But when you go without eating, put olive oil on your head. Wash your face. Then others will not know that you are fasting. Only your Father, who can't be seen, will know it. He will reward you. Your Father sees what is done secretly.

WORDS TO TREASURE

Our Father in heaven, may your name by honored.
Matthew 6:9

WORDS TO TREASURE

Do not put away riches for yourselves on earth. Moths and rust can destroy them. Thieves can break in and steal them. Instead, put away riches for yourselves in heaven.
Matthew 6:19–20

Put Away Riches in Heaven

"Do not put away riches for yourselves on earth. Moths and rust can destroy them. Thieves can break in and steal them. Instead, put away riches for yourselves in heaven. There, moths and rust do not destroy them. There, thieves do not break in and steal them. Your heart will be where your riches are.

"The eye is like a lamp for the body. Suppose your eyes are good. Then your whole body will be full of light. But suppose your eyes are bad. Then your whole body will be full of darkness. If the light inside you is darkness, then it is very dark!

"No one can serve two masters at the same time. He will hate one of them and love the other. Or he will be faithful to one and dislike the other. You can't serve God and Money at the same time.

Do Not Worry

"I tell you, do not worry. Don't worry about your life and what you will eat or drink. And don't worry about your body and what you will wear. Isn't there more to life than eating? Aren't there more important things for the body than clothes?

"Look at the birds of the air. They don't plant or gather crops. They don't put away crops in storerooms. But your Father who is in heaven feeds them. Aren't you worth much more than they are?

"Can you add even one hour to your life by worrying?

"And why do you worry about clothes? See how the wild flowers grow. They don't work or make clothing. But here is what I tell you. Not even Solomon in all of his glory was dressed like one of those flowers.

Lilies of the Field

Flowers grew wild all over Galilee. No one planted or weeded them. Yet God "dressed" them with beautiful petals. God will care for us too, because we are more important to God than flowers.

"If that is how God dresses the wild grass, won't he dress you even better? After all, the grass is here only today. Tomorrow it is thrown into the fire. Your faith is so small!

"So don't worry. Don't say, 'What will we eat?' Or, 'What will we drink?' Or, 'What will we wear?' People who are ungodly run after all of those things. Your Father who is in heaven knows that you need them.

"But put God's kingdom first. Do what he wants you to do. Then all of those things will also be given to you.

"So don't worry about tomorrow. Tomorrow will worry about itself. Each day has enough trouble of its own.

Be Fair When You Judge Others

"Do not judge others. Then you will not be judged. You will be judged in the same way you judge others. You will be measured in the same way you measure others.

"You look at the bit of sawdust in your friend's eye. But you pay no attention to the piece of wood in your own eye. How can you say to your friend, 'Let me take the bit of sawdust out of your eye'? How can you say this while there is a piece of wood in your own eye?

"You pretender! First take the piece of wood out of your own eye. Then you will be able to see clearly to take the bit of sawdust out of your friend's eye.

"Do not give holy things to dogs. Do not throw your pearls to pigs. If you do, they might walk all over them. Then they might turn around and tear you to pieces.

Ask, Search, Knock

"Ask, and it will be given to you. Search, and you will find. Knock, and the door will be opened to you. Everyone who asks will receive. He who searches will find. The door will be opened to the one who knocks.

"Suppose your son asks for bread. Which of you will give him a stone? Or suppose he asks for a fish. Which of you will give him a snake? Even though you are evil, you know how

WORDS TO TREASURE

Ask, and it will be given to you. Search, and you will find. Knock, and the door will be opened to you.
Matthew 7:7

to give good gifts to your children. How much more will your Father who is in heaven give good gifts to those who ask him!

"In everything, do to others what you would want them to do to you. This is what is written in the Law and in the Prophets.

The Large and Small Gates

"Enter God's kingdom through the narrow gate. The gate is large and the road is wide that lead to death and hell. Many people go that way. But the gate is small and the road is narrow that lead to life. Only a few people find it.

A Tree and Its Fruit

"Watch out for false prophets. They come to you pretending to be sheep. But on the inside they are hungry wolves. You can tell what they really are by what they do.

"Do people pick grapes from bushes? Do they pick figs from thorns? In the same way, every good tree bears good fruit. But a bad tree bears bad fruit. A good tree can't bear bad fruit. And a bad tree can't bear good fruit. Every tree that does not bear good fruit is cut down. It is thrown into the fire. You can tell each tree by its fruit.

"Not everyone who says to me, 'Lord, Lord,' will enter the kingdom of heaven. Only those who do what my Father in heaven wants will enter.

"Many will say to me on that day, 'Lord! Lord! Didn't we prophesy in your name? Didn't we drive out demons in your name? Didn't we do many miracles in your name?' Then I will tell them clearly, 'I never knew you. Get away from me, you who do evil!'

The Wise and Foolish Builders

"So then, everyone who hears my words and puts them into practice is like a wise man. He builds his house on the rock. The rain comes down. The water rises. The

WORDS TO TREASURE

Everyone who hears my words and puts them into practice is like a wise man. He builds his house on the rock. The rain comes down. The water rises. The winds blow and beat against that house. But it does not fall. It is built on the rock.

Matthew 7:24–25

winds blow and beat against that house. But it does not fall. It is built on the rock.

"But everyone who hears my words and does not put them into practice is like a foolish man. He builds his house on sand. The rain comes down. The water rises. The winds blow and beat against that house. And it falls with a loud crash."

Jesus finished saying all these things. The crowds were amazed at his teaching. He taught like one who had authority. He did not speak like their teachers of the law.

A Man With Great Faith

Matthew 8

A Roman Commander Has Faith

When Jesus entered Capernaum, a Roman commander came to him. He asked Jesus for help. "Lord," he said, "my servant lies at home and can't move. He is suffering terribly."

Jesus said, "I will go and heal him."

The commander replied, "Lord, I am not good enough to have you come into my house. But just say the word, and my servant will be healed. I myself am a man under authority. And I have soldiers who obey my orders. I tell this one, 'Go,' and he goes. I tell that one, 'Come,' and he comes. I say to my servant, 'Do this,' and he does it."

PEOPLE IN BIBLE TIMES

Roman Commander

The Roman commander was sad. He was a leader in the Roman army. But his servant was sick. He asked Jesus to heal the servant. The commander believed in Jesus. He knew that Jesus could heal the servant without even touching him. Jesus said that the commander had a strong faith. His faith was stronger than the faith of anyone else Jesus had ever met.

When Jesus heard this, he was amazed. He said to those following him, "What I'm about to tell you is true. In Israel I have not found anyone whose faith is so strong.

"I say to you that many will come from the east and the west. They will take their places at the feast in the kingdom of heaven. They will sit with Abraham, Isaac and Jacob. But those who think they belong to the kingdom will be thrown outside, into the darkness. There they will sob and grind their teeth."

Then Jesus said to the Roman commander, "Go! It will be done just as you believed it would."

And his servant was healed at that very hour.

The Story of the Farmer

Matthew 13

Jesus sat by the Sea of Galilee. Large crowds gathered around him. So he got into a boat. He sat down in it. All the people stood on the shore. Then he told them many things by using stories.

He said, "A farmer went out to plant his seed. He scattered the seed on the ground. Some fell on a path. Birds came and ate it up. Some seed fell on rocky places, where there wasn't much soil. The plants came up quickly, because the soil wasn't deep. When the sun came up, it burned the plants. They dried up because they had no roots. Other seed fell among thorns. The thorns grew up and crowded out the plants. Still other seed fell on good soil. It produced a crop 100, 60 or 30 times more than what was planted. Those who have ears should listen."

The disciples came to him. They asked, "Why do you use stories when you speak to the people?"

He replied, "You have been given the chance to understand the secrets of the kingdom of heaven. It has not been given to outsiders.

Planting Seeds

Farmers in Jesus' time didn't use machines to plant, or sow, their fields with seed. They took handfuls of seeds and threw them on the ground they had plowed. A skillful farmer could spread grain seeds very evenly.

314

Everyone who has that kind of knowledge will be given more. In fact, they will have very much. If anyone doesn't have that kind of knowledge, even what little he has will be taken away from him. Here is why I use stories when I speak to the people. I say,

"They look, but they don't really see.
    They listen, but they don't really hear or understand.

"In them the words of the prophet Isaiah come true. He said,

" 'You will hear but never understand.
    You will see but never know what you are seeing.
The hearts of these people have become stubborn.
    They can barely hear with their ears.
    They have closed their eyes.
Otherwise they might see with their eyes.
    They might hear with their ears.
    They might understand with their hearts.
They might turn to the Lord, and then he would heal them.'
                                                    (Isaiah 6:9,10)

"But blessed are your eyes because they see. And blessed are your ears because they hear. What I'm about to tell you is true. Many prophets and godly people wanted to see what you see. But they didn't see it. They wanted to hear what you hear. But they didn't hear it.

"Listen! Here is the meaning of the story of the farmer. People hear the message about the kingdom but do not understand it. Then the evil one comes. He steals what was planted in their hearts. Those people are like the seed planted on a path. Others received the seed that fell on rocky places. They are those who hear the message and at once receive it with joy. But they have no roots. So they last only a short time. They quickly fall away from the faith when trouble or suffering comes because of the message. Others received the seed that fell among the thorns. They are those who hear the message. But then the worries of this life and the false promises of wealth crowd it out. They keep it from producing fruit. But still others received the seed that fell on good soil. They are those who hear the message and understand it. They produce a crop 100, 60 or 30 times more than the farmer planted."

The Story of the Weeds

Matthew 13

Jesus told the crowd another story. "Here is what the kingdom of heaven is like," he said. "A man planted good seed in his field. But while everyone was sleeping, his enemy came. The enemy planted weeds among the wheat and then went away. The wheat began to grow and form grain. At the same time, weeds appeared.

"The owner's servants came to him. They said, 'Sir, didn't you plant good seed in your field? Then where did the weeds come from?'

"'An enemy did this,' he replied.

"The servants asked him, 'Do you want us to go and pull the weeds up?'

"'No,' the owner answered. 'While you are pulling up the weeds, you might pull up the wheat with them. Let both grow together until the harvest. At that time I will tell the workers what to do. Here is what I will say to them. First collect the weeds. Tie them in bundles to be burned. Then gather the wheat. Bring it into my storeroom.'"

DID YOU KNOW?

What is the story of the weeds about?

The story of the weeds is about people. Some people are real Christians. Some people only pretend to be Christians. Jesus says that it can be hard to tell the difference. He tells us to wait. Let God decide who is a real Christian when Jesus returns.

The Stories of the Mustard Seed and the Yeast

Jesus told the crowd another story. He said, "The kingdom of heaven is like a mustard seed. Someone took the seed and planted it in a field. It is the smallest of all your seeds. But when it grows, it is the largest of all garden plants. It becomes a tree. Birds come and rest in its branches."

Jesus told them still another story. "The kingdom of heaven is like yeast," he said. "A woman mixed it into a large amount of flour. The yeast worked its way all through the dough."

Jesus spoke all these things to the crowd by using stories. He did not say anything to them without telling a story. So the words spoken by the prophet came true. He had said,

"I will open my mouth and tell stories.

I will speak about things that were hidden since the world was made." *(Psalm 78:2)*

Jesus Explains the Story of the Weeds

Then Jesus left the crowd and went into the house. His disciples came to him. They said, "Explain to us the story of the weeds in the field."

He answered, "The one who planted the good seed is the Son of Man. The field is the world. The good seed stands for the people who belong to the kingdom. The weeds are the people who belong to the evil one. The enemy who plants them is the devil. The harvest is judgment day. And the workers are angels.

"The weeds are pulled up and burned in the fire. That is how it will be on judgment day. The Son of Man will send out his angels. They will weed out of his kingdom everything that causes sin. They will also get rid of all who do evil. They will throw them into the blazing furnace. There people will sob and grind their teeth. Then God's people will shine like the sun in their Father's kingdom. Those who have ears should listen.

Jesus Calms the Storm

Mark 4

When evening came, Jesus said to his disciples, "Let's go over to the other side of the lake." They left the crowd behind. And they took him along in a boat, just as he was. There were also other boats with him.

A wild storm came up. Waves crashed over the boat. It was about to sink. Jesus was in the back, sleeping on a cushion. The disciples woke him up. They said, "Teacher! Don't you care if we drown?"

He got up and ordered the wind to stop. He said to the waves, "Quiet! Be still!" Then the wind died down. And it was completely calm.

He said to his disciples, "Why are you so afraid? Don't you have any faith at all yet?"

They were terrified. They asked each other, "Who is this? Even the wind and the waves obey him!"

A Dying Girl and a Suffering Woman

Mark 5

[One day] a man named Jairus came. He was a synagogue ruler. Seeing Jesus, he fell at his feet. He begged Jesus, "Please come. My little daughter is dying. Place your hands on her to heal her. Then she will live." So Jesus went with him.

A large group of people followed. They crowded around him. A woman was there who had a sickness that made her bleed. It had lasted for 12 years. She had suffered a great deal, even though she had gone to many doctors. She had spent all the money she had. But she was getting worse, not better. Then she heard about Jesus. She came up behind him in the crowd and touched his clothes. She thought, "I just need to touch his clothes. Then I will be healed." Right away her bleeding stopped. She felt in her body that her suffering was over.

At once Jesus knew that power had gone out from him. He turned around in the crowd. He asked, "Who touched my clothes?"

Then the woman came and fell at his feet. She knew what had happened to her. She was shaking with fear. But she told him the whole truth.

He said to her, "Dear woman, your faith has healed you. Go in peace. You are free from your suffering."

While Jesus was still speaking, some people came from the house of Jairus. He was the synagogue ruler. "Your daughter is dead," they said. "Why bother the teacher anymore?"

But Jesus didn't listen to them. He told the synagogue ruler, "Don't be afraid. Just believe."

Parents Who Pray

This story tells about a man who begged Jesus to heal his daughter. She was dying. The man believed that Jesus could heal her.

Ask your parents to tell you about a time that they prayed for you. Why did they pray? What did they say in their prayer? How did God answer their prayer? Do they still pray for you every day?

He let only Peter, James, and John, the brother of James, follow him. They came to the home of the synagogue ruler. There Jesus saw a lot of confusion. People were crying and sobbing loudly. He went inside. Then he said to them, "Why all this confusion and sobbing? The child is not dead. She is only sleeping." But they laughed at him.

He made them all go outside. He took only the child's father and mother and the disciples who were with him. And he went in where the child was. He took her by the hand. Then he said to her, *"Talitha koum!"* This means, "Little girl, I say to you, get up!" The girl was 12 years old. Right away she stood up and walked around. They were totally amazed at this. Jesus gave strict orders not to let anyone know what had happened. And he told them to give her something to eat.

Jesus Feeds the Five Thousand

John 6

Some time after this, Jesus crossed over to the other side of the Sea of Galilee. It is also called the Sea of Tiberias. A large crowd of people followed him. They had seen the miraculous signs he had done on those who were sick.

Then Jesus went up on a mountainside. There he sat down with his disciples. The Jewish Passover Feast was near.

Jesus looked up and saw a large crowd coming toward him. So he said to Philip, "Where can we buy bread for these people to eat?" He asked this only to put Philip to the test. He already knew what he was going to do.

Philip answered him, "Eight months' pay would not buy enough bread for each one to have a bite!"

Another of his disciples spoke up. It was Andrew, Simon Peter's brother. He

DID YOU KNOW?

Why did Jesus feed 5,000 people?

The people had come to hear Jesus. But they were hungry. Jesus was worried about them. He cares about people who are poor and hungry. It is good for Christians to care about others just like Jesus did.

said, "Here is a boy with five small loaves of barley bread. He also has two small fish. But how far will that go in such a large crowd?"

Barley Loaves

Two kinds of grain, wheat and barley, were used to make bread. Wheat was expensive. Most people were poor, so they ate small round loaves of coarse barley bread. The little boy in this story had five of these loaves.

Jesus said, "Have the people sit down." There was plenty of grass in that place, and they sat down. The number of men among them was about 5,000.

Then Jesus took the loaves and gave thanks. He handed out the bread to those who were seated. He gave them as much as they wanted. And he did the same with the fish.

When all of them had enough to eat, Jesus spoke to his disciples. "Gather the leftover pieces," he said. "Don't waste anything."

So they gathered what was left over from the five barley loaves. They filled 12 baskets with the pieces left by those who had eaten.

The people saw the miraculous sign that Jesus did. Then they began to say, "This must be the Prophet who is supposed to come into the world." But Jesus knew that they planned to come and force him to be their king. So he went away again to a mountain by himself.

Jesus Walks on the Water

Matthew 14

[Jesus sent his disciples] to the other side of the Sea of Galilee. The he went up on a mountainside by himself to pray. When evening came, he was there alone. The boat was already a long way from land. It was being pounded by the waves because the wind was blowing against it.

Early in the morning, Jesus went out to the disciples. He walked on the lake. They saw him walking on the lake and were terrified. "It's a ghost!" they said. And they cried out in fear.

Right away Jesus called out to them, "Be brave! It is I. Don't be afraid."

"Lord, is it you?" Peter asked. "If it is, tell me to come to you on the water."

"Come," Jesus said.

So Peter got out of the boat. He walked on the water toward Jesus. But when Peter saw the wind, he was afraid. He began to sink. He cried out, "Lord! Save me!"

Right away Jesus reached out his hand and caught him. "Your faith is so small!" he said. "Why did you doubt me?"

When they climbed into the boat, the wind died down. Then those in the boat worshiped Jesus. They said, "You really are the Son of God!"

They crossed over the lake and landed at Gennesaret. The men who lived there recognized Jesus. So they sent a message all over the nearby countryside. People brought all their sick to Jesus. And all who touched him were healed.

Peter Says That Jesus Is the Christ

Luke 9

One day Jesus was praying alone. Only his disciples were with him. He asked them, "Who do the crowds say I am?"

They replied, "Some say John the Baptist. Others say Elijah. Still others say that one of the prophets of long ago has come back to life."

"But what about you?" he asked. "Who do you say I am?"

Peter answered, "The Christ of God."

Jesus strongly warned them not to tell this to anyone. He said, "The Son of Man must suffer many things. The elders will not accept him. The chief priests and teachers of the law will not accept him

DID YOU KNOW?

What does "Christ" mean?

"Christ" is a special person. He is the one God sent to save his people. When a person called Jesus the "Christ," it meant that the person believed in Jesus. The person believed that Jesus was the One God's Word said would save them.

either. He must be killed and on the third day rise from the dead."

Then he said to all of them, "If anyone wants to follow me, he must say no to himself. He must pick up his cross every day and follow me. If he wants to save his life, he will lose it. But if he loses his life for me, he will save it. What good is it if someone gains the whole world but loses or gives up his very self?

"Suppose you are ashamed of me and my words. The Son of Man will come in his glory and in the glory of the Father and the holy angels. Then he will be ashamed of you.

"What I'm about to tell you is true. Some who are standing here will not die before they see God's kingdom."

The Servant Who Had No Mercy
Matthew 18

Peter came to Jesus. He asked, "Lord, how many times should I forgive my brother when he sins against me? Up to seven times?"

Jesus answered, "I tell you, not seven times, but 77 times.

"The kingdom of heaven is like a king who wanted to collect all the money his servants owed him. As the king began to do it, a man who owed him millions of dollars was brought to him. The man was not able to pay. So his master gave an order. The man, his wife, his children, and all he owned had to be sold to pay back what he owed.

"The servant fell on his knees in front of him. 'Give me time,' he begged. 'I'll pay everything back.'

"His master felt sorry for him. He forgave him what he owed and let him go.

"But then that servant went out and found one of the other servants who owed him a few dollars. He grabbed him and began to choke him. 'Pay back what you owe me!' he said.

"The other servant fell on his knees. 'Give me time,' he begged him. 'I'll pay you back.'

"But the first servant refused. Instead, he went and had the man thrown into prison. The man would be held there until he could pay back what he owed. The other servants saw what had happened. It troubled them greatly. They went and told their master everything that had happened.

"Then the master called the first servant in. 'You evil servant,' he said. 'I forgave all that you owed me because you begged me to. Shouldn't you have had mercy on the other servant just as I had mercy on you?' In anger his master turned him over to the jailers. He would be punished until he paid back everything he owed.

"This is how my Father in heaven will treat each of you unless you forgive your brother from your heart."

The Story of the Good Samaritan

Luke 10

One day an authority on the law stood up to put Jesus to the test. "Teacher," he asked, "what must I do to receive eternal life?"

"What is written in the Law?" Jesus replied. "How do you understand it?"

He answered, "'Love the Lord your God with all your heart and with all your soul. Love him with all your strength and with all your mind.' *(Deuteronomy 6:5)* And, 'Love your neighbor as you love yourself.'" *(Leviticus 19:18)*

"You have answered correctly," Jesus replied. "Do that, and you will live."

But the man wanted to make himself look good. So he asked Jesus, "And who is my neighbor?"

Jesus replied, "A man was going down from Jerusalem to Jericho. Robbers attacked him. They stripped off his clothes and beat him. Then they went away, leaving him almost dead. A priest happened to be going down that same road. When he saw the man, he passed by on the other side. A Levite also came by. When he saw the man, he passed by on the other side too.

What was a Samaritan?

A Samaritan was a person who lived in a country next to Israel. The Jews did not like these people. But Jesus' story shows that we can all be good neighbors. It doesn't matter if people are different from us. We can help all people in trouble.

But a Samaritan came to the place where the man was. When he saw the man, he felt sorry for him. He went to him, poured olive oil and wine on his wounds and bandaged them. Then he put the man on his own donkey. He took him to an inn and took care of him. The next day he took out two silver coins. He gave them to the owner of the inn. 'Take care of him,' he said. 'When I return, I will pay you back for any extra expense you may have.'

"Which of the three do you think was a neighbor to the man who was attacked by robbers?"

The authority on the law replied, "The one who felt sorry for him." Jesus told him, "Go and do as he did."

Jesus Heals a Man Born Blind

John 9

As Jesus went along, he saw a man who was blind. He had been blind since he was born. Jesus' disciples asked him, "Rabbi, who sinned? Was this man born blind because he sinned? Or did his parents sin?"

"It isn't because this man sinned," said Jesus. "It isn't because his parents sinned. This happened so that God's work could be shown in his life. While it is still day, we must do the work of the One who sent me. Night is coming. Then no one can work. While I am in the world, I am the light of the world."

After he said this, he spit on the ground. He made some mud with the spit. Then he put the mud on the man's eyes.

Does Sin Make You Sick?

Some people think that if they're sick it means God is punishing them. Jesus says that's not true. The man in this story wasn't blind because of sin. He was blind so that Jesus could heal him and show how great God is.

Think of the last time you were sick. Was it because you had done something wrong? Of course not. And who made you better? Doctors and nurses can help. But it was God's touch that healed your body. He deserves the praise. Write him a thank-you note.

"Go," he told him. "Wash in the Pool of Siloam." Siloam means Sent. So the man went and washed. And he came home able to see.

His neighbors and those who had earlier seen him begging asked questions. "Isn't this the same man who used to sit and beg?" they asked.

Some claimed that he was.

Others said, "No. He only looks like him."

But the man who had been blind kept saying, "I am the man."

"Then how were your eyes opened?" they asked.

He replied, "The man they call Jesus made some mud and put it on my eyes. He told me to go to Siloam and wash. So I went and washed. Then I could see."

"Where is this man?" they asked him.

"I don't know," he said.

The Pharisees Want to Know What Happened

They brought to the Pharisees the man who had been blind. The day Jesus made the mud and opened the man's eyes was a Sabbath. So the Pharisees also asked him how he was able to see.

"He put mud on my eyes," the man replied. "Then I washed. And now I can see."

Some of the Pharisees said, "Jesus has not come from God. He does not keep the Sabbath day."

But others asked, "How can a sinner do such miraculous signs?"

So the Pharisees did not agree with each other.

Finally they turned again to the blind man. "What do you have to say about him?" they asked. "It was your eyes he opened."

The man replied, "He is a prophet."

The Jews still did not believe that the man had been blind and now could see. So they sent for his parents. "Is this your son?" they asked. "Is this the one you say was born blind? How is it that now he can see?"

"We know he is our son," the parents answered. "And we know he was born blind. But we don't know how he can now see. And we don't know who opened his eyes. Ask him. He is an adult. He can speak for himself."

His parents said this because they were afraid of the Jews. The Jews had already decided that anyone who said Jesus was the Christ would be put out of the synagogue. That was why the man's parents said, "He is an adult. Ask him."

Again they called the man who had been blind to come to them. "Give glory to God by telling the truth!" they said. "We know that the man who healed you is a sinner."

He replied, "I don't know if he is a sinner or not. I do know one thing. I was blind, but now I can see!"

Then they asked him, "What did he do to you? How did he open your eyes?"

He answered, "I have already told you. But you didn't listen. Why do you want to hear it again? Do you want to become his disciples too?"

Then they began to attack him with their words. "You are this fellow's disciple!" they said. "We are disciples of Moses! We know that God spoke to Moses. But we don't even know where this fellow comes from."

The man answered, "That is really surprising! You don't know where he comes from, and yet he opened my eyes. We know that God does not listen to sinners. He listens to godly people who do what he wants them to do. Nobody has ever heard of anyone opening the eyes of a person born blind. If this man had not come from God, he could do nothing."

Then the Pharisees replied, "When you were born, you were already deep in sin. How dare you talk like that to us!" And they threw him out of the synagogue.

The Blind Will See

Jesus heard that the Pharisees had thrown the man out. When he found him, he said, "Do you believe in the Son of Man?"

"Who is he, sir?" the man asked. "Tell me, so I can believe in him."

Jesus said, "You have now seen him. In fact, he is the one speaking with you."

Then the man said, "Lord, I believe." And he worshiped him.

Jesus said, "I have come into this world to judge it. I have come so that the blind will see and those who see will become blind."

Some Pharisees who were with him heard him say this. They asked, "What? Are we blind too?"

Jesus said, "If you were blind, you would not be guilty of sin. But since you claim you can see, you remain guilty."

The Story of the Lost Son

Luke 15

Jesus continued, "There was a man who had two sons. The younger son spoke to his father. He said, 'Father, give me my share of the family property.' So the father divided his property between his two sons.

"Not long after that, the younger son packed up all he had. Then he left for a country far away. There he wasted his money on wild living. He spent everything he had.

"Then the whole country ran low on food. So the son didn't have what he needed. He went to work for someone who lived in that country, who sent him to the fields to feed the pigs. The son wanted to fill his stomach with the food the pigs were eating. But no one gave him anything.

"Then he began to think clearly again. He said, 'How many of my father's hired workers have more than enough food! But here I am dying from hunger! I will get up and go back to my father. I will say to him, "Father, I have sinned against heaven. And I have sinned against you. I am no longer fit to be called your son. Make me like one of your hired workers."' So he got up and went to his father.

"While the son was still a long way off, his father saw him. He was filled with tender love for his son. He ran to him. He threw his arms around him and kissed him.

"The son said to him, 'Father, I have sinned against heaven and against you. I am no longer fit to be called your son.'

"But the father said to his servants, 'Quick! Bring the best robe and put it on him. Put a ring on his finger and sandals on his feet. Bring the fattest calf and kill it. Let's have a big dinner and celebrate. This son of mine was dead. And now he is alive again. He was lost. And now he is found.'

"So they began to celebrate.

"The older son was in the field. When he came near the house, he heard music and dancing. So he called one of the servants. He asked him what was going on.

WORDS TO TREASURE

While the son was still a long way off, his father saw him. He was filled with tender love for his son. He ran to him. He threw his arms around him and kissed him.

Luke 15:20

327

"'Your brother has come home,' the servant replied. 'Your father has killed the fattest calf. He has done this because your brother is back safe and sound.'

"The older brother became angry. He refused to go in. So his father went out and begged him.

"But he answered his father, 'Look! All these years I've worked like a slave for you. I have always obeyed your orders. You never gave me even a young goat so I could celebrate with my friends. But this son of yours wasted your money with some prostitutes. Now he comes home. And for him you kill the fattest calf!'

"'My son,' the father said, 'you are always with me. Everything I have is yours. But we had to celebrate and be glad. This brother of yours was dead. And now he is alive again. He was lost. And now he is found.'"

The Story of Three Servants

Luke 19

While the people were listening to these things, Jesus told them a story. He was near Jerusalem. The people thought that God's kingdom was going to appear right away.

Jesus said, "A man from an important family went to a country far away. He went there to be made king and then return home. So he sent for ten of his servants. He gave them each about three months' pay. 'Put this money to work until I come back,' he said.

"But those he ruled over hated him. They sent some messengers after him. They were sent to say, 'We don't want this man to be our king.'

"But he was made king and returned home. Then he sent for the servants he had given the money to. He wanted to find out what they had earned with it.

"The first one came to him. He said, 'Sir, your money has earned ten times as much.'

"'You have done well, my good servant!' his master replied. 'You have been faithful in a very small matter. So I will put you in charge of ten towns.'

"The second servant came to his master. He said, 'Sir, your money has earned five times as much.'

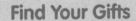

Find Your Gifts

This passage has some important lessons for us to learn. God gives each one of us at least one gift. That means he makes us able to do something really well. He wants us to use our gifts for him. God will praise us when we use our gifts for him.

List some things you can do well. Can you sing? Draw? Write? Play sports? Help others? Each gift is important in its own way. Ask your parents what gifts they think God has given you. Talk about ways you can use these gifts to serve God.

"His master answered, 'I will put you in charge of five towns.'

"Then another servant came. He said, 'Sir, here is your money. I have kept it hidden in a piece of cloth. I was afraid of you. You are a hard man. You take out what you did not put in. You harvest what you did not plant.'

"His master replied, 'I will judge you by your own words, you evil servant! So you knew that I am a hard man? You knew that I take out what I did not put in? You knew that I harvest what I did not plant? Then why didn't you put my money in the bank? When I came back, I could have collected it with interest.'

"Then he said to those standing by, 'Take his money away from him. Give it to the one who has ten times as much.'

"'Sir,' they said, 'he already has ten times as much!'

"He replied, 'I tell you that everyone who has will be given more. But here is what will happen to anyone who has nothing. Even what he has will be taken away from him. And what about my enemies who did not want me to be king over them? Bring them here! Kill them in front of me!'"

Jesus Brings Lazarus Back to Life

John 11

Lazarus Dies

A man named Lazarus was sick. He was from Bethany, the village where Mary and her sister Martha lived. Mary would later pour perfume on the Lord. She would also wipe his feet with her hair. Her brother Lazarus was sick in bed. So the sisters sent a message to Jesus. "Lord," they told him, "the one you love is sick."

When Jesus heard this, he said, "This sickness will not end in death. No, it is for God's glory. God's Son will receive glory because of it."

Jesus loved Martha and her sister and Lazarus. But after he heard Lazarus was sick, he stayed where he was for two more days.

Then he said to his disciples, "Let us go back to Judea."

"But Rabbi," they said, "a short time ago the Jews tried to kill you with stones. Are you still going back there?"

Jesus answered, "Aren't there 12 hours of daylight? A person who walks during the day won't trip and fall. He can see because of this world's light. But when he walks at night, he'll trip and fall. He has no light."

After he said this, Jesus went on speaking to them. "Our friend Lazarus has fallen asleep," he said. "But I am going there to wake him up."

His disciples replied, "Lord, if he's sleeping, he will get better."

Jesus had been speaking about the death of Lazarus. But his disciples thought he meant natural sleep.

So then he told them plainly, "Lazarus is dead. For your benefit, I am glad I was not there. Now you will believe. But let us go to him."

PEOPLE IN BIBLE TIMES

Mary and Martha

Mary and Martha were sisters. They loved God and invited Jesus into their home when he came to their city. Mary and Martha had a brother named Lazarus. He became very sick, and he died. Mary and Martha were sad. Jesus cried with them. Then Jesus raised Lazarus from the dead.

Then Thomas, who was called Didymus, spoke to the rest of the disciples. "Let us go also," he said. "Then we can die with Jesus."

Jesus Comforts the Sisters

When Jesus arrived, he found out that Lazarus had already been in the tomb for four days. Bethany was less than two miles from Jerusalem. Many Jews had come to Martha and Mary. They had come to comfort them because their brother was dead.

When Martha heard that Jesus was coming, she went out to meet him. But Mary stayed at home.

"Lord," Martha said to Jesus, "I wish you had been here! Then my brother would not have died. But I know that even now God will give you anything you ask for."

Jesus said to her, "Your brother will rise again."

Martha answered, "I know he will rise again. This will happen when people are raised from the dead on the last day."

Jesus said to her, "I am the resurrection and the life. Anyone who believes in me will live, even if he dies. And those who live and believe in me will never die. Do you believe this?"

"Yes, Lord," she told him. "I believe that you are the Christ, the Son of God. I believe that you are the One who was supposed to come into the world."

After she said this, she went back home. She called her sister Mary to one side to talk to her. "The Teacher is here," Martha said. "He is asking for you."

When Mary heard this, she got up quickly and went to him. Jesus had not yet entered the village. He was still at the place where Martha had met him. Some Jews had been comforting Mary in the house. They noticed how quickly she got up and went out. So they followed her. They thought she was going to the tomb to cry there.

DID YOU KNOW?

Why didn't Jesus come before Lazarus died?

Jesus didn't come right away when Lazarus's sisters sent for him. When Jesus got there, his friend had already died. But Jesus brought Lazarus back to life. He did this to show his power over death.

Mary reached the place where Jesus was. When she saw him, she fell at his feet. She said, "Lord, I wish you had been here! Then my brother would not have died."

Jesus saw her crying. He saw that the Jews who had come along with her were crying also. His spirit became very sad, and he was troubled.

"Where have you put him?" he asked.

"Come and see, Lord," they replied.

Jesus sobbed.

Then the Jews said, "See how much he loved him!"

But some of them said, "He opened the eyes of the blind man. Couldn't he have kept this man from dying?"

Jesus Raises Lazarus From the Dead

Once more Jesus felt very sad. He came to the tomb. It was a cave with a stone in front of the entrance.

"Take away the stone," he said.

"But, Lord," said Martha, the sister of the dead man, "by this time there is a bad smell. Lazarus has been in the tomb for four days."

Then Jesus said, "Didn't I tell you that if you believed, you would see God's glory?"

So they took away the stone.

Then Jesus looked up. He said, "Father, I thank you for hearing me. I know that you always hear me. But I said this for the benefit of the people standing here. I said it so they will believe that you sent me."

Then Jesus called in a loud voice. He said, "Lazarus, come out!"

The dead man came out. His hands and feet were wrapped with strips of linen. A cloth was around his face.

Jesus said to them, "Take off the clothes he was buried in and let him go."

Jesus Heals Ten Men

Luke 17

Jesus was on his way to Jerusalem. He traveled along the border between Samaria and Galilee. As he was going into a village, ten men met him. They had a skin disease. They were standing close by. And they called out in a loud voice, "Jesus! Master! Have pity on us!"

Jesus saw them and said, "Go. Show yourselves to the priests." While they were on the way, they were healed.

When one of them saw that he was healed, he came back. He praised God in a loud voice. He threw himself at Jesus' feet and thanked him. The man was a Samaritan.

Jesus asked, "Weren't all ten healed? Where are the other nine? Didn't anyone else return and give praise to God except this outsider?"

Then Jesus said to him, "Get up and go. Your faith has healed you."

Saying Thank You

Saying thank you to God is one important way we can praise him and show our love for him. In this story Jesus healed ten men. But only one came back to thank Jesus.

Have a grown-up help you with this project. Cut a piece of paper in half the long way. Tape two of the short ends together. Now fold the paper back and forth about every two inches, as if you were making a fan. On one of the folded ends draw a simple shape of a man. Draw his arms going up to the folds. Cut out the shape without cutting off the ends of the arms. Unfold the paper. You have a string of ten men attached to each other! Color one of the men to stand for the one man who thanked Jesus. Tape the figures to your wall. Remember to be like that one man who said thank you.

Children Come to Jesus

Matthew 18

Who Is the Most Important Person in the Kingdom?

At that time the disciples came to Jesus. They asked him, "Who is the most important person in the kingdom of heaven?"

Jesus called a little child over to him. He had the child stand among them. Jesus said, "What I'm about to tell you is true. You need to change

Jesus Loves the Children

Jesus loved the little children in this story. He wanted them close to him. He loves you just as much. You can't feel his arms around you like these children did. But you can know they are there, holding you close.

Make some special placemats for your table. Do this with your family. Get some pieces of colored art paper. Each person should trace around his or her hands on the paper. Color and decorate the hands any way you wish. Use the mats for your next meal. Talk about the way Jesus has his arms around your family. What are some ways he shows his love to your family?

and become like little children. If you don't, you will never enter the kingdom of heaven. Anyone who becomes as free of pride as this child is the most important in the kingdom of heaven.

"Anyone who welcomes a little child like this in my name welcomes me.

"But what if someone leads one of these little ones who believe in me to sin? If he does, it would be better for him to have a large millstone hung around his neck and be drowned at the bottom of the sea.

"How terrible it will be for the world because of the things that lead people to sin! Things like that must come. But how terrible for those who cause them!

"If your hand or foot causes you to sin, cut it off and throw it away. It would be better for you to enter the kingdom of heaven with only one hand or one foot than to go into hell with two hands and two feet. In hell the fire burns forever. If your eye causes you to sin, poke it out and throw it away. It would be better for you to enter the kingdom of heaven with one eye than to have two eyes and be thrown into the fire of hell.

The Story of the Lost Sheep

"See that you don't look down on one of these little ones. Here is what I tell you. Their angels in heaven can go at any time to see my Father who is in heaven.

God's Not Mad at Me!

When this story talks about a shepherd and his sheep, it is really talking about God and his children. You are God's child if you believe in Jesus and ask him into your heart. But even though you are God's child, you still sin sometimes. That's like the sheep that goes away and gets lost. The shepherd loves that sheep so much. He goes out searching until he finds the sheep and brings it home. That is just what God does for you. He loves you no matter what you do. He wants you to be close to him.

Draw a sheep on a piece of poster board. Glue on cotton balls for wool. Write "He is happy about the one that he finds" under your picture. Put the picture in your room. Remember that God loves you even when you have done something wrong.

"What do you think? Suppose a man owns 100 sheep and one of them wanders away. Won't he leave the 99 sheep on the hills? Won't he go and look for the one that wandered off? What I'm about to tell you is true. If he finds that sheep, he is happier about the one than about the 99 that didn't wander off. It is the same with your Father in heaven. He does not want any of these little ones to be lost."

Jesus and the Rich Young Man

Mark 10

As Jesus started on his way, a man ran up to him. He fell on his knees before Jesus. "Good teacher," he said, "what must I do to receive eternal life?"

"Why do you call me good?" Jesus answered. "No one is good except God. You know what the commandments say. 'Do not commit murder. Do not commit adultery. Do not steal. Do not give false witness. Do not cheat. Honor your father and mother.'" *(Exodus 20:12–16; Deuteronomy 5:16–20)*

"Teacher," he said, "I have obeyed all those commandments since I was a boy."

Jesus looked at him and loved him. "You are missing one thing," he said. "Go and sell everything you have. Give the money to those who are poor. You will have treasure in heaven. Then come and follow me."

The man's face fell. He went away sad, because he was very rich.

Jesus looked around. He said to his disciples, "How hard it is for rich people to enter God's kingdom!"

The disciples were amazed at his words. But Jesus said again, "Children, how hard it is to enter God's kingdom! Is it hard for a camel to go through the eye of a needle? It is even harder for the rich to enter God's kingdom!"

The disciples were even more amazed. They said to each other, "Then who can be saved?"

Jesus looked at them and said, "With man, that is impossible. But not with God. All things are possible with God."

Peter said to him, "We have left everything to follow you!"

"What I'm about to tell you is true," Jesus replied. "Has anyone left home or family or fields for me and the good news? They will receive 100 times as much in this world. They will have homes and families and fields. But they will also be treated badly by others. In the world to come they will live forever. But many who are first will be last. And the last will be first."

The Story of Zacchaeus

Luke 19

Zacchaeus the Tax Collector

Jesus entered Jericho and was passing through. A man named Zacchaeus lived there. He was a chief tax collector and was very rich.

Zacchaeus wanted to see who Jesus was. But he was a short man. He could not see Jesus because of the crowd. So he ran ahead and climbed a sycamore-fig tree. He wanted to see Jesus, who was coming that way.

Jesus reached the spot where Zacchaeus was. He looked up and said, "Zacchaeus, come down at once. I must stay at your house today." So Zacchaeus came down at once and welcomed him gladly.

All the people saw this. They began to whisper among themselves. They said, "Jesus has gone to be the guest of a 'sinner.'"

But Zacchaeus stood up. He said, "Look, Lord! Here and now I give half of what I own to those who are poor. And if I have cheated anybody out of anything, I will pay it back. I will pay back four times the amount I took."

Jesus said to Zacchaeus, "Today salvation has come to your house. You are a member of Abraham's family line. The Son of Man came to look for the lost and save them."

PEOPLE IN BIBLE TIMES

Zacchaeus

Zacchaeus was a very short man. He was a tax collector in the city of Jericho, and he had cheated many people out of their money. He was so short that he climbed up a tree to see Jesus. Jesus asked him to come down from the tree. Zacchaeus obeyed. Then he gave half of everything he owned to the poor. He was sorry for his sins. And Jesus forgave him.

Mary Pours Perfume on Jesus

John 12

It was six days before the Passover Feast. Jesus arrived at Bethany, where Lazarus lived. Lazarus was the one Jesus had raised from the dead. A dinner was given at Bethany to honor Jesus. Martha served the food. Lazarus was among those at the table with Jesus.

Then Mary took about a pint of pure nard. It was an expensive perfume. She poured it on Jesus' feet and wiped them with her hair. The house was filled with the sweet smell of the perfume.

But Judas Iscariot didn't like what Mary did. He was one of Jesus' disciples. Later he was going to hand Jesus over to his enemies. Judas said, "Why wasn't this perfume sold? Why wasn't the money given to poor people? It was worth a year's pay."

He didn't say this because he cared about the poor. He said it because he was a thief. Judas was in charge of the money bag. He used to help himself to what was in it.

"Leave her alone," Jesus replied. "The perfume was meant for the day I am buried. You will always have the poor among you. But you won't always have me."

Meanwhile a large crowd of Jews found out that Jesus was there, so they came. But they did not come only because of Jesus. They also came to see Lazarus. After all, Jesus had raised him from the dead.

So the chief priests made plans to kill Lazarus too. Because of Lazarus, many of the Jews were starting to follow Jesus. They were putting their faith in him.

Jesus Enters Jerusalem

Matthew 21; Luke 19

As [Jesus and his disciples] approached Jerusalem, they came to Bethphage. It was on the Mount of Olives. Jesus sent out two of his disciples. He said to them, "Go to the village ahead of you. As soon as you get there, you will find a donkey's colt tied up. No one has ever ridden it. Untie it and bring it here. Someone may ask you, 'Why are you untying it?' If so, say, 'The Lord needs it.'"

Those who were sent ahead went and found the young donkey. It was there just as Jesus had told them. They were untying the colt when its owners came. The owners asked them, "Why are you untying the colt?"

They replied, "The Lord needs it."

Then the disciples brought the colt to Jesus. They threw their coats on the young donkey and put Jesus on it. As he went along, people spread their coats on the road.

Jesus came near the place where the road goes down the Mount of Olives. There the whole crowd of disciples began to praise God with joy. In loud voices they praised him for all the miracles they had seen. They shouted,

"Blessed is the king who comes in the name of the Lord!"

(Psalm 118:26)

"May there be peace and glory in the highest heaven!"

Some of the Pharisees in the crowd spoke to Jesus. "Teacher," they said, "tell your disciples to stop!"

"I tell you," he replied, "if they keep quiet, the stones will cry out."

Jesus Clears the Temple

Mark 11

When Jesus reached Jerusalem, he entered the temple area. He began chasing out those who were buying and selling there. He turned

Clearing the Temple

The great temple in Jerusalem had several courtyards, or patios, inside fences. In the outer court people often bought or sold animals to sacrifice. Jesus was angry about this. God's temple was for prayer, not for doing business.

over the tables of the people who were exchanging money. He also turned over the benches of those who were selling doves. He would not allow anyone to carry items for sale through the temple courtyards.

Then he taught them. He told them, "It is written that the Lord said,

"'My house will be called
　　a house where people from all nations can pray.'　　*(Isaiah 56:7)*

But you have made it a 'den for robbers.'" *(Jeremiah 7:11)*

The chief priests and the teachers of the law heard about this. They began looking for a way to kill Jesus. They were afraid of him, because the whole crowd was amazed at his teaching.

The Story of the Pharisee and the Tax Collector

Luke 18

Jesus told a story to some people who were sure they were right with God. They looked down on everybody else. He said to them, "Two men went up to the temple to pray. One was a Pharisee. The other was a tax collector.

"The Pharisee stood up and prayed about himself. 'God, I thank you that I am not like other people,' he said. 'I am not like robbers or those who do other evil things. I am not like those who commit adultery. I am not even like this tax collector. I fast twice a week. And I give a tenth of all I get.'

"But the tax collector stood not very far away. He would not even look up to heaven. He beat his chest and said, 'God, have mercy on me. I am a sinner.'

"I tell you, the tax collector went home accepted by God. But not the Pharisee.

PEOPLE IN BIBLE TIMES

Tax Collectors

Tax collectors were Jewish men who collected money for the Roman government taxes. The other Jews hated them, because many tax collectors cheated the people and took too much of their money. Some of the tax collectors had outdoor offices by highways. People who traveled had to stop and pay taxes on the things they were carrying.

Everyone who lifts himself up will be brought down. And anyone who is brought down will be lifted up."

DID YOU KNOW?

Why did Jesus say it would be terrible for the Pharisees?

Jesus was warning the Pharisees. He told them that they were in trouble with God. They didn't do what they told other people to do. They did everything for show. And they stopped other people from knowing God. Jesus gave seven reasons why they were in trouble with God.

The Widow's Offering
Mark 12

Jesus sat down across from the place where people put their temple offerings. He watched the crowd putting their money into the offering boxes. Many rich people threw large amounts into them.

But a poor widow came and put in two very small copper coins. They were worth much less than a penny.

Jesus asked his disciples to come to him. He said, "What I'm about to tell you is true. That poor widow has put more into the offering box than all the others. They all gave a lot because they are rich. But she gave even though she is poor. She put in everything she had. She gave all she had to live on."

Jesus Tells About His Coming Death
John 12

There were some Greeks among the people who went up to worship during the [Passover] Feast. They came to ask Philip for a favor. Philip was from Bethsaida in Galilee.

"Sir," they said, "we would like to see Jesus."

Philip went to tell Andrew. Then Andrew and Philip told Jesus.

Jesus replied, "The hour has come for the Son of Man to receive glory. What I'm about to tell you is true. Unless a grain of wheat falls to the ground and dies, it remains only one seed. But if it dies, it produces many seeds.

"Anyone who loves his life will lose it. But anyone who hates his life in this world will keep it and have eternal life. Anyone who serves me must follow me. And where I am, my servant will also be. My Father will honor the one who serves me.

"My heart is troubled. What should I say? 'Father, save me from this hour'? No. This is the very reason I came to this hour. Father, bring glory to your name!"

Then a voice came from heaven. It said, "I have brought glory to my name. I will bring glory to it again."

The crowd there heard the voice. Some said it was thunder. Others said an angel had spoken to Jesus.

Jesus said, "This voice was for your benefit, not mine. Now it is time for the world to be judged. Now the prince of this world will be thrown out. But I am going to be lifted up from the earth. When I am, I will bring all people to myself." He said this to show them how he was going to die.

The crowd spoke up. "The Law tells us that the Christ will remain forever," they said. "So how can you say, 'The Son of Man must be lifted up'? Who is this 'Son of Man'?"

Then Jesus told them, "You are going to have the light just a little while longer. Walk while you have the light. Do this before darkness catches up with you. Anyone who walks in the dark does not know where he is going. While you have the light, put your trust in it. Then you can become sons of light."

When Jesus had finished speaking, he left and hid from them.

Jesus Will Judge the Good From the Bad

Matthew 24—25

Jesus was sitting on the Mount of Olives. There the disciples came to him in private. [He said to them,] "The Son of Man will come in all his glory. All the angels will come with him. Then he will sit on his throne in the glory of heaven. All the nations will be gathered in front of him. He will separate the people into two groups. He will be like a shepherd who separates the sheep from the goats. He will put the sheep to his right and the goats to his left.

"Then the King will speak to those on his right. He will say, 'My Father has blessed you. Come and take what is yours. It is the kingdom prepared for you since the world was created. I was hungry. And you gave me something to eat. I was thirsty. And you gave me something to drink. I was a stranger. And you invited me in. I needed clothes. And you gave them to me. I was sick. And you took care of me. I was in prison. And you came to visit me.'

"Then the people who have done what is right will answer him. 'Lord,' they will ask, 'when did we see you hungry and feed you? When did we see you thirsty and give you something to drink? When did we see you as a stranger and invite you in? When did we see you needing clothes and give them to you? When did we see you sick or in prison and go to visit you?'

"The King will reply, 'What I'm about to tell you is true. Anything you did for one of the least important of these brothers of mine, you did for me.'

"Then he will say to those on his left, 'You are cursed! Go away from me into the fire that burns forever. It has been prepared for the devil and his angels. I was hungry. But you gave me nothing to eat. I was thirsty. But you gave me nothing to drink. I was a stranger. But you did not invite me in. I needed clothes. But you did not give me any. I was sick and in prison. But you did not take care of me.'

"They also will answer, 'Lord, when did we see you hungry or thirsty and not help you? When did we see you as a stranger or needing clothes or sick or in prison and not help you?'

"He will reply, 'What I'm about to tell you is true. Anything you didn't do for one of the least important of these, you didn't do for me.'

"Then they will go away to be punished forever. But those who have done what is right will receive eternal life."

WORDS TO TREASURE

Anything you did for one of the least important of these brothers of mine, you did for me.

Matthew 25:40

Jesus Washes His Disciples' Feet

John 13

It was just before the Passover Feast. Jesus knew that the time had come for him to leave this world. It was time for him to go to the Father. Jesus loved his disciples who were in the world. So he now showed them how much he really loved them.

The evening meal was being served. The devil had already tempted Judas Iscariot, son of Simon. He had told Judas to hand Jesus over to his enemies. Jesus knew that the Father had put everything under his power. He also knew he had come from God and was returning to God.

So he got up from the meal and took off his outer clothes. He wrapped a towel around his waist. After that, he poured water into a large bowl. Then he began to wash his disciples' feet. He dried them with the towel that was wrapped around him.

He came to Simon Peter.

"Lord," Peter said to him, "are you going to wash my feet?"

Jesus replied, "You don't realize now what I am doing. But later you will understand."

"No," said Peter. "You will never wash my feet."

Jesus answered, "Unless I wash you, you can't share life with me."

"Lord," Simon Peter replied, "not just my feet! Wash my hands and my head too!"

Foot Washing

When visitors came into a house, they took off their sandals. The person who lived there brought out water to wash their dusty feet. Usually the lowest servant in the house was ordered to wash the guests' feet. Jesus was showing us how to be humble when he took the job of washing his disciples' feet.

Jesus answered, "A person who has had a bath needs to wash only his feet. The rest of his body is clean. And you are clean. But not all of you are."

Jesus knew who was going to hand him over to his enemies. That was why he said not every one was clean.

When Jesus finished washing their feet, he put on his clothes. Then he returned to his place.

"Do you understand what I have done for you?" he asked them. "You call me 'Teacher' and 'Lord.' You are right. That is what I am. I, your Lord and Teacher, have washed your feet. So you also should wash one another's feet. I have given you an example. You should do as I have done for you.

"What I'm about to tell you is true. A servant is not more important than his master. And a messenger is not more important than the one who sends him. Now you know these things. So you will be blessed if you do them.

PEOPLE IN BIBLE TIMES

Judas

Judas was one of Jesus' disciples. But he made a deal with Jesus' enemies. He said that he would hand Jesus over to them for money. Judas was not brave. He handed Jesus over to his enemies at night so the people who believed in Jesus would not see them.

Jesus Tells What Judas Will Do

"I am not talking about all of you. I know those I have chosen. But this will happen so that Scripture will come true. It says, 'The one who shares my bread has deserted me.' *(Psalm 41:9)*

"I am telling you now, before it happens. When it does happen, you will believe that I am he. What I'm about to tell you is true. Anyone who accepts someone I send accepts me. And anyone who accepts me accepts the One who sent me."

The Lord's Supper

Mark 14; John 13

It was the first day of the Feast of Unleavened Bread. That was the time to sacrifice the Passover lamb.

Jesus' disciples asked him, "Where do you want us to go and prepare for you to eat the Passover meal?"

So he sent out two of his disciples. He told them, "Go into the city. A man carrying a jar of water will meet you. Follow him. He will enter a house. Say to its owner, 'The Teacher asks, "Where is my guest room? Where can I eat the Passover meal with my disciples?"' He will show you a large upstairs room. It will have furniture and will be ready. Prepare for us to eat there."

DID YOU KNOW?

What was the Last Supper?

It was the last meal Jesus ate with his followers. It was the night before Jesus died. Jesus told his friends he was about to die. He told them to eat the Lord's Supper again and again until he came back.

The disciples left and went into the city. They found things just as Jesus had told them. So they prepared the Passover meal.

When evening came, Jesus arrived with the Twelve. While they were at the table eating, Jesus said, "What I'm about to tell you is true. One of you who is eating with me will hand me over to my enemies."

The Son of Man will go just as it is written about him. But how terrible it will be for the one who hands over the Son of Man! It would be better for him if he had not been born."

After he had said this, Jesus' spirit was troubled. Here is the witness he gave. "What I'm about to tell you is true," he said. "One of you is going to hand me over to my enemies."

His disciples stared at one another. They had no idea which one of them he meant. The disciple Jesus loved was next to him at the table. Simon Peter motioned to that disciple. He said, "Ask Jesus which one he means."

The disciple was leaning back against Jesus. He asked him, "Lord, who is it?"

Jesus answered, "It is the one I will give this piece of bread to. I will give it to him after I have dipped it in the dish."

He dipped the piece of bread. Then he gave it to Judas Iscariot, son of Simon. As soon as Judas took the bread, Satan entered into him.

"Do quickly what you are going to do," Jesus told him.

But no one at the meal understood why Jesus said this to him. Judas was in charge of the money. So some of the disciples thought Jesus was telling him to buy what was needed for the Feast. Others thought Jesus was talking about giving something to poor people.

As soon as Judas had taken the bread, he went out. And it was night.

Jesus Says That Peter Will Fail

After Judas was gone, Jesus spoke. He said, "Now the Son of Man receives glory. And he brings glory to God. If the Son brings glory to God, God himself will bring glory to the Son. God will do it at once.

"My children, I will be with you only a little longer. You will look for me. Just as I told the Jews, so I am telling you now. You can't come where I am going.

"I give you a new command. Love one another. You must love one another, just as I have loved you. If you love one another, everyone will know you are my disciples."

Simon Peter asked him, "Lord, where are you going?"

Jesus replied, "Where I am going you can't follow now. But you will follow me later."

"Lord," Peter asked, "why can't I follow you now? I will give my life for you."

Then Jesus answered, "Will you really give your life for me? What I'm about to tell you is true. Before the rooster crows, you will say three times that you don't know me!"

While they were eating, Jesus took bread. He gave thanks and broke it. He handed it to his disciples and said, "Take it. This is my body."

Then he took the cup. He gave thanks and handed it to them. All of them drank from it.

"This is my blood of the new covenant," he said to them. "It is poured out for many. What I'm about to tell you is true. I won't drink wine with you again until the day I drink it in God's kingdom."

Then they sang a hymn and went out to the Mount of Olives.

Judas Hands Jesus Over

Mark 14

Jesus Prays in Gethsemane

Jesus and his disciples went to a place called Gethsemane. Jesus said to them, "Sit here while I pray."

He took Peter, James and John along with him. He began to be very upset and troubled. "My soul is very sad. I feel close to death," he said to them. "Stay here. Keep watch."

He went a little farther. Then he fell to the ground. He prayed that, if possible, the hour might pass by him. *"Abba,"* he said, "everything is possible for you. Take this cup of suffering away from me. But let what you want be done, not what I want." *Abba* means Father.

Then he returned to his disciples and found them sleeping. "Simon," he said to Peter, "are you asleep? Couldn't you keep watch for one hour? Watch and pray. Then you won't fall into sin when you are tempted. The spirit is willing. But the body is weak."

Once more Jesus went away and prayed the same thing. Then he came back. Again he found them sleeping. They couldn't keep their eyes open. They did not know what to say to him.

Jesus returned the third time. He said to them, "Are you still sleeping and resting? Enough! The hour has come. Look! The Son of Man is about to be handed over to sinners. Get up! Let us go! Here comes the one who is handing me over to them!"

Pray When You Are Hurting

The Bible passage tells about a time that Jesus prayed. He knew that he would soon be nailed to a cross. The "cup" Jesus prayed about stood for suffering and death. Jesus was very sad and troubled as he prayed. God sent an angel to him to give him strength.

The best thing you can do when something terrible happens is to pray. Tell God how you feel. He will give you strength to help you through your problem.

Jesus Is Arrested

Just as Jesus was speaking, Judas appeared. He was one of the Twelve. A crowd was with him. They were carrying swords and clubs. The chief priests, the teachers of the law, and the elders had sent them.

Judas, who was going to hand Jesus over, had arranged a signal with them. "The one I kiss is the man," he said. "Arrest him and have the guards lead him away."

So Judas went to Jesus at once. He said, "Rabbi!" And he kissed him. The men grabbed Jesus and arrested him.

Then one of those standing nearby pulled his sword out. He struck the servant of the high priest and cut off his ear.

"Am I leading a band of armed men against you?" asked Jesus. "Do you have to come out with swords and clubs to capture me? Every day I was with you. I taught in the temple courtyard, and you didn't arrest me. But the Scriptures must come true."

Then everyone left him and ran away.

A young man was following Jesus. The man was wearing nothing but a piece of linen cloth. When the crowd grabbed him, he ran away naked. He left his clothing behind.

Jesus Is Taken to the Sanhedrin

The crowd took Jesus to the high priest. All of the chief priests, the elders, and the teachers of the law came together.

What was the Sanhedrin?

The Sanhedrin was a group of men that led the Jews. They were all Jews. The Sanhedrin could make laws. The Sanhedrin could send people to jail. The Sanhedrin had a lot of power.

Not too far away, Peter followed Jesus. He went right into the courtyard of the high priest. There he sat with the guards. He warmed himself at the fire.

The chief priests and the whole Sanhedrin were looking for something to use against Jesus. They wanted to put him to death. But they did not find any proof. Many witnesses lied about him. But their stories did not agree.

Then some stood up. They gave false witness about him. "We heard him say, 'I will destroy this temple made by human hands. In three days I will build another temple, not made by human hands.'" But what they said did not agree.

Then the high priest stood up in front of them. He asked Jesus, "Aren't you going to answer? What are these charges these men are bringing against you?"

But Jesus remained silent. He gave no answer.

Again the high priest asked him, "Are you the Christ? Are you the Son of the Blessed One?"

"I am," said Jesus. "And you will see the Son of Man sitting at the right hand of the Mighty One. You will see the Son of Man coming on the clouds of heaven."

The high priest tore his clothes. "Why do we need any more witnesses?" he asked. "You have heard him say a very evil thing against God. What do you think?"

They all found him guilty and said he must die.

Then some began to spit at him. They blindfolded him. They hit him with their fists. They said, "Prophesy!" And the guards took him and beat him.

Peter Says He Does Not Know Jesus

Peter was below in the courtyard. One of the high priest's female servants came by. When she saw Peter warming himself, she looked closely at him.

"You also were with Jesus, that Nazarene," she said.

But Peter said he had not been with him. "I don't know or understand

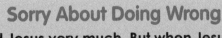

Sorry About Doing Wrong

Peter loved Jesus very much. But when Jesus was arrested, Peter was afraid. He even told people that he didn't know Jesus. Afterward he felt so bad that he broke down and cried.

How do you feel when you do something wrong? Very unhappy, right? The best thing to do is to tell God all about it. Tell him you're sorry. He will forgive you. Then you will feel better.

what you're talking about," he said. He went out to the entrance to the courtyard.

The servant saw him there. She said again to those standing around, "This fellow is one of them."

Again he said he was not.

After a little while, those standing nearby said to Peter, "You must be one of them. You are from Galilee."

He began to call down curses on himself. He took an oath and said to them, "I don't know this man you're talking about!"

Right away the rooster crowed the second time. Then Peter remembered what Jesus had spoken to him. "The rooster will crow twice," he had said. "Before it does, you will say three times that you don't know me." Peter broke down and sobbed.

Jesus Goes Before Pilate
Matthew 27; Luke 23

Judas Hangs Himself

It was early in the morning. All the chief priests and the elders of the people decided to put Jesus to death. They tied him up and led him away. Then they handed him over to Pilate, who was the governor.

Judas, who had handed him over, saw that Jesus had been sentenced to die. He felt deep shame and sadness for what he had done. So he returned the 30 silver coins to the chief priests and the elders. "I have sinned," he said. "I handed over a man who is not guilty."

"What do we care?" they replied. "That's your problem."

So Judas threw the money into the temple and left. Then he went away and hanged himself.

The chief priests picked up the coins. They said, "It's against the law to put this money into the temple fund. It is blood money. It has paid for a man's death." So they decided to use the money to buy a potter's field. People from other countries would be buried there. That is why it has been called The Field of Blood to this very day. Then the words spoken by Jeremiah the prophet came true. He had said, "They took the 30 silver coins.

That price was set for him by the people of Israel. They used the coins to buy a potter's field, just as the Lord commanded me."

(Zechariah 11:12,13; Jeremiah 19:1–13; 32:6–9)

Then the whole group got up and led Jesus off to Pilate. They began to bring charges against Jesus. They said, "We have found this man misleading our people. He is against paying taxes to Caesar. And he claims to be Christ, a king."

So Pilate asked Jesus, "Are you the king of the Jews?"

"Yes. It is just as you say," Jesus replied.

Then Pilate spoke to the chief priests and the crowd. He announced, "I find no basis for a charge against this man."

But they kept it up. They said, "His teaching stirs up the people all over Judea. He started in Galilee and has come all the way here."

PEOPLE IN BIBLE TIMES

Pontius Pilate

Pontius Pilate was the man in charge of Judea. Pilate was not a Jew. He was a Roman. Pilate was the only one who could decide that Jesus should be put to death. Pilate asked Jesus to defend himself. Jesus did not say a word. Pilate knew that Jesus was innocent. But he was afraid of the people and was not brave enough to let Jesus go. He let the people crucify Jesus.

When Pilate heard this, he asked if the man was from Galilee. He learned that Jesus was from Herod's area of authority. So Pilate sent Jesus to Herod. At that time Herod was also in Jerusalem.

When Herod saw Jesus, he was very pleased. He had been wanting to see Jesus for a long time. He had heard much about him. He hoped to see Jesus do a miracle.

Herod asked him many questions, but Jesus gave him no answer. The chief priests and the teachers of the law were standing there. With loud shouts they brought charges against him.

Herod and his soldiers laughed at him and made fun of him. They dressed him in a beautiful robe. Then they sent him back to Pilate. That day Herod and Pilate became friends. Before this time they had been enemies.

Pilate called together the chief priests, the rulers and the people. He said to them, "You brought me this man. You said he was turning the people against the authorities. I have questioned him in front of you. I

Flogging

Before Roman prisoners were crucified, they were beaten with a leather whip. This whip had sharp pieces of metal or bone near the ends. This kind of whip made the prisoners' backs bleed so much that prisoners who were flogged sometimes died.

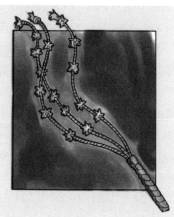

have found no basis for your charges against him. Herod hasn't either. So he sent Jesus back to us. As you can see, Jesus has done nothing that is worthy of death. So I will just have him whipped and let him go."

With one voice the crowd cried out, "Kill this man! Give Barabbas to us!" Barabbas had been thrown into prison. He had taken part in a struggle in the city against the authorities. He had also committed murder.

Pilate wanted to let Jesus go. So he made an appeal to the crowd again. But they kept shouting, "Crucify him! Crucify him!"

Pilate spoke to them for the third time. "Why?" he asked. "What wrong has this man done? I have found no reason to have him put to death. So I will just have him whipped and let him go."

But with loud shouts they kept calling for Jesus to be crucified. The people's shouts won out.

So Pilate decided to give them what they wanted. He set free the man they asked for. The man had been thrown in prison for murder and for fighting against the authorities. Pilate gave Jesus over to them so they could carry out their plans.

Jesus Is Nailed to a Cross

As they led Jesus away, they took hold of Simon. Simon was from Cyrene. He was on his way in from the country. They put a

PEOPLE IN BIBLE TIMES

Simon

Simon was a man from Cyrene. He was walking by when Jesus was taken out to be killed on the cross. Jesus' enemies forced Simon to carry Jesus' cross. He took the cross to Golgotha. Jesus died on the cross there.

wooden cross on his shoulders. Then they made him carry it behind Jesus.

A large number of people followed Jesus. Some were women whose hearts were filled with sorrow. They cried loudly because of him.

Jesus turned and said to them, "Daughters of Jerusalem, do not cry for me. Cry for yourselves and for your children. The time will come when you will say, 'Blessed are the women who can't have children! Blessed are those who never gave birth or nursed babies!' It is written,

> "'The people will say to the mountains, "Fall on us!"
>   They'll say to the hills, "Cover us!"'"   *(Hosea 10:8)*

People do these things when trees are green. So what will happen when trees are dry?"

Two other men were also led out with Jesus to be killed. Both of them had broken the law. The soldiers brought them to the place called The Skull. There they nailed Jesus to the cross. He hung between the two criminals. One was on his right and one was on his left.

Jesus said, "Father, forgive them. They don't know what they are doing." The soldiers divided up his clothes by casting lots.

The people stood there watching. The rulers even made fun of Jesus. They said, "He saved others. Let him save himself if he is the Christ of God, the Chosen One."

The Cross

The Romans killed only the worst criminals by hanging them on crosses. Even though he had done nothing wrong, Jesus was crucified along with two such criminals. Crucifixion was a very painful way to die. The hands of the person being crucified were nailed or tied to the wooden cross. It usually took a long time to die on a cross.

The soldiers also came up and poked fun at him. They offered him wine vinegar. They said, "If you are the king of the Jews, save yourself."

A written sign had been placed above him. It read, THIS IS THE KING OF THE JEWS.

One of the criminals hanging there made fun of Jesus. He said, "Aren't you the Christ? Save yourself! Save us!"

But the other criminal scolded him. "Don't you have any respect for God?" he said. "Remember, you are under the same sentence of death. We are being punished fairly. We are getting just what our actions call for. But this man hasn't done anything wrong."

Then he said, "Jesus, remember me when you come into your kingdom."

Jesus answered him, "What I'm about to tell you is true. Today you will be with me in paradise."

Jesus Dies

It was now about noon. The whole land was covered with darkness until three o'clock. The sun had stopped shining. The temple curtain was torn in two. Jesus called out in a loud voice, "Father, into your hands I commit my very life." After he said this, he took his last breath.

The Roman commander saw what had happened. He praised God and said, "Jesus was surely a man who did what was right."

Jesus Is Buried

John 19

It was Preparation Day. The next day would be a special Sabbath. The Jews did not want the bodies left on the crosses during the Sabbath. So they asked Pilate to have the legs broken and the bodies taken down. The soldiers came and broke the legs of the first man who had been crucified with Jesus. Then they broke the legs of the other man.

But when they came to Jesus, they saw that he was already dead. So they did not break his legs. Instead, one of the soldiers stuck his spear into Jesus' side. Right away, blood and water flowed out. The man who saw it has given witness. And his witness is true. He knows that he tells the truth. He gives witness so that you also can believe.

These things happened in order that Scripture would come true. It says, "Not one of his bones will be broken." *(Exodus 12:46; Numbers 9:12; Psalm 34:20)* Scripture also says, "They will look to the one they have pierced." *(Zechariah 12:10)*

Jesus Is Buried

Later Joseph asked Pilate for Jesus' body. Joseph was from the town of Arimathea. He was a follower of Jesus. But he followed Jesus secretly because he was afraid of the Jews. After Pilate gave him permission, Joseph came and took the body away.

Nicodemus went with Joseph. He was the man who had earlier visited Jesus at night. Nicodemus brought some mixed spices, about 75 pounds. The two men took Jesus' body. They wrapped it in strips of linen cloth, along with the spices. That was the way the Jews buried people's bodies.

PEOPLE IN BIBLE TIMES

Joseph of Arimathea

Joseph of Arimathea was a Jewish ruler. He believed in Jesus. But he did not tell anyone else. He followed Jesus in secret. He was afraid of Jesus' enemies. When Jesus died, Joseph asked Pilate if he could have Jesus' body. Then Joseph buried Jesus in Joseph's own tomb.

At the place where Jesus was crucified, there was a garden. A new tomb was there. No one had ever been put in it before. That day was the Jewish Preparation Day, and the tomb was nearby. So they placed Jesus there.

Burial

The Jews buried people the same day they died. The body was wrapped in strips of cloth and placed in a tomb, often a cave with a large stone in front of the opening. For special people, sweet-smelling spices were wrapped with the cloth.

Jesus Rises From the Dead!

John 20

The Tomb Is Empty

Early on the first day of the week, Mary Magdalene went to the tomb. It was still dark. She saw that the stone had been moved away from the entrance. So she ran to Simon Peter and another disciple, the one Jesus loved. She said, "They have taken the Lord out of the tomb! We don't know where they have put him!"

So Peter and the other disciple started out for the tomb. Both of them were running. The other disciple ran faster than Peter. He reached the tomb first. He bent over and looked in at the strips of linen lying there. But he did not go in.

Then Simon Peter, who was behind him, arrived. He went into the tomb. He saw the strips of linen lying there. He also saw the burial cloth that had been around Jesus' head. The cloth was folded up by itself. It was separate from the linen.

The disciple who had reached the tomb first also went inside. He saw and believed. They still did not understand from Scripture that Jesus had to rise from the dead.

Jesus Appears to Mary Magdalene

Then the disciples went back to their homes. But Mary stood outside the tomb crying. As she cried, she bent over to look into the tomb. She saw two angels dressed in white. They were seated where Jesus' body

Jesus' Tomb

The tombs of rich people were cut into rocky hillsides. A large round stone was rolled in front of the opening to close it. This is the kind of tomb in which Jesus was buried.

had been. One of them was where Jesus' head had been laid. The other sat where his feet had been placed.

They asked her, "Woman, why are you crying?"

"They have taken my Lord away," she said. "I don't know where they have put him."

Then she turned around and saw Jesus standing there. But she didn't realize that it was Jesus.

"Woman," he said, "why are you crying? Who are you looking for?"

She thought he was the gardener. So she said, "Sir, did you carry him away? Tell me where you put him. Then I will go and get him."

Jesus said to her, "Mary."

She turned toward him. Then she cried out in the Aramaic language, "Rabboni!" Rabboni means Teacher.

Jesus said, "Do not hold on to me. I have not yet returned to the Father. Instead, go to those who believe in me. Tell them, 'I am returning to my Father and your Father, to my God and your God.'"

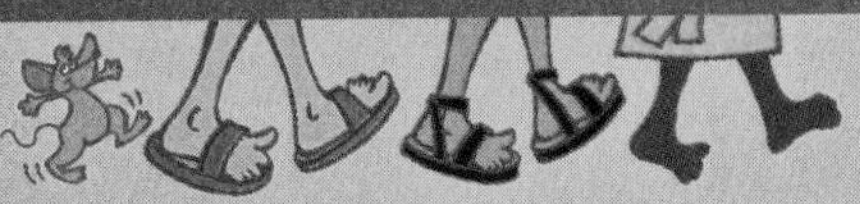

Mary Magdalene went to the disciples with the news. She said, "I have seen the Lord!" And she told them that he had said these things to her.

PEOPLE IN BIBLE TIMES

Mary Magdalene

Mary Magdalene was with Jesus' mother when Jesus died on the cross. She went to Jesus' tomb too. Mary saw that the stone was rolled away from the door of the tomb. Jesus came to Mary at the empty tomb. He spoke to her. She was the first person to see Jesus after he came back to life. Mary told Jesus' followers the good news.

Others See Jesus

Luke 24

On the Road to Emmaus

That same day two of Jesus' followers were going to a village called Emmaus. It was about seven miles from Jerusalem. They were talking with each other about everything that had happened.

As they talked about those things, Jesus himself came up and walked along with them. But God kept them from recognizing him.

Jesus asked them, "What are you talking about as you walk along?"

They stood still, and their faces were sad. One of them was named Cleopas. He said to Jesus, "You must be a visitor to Jerusalem. If you lived there, you would know the things that have happened there in the last few days."

"What things?" Jesus asked.

"About Jesus of Nazareth," they replied. "He was a prophet. He was powerful in what he said and did in the eyes of God and all of the people. The chief priests and our rulers handed Jesus over to be sentenced to death. They nailed him to a cross. But we had hoped that he was the one who was going to set Israel free. Also, it is the third day since all this happened.

"Some of our women amazed us too. Early this morning they went to the tomb. But they didn't find his body. So they came and told us what they had seen. They saw angels, who said Jesus was alive. Then some of our friends went to the tomb. They saw it was empty, just as the women had said. They didn't see Jesus' body there."

Jesus said to them, "How foolish you are! How long it takes you to believe all that the prophets said! Didn't the Christ have to suffer these things and then receive his glory?"

Jesus explained to them what was said about himself in all the Scriptures. He began with Moses and all the Prophets.

The two men approached the village where they were going. Jesus acted as if he were going farther. But they tried hard to keep him from leaving. They said, "Stay with us. It is nearly evening. The day is almost over." So he went in to stay with them.

He joined them at the table. Then he took bread and gave thanks. He broke it and began to give it to them. Their eyes were opened, and they recognized him. But then he disappeared from their sight.

They said to each other, "He talked with us on the road. He opened the Scriptures to us. Weren't our hearts burning inside us during that time?"

They got up and returned at once to Jerusalem. There they found the Eleven and those with them. They were all gathered together. They were saying, "It's true! The Lord has risen! He has appeared to Simon!"

Then the two of them told what had happened to them on the way. They told how they had recognized Jesus when he broke the bread.

The Disciples See Jesus

John 20

Jesus Appears to His Disciples

On the evening of that first day of the week, the disciples were together. They had locked the doors because they were afraid of the Jews.

Jesus came in and stood among them. He said, "May peace be with you!" Then he showed them his hands and his side. The disciples were very happy when they saw the Lord.

Again Jesus said, "May peace be with you! The Father has sent me. So now I am sending you." He then breathed on them. He said, "Receive the Holy Spirit. If you forgive anyone's sins, they are forgiven. If you do not forgive them, they are not forgiven."

Jesus Appears to Thomas

Thomas was one of the Twelve. He was called Didymus. He was not with the other disciples when Jesus came. So they told him, "We have seen the Lord!"

But he said to them, "First I must see the nail marks in his hands. I must put my finger where the nails were. I must put my hand into his side. Only then will I believe what you say."

A week later, Jesus' disciples were in the house again. Thomas was with them. Even though the doors were locked, Jesus came in and stood among them.

He said, "May peace be with you!" Then he said to Thomas, "Put your finger here. See my hands. Reach out your hand and put it into my side. Stop doubting and believe."

Thomas said to him, "My Lord and my God!"

Then Jesus told him, "Because you have seen me, you have believed. Blessed are those who have not seen me but still have believed."

Jesus did many other miraculous signs in front of his disciples. They are not written down in this book. But these are written down so that you may believe that Jesus is the Christ, the Son of God. If you believe this, you will have life because you belong to him.

Jesus Goes to Heaven

Matthew 28; Mark 16

Then the 11 disciples went to Galilee. They went to the mountain where Jesus had told them to go. When they saw him, they worshipped him.

He said to them, "Go into all the world. Preach the good news to everyone. Anyone who believes and is baptized will be saved. But anyone who does not believe will be punished. Here are the miraculous signs that those who believe will do. In my name they will drive out demons. They will speak in languages they had not known before. They will pick up snakes with their hands. And when they drink deadly poison, it will not hurt them at all. They will place their hands on sick people. And the people will get well."

When the Lord Jesus finished speaking to them, he was taken up into heaven. He sat down at the right hand of God.

WORDS TO TREASURE

Go into all the world. Preach the good news to everyone. Anyone who believes and is baptized will be saved.

Mark 16:15–16

The Life of CHRIST

JESUS is born

JESUS goes to the temple ● JESUS is baptized

JESUS is tempted by Satan ● JESUS chooses his disciples

JESUS feeds 5,000 people ● JESUS walks on water

JESUS raises Lazarus from the dead ● JESUS talks to Zacchaeus

JESUS enters Jerusalem ● JESUS clears the temple

JESUS eats the last supper ● JESUS prays in Gethsemane

JESUS is arrested ● JESUS is crucified ● JESUS is buried

JESUS is raised ● JESUS appears to the disciples

JESUS goes to heaven

The Book of History

Acts

Acts is the only book of history in the New Testament of the Bible. It comes after the Gospels. At the beginning of the book, Jesus goes up into heaven. Acts tells how Jesus' followers met together and prayed. The Holy Spirit came down from heaven. Jesus' followers were filled with the Holy Spirit. They praised God. They were joyful. And they ran out to tell everyone about Jesus. That's how the church spread to the whole world.

Peter and Paul are two important people in this book. They were apostles. They became the leaders of Jesus' followers after Jesus went up to heaven. They went to many cities to tell the people about Jesus. Jesus came to save us from our sins!

Luke wrote this book. He was a doctor who traveled with Paul. The stories in this book happened from A.D. 30 to 61. These things happened in many cities all over the Roman world.

The Holy Spirit Comes at Pentecost

Acts 2

The day of Pentecost came. The believers all gathered in one place. Suddenly a sound came from heaven. It was like a strong wind blowing. It filled the whole house where they were sitting. They saw something that looked like tongues of fire. The flames separated and settled on each of them. All of them were filled with the Holy Spirit. They began to speak in languages they had not known before. The Spirit gave them the ability to do this.

Godly Jews from every country in the world were staying in Jerusalem. A crowd came together when they heard the sound. They were bewildered because they each heard the believers speaking in their own language. The crowd was really amazed. They asked, "Aren't all these people from Galilee? Why, then, do we each hear them speaking in our own native language? We are Parthians, Medes and Elamites. We live in Mesopotamia, Judea and Cappadocia. We are from Pontus, Asia, Phrygia and Pamphylia. Others of us are from Egypt and the parts of Libya near Cyrene. Still others are visitors from Rome. Some of the visitors are Jews. Others have accepted the Jewish faith. Also, Cretans and Arabs are here. We hear all these people speaking about God's wonders in our own languages!" They were amazed and bewildered. They asked one another, "What does this mean?"

But some people in the crowd made fun of the believers. "They've had too much wine!" they said.

DID YOU KNOW?

What was Pentecost?

God gave Jesus' followers the Holy Spirit that day. They spoke in languages they didn't know. Flames of fire were over their heads. These were special signs of the Holy Spirit. Many people came to see what was happening. They each heard about Jesus in their own language. Peter told them about Jesus.

Peter Speaks to the Crowd

Then Peter stood up with the Eleven. In a loud voice he spoke to the crowd. "My Jewish friends," he said, "let me explain this to you. All of you who live in Jerusalem, listen carefully to what I say. You think these

people are drunk. But they aren't. It's only nine o'clock in the morning!
No, here is what the prophet Joel meant. He said,

"'In the last days, God says,
    I will pour out my Holy Spirit on all people.
Your sons and daughters will prophesy.
    Your young men will see visions.
    Your old men will have dreams.
In those days I will pour out my Spirit
    even on those who serve me, both men and women.
    When I do, they will prophesy.
I will show wonders in the heavens above.
    I will show miraculous signs on the earth below.
    There will be blood and fire and clouds of smoke.
The sun will become dark.
    The moon will turn red like blood.
    This will happen before the coming of the great and glorious
    day of the Lord.
Everyone who calls
    on the name of the Lord will be saved.'"

(Joel 2:28–32)

Power to Love

Do you have a special love for your Christian friends? The first Christians loved each other very much too. The Holy Spirit gave them power to show love in many ways.

Think about some ways that the first Christians showed love to each other. Then think about some ways that your family and friends could show Christian love today. Here are some ideas:

1. Have a garage sale. Give the money to needy people.

2. Invite a lonely person to your house for a meal.

3. Have friends over to sing and praise God.

How are these ideas like the things that the first Christians did?

The believers studied what the apostles taught. They shared life together. They broke bread and ate together. And they prayed. Everyone felt that God was near. The apostles did many wonders and miraculous signs. All the believers were together. They shared everything they had. They sold what they owned. They gave each other everything they needed. Every day they met together in the temple courtyard. In their homes they broke bread and ate together. Their hearts were glad and honest and true. They praised God. They were respected by all the people. Every day the Lord added to their group those who were being saved.

Peter Heals the Disabled Beggar

Acts 3

One day Peter and John were going up to the temple. It was three o'clock in the afternoon. It was the time for prayer. A man unable to walk was being carried to the temple gate called Beautiful. He had been that way since he was born. Every day someone put him near the gate. There he would beg from people going into the temple courtyards.

He saw that Peter and John were about to enter. So he asked them for money. Peter looked straight at him, and so did John. Then Peter said, "Look at us!" So the man watched them closely. He expected to get something from them.

Peter said, "I don't have any silver or gold. But I'll give you what I have. In the name of Jesus Christ of Nazareth, get up and walk." Then Peter took him by the right hand and helped him up. At once the man's feet and ankles became strong. He jumped to his feet and began to walk. He went with Peter and John into the temple courtyards. He walked and jumped

DID YOU KNOW?

How were Peter and John able to heal?

God gave Peter and John special power. They healed in Jesus' name. This proved that Jesus really was the Son of God. After healing the people, Peter told them about Jesus.

and praised God. All the people saw him walking and praising God. They recognized him as the same man who used to sit and beg at the temple gate called Beautiful. They were filled with wonder. They were amazed at what had happened to him.

Peter Speaks to the Jews

The beggar was holding on to Peter and John. All the people were amazed. They came running to them at Solomon's Porch. When Peter saw this, he said, "Men of Israel, why does this surprise you? Why do you stare at us? We haven't made this man walk by our own power or godliness. The God of our fathers, Abraham, Isaac and Jacob, has done this. He has brought glory to Jesus, who serves him. But you handed Jesus over to be killed. Pilate had decided to let him go. But you spoke against Jesus when he was in Pilate's court. You spoke against the Holy and Blameless One. You asked for a murderer to be set free instead. You killed the one who gives life. But God raised him from the dead. We are witnesses of this. This man whom you see and know was made strong because of faith in Jesus' name. Faith in Jesus has healed him completely. You can see it with your own eyes."

The Believers Share What They Own

Acts 4

All the believers were agreed in heart and mind. They didn't claim that anything they had was their own. They shared everything they owned. With great power the apostles continued their teaching. They gave witness that the Lord Jesus had risen from the dead. And they were greatly blessed by God.

There were no needy persons among them. From time to time, those who owned land or houses sold them. They brought the money from the sales. They put it down at the apostles' feet. It was then given out to anyone who needed it.

Joseph was a Levite from Cyprus. The apostles called him Barnabas. The name Barnabas means Son of Help. Barnabas sold a field he owned. He brought the money from the sale. He put it down at the apostles' feet.

Power Through Prayer

Peter and John had very important work to do for God. They knew they needed power. So they prayed for it. God gave them power to keep on preaching and doing wonderful things.

Ask your mom or dad if they ever asked God for power or strength to do something. Tell them how God helped Peter and John. Talk about times that you might need to ask God for power.

Ananias and Sapphira

Acts 5

A man named Ananias and his wife, Sapphira, also sold some land. He kept part of the money for himself. Sapphira knew he had kept it. He brought the rest of it and put it down at the apostles' feet.

Then Peter said, "Ananias, why did you let Satan fill your heart? He made you lie to the Holy Spirit. You have kept some of the money you received for the land. Didn't the land belong to you before it was sold? After it was sold, you could have used the money as you wished. What made you think of doing such a thing? You haven't lied to just anyone. You've lied to God."

When Ananias heard this, he fell down and died. All who heard what had happened were filled with fear. Some young men came and wrapped up his body. They carried him out and buried him.

What was the sin of Ananias and Sapphira?

Ananias and Sapphira lied. They got money from selling some land. They could use the money any way they wanted. But they agreed to lie to the church. Lying to the church is like lying to God. So God punished them.

About three hours later, the wife of Ananias came in. She didn't know what had happened. Peter asked her, "Tell me. Is this the price you and Ananias sold the land for?"

"Yes," she said. "That's the price."

Peter asked her, "How could you agree to test the Spirit of the Lord? Listen! You can hear the steps of the men who buried your husband. They are at the door. They will carry you out also."

At that very moment she fell down at his feet and died. Then the young men came in. They saw that Sapphira was dead. So they carried her out and buried her beside her husband. The whole church and all who heard about these things were filled with fear.

The Apostles Heal Many People

Acts 5

The apostles did many miraculous signs and wonders among the people. All the believers used to meet together at Solomon's Porch. No outsider dared to join them. But the people thought highly of them. More and more men and women believed in the Lord. They joined the other believers. So people brought those who were sick into the streets. They placed them on beds and mats. They hoped that at least Peter's shadow might fall on some of them as he walked by. Crowds even gathered from the towns around Jerusalem. They brought their sick. They also brought those who were suffering because of evil spirits. All of them were healed.

The Story of Stephen, the First Martyr

Acts 6—7

So God's word spread. The number of believers in Jerusalem grew quickly. Also, a large number of priests began to obey Jesus' teachings.

Stephen Is Arrested

Stephen was full of God's grace and power. He did great wonders and miraculous signs among the people. But members of the group called the Synagogue of the Freedmen began to oppose him. Some of them were Jews from Cyrene and Alexandria. Others were Jews from Cilicia and Asia Minor. They all began to argue with Stephen. But he was too wise for them. They couldn't stand up against the Holy Spirit who spoke through him.

Then in secret they talked some men into lying about Stephen. They said, "We heard Stephen speak evil things against Moses. He also spoke evil things against God."

So the people were stirred up. The elders and the teachers of the law were stirred up too. They arrested Stephen and brought him to the Sanhedrin. The false witnesses said, "This fellow never stops speaking against this holy place. He also speaks against the law. We have heard him say that this Jesus of Nazareth will destroy this place. He says Jesus will change the practices that Moses handed down to us."

All who were sitting in the Sanhedrin looked right at Stephen. They saw that his face was like the face of an angel.

[Stephen said to them,] "You people! You won't obey! You are stubborn! You won't listen! You are just like your people of long ago! You always oppose the Holy Spirit! Was there ever a prophet your people didn't try to hurt? They even killed those who told about the coming of the Blameless One. And now you have handed him over to his enemies. You have murdered him. The law you received was brought by angels. But you haven't obeyed it."

Stephen Is Killed

When the Sanhedrin heard this, they became very angry. They ground their teeth at Stephen. But he was full of the Holy Spirit. He looked up to heaven and saw God's glory. He saw Jesus standing at

Power to Do Right

Stephen was very brave. He was the first person to die for preaching about Jesus. God gave Stephen the power to do what was right. He even gave Stephen the power to pray for the people who were killing him.

People won't always agree with you when you tell them about Jesus. But God wants you to stand up for what you know is right. Stand up even when it is hard. God will make you brave like Stephen.

God's right hand. "Look!" he said. "I see heaven open. The Son of Man is standing at God's right hand."

When the Sanhedrin heard this, they covered their ears. They yelled at the top of their voices. They all rushed at him. They dragged him out of the city. They began to throw stones at him to kill him. The witnesses took off their coats. They placed them at the feet of a young man named Saul.

While the members of the Sanhedrin were throwing stones at Stephen, he prayed. "Lord Jesus, receive my spirit," he said. Then he fell on his knees. He cried out, "Lord! Don't hold this sin against them!" When he had said this, he died.

Philip and the Man From Ethiopia

Acts 8

An angel of the Lord spoke to Philip. "Go south to the desert road," he said. "It's the road that goes down from Jerusalem to Gaza." So Philip started out. On his way he met an Ethiopian official. The man had an important position. He was in charge of all the wealth of Candace. She was the queen of Ethiopia. He had gone to Jerusalem to worship. On his way home he was sitting in his chariot. He was reading the book of Isaiah the prophet. The Holy Spirit told Philip, "Go to that chariot. Stay near it."

So Philip ran up to the chariot. He heard the man reading Isaiah the prophet. "Do you understand what you're reading?" Philip asked.

"How can I?" he said. "I need someone to explain it to me." So he invited Philip to come up and sit with him.

Here is the part of Scripture the official was reading. It says,

"He was led like a sheep to be killed.
   Just as lambs are silent while their wool is being cut off,
   he did not open his mouth.

When he was treated badly, he was refused a fair trial.
> Who can say anything about his children?
> His life was cut off from the earth." *(Isaiah 53:7,8)*

The official said to Philip, "Tell me, please. Who is the prophet talking about? Himself, or someone else?" Then Philip began with that same part of Scripture. He told him the good news about Jesus.

As they traveled along the road, they came to some water. The official said, "Look! Here is water! Why shouldn't I be baptized?" He gave orders to stop the chariot. Then both Philip and the official went down into the water. Philip baptized him. When they came up out of the water, the Spirit of the Lord suddenly took Philip away. The official did not see him again. He went on his way full of joy. Philip was seen next at Azotus. From there he traveled all around. He preached the good news in all the towns. Finally he arrived in Caesarea.

The Story of Saul Who Became Paul

Acts 9

Saul Becomes a Believer

Meanwhile, [a man named] Saul continued to oppose the Lord's followers. He said they would be put to death. He went to the high priest. He asked the priest for letters to the synagogues in Damascus. He wanted to find men and women who belonged to the Way of Jesus. The letters would allow him to take them as prisoners to Jerusalem.

On his journey, Saul approached Damascus. Suddenly a light from heaven flashed around him. He fell to the ground. He heard a voice speak to him. "Saul! Saul!" the voice said. "Why are you opposing me?"

"Who are you, Lord?" Saul asked.

PEOPLE IN BIBLE TIMES

Saul/Paul

The Saul who is in the New Testament hated Christians. Jesus changed Saul. He made Saul into a Christian. Jesus changed Saul's name to Paul. Paul was a great missionary. He wrote 13 books of the Bible, all in the New Testament.

"I am Jesus," he replied. "I am the one you are opposing. Now get up and go into the city. There you will be told what you must do."

The men traveling with Saul stood there. They weren't able to speak. They had heard the sound. But they didn't see anyone. Saul got up from the ground. He opened his eyes, but he couldn't see. So they led him by the hand into Damascus.

Saul Becomes a Believer

For three days he was blind. He didn't eat or drink anything.

In Damascus there was a believer named Ananias. The Lord called out to him in a vision. "Ananias!" he said.

"Yes, Lord," he answered.

The Lord told him, "Go to the house of Judas on Straight Street. Ask for a man from Tarsus named Saul. He is praying. In a vision he has seen a man named Ananias. The man has come and placed his hands on him. Now he will be able to see again."

"Lord," Ananias answered, "I've heard many reports about this man. They say he has done great harm to God's people in Jerusalem. Now he has come here to arrest all those who worship you. The chief priests have given him authority to do this."

But the Lord said to Ananias, "Go! I have chosen this man to work for me. He will carry my name to those who aren't Jews and to their kings. He will bring my name to the people of Israel. I will show him how much he must suffer for me."

Power to Change

Saul hated Christians. He was mean to them and arrested as many as he could. Then Saul met Jesus. Saul's heart was changed. He even got a new name. Now he was called Paul. He became a great missionary. Only God has the power to change a heart like that.

Draw "before" and "after" pictures of Paul. How do you think he looked when he hated Christians? How do you think his love for Jesus changed the way he looked? Put your pictures on your wall. Let them remind you of the change that loving Jesus can make in a person. Pray for someone who needs to change.

Then Ananias went to the house and entered it. He placed his hands on Saul. "Brother Saul," he said, "you saw the Lord Jesus. He appeared to you on the road as you were coming here. He has sent me so that you will be able to see again. You will be filled with the Holy Spirit."

Right away something like scales fell from Saul's eyes. And he could see again. He got up and was baptized. After eating some food, he got his strength back.

Saul in Damascus and Jerusalem

At once he began to preach in the synagogues. He taught that Jesus is the Son of God. All who heard him were amazed. They asked, "Isn't he the man who caused great trouble in Jerusalem for those who worship Jesus? Hasn't he come here to take them as prisoners to the chief priests?" But Saul grew more and more powerful. The Jews living in Damascus couldn't believe what was happening. Saul proved to them that Jesus is the Christ.

After many days, the Jews had a meeting. They planned to kill Saul. But he learned about their plan. Day and night they watched the city gates closely in order to kill him. But his followers helped him escape by night. They lowered him in a basket through an opening in the wall.

When Saul came to Jerusalem, he tried to join the believers. But they were all afraid of him. They didn't believe he was really one of Jesus' followers. But Barnabas took him to the apostles. He told them about Saul's journey. He said that Saul had seen the Lord. He told how the Lord had spoken to Saul. Barnabas also said that Saul had preached without fear in Jesus' name in Damascus.

So Saul stayed with the believers. He moved about freely in Jerusalem. He spoke boldly in the Lord's name. He talked and argued with Jews who followed Greek practices. But they tried to kill him. The other believers heard about this. They took Saul down to Caesarea. From there they sent him off to Tarsus.

PEOPLE IN BIBLE TIMES

Barnabas

Barnabas loved to tell people about Jesus. He went to many cities to share the good news of Jesus Christ. He went on trips with Paul too. They both told people about Jesus. They were brave, even when people were angry with them.

Then the church throughout Judea, Galilee and Samaria enjoyed a time of peace. The Holy Spirit gave the church strength and boldness. So they grew in numbers. And they worshiped the Lord.

Peter Heals a Woman

Acts 9

Peter Goes to Lydda and Joppa

In Joppa there was a believer named Tabitha. Her name in the Greek language was Dorcas. She was always doing good and helping poor people.

About that time she became sick and died. Her body was washed and placed in a room upstairs. Lydda was near Joppa. The believers heard that Peter was in Lydda. So they sent two men to him. They begged him, "Please come at once!"

Peter went with them. When he arrived, he was taken upstairs to the room. All the widows stood around him crying. They showed him the robes and other clothes Dorcas had made while she was still alive.

Peter sent them all out of the room. Then he got down on his knees and prayed. He turned toward the dead woman. He said, "Tabitha, get up." She opened her eyes. When she saw Peter, she sat up. He took her by the hand and helped her to her feet. Then he called the believers and the widows. He brought her to them. They saw that she was alive. This became known all over Joppa. Many people believed in the Lord. Peter stayed in Joppa for some time. He stayed with Simon, a man who worked with leather.

The Story of Cornelius

Acts 10

Cornelius Calls for Peter

A man named Cornelius lived in Caesarea. He was a Roman commander in the Italian Regiment. Cornelius and all his family were faithful and worshiped God. He gave freely to people who were in need. He prayed to God regularly. One day about three o'clock in the afternoon he had a vision. He saw an angel of God clearly. The angel came to him and said, "Cornelius!"

Cornelius was afraid. He stared at the angel. "What is it, Lord?" he asked.

The angel answered, "Your prayers and gifts to poor people have come up like an offering to God. So he has remembered you. Now send men to Joppa. Have them bring back a man named Simon. He is also called Peter. He is staying with another Simon, a man who works with leather. His house is by the sea."

The angel who spoke to him left. Then Cornelius called two of his servants. He also called a godly soldier who was one of his attendants. He told them everything that had happened. Then he sent them to Joppa. [They asked Peter to come home with them.]

Peter Goes to the House of Cornelius

The next day Peter went with the three men. Some of the believers from Joppa went along. The following day he arrived in Caesarea. Cornelius was expecting them.

When Peter entered the house, Cornelius met him. As a sign of respect, he fell at Peter's feet. But Peter made him get up. "Stand up," he said. "I am only a man myself."

Talking with Cornelius, Peter went inside. There he found a large group of people. He said to them, "You know that it is against our law for a Jew to have anything to do with those who aren't Jews. But God has shown me that I should not say anyone is not pure and 'clean.' So when you sent for me, I came without asking any questions. May I ask why you sent for me?"

Cornelius answered, "Four days ago at this very hour I was in my house praying. It was three o'clock in the afternoon. Suddenly a man in shining clothes stood in front of me. He said, 'Cornelius, God has heard your prayer. He has remembered your gifts to poor people. Send someone to Joppa to get Simon Peter. He is a guest in the home of another Simon, who works with leather. He lives by the sea.' So I sent for you right away. It was good of you to come. Now we are all here. And God is here with us. We are ready to listen to everything the Lord has commanded you to tell us."

Then Peter began to speak. "I now realize how true it is that God treats everyone the same," he said. "He accepts people from every nation. He accepts all who have respect for him and do what is right."

Believers Are Called Christians for the First Time

Acts 11

Some believers had been scattered by the suffering that came to them after Stephen's death. They traveled as far as Phoenicia, Cyprus and Antioch. But they told the message only to Jews. Some believers from Cyprus and Cyrene went to Antioch. There they began to speak to Greeks also. They told them the good news about the Lord Jesus. The Lord's power was with them. Large numbers of people believed and turned to the Lord.

The church in Jerusalem heard about this. So they sent Barnabas to Antioch. When he arrived and saw what the grace of God had done, he was glad. He told them all to remain true to the Lord with all their hearts. Barnabas was a good man. He was full of the Holy Spirit and of faith. Large numbers of people came to know the Lord.

Then Barnabas went to Tarsus to look for Saul. He found him there. Then he brought him to Antioch. For a whole year Barnabas and Saul met with the church. They taught large numbers of people. At Antioch the believers were called Christians for the first time.

In those days some prophets came down from Jerusalem to Antioch. One of them was named Agabus. He stood up and spoke through the Spirit. He said there would not be nearly enough food anywhere in the Roman world. This happened while Claudius was the emperor. The believers decided to provide help for the brothers and sisters living in Judea. All of them helped as much as they could. They sent their gift to the elders through Barnabas and Saul.

An Angel Helps Peter Escape From Prison

Acts 12

About this time, King Herod arrested some people who belonged to the church. He planned to make them suffer greatly. He had James killed with a sword. James was John's brother. Herod saw that the death of James pleased the Jews. So he arrested Peter also. This happened during the Feast of Unleavened Bread. After Herod arrested Peter, he put him in prison. Peter was placed under guard. He was watched by four groups of four soldiers each. Herod planned to put Peter on public trial. It would take place after the Passover Feast.

So Peter was kept in prison. But the church prayed hard to God for him.

It was the night before Herod was going to bring him to trial. Peter was sleeping between two soldiers. Two chains held him there. Lookouts stood guard at the entrance. Suddenly an angel of the Lord appeared. A light shone in the prison cell. The angel struck Peter on his side. Peter woke up. "Quick!" the angel said. "Get up!" The chains fell off Peter's wrists.

Then the angel said to him, "Put on your clothes and sandals." Peter did so. "Put on your coat," the angel told him. "Follow me." Peter followed him out of the prison. But he had no idea that what the angel was doing was really happening. He thought he was seeing a vision. They passed the first and second guards. Then they came to the iron gate leading to the city. It opened for them by itself. They went through it. They walked the length of one street. Suddenly the angel left Peter.

Then Peter realized what had happened. He said, "Now I know for sure that

How did Peter escape from prison?

An angel let Peter out of his chains. The angel led Peter outside the jail. All Peter's friends were praying for him. Peter came to their door. But they didn't believe he was really there! Sometimes God gives us surprise answers when we pray. We need to trust him and believe in his amazing answers.

the Lord sent his angel. He set me free from Herod's power. He saved me from everything the Jewish people were hoping for."

When Peter understood what had happened, he went to Mary's house. Mary was the mother of John Mark. Many people had gathered in her home. They were praying there. Peter knocked at the outer entrance. A servant named Rhoda came to answer the door. She recognized Peter's voice. She was so excited that she ran back without opening the door. "Peter is at the door!" she exclaimed.

"You're out of your mind," they said to her. But she kept telling them it was true. So they said, "It must be his angel."

Peter kept on knocking. When they opened the door and saw him, they were amazed. Peter motioned with his hand for them to be quiet. He explained how the Lord had brought him out of prison. "Tell James and the others about this," he said. Then he went to another place.

Paul and Silas Are Thrown Into Prison

Acts 16

One day [Paul and Silas] were going to the place of prayer. On the way [they] were met by a female slave. She had a spirit that helped her to tell ahead of time what was going to happen. She earned a lot of money for her owners by telling fortunes. The woman followed Paul around. She shouted, "These men serve the Most High God. They are telling you how to be saved." She kept this up for many days. Finally Paul became upset. Turning around, he spoke to the spirit. "In the name of Jesus Christ," he said, "I command you to come out of her!" At that very moment the spirit left her.

The female slave's owners realized that their hope of making money was gone. So they grabbed Paul and Silas. They dragged them into the market place to face the authorities. They brought them to the judges. "These men are Jews," her owners said. "They are making trouble in our city. They are suggesting practices that are against Roman law. These are practices we can't accept or take part in."

The crowd joined the attack against Paul and Silas. The judges ordered that Paul and Silas be stripped and beaten. They were whipped without mercy. Then they were thrown into prison. The jailer was commanded to guard them carefully. When he received his orders, he put Paul and Silas deep inside the prison. He fastened their feet so they couldn't get away.

About midnight Paul and Silas were praying. They were also singing hymns to God. The other prisoners were listening to them. Suddenly there was a powerful earthquake. It shook the prison from top to bottom. All at once the prison doors flew open. Everybody's chains came loose.

The jailer woke up. He saw that the prison doors were open. He pulled out his sword and was going to kill himself. He thought the prisoners had escaped. "Don't harm yourself!" Paul shouted. "We are all here!"

The jailer called out for some lights. He rushed in, shaking with fear. He fell down in front of Paul and Silas. Then he brought them out. He asked, "Sirs, what must I do to be saved?"

They replied, "Believe in the Lord Jesus. Then you and your family will be saved." They spoke the word of the Lord to him. They also spoke to all the others in his house.

At that hour of the night, the jailer took Paul and Silas and washed their wounds. Right away he and his whole family were baptized. The jailer brought them into his house. He set a meal in front of them. He and his whole family were filled with joy. They had become believers in God.

Power in Praise

Tommy was very unhappy. Dad had to work late and couldn't take him to the ball game. At supper Mom made him eat food he didn't like. And now he had to clean up the dinner table instead of watch TV. Do you ever have a day like Tommy's? Have a "Tommy contest." Let each member of your family act the way they think Tommy acted. You can make a face, or walk or sit like you think Tommy did.

Is there something Tommy could praise God for, even though he was unhappy? List some things you can praise God for no matter how badly you feel. Put the list where you can see it every day. When we praise God, he gives us the power to be happy no matter what.

Early in the morning the judges sent their officers to the jailer. They ordered him, "Let those men go." The jailer told Paul, "The judges have ordered me to set you and Silas free. You can leave now. Go in peace."

But Paul replied to the officers. "They beat us in public," he said. "We weren't given a trial. And we are Roman citizens! They threw us into prison. And now do they want to get rid of us quietly? No! Let them come themselves and personally lead us out."

The officers reported this to the judges. When the judges heard that Paul and Silas were Roman citizens, they became afraid. So they came and said they were sorry. They led them out of the prison. Then they asked them to leave the city. After Paul and Silas came out of the prison, they went to Lydia's house. There they met with the believers. They told them to be brave. Then they left.

Priscilla and Aquila Teach Apollos

Acts 18

At that time a Jew named Apollos came to Ephesus. He was an educated man from Alexandria. He knew the Scriptures very well. Apollos had been taught the way of the Lord. He spoke with great power. He taught the truth about Jesus. But he only knew about John's baptism.

Priscilla and Aquila

Priscilla and Aquila were married. They made tents. Paul stayed at their house in Corinth. He helped them make tents. Priscilla and Aquila went with Paul on a trip to tell people about Jesus.

He began to speak boldly in the synagogue. Priscilla and Aquila heard him. So they invited him to their home. There they gave him a better understanding of the way of God.

Apollos wanted to go to Achaia. The brothers agreed with him. They wrote to the believers there. They asked them to welcome him. When he arrived, he was a great help to those who had become believers by God's grace. He argued strongly against the Jews in public meetings. He proved from the Scriptures that Jesus was the Christ.

Eutychus Is Raised From the Dead

Acts 20

On the first day of the week ... Paul spoke to the people. He kept on talking until midnight because he planned to leave the next day. There were many lamps in the room upstairs where we were meeting. A young man named Eutychus was sitting in a window. He sank into a deep sleep as Paul talked on and on. Sound asleep, Eutychus fell from the third floor. When they picked him up from the ground, he was dead.

Paul went down and threw himself on the young man. He put his arms around him. "Don't be alarmed," he told them. "He's alive!" Then Paul went upstairs again. He broke bread and ate with them. He kept on talking until daylight. Then he left. The people took the young man home. They were greatly comforted because he was alive.

The Letters of Paul

Romans   1 Corinthians   2 Corinthians   Ephesians

Philippians   Colossians   1 Thessalonians   Galatians   2 Thessalonians

1 Timothy   2 Timothy   Titus   Philemon

God chose Paul to be a teacher. He spoke to many people who were not Jews. He traveled to many cities. He told the people about Jesus Christ. He started many new churches. These books are the letters that Paul wrote to the churches after he left them.

Paul taught the people that they must believe in Jesus to be saved from their sins. He taught them that having faith in Jesus was better than trying to keep the law. Sometimes he scolded the churches when they were doing wrong. He told them how to get along with each other. Paul is an important teacher in the Bible. The letters he wrote so long ago still help us follow Jesus today.

Paul wrote the first letter in A.D 48. He wrote the last letter in A.D. 64 or 65.

A Letter From Paul

Romans 1

I, Paul, am writing this letter. I serve Christ Jesus. I have been appointed to be an apostle. God set me apart to tell others his good news. He promised the good news long ago. He announced it through his prophets in the Holy Scriptures.

The good news is about God's Son. As a human being, the Son of God belonged to King David's family line. By the power of the Holy Spirit, he was appointed to be the mighty Son of God because he rose from the dead. He is Jesus Christ our Lord.

I received God's grace because of what Jesus did so that I could bring glory to him. He made me an apostle to all those who aren't Jews. I must invite them to have faith in God and obey him. You also are among those who are appointed to belong to Jesus Christ.

I am sending this letter to all of you in Rome who are loved by God and appointed to be his people.

May God our Father and the Lord Jesus Christ give you grace and peace.

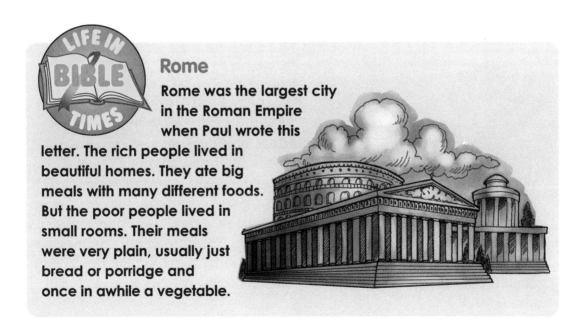

Rome

Rome was the largest city in the Roman Empire when Paul wrote this letter. The rich people lived in beautiful homes. They ate big meals with many different foods. But the poor people lived in small rooms. Their meals were very plain, usually just bread or porridge and once in awhile a vegetable.

Paul Longs to Visit Rome

First, I thank my God through Jesus Christ for all of you. People all over the world are talking about your faith. I serve God with my whole heart. I preach the good news about his Son. God knows that I always remember you in my prayers. I pray that now at last it may be God's plan to open the way for me to visit you.

I long to see you. I want to make you strong by giving you a gift from the Holy Spirit. I want us to cheer each other up by sharing our faith.

Brothers and sisters, I want you to know that I planned many times to visit you. But until now I have been kept from coming. My work has produced results among others who are not Jews. In the same way, I want to see results among you.

I have a duty both to Greeks and to non-Greeks. I have a duty both to wise people and to foolish people. So I really want to preach the good news also to you who live in Rome.

I am not ashamed of the good news. It is God's power. And it will save everyone who believes. It is meant first for the Jews. It is meant also for those who aren't Jews.

The good news shows how God makes people right with himself. From beginning to end, becoming right with God depends on a person's faith. It is written, "Those who are right with God will live by faith." *(Habakkuk 2:4)*

Praying for Others

Do you pray for Christians in other parts of the world? Paul did. He prayed for the Christians in Rome. He had never met them, but he prayed for them every day.

Your church probably helps several missionaries. Get the address of one of the missionary families. Look for one with a child about your age. Ask your family to write to them. Tell them you will try to pray for them every day. Ask them to send you a letter telling about their work. Maybe they could send a photograph too. Then you will know some special ways to pray for them.

Peace and Joy

Romans 5

We have been made right with God because of our faith. Now we have peace with him because of our Lord Jesus Christ. Through faith in Jesus we have received God's grace. In that grace we stand. We are full of joy because we expect to share in God's glory.

And that's not all. We are full of joy even when we suffer. We know that our suffering gives us the strength to go on. The strength to go on produces character. Character produces hope. And hope will never let us down. God has poured his love into our hearts. He did it through the Holy Spirit, whom he has given to us.

At just the right time Christ died for ungodly people. He died for us when we had no power of our own. It is unusual for anyone to die for a godly person. Maybe someone would be willing to die for a good person. But here is how God has shown his love for us. While we were still sinners, Christ died for us.

The blood of Christ has made us right with God. So we are even more sure that Jesus will save us from God's anger. Once we were God's enemies. But we have been brought back to him because his Son has died for us. Now that God has brought us back, we are even more secure. We know that we will be saved because Christ lives.

And that is not all. We are full of joy in God because of our Lord Jesus Christ. Because of him, God has brought us back to himself.

What is grace?

If you do something wrong, you should be punished. But grace changes that. Grace means you are forgiven even when you don't deserve to be. It means that God blesses you even though you should be punished.

Here is how God has shown his love for us. While we were still sinners, Christ died for us.

Romans 5:8

God Is On Our Side

Romans 8

We Will Win

We know that in all things God works for the good of those who love him. He appointed them to be saved in keeping with his purpose.

God planned that those he had chosen would become like his Son. In that way, Christ will be the first and most honored among many brothers. And those God has planned for, he has also appointed to be saved. Those he has appointed, he has made right with himself. To those he has made right with himself, he has given his glory.

What should we say then? Since God is on our side, who can be against us? God did not spare his own Son. He gave him up for us all. Then won't he also freely give us everything else?

Who can bring any charge against God's chosen ones? God makes us right with himself. Who can sentence us to death? Christ Jesus is at the right hand of God and is also praying for us. He died. More than that, he was raised to life.

Who can separate us from Christ's love? Can trouble or hard times or harm or hunger? Can nakedness or danger or war? It is written,

"Because of you, we face death all day long.
We are considered as sheep to be killed." *(Psalm 44:22)*

We know that in all things God works for the good of those who love him.

Romans 8:28

No! In all these things we will do even more than win! We owe it all to Christ, who has loved us.

I am absolutely sure that not even death or life can separate us from God's love. Not even angels or demons, the present or the future, or any powers can do that. Not even the highest places or the lowest, or anything else in all creation can do that. Nothing at all can ever separate us from God's love because of what Christ Jesus our Lord has done.

Hold on to What Is Good

Romans 12

Love

Love must be honest and true. Hate what is evil. Hold on to what is good. Love each other deeply. Honor others more than yourselves. Never let the fire in your heart go out. Keep it alive. Serve the Lord.

When you hope, be joyful. When you suffer, be patient. When you pray, be faithful. Share with God's people who are in need. Welcome others into your homes.

Bless those who hurt you. Bless them, and do not call down curses on them. Be joyful with those who are joyful. Be sad with those who are sad. Agree with each other. Don't be proud. Be willing to be a friend of people who aren't considered important. Don't think that you are better than others.

Don't pay back evil with evil. Be careful to do what everyone thinks is right. If possible, live in peace with everyone. Do that as much as you can.

WORDS TO TREASURE

Hate what is evil. Hold on to what is good.
Romans 12:9

DID YOU KNOW?

How can we show that we love God?

We show love for God when we love and help others. You can find ways to show love to others in this Bible passage.

My friends, don't try to get even. Leave room for God to show his anger. It is written, "I am the One who judges people. I will pay them back," *(Deuteronomy 32:35)* says the Lord. Do just the opposite. Scripture says,

> "If your enemies are hungry, give them food to eat.
>   If they are thirsty, give them something to drink.
> By doing those things, you will pile up burning coals on their
>   heads." *(Proverbs 25:21,22)*

Don't let evil overcome you. Overcome evil by doing good.

Paul Describes the Church

1 Corinthians 12

One Body but Many Parts

The body is not made up of just one part. It has many parts. Suppose the foot says, "I am not a hand. So I don't belong to the body." It is still part of the body. And suppose the ear says, "I am not an eye. So I don't belong to the body." It is still part of the body.

If the whole body were an eye, how could it hear? If the whole body were an ear, how could it smell? God has placed each part in the body just as he wanted it to be. If all the parts were the same, how could there be a body? As it is, there are many parts. But there is only one body.

The eye can't say to the hand, "I don't need you!" The head can't say to the feet, "I don't need you!" In fact, it is just the opposite. The parts of the body that seem to be weaker are the ones we can't do without. The parts that we think are less important we treat with special honor. The private parts aren't shown. But they are treated with special care. The parts that can be shown don't need special care.

What are the gifts of the Holy Spirit?

Gifts of the Holy Spirit are special talents. God gives these special talents to Christians. There are many different kinds of gifts. But all of the gifts of the Holy Spirit come from God. And all of the gifts can help others grow stronger in their faith.

But God has joined together all the parts of the body. And he has given more honor to the parts that didn't have any. In that way, the parts of the body will not take sides. All of them will take care of each other. If one part suffers, every part suffers with it. If one part is honored, every part shares in its joy.

You are the body of Christ. Each one of you is a part of it. First, God has appointed apostles in the church. Second, he has appointed prophets. Third, he has appointed teachers. Then he has appointed people who do miracles and those who have gifts of healing. He also appointed those able to help others, those able to direct things, and those who can speak in different kinds of languages they had not known before.

Is everyone an apostle? Is everyone a prophet? Is everyone a teacher? Do all work miracles? Do all have gifts of healing? Do all speak in languages they had not known before? Do all explain what is said in those languages? But above all, you should want the more important gifts.

Love Is Everything
1 Corinthians 13

Suppose I speak in the languages of human beings and of angels. If I don't have love, I am only a loud gong or a noisy cymbal. Suppose I have the gift of prophecy. Suppose I can understand all the secret things of God and know everything about him. And suppose I have enough faith to move mountains. If I don't have love, I am nothing at all. Suppose I give everything I have to poor people. And suppose I give my body to be burned. If I don't have love, I get nothing at all.

Love is patient. Love is kind. It does not want what belongs to others. It does not brag. It is not proud. It is not rude. It does not look out for its own interests. It does not easily become angry. It does not keep track of other people's wrongs.

Love is not happy with evil. But it is full of joy when the truth is spoken. It always protects. It always trusts. It always hopes. It never gives up.

Love Is

God wants us to show love more than anything else. He wants us to love him. He wants us to love others. This passage tells how a person who loves will treat others. What are the ways? Here is one answer to get you started: Love is patient.

Get some note cards. With your family's help, write something on each card that these verses say about love. At mealtime have each person pick a card. Have each one tell how someone in the family showed that kind of love.

The three most important things to have are faith, hope and love. But the greatest of them is love.

1 Corinthians 13:13

Love never fails. But prophecy will pass away. Speaking in languages that had not been known before will end. And knowledge will pass away.

What we know now is not complete. What we prophesy now is not perfect. But when what is perfect comes, the things that are not perfect will pass away.

When I was a child, I talked like a child. I thought like a child. I had the understanding of a child. When I became a man, I put childish ways behind me.

Now we see only a dim likeness of things. It is as if we were seeing them in a mirror. But someday we will see clearly. We will see face to face. What I know now is not complete. But someday I will know completely, just as God knows me completely.

The three most important things to have are faith, hope and love. But the greatest of them is love.

Forgive Those Who Make You Sad

2 Corinthians 2

Suppose someone has made us sad. In some ways, he hasn't made me sad so much as he has made all of you sad. But I don't want to put this too strongly. He has been punished because most of you decided he should be. That is enough for him.

Now you should forgive him and comfort him. Then he won't be sad more than he can stand. So I'm asking you to tell him again that you still love him.

I wrote to you for a special reason. I wanted to see if you could stand the test. I wanted to see if you could obey everything that was asked of you.

Anyone you forgive I also forgive. Was there anything to forgive? If so, I have forgiven it for your benefit, knowing that Christ is watching. We don't want Satan to outsmart us. We know how he does his evil work.

A Treasure in Clay Jars

2 Corinthians 4

So because of God's mercy, we have work to do. He has given it to us. And we don't give up. Instead, we have given up doing secret and shameful things. We don't twist God's word. In fact, we do just the opposite. We present the truth plainly. In the sight of God, we make our appeal to everyone's sense of what is right and wrong.

We do not preach about ourselves. We preach about Jesus Christ. We say that he is Lord. And we serve you because of him.

God said, "Let light shine out of darkness." *(Genesis 1:3)* He made his light shine in our hearts. It shows us the light of God's glory in the face of Christ.

Treasure is kept in clay jars. In the same way, we have the treasure of the good news in these earthly bodies of ours. That shows that the mighty power of the good news comes from God. It doesn't come from us.

We are pushed hard from all sides. But we are not beaten down. We are bewildered. But that doesn't make us lose hope. Others make us suffer. But God does not desert us. We are knocked down. But we are not knocked out.

It is written, "I believed, and so I have spoken." *(Psalm 116:10)* With that same spirit of faith we also believe. And we also speak.

We know that God raised the Lord Jesus from the dead. And he will also raise us up with Jesus. He will bring us with you to God in heaven. All of that is for your benefit. God's grace is reaching more and more people. So they will become more and more thankful. They will give glory to God.

Treasure!

Scientists (called archaeologists) have found treasures of silver in cheap clay pots. Clay pots were common, and thousands were made. But they were sometimes used to store valuable and precious things.

Christ Brings Us Back to God

2 Corinthians 5

Christ died for everyone. He died so that those who live should not live for themselves anymore. They should live for Christ. He died for them and was raised again.

So from now on we don't look at anyone the way the world does. At one time we looked at Christ in that way. But we don't anymore.

Anyone who believes in Christ is a new creation. The old is gone! The new has come! It is all from God. He brought us back to himself through Christ's death on the cross. And he has given us the task of bringing others back to him through Christ.

What task has God given us?

God wants us to be messengers. Jesus died for our sins so we could be friends with God. God wants us to tell our friends about Jesus. Then they can become God's friends too.

God was bringing the world back to himself through Christ. He did not hold people's sins against them. God has trusted us with the message that people may be brought back to him. So we are Christ's official messengers. It is as if God were making his appeal through us. Here is what Christ wants us to beg you to do. Come back to God!

Christ didn't have any sin. But God made him become sin for us. So we can be made right with God because of what Christ has done for us.

The Fruit of the Spirit

Galatians 5

Christ Sets Us Free

Christ has set us free. He wants us to enjoy freedom. So stand firm. Don't let the chains of slavery hold you again.

Here is what I, Paul, say to you. Don't let yourselves be circumcised. If you do, Christ won't be of any value to you. I say it again. Every man who lets himself be circumcised must obey the whole law.

Some of you are trying to be made right with God by obeying the law. You have been separated from Christ. You have fallen away from God's grace.

But we expect to be made completely holy because of our faith in Christ. Through the Holy Spirit we wait in hope. The only thing that really counts is faith that shows itself through love.

You were running a good race. Who cut in on you and kept you from obeying the truth? The One who chooses you does not keep you from obeying the truth. You should know that "just a little yeast works its way through the whole batch of dough."

Chosen to Be Free

My brothers and sisters, you were chosen to be free. But don't use your freedom as an excuse to live in sin. Instead, serve one another in love. The whole law can be found in a single command. "Love your neighbor as you love yourself." *(Leviticus 19:18)*

You must not keep on biting each other. You must not keep eating each other up. Watch out! You might destroy each other.

Living by the Holy Spirit's Power

So I say, live by the Holy Spirit's power. Then you will not do what your sinful nature wants you to do.

The sinful nature does not want what the Spirit delights in. And the Spirit does not want what the sinful nature delights in. The two are at war with each other. That's what makes you do what you don't want to do. But if you are led by the Spirit, you are not under the authority of the law.

What is Christian freedom?

Christians are not free to do whatever they want. Because God helps us, we are free to do what is right.

The fruit the Holy Spirit produces is love, joy and peace. It is being patient, kind and good. It is being faithful and gentle and having control of oneself. There is no law against things of that kind.

Galatians 5:22–23

The fruit the Holy Spirit produces is love, joy and peace. It is being patient, kind and good. It is being faithful and gentle and having control of oneself. There is no law against things of that kind.

Those who belong to Christ Jesus have nailed their sinful nature to his cross. They don't want what their sinful nature loves and longs for.

Since we live by the Spirit, let us march in step with the Spirit. Let us not become proud. Let us not make each other angry. Let us not want what belongs to others.

God Gives Spiritual Blessings

Ephesians 1

Give praise to the God and Father of our Lord Jesus Christ. He has blessed us with every spiritual blessing. Those blessings come from the heavenly world. They belong to us because we belong to Christ.

God chose us to belong to Christ before the world was created. He chose us to be holy and without blame in his eyes. He loved us. So he decided long ago to adopt us as his children. He did it because of what Jesus Christ has done. It pleased God to do it. All those things bring praise to his glorious grace. God freely gave us his grace because of the One he loves.

What has God done to bless you?

Ephesians 1 tells how God chose you. Christ died to forgive you. And the Holy Spirit stays with you to help you. Paul wanted us to remember that we have many "spiritual blessings."

We have been set free because of what Christ has done. Through his blood our sins have been forgiven. We have been set free because God's grace is so rich. He poured his grace on us by giving us great wisdom and understanding.

He showed us the mystery of his plan. It was in keeping with what he wanted to do. It was what he had planned through Christ. It will all come about when history has been completed. God will then bring together all things in heaven and on earth under one ruler. The ruler is Christ.

We were also chosen to belong to him. God decided to choose us long ago in keeping with his plan. He works out everything to fit his plan and purpose. We were the first to put our hope in Christ. We were chosen to bring praise to his glory.

You also became believers in Christ. That happened when you heard the message of truth. It was the good news about how you could be saved. When you believed, he marked you with a seal. The seal is the Holy Spirit that he promised.

The Spirit marks us as God's own. We can now be sure that someday we will receive all that God has promised. That will happen after God sets all of his people completely free. All of those things will bring praise to his glory.

God's Grace

Ephesians 2

God Has Given Us New Life Through Christ

God loves us deeply. He is full of mercy. So he gave us new life because of what Christ has done. He gave us life even when we were dead in sin. God's grace has saved you.

God raised us up with Christ. He has seated us with him in his heavenly kingdom because we belong to Christ Jesus. He has done it to show the riches of his grace for all time to come. His grace can't be compared with anything else. He has shown it by being kind to us because of what Christ Jesus has done.

WORDS TO TREASURE

God's grace has saved you because of your faith in Christ. Your salvation doesn't come from anything you do. It is God's gift.
Ephesians 2:8

God's grace has saved you because of your faith in Christ. Your salvation doesn't come from anything you do. It is God's gift. It is not based on anything you have done. No one can brag about earning it.

God made us. He created us to belong to Christ Jesus. Now we can do good things.

A Soldier's Armor

The apostle Paul's description of a Roman soldier's armor shows how much Paul knew about Roman soldiers and what they wore. Each part of the soldier's armor was important to protect him from the weapons of his enemy. Read this passage to learn all the parts of the soldier's armor. Now compare that soldier's armor with what you need to do as a Christian.

God's Armor

Ephesians 6

Put on all of God's armor. Evil days will come. But you will be able to stand up to anything. And after you have done everything you can, you will still be standing.

So stand firm. Put the belt of truth around your waist. Put the armor of godliness on your chest. Wear on your feet what will prepare you to tell the good news of peace. Also, pick up the shield of faith. With it you can put out all of the flaming arrows of the evil one. Put on the helmet of salvation. And take the sword of the Holy Spirit. The sword is God's word.

At all times, pray by the power of the Spirit. Pray all kinds of prayers. Be watchful, so that you can pray. Always keep on praying for all of God's people.

Thinking Like Christ

Philippians 2

Are you cheerful because you belong to Christ? Does his love comfort you? Is the Holy Spirit your companion? Has Christ been gentle and loving toward you? Then make my joy complete by agreeing with each other. Have the same love. Be one in spirit and purpose.

Don't do anything only to get ahead. Don't do it because you are proud. Instead, be free of pride. Think of others as better than yourselves.

None of you should look out just for your own good. You should also look out for the good of others.

You should think in the same way Christ Jesus does.

In his very nature he was God.
But he did not think that being equal with God was something he should hold on to.
Instead, he made himself nothing.
He took on the very nature of a servant.
He was made in human form.
He appeared as a man.
He came down to the lowest level.
He obeyed God completely, even though it led to his death.
In fact, he died on a cross.
So God lifted him up to the highest place.
He gave him the name that is above every name.
When the name of Jesus is spoken, everyone's knee will bow to worship him.
Every knee in heaven and on earth and under the earth will bow to worship him.
Everyone's mouth will say that Jesus Christ is Lord.
And God the Father will receive the glory.

Follow Jesus' Example

Jesus knew he was equal with God. But he acted like a servant. He wasn't selfish. He put others first. He cared about how others felt. He was obedient.

What a wonderful example Jesus set for us! Discuss these three problems with your family. How would Jesus act? How will you try to act?

1. A child falls down and gets hurt in the park.
2. A new family moves into your neighborhood and doesn't have any friends.
3. You and your sister both want to play a new computer game.

Running a Race
In Greek Olympic games and at other games, runners tried to be the first to reach the finish line. The prize was a wreath of leaves for the runner's head.

The Heavenly Prize Is Jesus

Philippians 3

I consider everything to be nothing compared to knowing Christ Jesus my Lord. To know him is the best thing of all. Because of him I have lost everything. But I consider all of it to be garbage so I can get to know Christ. I want to be joined to him.

For me, being right with God does not come from the law. It comes because I believe in Christ. It comes from God. It is received by faith.

Moving on Toward the Goal

I have not yet received all of those things. I have not yet been made perfect. But I move on to take hold of what Christ Jesus took hold of me for.

Brothers and sisters, I don't consider that I have taken hold of it yet. But here is the one thing I do. I forget what is behind me. I push hard toward what is ahead of me. I move on toward the goal to win the prize. God has appointed me to win it. The heavenly prize is Christ Jesus himself.

Rules for Holy Living

Colossians 3

You are God's chosen people. You are holy and dearly loved. So put on tender mercy and kindness as if they were your clothes. Don't be proud. Be gentle and patient. Put up with each other. Forgive the things you are holding against one another. Forgive, just as the Lord forgave you.

And over all of those good things put on love. Love holds them all together perfectly as if they were one.

Let the peace that Christ gives rule in your hearts. As parts of one body, you were appointed to live in peace. And be thankful.

Let Christ's word live in you like a rich treasure. Teach and correct each other wisely. Sing psalms, hymns and spiritual songs. Sing with thanks in your hearts to God. Do everything you say or do in the name of the Lord Jesus. Always give thanks to God the Father through Christ.

DID YOU KNOW?

What does it mean to be "holy"?

Being holy means living right and doing good things. We should do these things because we love Jesus. You can find some rules for living a holy life in Colossians chapter 3.

God Is Fair

2 Thessalonians 1

God is fair. He will pay back trouble to those who give you trouble. He will help you who are troubled. And he will also help us.

All of those things will happen when the Lord Jesus appears from heaven. He will come in blazing fire. He will come with the angels who are given the power to do what God wants. He will punish those who don't know God. He will punish those who don't obey the good news about our Lord Jesus. They will be destroyed forever. They will be shut out of heaven. They will never see the glory of the Lord's power.

DID YOU KNOW?

When will God punish people for their sins?

God will punish wicked people when Jesus comes back to earth. Until then, people can decide to trust Jesus. If they do, their sins are forgiven. When people become Christians, they love Jesus and begin to do good things.

All of those things will happen when he comes. On that day his glory
[wil]l be seen in his holy people. Everyone who has believed will be
[am]azed when they see him. That includes you, because you believed
[th]e witness we gave you.

WORDS TO TREASURE

Don't let anyone look down
on you because you are
young. Set an example for
the believers in what you say
and in how you live.
1 Timothy 4:12

Paul Gives Timothy Advice

1 Timothy 4

Directions for Timothy

Don't let anyone look down on you
because you are young. Set an example for
the believers in what you say and in how
you live. Also set an example in how you
love and in what you believe. Show the
believers how to be pure.

Until I come, spend your time reading
Scripture out loud to one another. Spend
your time preaching and teaching. Don't fail

Be an Example

How can a child who is your age set a Christian example for others? Have your family help you find the five
ways listed here. Do you know what a pledge is? It's
like a promise. Can you promise to be a good example
with God's help? Make a poster for your wall. It could
say something like this:

I will be a Christian example
in speech—I will not say mean things or bad words;
in life—I will do what pleases God;
in love—I will care about others;
in faith—I will pray and trust God;
in purity—I will choose what is right.

to use the gift the Holy Spirit gave you. He gave it to you through a message from God. It was given when the elders placed their hands on you.

Keep on doing those things. Give them your complete attention. Then everyone will see how you are coming along. Be careful of how you live and what you believe. Never give up. Then you will save yourself and those who hear you.

Love for Money

1 Timothy 6

Suppose someone teaches ideas that are false. He doesn't agree with the true teaching of our Lord Jesus Christ. He doesn't agree with godly teaching. People like that are proud. They don't understand anything. They like to argue more than they should. They can't agree about what words mean.

All of that results in wanting what others have. It causes fighting, harmful talk, and evil distrust. It stirs up trouble all the time among people whose minds are twisted by sin. The truth they once had has been taken away from them. They think they can get rich by being godly.

You gain a lot when you live a godly life. But you must be happy with what you have. We didn't bring anything into the world. We can't take anything out of it. If we have food and clothing, we will be happy with that.

Being Happy With What You Have

Make a list of the things you would like the most, something like a Christmas list.

What is most important in life? It's being godly, which means living like God wants us to. It's also having enough to eat and to wear. Those things should be enough to make us content, or happy.

It's easy to think we need a lot more than that to be happy. But getting more things usually doesn't make us happier. Look back at your list. Do you want to make any changes?

People who want to get rich are tempted. They fall into a trap. They are tripped up by wanting many foolish and harmful things. Those who live like that are dragged down by what they do. They are destroyed and die.

Love for money causes all kinds of evil. Some people want to get rich. They have wandered away from the faith. They have wounded themselves with many sorrows.

Paul Tells Timothy to Be Faithful

2 Timothy 1

God didn't give us a spirit that makes us weak and fearful. He gave us a spirit that gives us power and love. It helps us control ourselves.

WORDS TO TREASURE

Don't be ashamed to give witness about our Lord.

2 Timothy 1:8

So don't be ashamed to give witness about our Lord. And don't be ashamed of me, his prisoner. Instead, join with me as I suffer for the good news. God's power will help us do that.

God has saved us. He has chosen us to live a holy life. It wasn't because of anything we have done. It was because of his own purpose and grace. Through Christ Jesus, God gave us that grace even before time began. It has now been made known through the coming of our Savior, Christ Jesus. He has destroyed death. Because of the good news, he has brought life out into the light. That life never dies.

I was appointed to announce the good news. I was appointed to be an apostle and a teacher. That's why I'm suffering the way I am. But I'm not ashamed. I know the One I have believed in. I am sure he is able to take care of what I have given him. I can trust him with it until the day he returns as judge.

Follow what you heard from me as the pattern of true teaching. Follow it with faith and love because you belong to Christ Jesus. Guard the truth of the good news that you were trusted with. Guard it with the help of the Holy Spirit who lives in us.

Do What Is Good

Titus 3

At one time we too acted like fools. We didn't obey God. We were tricked. We were controlled by all kinds of longings and pleasures. We were full of evil. We wanted what belongs to others. People hated us, and we hated one another.

But the kindness and love of God our Savior appeared. He saved us. It wasn't because of the good things we had done. It was because of his mercy. He saved us by washing away our sins. We were born again. The Holy Spirit gave us new life.

God poured out the Spirit on us freely because of what Jesus Christ our Savior has done. His grace made us right with God. So now we have received the hope of eternal life as God's children.

You can trust that saying. Those things are important. Treat them that way. Then those who have trusted in God will be careful to commit themselves to doing what is good. Those things are excellent. They are for the good of everyone.

WORDS TO TREASURE

He saved us. It wasn't because of the good things we had done. It was because of his mercy.

Titus 3:5

Just Say No

What should you say if someone tries to get you to do something wrong? The book of Titus says not to argue. It's best to just say a simple no. Look in a mirror and practice saying no. Try saying no with a smile. Then try to look very serious when you say no. Try an angry look with your no. Which do you think is the best way to say no?

Talk to your mom or dad about things you should say no to. Show them the different faces you can make with your no. What look do they think will work the best?

The General Letters

Hebrews   James
                    1 Peter   2 Peter
1 John   2 John   3 John   Jude

In New Testament times, Christians lived in many different cities. Trips took a long time. Travel was hard. When the leaders wanted to talk to the people in the churches, the leaders wrote letters to them. God told them what to say in the letters. God had a special plan for those letters. These books of the Bible are the letters that the leaders wrote.

The General Letters were sent from church to church. Peter wrote some of them. So did James, Jude and John. Being a Christian was hard. So sometimes the writers cheered the people up. Sometimes they said, "Be careful of false teachers!" Sometimes they taught the people how to live the way God wanted them to live. These letters still teach us how to live today. They show us how to follow Jesus every day! These letters were written between A.D 48 and 90.

Living by Faith

Hebrews 11

Faith is being sure of what we hope for. It is being certain of what we do not see. That is what the people of long ago were praised for.

We have faith. So we understand that everything was made when God commanded it. That's why we believe that what we see was not made out of what could be seen.

Abel had faith. So he offered to God a better sacrifice than Cain did. Because of his faith Abel was praised as a godly man. God said good things about his offerings. Because of his faith Abel still speaks. He speaks even though he is dead.

Enoch had faith. So he was taken from this life. He didn't die. He just couldn't be found. God had taken him away. Before God took him, Enoch was praised as one who pleased God.

Without faith it isn't possible to please God. Those who come to God must believe that he exists. And they must believe that he rewards those who look to him.

Noah had faith. So he built an ark to save his family. He built it because of his great respect for God. God had warned him about things that could not yet be seen. Because of his faith he showed the world that it was guilty. Because of his faith he was considered right with God.

Abraham had faith. So he obeyed God. God called him to go to a place he would later receive as his own. So he went. He did it even

Show Your Faith

Remember Abraham way back in the book of Genesis? (page 16). Well, Abraham had faith in God. Faith means believing and trusting in God. What were some of the great things Abraham did?

What are some things your family has done because of their faith in God? Did God ever lead your dad to a new job? Did your mom ever stop her chores to help a friend in trouble? Did you ever walk away from your friends because they were doing something wrong? When you obey God, you show that you have faith in him. You show that he knows what's best for you.

though he didn't know where he was going. Because of his faith he made his home in the land God had promised him. He was like an outsider in a strange country. He lived there in tents. So did Isaac and Jacob. They received the same promise he did. Abraham was looking forward to the city that has foundations. He was waiting for the city that God planned and built.

Abraham had faith. So God made it possible for him to become a father. He became a father even though he was too old. Sarah also was too old to have children. But Abraham believed that the One who made the promise was faithful. Abraham was past the time when he could have children. But many children came from that one man. They were as many as the stars in the sky. They were as many as the sand on the seashore. No one could count them.

All those people were still living by faith when they died. They didn't receive the things God had promised. They only saw them and welcomed them from a long way off. They openly said that they were outsiders and strangers on earth.

Isaac had faith. So he blessed Jacob and Esau. He told them what was ahead for them.

Jacob had faith. So he blessed each of Joseph's sons. He blessed them when he was dying. Because of his faith he worshiped God as he leaned on the top of his wooden staff.

Joseph had faith. So he spoke to the people of Israel about their leaving Egypt. He gave directions about his bones. He did that toward the end of his life.

Moses' parents had faith. So they hid him for three months after he was born. They saw he was a special child. They were not afraid of the king's command.

Moses had faith. So he refused to be called the son of Pharaoh's daughter. That happened after he had grown up. He chose to be treated badly together with the people of God. He chose that instead of enjoying sin's pleasures for a short time. He suffered shame because of Christ. He thought it had great value. He considered it better than the riches of Egypt. He was looking ahead to God's reward.

Because of his faith he left Egypt. It wasn't because he was afraid of the king's anger. He didn't let anything stop him. He saw the One who can't be seen.

Because of his faith he was the first to keep the Passover Feast. He commanded the people of Israel to sprinkle blood on their doorways. He did it so that the destroying angel would not touch their oldest sons.

The people had faith. So they passed through the Red Sea. They went through it as if it were dry land. The Egyptians tried to do it also. But they drowned.

The people had faith. So the walls of Jericho fell down. It happened after they had marched around the city for seven days.

Rahab, the prostitute, had faith. So she welcomed the spies. That's why she wasn't killed with those who didn't obey God.

What more can I say? I don't have time to tell about all the others. I don't have time to talk about Gideon, Barak, Samson and Jephthah. I don't have time to tell about David, Samuel and the prophets. Because of their faith they took over kingdoms. They ruled fairly. They received the blessings God had promised. They shut the mouths of lions. They put out great fires. They escaped being killed by the sword. Their weakness was turned to strength. They became powerful in battle. They beat back armies from other countries.

Some were laughed at. Some were whipped. Still others were held by chains. They were put in prison. Some were killed with stones. They were sawed in two. They were put to death by the sword. They went around wearing the skins of sheep and goats. They were poor. They were attacked. They were treated badly. The world was not worthy of them. They wandered in deserts and mountains. They lived in caves. They lived in holes in the ground.

All of those people were praised because they had faith. But none of them received what God had promised. God had planned something better for us. So they would only be made perfect together with us.

DID YOU KNOW?

What difference does faith make?

Faith helps believers do great things. This chapter in the book of Hebrews lists many heroes of faith. It tells what they were able to do because they trusted God.

Control What You Say

James 3

My brothers and sisters, most of you shouldn't want to be teachers. You know that those of us who teach will be held more accountable.

All of us get tripped up in many ways. Suppose someone is never wrong in what he says. Then he is a perfect man. He is able to keep his whole body under control.

We put a bit in the mouth of a horse to make it obey us. We can control the whole animal with it. And how about ships? They are very big. They are driven along by strong winds. But they are steered by a very small rudder. It makes them go where the captain wants to go.

In the same way, the tongue is a small part of the body. But it brags a lot. Think about how a small spark can set a big forest on fire.

The tongue also is a fire. The tongue is the most evil part of the body. It pollutes the whole person. It sets a person's whole way of life on fire. And the tongue is set on fire by hell.

People have controlled all kinds of animals, birds, reptiles and creatures of the sea. They still control them. But no one can control the tongue. It is an evil thing that never rests. It is full of deadly poison.

With our tongues we praise our Lord and Father. With our tongues we call down curses on people. We do it even though they have been

Count to Three First

Does your tongue ever get you into trouble? Do you say things and then feel sorry for saying them? James understood this problem. He said the tongue is such a small thing. But it's the most evil part of the body.

James compared the tongue to three things. With a small bit you can make a horse go where you want. With a small rudder you can steer a large ship. With a small spark you can start a forest fire.

Try this the next time you want to say something mean. Count to three silently, saying "bit, rudder, fire." Think of how those small things control big things. See if you can keep your tongue from getting you into trouble!

created to be like God. Praise and cursing come out of the same mouth. My brothers and sisters, it shouldn't be that way.

Stand Firm in Your Faith

1 Peter 5

So don't be proud. Put yourselves under God's mighty hand. Then he will honor you at the right time. Turn all your worries over to him. He cares about you.

Control yourselves. Be on your guard. Your enemy the devil is like a roaring lion. He prowls around looking for someone to chew up and swallow. Stand up to him. Stand firm in what you believe. All over the world you know that your brothers and sisters are going through the same kind of suffering.

God always gives you all the grace you need. So you will only have to suffer for a little while. Then God himself will build you up again. He will make you strong and steady. And he has chosen you to share in his eternal glory because you belong to Christ.

Give him the power for ever and ever. Amen.

WORDS TO TREASURE

Turn all your worries over to him. He cares about you.
1 Peter 5:7

We Are Children of God

1 John 3

How great is the love the Father has given us so freely! Now we can be called children of God. And that's what we really are! The world doesn't know us because it didn't know him.

Dear friends, now we are children of God. He still hasn't let us know what we will be. But we know that when Christ appears, we will be like him. We will see him as he really is. He is pure. All who hope to be like him make themselves pure.

Everyone who sins breaks the law. In fact, breaking the law is sin. But you know that Christ came to take our sins away. And there is no sin in him. No one who remains joined to him keeps on sinning. No one who keeps on sinning has seen him or known him.

Dear children, don't let anyone lead you down the wrong path. Those who do what is right are holy, just as Christ is holy. Those who do what is sinful belong to the devil. They are just like him. He has been sinning from the beginning. But the Son of God came to destroy the devil's work.

Those who are born again because of what God has done will not keep on sinning. God's very nature remains in them. They can't go on sinning. They have been born again because of what God has done.

Here is how you can tell the difference between the children of God and the children of the devil. Those who don't do what is right do not belong to God. Those who don't love their brothers and sisters do not belong to him either.

Dear children, don't just talk about love. Put your love into action. Then it will truly be love. That's how we know that we hold to the truth.

How do you know if a person is a child of God?

Children of God believe in Jesus. They believe that he died on the cross to take our punishment for sin. Then he rose from the grave to defeat sin and Satan. They show that they trust Jesus by obeying God's commands. And they love others.

Love and Actions

God loves us very much. We know that because he gave his Son, Jesus, to die for our sins. We need to show that God's love is in us. How? By the things we do and say.

Try this game with your family. Say "Love is. . ." and then give each person a chance to finish the sentence. Here are some ideas. "Love is helping with the dishes." "Love is praying with me at night." "Love is helping a sick neighbor." Each person gets ten seconds to answer, or it's the next person's turn.

How many "love is" actions can your family name? Now see how many of them your family can put into practice.

And that's how we put our hearts at rest, knowing that God is watching. Our hearts may judge us. But God is greater than our hearts. He knows everything.

A Letter From John

3 John

I, the elder, am writing this letter.

I am sending it to you, my dear friend Gaius. I love you because of the truth.

Dear friend, I know that your spiritual life is going well. I pray that you also may enjoy good health. And I pray that everything else may go well with you.

Some believers came to me and told me that you are faithful to the truth. They told me that you continue to live by it. That gave me great joy. I have no greater joy than to hear that my children are living by the truth.

Dear friend, you are faithful in what you are doing for the believers. You are faithful even though they are strangers to you. They have told the church about your love. Please help them by sending them on their way in a manner that honors God.

They started on their journey to serve Jesus Christ. They didn't receive any help from those who aren't believers. So we should welcome people like them. We should work together with them for the truth.

Great Joy

The book of John 3 says, "I have no greater joy than to hear that my children are living by the truth." Living by the truth means obeying Jesus and living for him.

Talk with your parents about this verse. Do they have great joy when they see you live by the truth? Ask them why. Ask them to help you live by the truth.

I wrote to the church. But Diotrephes won't have anything to do with us. He loves to be the first in everything. So if I come, I will point out what he is doing. He is saying evil things about us to others. Even that doesn't satisfy him. He refuses to welcome other believers. He also keeps others from welcoming them. In fact, he throws them out of the church.

Dear friend, don't be like those who do evil. Be like those who do good. Anyone who does what is good belongs to God. Anyone who does what is evil hasn't really seen or known God.

Everyone says good things about Demetrius. He lives in keeping with the truth. We also say good things about him. And you know that our witness is true.

I have a lot to write to you. But I don't want to write with pen and ink. I hope I can see you soon. Then we can talk face to face.

May you have peace. The friends here send their greetings. Greet the friends there by name.

WORDS TO TREASURE

Dear friend, don't be like those who do evil. Be like those who do good.

3 John 11

A Letter From Jude

Jude

I, Jude, am writing this letter. I serve Jesus Christ. I am a brother of James.

I am sending this letter to you who have been chosen by God. You are loved by God the Father. You are kept safe by Jesus Christ.

May more and more mercy, peace, and love be given to you.

A Warning Against Ungodly Teachers

Dear friends, I really wanted to write to you about the salvation we share. But now I feel I should write and ask you to stand up for the faith. God's people were trusted with it once and for all time.

Certain people have slipped in among you in secret. Long ago it was written that they would be judged. They are godless people. They use the grace of our God as an excuse for sexual sins. They say no to Jesus Christ. He is our only Lord and King.

Remain in God's Love

Dear friends, remember what the apostles of our Lord Jesus Christ said was going to happen. They told you, "In the last days, some people will make fun of the truth. They will follow their own ungodly longings." They are the people who separate you from one another. They do only what comes naturally. They are not led by the Holy Spirit.

Dear friends, build yourselves up in your most holy faith. Let the Holy Spirit guide and help you when you pray. The mercy of our Lord Jesus Christ will bring you eternal life. As you wait for his mercy, remain in God's love.

WORDS TO TREASURE

Remain in God's love.
Jude 21

Show mercy to those who doubt. Pull others out of the fire. Save them. To others, show mercy mixed with fear. Hate even the clothes that are stained by the sins of those who wear them.

Praise to God

Give praise to the One who is able to keep you from falling into sin. He will bring you into his heavenly glory without any fault. He will bring you there with great joy. Give praise to the only God. He is our Savior. Glory, majesty, power and authority belong to him. Give praise to him through Jesus Christ our Lord. Give praise to the One who was before all time, who now is, and who will be forever. Amen.

The Book of Prophecy

Revelation

The book of Revelation is the only book of prophecy in the New Testament. It is also the last book of the Bible. The apostle John wrote it. He was sent away to an island called Patmos. While he was there, God gave him a vision. The vision was about Jesus. It was also about what "will happen soon" (Revelation 1:1). God told John to write it all down for the churches to read. But the book was also written for all people everywhere.

Some things in Revelation are hard to understand. But some things are very clear. Jesus is the King of kings. He will win the battle over death and evil. And he will come back again someday!

John wrote this book in A.D. 90.

John Is Told What Heaven Will Be Like

Revelation 1—2; 4; 19; 20—22

One Who Looks Like a Son of Man

I, John, am a believer like you. I am a friend who suffers like you. As members of Jesus' royal family, we can put up with anything that happens to us.

I was on the island of Patmos because I taught God's word and what Jesus said. The Holy Spirit took complete control of me on the Lord's Day. I heard a loud voice behind me that sounded like a trumpet. The voice said, "Write on a scroll what you see."

I turned around to see who was speaking to me. When I turned, I saw seven golden lampstands. In the middle of them was someone who looked "like a son of man." *(Daniel 7:13)*

He was dressed in a long robe with a gold strip of cloth around his chest. The hair on his head was white like wool, as white as snow. His eyes were like a blazing fire. His feet were like bronze metal glowing in a furnace. His voice sounded like rushing waters. When I saw him, I fell at his feet as if I were dead.

Then he put his right hand on me and said, "Do not be afraid. I am the First and the Last. I am the Living One. I was dead. But look! I am alive for ever and ever!"

The Lord Who Rules Over All

John was a close friend of Jesus. The book of Revelation tells of a vision John had. In his vision John saw Jesus as he truly is in heaven. John fell at Jesus' feet in fear. Then Jesus put his hand on John. He told him not to be afraid. Jesus is almighty God. But he was still John's friend.

Find or draw some pictures of Jesus. Show how he might have looked as a baby, as a grown-up teacher, and as he looks in heaven now. Put the three pictures together. Remember that Jesus is God as well as your loving friend.

The Letter to the Church in Smyrna

Here are the words of the One who is the First and the Last. He is the One who died and came to life again. He says, "I know that you suffer and are poor. But you are rich!

"Don't be afraid of what you are going to suffer. I tell you, the devil will put some of you in prison to test you. You will be treated badly for ten days. Be faithful, even if it means you must die. Then I will give you a crown. The crown is life itself.

"Those who have ears should listen to what the Holy Spirit says to the churches. Those who overcome will not be hurt at all by the second death."

The Throne in Heaven

After this I looked, and there in front of me was a door standing open in heaven. I heard the voice I had heard before. It sounded like a trumpet. The voice said, "Come up here. I will show you what must happen after this."

At once the Holy Spirit took complete control of me. There in front of me was a throne in heaven with someone sitting on it. The One who sat there shone like jewels. Around the throne was a rainbow that looked like an emerald.

Twenty-four other thrones surrounded that throne. Twenty-four elders were sitting on them. The elders were dressed in white. They had gold crowns on their heads.

What did John see in heaven?

John saw God on his throne. He saw creatures praise God. Then John saw Jesus. John knew he was the Lamb of God. John saw that Jesus was ready to punish bad people for their sins

From the throne came flashes of lightning, rumblings and thunder. Seven lamps were blazing in front of the throne. These stand for the seven spirits of God. There was something that looked like a sea of glass in front of the throne. It was as clear as crystal.

In the inner circle, around the throne, were four living creatures. They were covered with eyes, in front and in back. The first creature looked like a lion. The second looked like an ox. The third had a man's face. The fourth looked like a flying eagle. Each of the four living creatures had six wings. Each creature was covered all over with eyes, even under the wings. Day and night, they never stop saying,

> "Holy, holy, holy
> is the Lord God who rules over all.
> He was, and he is, and he will come."

The living creatures give glory, honor and thanks to the One who sits on the throne and who lives for ever and ever. At the same time, the 24 elders fall down and worship the One who sits on the throne and who lives for ever and ever. They lay their crowns in front of the throne. They say,

> "You are worthy, our Lord and God!
>> You are worthy to receive glory and honor and power.
> You are worthy because you created all things.
>> They were created and they exist.
>> That is the way you planned it."

Hallelujah!

After these things I heard a roar in heaven. It sounded like a huge crowd shouting,

> "Hallelujah!
> Salvation and glory and power belong to our God.
>> The way he judges is true and fair.
> He has judged the great prostitute.
>> She polluted the earth with her terrible sins.
> God has paid her back for killing those who served him."

Again they shouted,

> "Hallelujah!
> The smoke from her fire goes up for ever and ever."

The 24 elders and the four living creatures bowed down. They worshiped God, who was sitting on the throne. They cried out,

> "Amen! Hallelujah!"

Then a voice came from the throne. It said,

"Praise our God,
all you who serve him!
Praise God, all you who have respect for him,
both great and small!"

Then I heard the noise of a huge crowd. It sounded like the roar of rushing waters and like loud thunder. The people were shouting,

"Hallelujah!

Our Lord God is the King who rules over all.
Let us be joyful and glad!
Let us give him glory!
It is time for the Lamb's wedding.
His bride has made herself ready.
Fine linen, bright and clean,
was given to her to wear."

Fine linen stands for the right things that God's people do.

Here is what the angel told me to write. "Blessed are those who are invited to the wedding supper of the Lamb!" Then he added, "These are the true words of God."

The Rider on the White Horse

I saw heaven standing open. There in front of me was a white horse. Its rider is called Faithful and True. When he judges or makes war, he is always fair. His eyes are like blazing fire. On his head are many crowns. A name is written on him that only he knows. He is dressed in a robe dipped in blood. His name is The Word of God.

The armies of heaven were following him, riding on white horses. They were dressed in fine linen, white and clean.

Out of the rider's mouth comes a sharp sword. He will strike down the nations with it. Scripture says, "He will rule them with an iron rod." *(Psalm 2:9)* He stomps on the grapes of God's winepress. The winepress stands for the terrible anger of the God who rules over all.

Here is the name that is written on the rider's robe and on his thigh.

> THE GREATEST KING OF ALL AND THE
> MOST POWERFUL LORD OF ALL

The Dead Are Judged

I saw a great white throne and the One who was sitting on it. When the earth and sky saw his face, they ran away. There was no place for them.

I saw the dead, great and small, standing in front of the throne. Books were opened. Then another book was opened. It was the Book of Life. The dead were judged by what they had done. The things they had done were written in the books. Anyone whose name was not written in the Book of Life was thrown into the lake of fire.

The New Jerusalem

I saw a new heaven and a new earth. The first heaven and the first earth were completely gone. There was no longer any sea.

How will Jesus come back to earth?

Jesus will come back when it is time to judge the world. He will come back as a strong soldier. He will come with all the armies of heaven. He will punish God's enemies. Then he will defeat Satan.

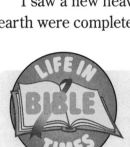

Horses

When rulers rode on horses, it meant they were going to war. When rulers came in peace they rode donkeys. Jesus is pictured here in Revelation as a warrior coming on a horse to conquer Satan finally and forever.

He who was sitting on the throne said, "I am making everything new!" Then he said, "Write this down. You can trust these words. They are true."

He said to me, "It is done. I am the Alpha and the Omega, the First and the Last. I am the Beginning and the End. Anyone who is thirsty may drink from the spring of the water of life. It doesn't cost anything! Anyone who overcomes will receive all this from me. I will be his God, and he will be my child.

"But others will have their place in the lake of fire that burns with sulfur. Those who are afraid and those who do not believe will be there. Murderers and those who pollute themselves will join them. Those who commit sexual sins and those who practice witchcraft will go there. Those who worship statues of gods and all who tell lies will be there too. It is the second death."

One of the seven angels who had the seven bowls came and spoke to me. The bowls were filled with the seven last plagues. The angel said, "Come. I will show you the bride, the wife of the Lamb."

Then he carried me away in a vision. The Spirit took me to a huge, high mountain. He showed me Jerusalem, the Holy City. It was coming down out of heaven from God. It shone with the glory of God. It gleamed like a very valuable jewel. It was like a jasper, as clear as crystal.

The city had a huge, high wall with 12 gates. Twelve angels were at the gates, one at each of them. On the gates were written the names of the 12 tribes of Israel. There were three gates on the east and three on

What Is Heaven Like?

Have you ever tried to picture what heaven looks like? These verses tell us a lot about heaven. The streets are made of pure gold. The gates are made of pearls. There is no need for the sun because God's glory is the light.

Four things will not be in heaven. Can you find them? Won't heaven be a wonderful place to live forever? Would you like your friends to be in heaven with you? Tell them that Jesus died for their sins. Tell them what heaven is like.

the north. There were three gates on the south and three on the west. The wall of the city had 12 foundations. Written on them were the names of the 12 apostles of the Lamb.

The angel who talked with me had a gold measuring rod. He used it to measure the city, its gates and its walls.

The city was laid out like a square. It was as long as it was wide. The angel measured the city with the rod. It was 1,400 miles long. It was as wide and high as it was long.

He measured the wall of the city. It was 200 feet thick. The angel did the measuring as a man would. The wall was made out of jasper. The city was made out of pure gold, as pure as glass.

The foundations of the city walls were decorated with every kind of jewel. The first foundation was made out of jasper. The second was made out of sapphire. The third was made out of chalcedony. The fourth was made out of emerald. The fifth was made out of sardonyx. The sixth was made out of carnelian. The seventh was made out of chrysolite. The eighth was made out of beryl. The ninth was made out of topaz. The tenth was made out of chrysoprase. The eleventh was made out of jacinth. The twelfth was made out of amethyst.

The 12 gates were made from 12 pearls. Each gate was made out of a single pearl. The main street of the city was made out of pure gold, as clear as glass.

I didn't see a temple in the city. This was because the Lamb and the Lord God who rules over all are its temple. The city does not need the sun or moon to shine on it. God's glory is its light, and the Lamb is its lamp.

The nations will walk by the light of the city. The kings of the world will bring their glory into it. Its gates will never be shut, because there will be no night there. The glory and honor of the nations will be brought into it.

Only what is pure will enter it. No one who fools others or does shameful things will enter it. Only those whose names are written in the Lamb's Book of Life will enter the city.

The River of Life

Then the angel showed me the river of the water of life. It was as clear as crystal. It flowed from the throne of God and of the Lamb. It flowed down the middle of the city's main street.

On each side of the river stood the tree of life, bearing 12 crops of fruit. Its fruit was ripe every month. The leaves of the tree bring healing to the nations.

There will no longer be any curse. The throne of God and of the Lamb will be in the city. God's servants will serve him. They will see his face. His name will be on their foreheads.

There will be no more night. They will not need the light of a lamp or the light of the sun. The Lord God will give them light. They will rule for ever and ever.

The angel said to me, "You can trust these words. They are true. The Lord is the God of the spirits of the prophets. He sent his angel to show those who serve him the things that must soon take place."

Jesus Is Coming

"Look! I am coming soon! I bring my rewards with me. I will reward each person for what he has done. I am the Alpha and the Omega. I am the First and the Last. I am the Beginning and the End.

"Blessed are those who wash their robes. They will have the right to come to the tree of life. They will be allowed to go through the gates into the city.

Look! I am coming soon!
Revelation 22:12

"Outside the city are the dogs and those who practice witchcraft. Outside are also those who commit sexual sins and murder. Those who worship statues of gods, and everyone who loves and does what is false, are outside too.

"I, Jesus, have sent my angel to give you this witness for the churches. I am the Root and the Son of David. I am the bright Morning Star."

The Holy Spirit and the bride say, "Come!" Let those who hear say, "Come!" Anyone who is thirsty should come. Anyone who wants to take the free gift of the water of life should do so.

I am warning everyone who hears the words of the prophecy of this book. If you add anything to them, God will add to you the plagues told about in this book. If you take any words away from this book of prophecy, God will take away from you your share in the tree of life. He will also take away your place in the Holy City. This book tells about these things.

He who gives witness to these things says, "Yes. I am coming soon." Amen. Come, Lord Jesus!

May the grace of the Lord Jesus be with God's people. Amen.

Activities

If you want to not only read *The Little Kids' Adventure Bible* but also do something with what you've learned, these next pages are just for you. Some of these activities can be done alone; some can be done with your friends and family. Take your pick . . . then turn to one of the pages listed for some great ideas for things to discuss, things to do, or things to make.

Dictionary

A

abyss—A deep pit where evil spirits live. Satan will be held there in chains.

adultery—Having a sexual relationship with someone who is not your husband or wife.

altar—A table or raised place on which a gift, or sacrifice, was offered to God.

amen—A word that means "it is true" or "let it be true."

angel—A spirit who is God's helper. A spirit who tells people God's words. See also cherubim.

anoint—1. To pour olive oil on people or things. This sets them apart for God. 2. To pour oil on people as part of praying for their healing.

anointed—To be set apart as God's special servant.

apostle—One of the twelve men who spent about three years with Jesus. They taught others about Jesus, too. See also disciple.

Aramaic—A language spoken by many people during Bible times. The Jews in Jesus' time most often spoke this language.

ark of the covenant—A large gold box that held the stone tablets of the Ten Commandments. The ark was God's throne on earth.

armor—A special outer covering like clothes made of metal. People wore it to help keep them safe in battle.

Asherah—A false god. People thought she was the Canaanite mother goddess and goddess of the sea.

B

Baal—The name of the most popular false god of Canaan.

Babel—A city where people tried to build a tower up to the sky.

Babylon—1. The capital city of the empire of Babylonia. 2. Any powerful, sinful city.

baptize—To sprinkle, pour on or cover a person with water. It is a sign that the person belongs to Jesus.

Beelzebub—Another name for the devil. Satan.

believe—To accept as true. To trust. See also faith.

blessed—1. Made joyful. 2. Helped by God.

C

cast lots—Something done to find out what God wants. It is like drawing straws to see who will go first.

chariot—A cart with two wheels pulled by horses. People, especially soldiers, rode in them.

cherubim—1. Spirits like angels who have large wings. They were and are a sign that God is sitting on his throne. 2. Spirits who serve God.

chief priest—See high priest.

Christ—A Greek word that means "the Anointed One." It is one of the names given to Jesus. It means the same thing as the Hebrew word Messiah. See also Jesus.

circumcision—Cutting off a male's foreskin (a piece of skin at the end of a penis). It was a sign that the person belonged to God.

clean—1. Something that God accepts. 2. Something that doesn't have sin.

clean animals—Animals that God said were acceptable to eat or to give as offerings.

commandment—A law or rule that God gives. See also law.

concubine—A woman who belonged to a man but was not his legal wife.

Council—See Sanhedrin.

covenant—1. A treaty, or promise, between two persons or groups. In the Bible it is a promise made between God and the people. 2. Promises from God for salvation.

cross—A wooden post with a bar near the top that extends to the right and left. A cross looks like the letter "T." The Romans killed people by nailing them to crosses.

crucify—To kill people by nailing them to crosses.

cud—Food that is chewed again. An animal such as a cow brings its food back from its stomach to its mouth. This food, or cud, can be chewed again. God told the people of Israel they could eat any animal that chews the cud and has hoofs that are separated.

curse—1. A call for God to punish someone. 2. A command of God that punishment will come on someone or something.

D

deacon—A church leader who helps people in Jesus' name.

dedicate—To set apart for a special purpose, often for God's use.

demon—An evil spirit.

devil—The one who tempts people to sin. See also Satan.

disciple—A person who follows a teacher. This person does what their teacher says to do. See also apostle. See also Twelve, the.

divorce—The end of a husband and wife's marriage.

doubt—A lack of faith or trust in something or someone. To not be sure.

E

Eden—The place where God made a garden for Adam and Eve.

elder—The leader of a church, town or nation. This person makes important decisions.

eternal—Forever. Without beginning or end.

evangelist—A person who tells others the Good News of Jesus.

evil—Bad. Wicked. Doing things that do not please God.

evil spirit—A demon. One of the devil's helpers.

F

faith—Trust and belief in God. Knowing that God is real, even though we can't see him. See also believe.

faithful—Able to be trusted or counted on.

famine—A time when there is not enough food to eat.

fast—Going without food and/or drink for a special reason.

Feast of Booths—A celebration or festival when the Israelites thanked God for the harvest of their crops. During the feast they lived in little tents for seven days to help remember when they traveled to Canaan.

Feast of Hanukkah—A celebration praising God that the Israelites and Jews today have to remember the cleaning and rededication of the temple. The temple had been made "unclean" by an enemy.

Feast of Weeks—A festival or celebration day at the beginning of the wheat harvest when the Israelites gave thanks to God. See also Pentecost.

Feast of Passover—See Passover.

Feast of Unleavened Bread—A week for remembering when God set the Israelites free from Egypt. It began the day after the Feast of Passover. During this time the people ate bread made without yeast, like they did when they left Egypt in a hurry.

fig—A sweet fruit that grows on trees in warm countries like Israel.

G

glory—1. God's greatness. 2. Praise and honor.

God—The maker and ruler of the world and all people.

grace—The kindness and forgiveness God gives to people. This is a gift. It cannot be earned.

hallelujah—A Hebrew word that means "praise the LORD."

Hanukkah—See Feast of Hanukkah.

harvest—Picking a crop when it is ripe.

heaven—1. God's home. 2. The sky. 3. Where Christians go after they die.

Hebrew—1. Another name for an Israelite. 2. The language spoken by the Israelites. The Old Testament is written in this language.

hell—A place of punishment for people who don't follow Jesus. They go there after they die.

Herod—The first name of five rulers from the same family. They ruled over Israel during the time of the New Testament.

high places—Places where people worshiped false gods. These places were found on top of hills.

high priest—A person from the family line of Aaron. He was in charge of everything in the holy tent or in the temple. He was in charge of everyone who came there to work and worship, too.

holy—Set apart for God. Belonging to God. Pure.

holy bread—Twelve loaves of bread placed in the Holy Room of the holy tent each week. They were a gift to God.

Holy Spirit—God's Spirit who creates life. He helps people do God's work. He helps people to believe in Jesus, to love him and to live like him.

holy tent—Also called the Tent of Meeting. A place where the Israelites worshiped God. They used this tent after they left Egypt and while they were in the desert for 40 years. Years later Solomon built the first temple. Then the people worshiped God there and not in the tent.

honor—To show respect to. To give credit to.

hosanna—A Hebrew word used to praise God.

hymn—A song of praise to God.

hyssop—A plant that smelled like mint. Its branches were used to shake water or blood on something to make it pure.

Immanuel—A name for Jesus that means "God with us."

incense—Spices that give a pleasing smell when they are burned. It was placed on the altar in the holy tent.

Israel—1. The new name God gave to Abraham's grandson Jacob. 2. The nation that came from the family line of Jacob. 3. The northern tribes that broke away from Judah to serve their own king.

Israelites—People from the nation of Israel. God's chosen people.

jealous—1. How God feels when people worship other things. 2. How we feel when someone else has something we want.

Jesus—The Greek form of the Hebrew name Joshua. It means "the LORD saves." See also Christ. See also Immanuel. See also Savior.

Jews—Another name for the people of Israel. This name was used after 600 B.C.

Jubilee—See Year of Jubilee.

judge—1. To decide if something is right or wrong. 2. A person who decides what is right or wrong in legal matters.

kingdom—An area or group of people ruled by a king.

law—Rules about what is right and wrong that God gave the people of Israel. See also law, the.

Law, the—The first five books of the Bible.

Levites—Men from the tribe of Levi. They took care of the holy tent and the temple.

locust—A type of insect similar to a grasshopper. A huge number of them sometimes eats and destroys crops.

Lord—A personal name for God or Christ. It shows respect to him as our master and ruler.

lots—See cast lots.

manger—A food box for animals.

manna—Special food sent from heaven. It tasted like wafers, or crackers, sweetened with honey. God gave it to the Israelites in the desert, after they left Egypt.

mercy—More kindness and forgiveness than people deserve to get.

Messiah—A Hebrew word that means, "The Anointed One." It means the same thing as the Greek word *Christ*. See also Jesus.

millstone—A heavy rock used to crush grain to make flour.

miracle—An amazing thing that happens that only God can do. This includes such things as calming a storm or bringing someone back to life.

miraculous signs—Amazing things that God does to point us to him. These things cannot be explained by the laws of nature.

myrrh—A spice with a sweet smell. It came from plants and was made into perfume, incense and medicine.

nard—A costly oil made from a plant grown in India. It was used as a perfume to make skin smell good.

Nazarene—A person who came from the town of Nazareth. Jesus was called a Nazarene.

Nazirite—A person who was set apart to God in a special way. Or, a person who promised to do something special for God. They were not allowed to cut their hair, drink any wine or grape juice, eat grapes or raisins, or touch a dead body.

oath—A promise made before God.

obey—To do what you are told to do. To carry out God's commands.

offering—Something people give to God. It was and is a part of their worship. See also sacrifice.

oxen—Large cattle that are very strong. They were used to pull carts or plows.

papyrus—A tall, grassy plant that grows in shallow water. People made boats with these plants and paper from their stems.

Passover—A feast that happened every year. It reminded the people of the time when God "passed over" their homes in Egypt. Since the people put blood on the doorways, God did not hurt them.

paradise—A perfect place. Another name used for heaven.

pasture—A field of grassy land where cows or sheep may eat.

Pentecost—1. A Jewish celebration held 50 days after Passover. 2. The day the Holy Spirit came in a special way to live in Christians.

Pharaoh—The title of the ruler of Egypt in Bible times.

Pharisees—A group of Jews who carefully followed God's laws and their own rules about God's laws. Some Pharisees were also known as "teachers of the law."

Philistines—Strong enemies of Israel, especially during Saul and David's time.

pierce—To poke through with a sharp instrument.

pillar—1. A tall, upright post that helped to hold up a building. 2. A pillar could also mark a special place.

pillar of cloud—A cloud God used to lead the people of Israel. They could see it all day long when they were in the desert.

pillar of fire—A column of fire God used to lead the people of Israel. They could see it all night long when they were in the desert.

plague—1. A sickness that kills many people. 2. Anything that brings a lot of suffering or loss.

plumb line—A string that has a weight tied to the end of it. It is used to tell whether a wall is straight or not.

pomegranate—A round fruit with a tough skin, many seeds and a juicy red center.

praise—To give glory or honor to someone. To say good things about someone or something.

pregnant—Carrying a baby inside a woman's body until the baby is born.

Preparation Day—The day before the Sabbath day. A day to get all work done so that a person could rest on the Sabbath.

priest—A person who worked in the holy tent or the temple. He was responsible to give his own as well as other people's gifts and prayers to God.

prophecy—Important words or messages that God gives to his people. God gives these words through a special person called a prophet.

prophesy—1. To give a message from God. 2. To tell what the future will be.

prophet—A person who hears messages from God and tells them to others.

prostitutes—People who get paid to let other people have sexual relationships with them.

proverb—A wise saying.

psalm—A poem of praise, prayer or teaching. The book of Psalms is full of these poems.

Purim—A feast in which the Israelites remembered when God helped Queen Esther save the Jews.

R

Rabbi—The title of a teacher of Jewish law.

resurrection—Coming back to life in a whole new way and never dying again.

right hand—A place of honor and power. Jesus is at the right hand of God.

Rome—1. The empire that controlled a lot of the world when Jesus lived here on the earth. 2. The capital city of that empire. It is in Italy.

S

Sabbath—The seventh day of the week. On that day the Israelites rested from their work and turned their thoughts toward God.

sacred—Set apart for God. Holy.

sacrifice—1. To give something to God as a gift. 2. Something that is given to God as a gift of worship. See also offering.

Sadducees—A group of Jewish leaders. They followed only the first five books of the Bible. They did not believe that people rise from the dead.

salvation—Free from the guilt of sin. Jesus died for our sins and rose up from the dead. With this sacrifice, he paid for our sin. He has saved us if we believe in him.

Sanhedrin—A group of 71 Jewish leaders. They were led by the high priest. They were the most important Jewish court of law in Jesus' time.

Satan—God's most powerful enemy in the spirit world. Also called the devil.

saved—Set free from danger or sin.

Savior—The One who sets us free from our sins. A name belonging to Jesus Christ. See also Jesus.

Scripture—God's written Word to us. We also call this the Bible.

scroll—A long strip of paper or animal skin to write on. It was rolled up on two sticks to make it easy to use and store.

seal—1. A tool or a ring with a drawing or pattern cut into it. 2. A mark made by pressing this tool into clay, wax or paper.

seer—A person who can tell the future with God's help. See also prophet.

shepherd—A person who takes care of sheep or goats.

sin—To disobey or displease God.

Sodom and Gomorrah—Two cities that God destroyed. The people who lived there were very evil.

Son of Man—A name Jesus gave to himself. It shows he is the Messiah. See also Messiah.

soul—A person's true inner self.

spiritual—Having to do with the things of God or the Bible.

staff—A stick a shepherd uses to take care of sheep or goats.

synagogue—A Jewish place of worship and teaching.

T

tambourine—A hand-held drum with metal pieces around the edge. It rattles when it is shaken or tapped.

tassels—Hanging groups of thread that are tied together at one end. God told the Israelites to sew tassels onto their clothing to remind them of God's commands.

temple—1. Any place of worship. 2. The building where the people of Israel worshiped God and brought their sacrifices. God was present there in a special way.

tempt—To try to get someone to do bad things.

Tent of Meeting—See holy tent.

threshing floor—A place where heads, or tops, of grain are beaten or stepped on. This is done to knock the seeds of grain from the stems.

tomb—A place to put dead bodies. It was often a cave with a big, stone door.

treaty—An agreement between two people or groups or nations.

Twelve, the—The men who Jesus chose to be his special followers. See also disciples.

U

unclean—Something that God does not accept. Not pure. Not pleasing to God.

Urim and Thummim—Objects that were worn on the high priest's vest. They were used by the high priest to get a message from God.

V

vineyard—A place where grapes grow and are picked.

virgin—A woman who has never had a sexual relationship with a man.

vision—A dream from God. The person who saw it was usually awake. God gave these kinds of dreams to people to show them what he was going to do.

W

wafer—A thin, crisp cracker. Wafers were one kind of offering the Israelites brought to the Lord.

widow—A woman whose husband has died.

winepress—A place where juice is pressed out of grapes to make wine.

wisdom—Understanding that comes from God. Wise thinking.

worship—To give praise, honor and glory to God.

Y

Year of Jubilee—A special year that was to happen every 50 years in Israel. No crops could be planted. Any money that was owed was forgiven. Slaves were set free. Property was given back to its first owner.

yeast—Something added to bread dough to make the bread rise.

yoke—1. A strong piece of wood. It fit on the necks of two oxen so that they could pull carts or plows. 2. A piece of wood put on the neck of a slave or a prisoner.

Z

Zealot—A Jew who was willing to fight to get rid of the Roman rulers. Simon may have been part of this group before becoming one of Jesus' twelve disciples.

Zion—1. The city of Jerusalem. 2. The hill on which King David's house and the temple once stood. 3. Another name sometimes used for heaven.

Three Ways to Read the Bible

Why should you read the Bible?

A man builds a big boat to get away from a flood. A slave becomes a ruler. Angels visit common people. A man walks on the water. A blind person sees again. A man chooses to die for his people. All of these stories are in the Bible. The Bible also tells us about Adam and Eve and how the world began. You can read about Abraham and Isaac and God's words to them. You will find out about Peter and Paul and how the church began. All these things are in this book.

The Bible is more than just a big book of stories, however. The Bible tells you how to live as God's child. The Bible tells you God's words of love. You will get to know God better as you read the Bible. As you get to know him better, you will see how much God loves you. Your love for him will grow too.

How should you begin?

- Take some time every day. Make it the same time every day, if you can. Find a quiet and comfortable place.
- Ask the Holy Spirit to help you as you read. He knows that you want to read the Bible. He knows that you want to learn.
- Don't worry if you don't understand everything you read the first time. You may have to read the same verse many times. You may find words you do not know. In the back of the Bible is a dictionary. It will tell you what the words mean.
- You might want to ask your mom or dad or another grownup to help you understand a verse or story.
- Use a notebook. Write down special things you learn.
- Pick out a plan for your reading. You can choose a plan from the ideas on the next few pages. The plan will help you as you read. When you are finished, try another plan!

1. READ A STORY AT A TIME.

You can read one story at a time. You don't have to read all the stories. You could pick out a story from the Table of Contents list on page v that sounds interesting. When you read a story from the Bible, ask yourself these questions:

Who are the people in the story?
What happens in the story?
What can I learn from this story?

Use your notebook. Write down the name of the story. Write down your answers to the questions. If you know where the book of the Bible is found, you can find the story that way. Or you may go to the page number listed.

2. READ A SUBJECT AT A TIME.

You might want to find out what the Bible says about one special subject. You could read about "Children" or about "Following Jesus." Read about a subject. Write down in your notebook what you think about the subject. Look up the word in the Bible dictionary on page 426 to learn more.

3. READ ABOUT A PERSON AT A TIME.

You can read about people in the Bible. In your notebook, write down the name of the person you want to read about. Read the story about that person. Write down one thing you learned. Look up the person you want to learn about in the Bible dictionary on page 426.

Project Management and Editorial: *Catherine DeVries*

Interior Design: *Sharon Wright, Belmont MI*

Cover Design: *Jody Langley*

Tip-in Design: *Michelle Lenger*

Illustrations: *Lyn Boyer Nelles, Nancy Munger*

Cover Illustration: *Matt LeBarre*

Typesetting: *Sherri L. Hoffman, Grand Rapids, MI*

Theological Review: *Andrew Sloan and Sarah M. Hupp*

Guarantee

Care

We suggest loosening the binding of your new Bible
by gently pressing on a small section of pages at a time
from the center. To ensure against breakage of the spine, it
is best not to bend the cover backward around the spine or
to carry study notes, church bulletins, pens, etc., inside the
cover. Because a felt-tipped marker will "bleed" through the
pages, we recommend use of a ball-point pen or pencil
to underline favorite passages. Your Bible should not
be exposed to excessive heat, cold or humidity.